WILD CAT

WILD CAT

LAURA BLACK

ST. MARTIN'S PRESS
NEW YORK

WILD CAT

1

The butler handed me over to the housekeeper, a big woman with a face as expressionless as a tree-stump. I expected her to conduct me to my bedroom, but she handed me over to a housemaid. A strange, unnerving thought went through my head. It occurred to me that the housekeeper wanted no part of leading me to my bedroom: as though she thought that I had no business to be going there: that I was wicked or foolish to be going there: that, although she could not stop it, she would not lend her countenance to it.

The housemaid was young, no more than twenty, two years older than myself. Her name was Phemie, and I had already met her when I visited the castle. I greeted her with a smile. She greeted me without one. She had borrowed a wooden face from the housekeeper. I did not think Phemie had reason to resent me personally, but something was going on of which she violently disapproved.

We passed other servants on the way upstairs. I had expected them to be assembled in the hall to greet me, but it seemed that was not the way of the castle. The men ducked their heads, the women curtseyed. They were respectful, and silent, and brought an air of despondency to what should have been a moment as joyful as larksong. I knew that all these servants were deft and skilful, tactful and discreet, soft-footed and smartly dressed, beyond any servants who had ever waited on me before: but they were in a conspiracy of gloom. It was all very puzzling and it made me rather angry. How dared they be sad? I smiled at all the servants I saw, and called greetings to those whose names I knew. I was not going to be downcast. Neither they nor anyone else was going to bully me, today or any other day.

It has always been a difficulty in my character, that whenever anyone tries to push me, I push harder in the opposite direction. The servants here, for some odd reason, were creating a dismal thundercloud in the atmosphere of the castle, and they were trying to push me under it. Consequently I became more blithe with each step I took, my smile became broader, my chin tilted at a higher angle of merry confidence.

I felt a twinge, and more than a twinge, of dismay and more than dismay: but I was very sure that no one should be allowed to see it.

The upstairs passages were all carpeted with thick Wilton broadloom, and lit with chandeliers that would have graced a duke's dining room. My bedroom, when I saw it, made me gasp. Nothing in my wretched experience had prepared me for such luxury. I cannot believe that in any other Scottish castle, in the year 1862, money could have been spent in such profusion, and in such perfect taste. Even the flowers looked as though they had been chosen, for the particular perfection of each, from among millions.

Though a little depressed by the curious demeanour of the servants, and by other things, I breathed a sigh of supreme content as I looked round the room, my room, my own new place. Silk, brocade, velvet, fur, French furniture, charming little Italian pictures, porcelain, the dulcet chiming of a dainty little miracle of a clock—these were my new things, my very own, the trappings of my new world.

The bed in the middle of the room was a four-poster, decked with sky-blue silk weeping from a gilded coronet. It was bigger than the bedroom in which I had been sleeping for the past year. I looked at it with particular attention, while trying not to appear to do so: for it was to be no small part of my new life.

A lady's-maid in black curtseyed creakily from the door of an enormous wardrobe. I knew that she was Ailsa Muir, forty, devout, a spinster, an accomplished hairdresser and skilful with her needle. She was to look after me on a trial basis, and if she pleased me she was to become my permanent personal maid. I expected to be pleased by her hairdressing and needlework, but less than enchanted by her dour personality. I wanted laughter about me, of the kind I thought the housemaid Phemie might have shown: I did not think there would be much laughter from Ailsa Muir. There had been so little laughter in the years since my childhood; I wanted to make up abundantly for all that dragging, mirthless time. That was one of the large reasons I was there.

But I had said that Ailsa Muir should have a fair trial, and a fair trial she would have. I had been betrayed so often myself, in the years since my childhood, that I would not break faith with any creature.

Had my situation been normal, I would, of course, have had already a lady's-maid of my own, and would have brought her with me to the castle. But I had no such thing. I never had had, since my childhood. Hence Ailsa Muir, and her creaking curtsey, and her peaked, sombre, Free Kirk face.

Well, if she was sombre herself, she presided over a very heaven of cheerful luxury. If my smile on the stairs had held something of defiance, my smile as I looked round my bedroom was of joy and relief and recognition. A room like this was my birthright, of which I had been cheated. Clothes such as those I was wearing, and others into which I would presently change, were my birthright: and the jewels Ailsa Muir would clip about my neck and wrists: and of all such I had been cheated, and I had won it all back. I had much to smile about, if I could forget just one or two small things . . .

Slanting rain threw itself against the great windows of the room. I raised a corner of the heavy brocade curtain, and looked out over the policies of the castle and the glorious countryside beyond. There was little enough I could see. It was still early in the evening, and our northern gloaming in midsummer lasts far towards midnight: but the dirty weather, the low scurrying clouds and driving rain, darkened the heavens and hid the land. The day had started as fair as such a day should start, but the wind changed at noon, and later the rain came down in sheets.

I shuddered at the thought of being abroad on such a night, of being a tinker or beggar or fugitive; but it made my bedroom seem the more snug and luxurious. Even in the Highlands, we are not used to having a fire in a bedroom on Midsummer Day: but a small fire twinkled in my grate, and I was glad of it. I was even glad of the need for it, for it made the room so very welcoming.

Turning away from the window, I saw a stranger looking at me from within a great golden frame. The frame rimmed a looking-glass larger than any door in the house where I had been living until that morning. The stranger was myself.

Closer inspection revealed that there was, to be sure, some familiarity in that reflected image. The pale gold hair was the same, the nose I thought even a little too small, and the blue eyes I thought even a little too large, and the figure that looked slender to the point of frailty. (But I was not frail. I knew little enough about myself, perhaps, but I knew that I was not frail. Had I been, I could not well have survived the grinding years since my childhood.) Most familiar— a kind of talisman, a mark that guaranteed that I was in truth myself— was the small mole by my left eye, inherited from my mother, who had an identical mole identically placed. A blemish, a disfigurement, perhaps: but I had known all my life, because I had been told all my life, that my mole was sited exactly where a court beauty of Queen Anne's time would have placed her beauty-spot, her 'patch'. Likewise I had known all my life, because I had been told all my life, that the mole made me even more beautiful. That is what people said—'*even* more beautiful'. But I had not heard the remark so very often since my childhood, because I had not seen so very many people.

But the familiar matters of my face and figure were transformed by great changes both without and within. Without, I was encased in an afternoon dress of a blue which matched my eyes, a garment absolutely new and frighteningly expensive, made for me by a French dressmaker brought all the way from Edinburgh, such as I had never worn and scarcely ever even seen in the whole of my life before. And there were pearls about my neck, and diamonds and sapphires on my fingers. Changes, indeed. Within, there was lit a lamp of victory. The miseries and indignities of the past were behind, trampled, dead. My joy and satisfaction showed. When I smiled at myself in the looking glass, a pampered queen smiled back. I thought I had a right to that smile. I thought I had a right to the happiness I had won.

I thought I had a right to ignore the shadows of uneasiness at the edges of my mind.

Phemie curtseyed herself out.

'Ye'll be wishfu' tae chenge, ma leddy?' asked Ailsa Muir.

'Yes, of course,' I said.

Since, for the first time in my life, I had wardrobes full of beautiful gowns, it would have been perverse not to wear them. They had all been made for me, most by the Frenchwoman, and brought to this room to await my triumphant arrival.

'There is a kind of gown,' I said, 'somewhere hanging up, in heavy cream-coloured silk, with ermine at the neck and wrists . . .'

'Ay, I ken yon goon. But I dinna richtly ken how tae ca' it.'

I shrugged and laughed. I did not know what to call it, either. It was not quite an evening gown, nor a dressing-robe, but something in between; it could have had no conceivable place in my life until this moment; but it was intended for just such an occasion as this, for a supper tête-à-tête in a boudoir. It was a garment of the most amazing luxury. Ever since I had tried it on, I had adored it, and looked forward avidly to this moment when I should wear it.

Ailsa Muir thought it was a garment devised by Satan. Events proved, I think, that she was right.

There was a cushioned annexe to the bedroom, in which great quantities of hot water were waiting for me, with sponges, and hot towels the size of bed-sheets; and cakes of soap scented with all the perfumes of Arabia. Ailsa Muir helped me to make myself adorable, by dint of scented soapsuds and a meticulous brushing and arranging of my hair. Dour she may have been, but her fingers were so deft they felt like moths. It was a totally new experience for me, to be looked after so expertly. I revelled in it.

She found for me such silk stockings and underclothes as I had not dreamed of, until my good fortune came: and soon I was swathed in the heavy cream silk with the ermine trim, with my hair in a golden knot low at the back of my neck, and a smile on my face which was the smile of the cat that had got at the cream.

Oh, the face and figure, the hair and the little mole, were still familiar in the enormous looking glass—but what was this robe of a particularly luxury-loving empress? What was this radiant contentment, this unconcealed enjoyment of it all?

And what were those little black question-marks, running like spiders about the shadows at the edge of my mind?

He had left me in the hall, with the butler, pleading arrangements he must make without delay about our journey in the morning. He said, rightly enough, that I would want to settle into my new quarters, and freshen myself after the fatigues of the day.

I had not expected him to have a bottle of brandy in the carriage. He drank from it the minute the rain started. He said it was to keep out the wet. He wanted me to drink some, but the neck of the bottle rattled against my teeth, and the strange burning taste made me feel sick. He had drunk half the bottle by the time we arrived. He held it well. There was no stutter in his speech or in his walk. Perhaps his cheeks were a little flushed, and there was a curious glitter in his eyes when he stared at me.

Well, a man should be flushed and bright-eyed when he stares at the woman he loves. Passion reddens cheeks and kindles eyes, as well as brandy. I put out of my mind the whispers I had heard, and followed Phemie upstairs.

Now, ninety minutes later, I was ready.

Ailsa Muir put more coals on the fire, and drew the curtains more snugly against the rain which hurled itself ill-temperedly against the windows. She began to collect together the clothes in which I had arrived, in order to take them away.

The door burst open. Ailsa Muir gave a little shriek of surprise: for in well-regulated households bedroom doors are opened demurely, after knocks. I did not shriek. I am not given to shrieking. But I was just as surprised as Ailsa Muir.

He stood in the doorway, swaying a little. He had not changed his clothes. But he had changed his bottle. He had a new one, three-quarters full. His hair was rumpled: it was the first time I had seen it unkempt by so much as a single strand. His eyelids sagged: but below them I saw that his eyes had a red gleam. His face was pale, and looked sweaty and unhealthy, but there were vivid scarlet blotches over his cheeks.

He walked slowly forward into the room. He walked with exceeding care, as though he knew he would fall if he stumbled. He was almost unrecognisable. I had never seen him like that before; I had never seen anyone like that before. The charming, polished gentleman had quite disappeared: and in his place was a disgusting stranger.

He raised his bottle and drank from it. He drank deep, swaying. When he lowered the bottle there was a dribble of spirit on his chin. I smelled the brandy across the room, over the scent of the flowers and my soaps and the lavender which had sweetened my clothes.

He made a gesture to Ailsa Muir, with his bottle. He was ordering her to leave the room, my room. She glanced at me, with a stricken face.

'Get out, you old crow, before I kick you out,' he said. He did not speak loudly, but the brutality of his words and tone was worse than a bellow.

Ailsa Muir curtseyed awkwardly, and scuttled out of the room. She left the door ajar, fearing, perhaps, to enrage him by banging it behind her.

'Now, little ladyship,' he said, with a smile that had no joy in it. 'What shall we do? What you want to do, or what I want to do?'

'What do you want to do?' I asked.

I tried to make my voice calm, partly in the hope of calming him, partly in the hope of calming myself, partly because I abhor the thought of anyone frightening me, and prefer to meet unpleasant things with resolution. I could not meet this unpleasant thing with quite enough resolution. My voice was a wretched little squeak. I knew I sounded frightened. I was frightened.

'What do I want to do?' he repeated. He laughed. There was no joy in his laugh. 'Let us think. Let us cat-catalogue the things I want to do. I want to possess you.' He did not say 'possess', but used a grosser word, a word of the most squalid and desperate tinker-folk.

'I want to teach you who you are and who I am,' he said, more clearly. 'You are very beautiful, and very ari-aristocratic, so you have not yet taken in who I *now* am, and what you *now* are. You are bred to arr-arrogance. You must be educated. You are spoiled. You mus' be dis-disciplined. That is my clear duty. We mus' start as we mean to go on. My clear duty.'

He turned, and stumbled to the door. He slammed it shut, and locked it. He drank deep from the bottle, spilling this time the spirit copiously down his shirt-front, so that he reeked of the brandy.

I stood stock-still, staring at him, too appalled to move so much as a finger. And where could I move? Even drunk, he was twice as strong as I. I am strong for my size, and can move very quick, but I could not be any match for him, whatever his condition, in a confined space where I could not run clear away.

The rain hurled itself against the windows out of the black sky. The flames hissed and gurgled in the grate. His breath was harsh in his throat, and his smile ugly on his transformed face. Suddenly his voice came out clear and rational, as though the force of an important thought had cleared his brain and his speech. 'I only like it if I'm hurting them,' he said in his new, reasonable voice. It seemed he knew I could not fail to be impressed with the excellence of his argument. 'And the more I'm hurting them, the more I like it. You understand? It is so simple. Of course you understand. You are the most beautiful girl I have ever seen, and you are a great ari-aristocrat, so it is necessary . . .' His voice thickened again, and his eyes glazed. 'You asked for it,' he finished, and drank deep from his bottle.

He was right. I had asked for it. This situation was all my own fault, all of my own making. I had chosen the road to this bedroom.

All my life, my road had been downhill—down, down, down, until I was in despair. I had chosen this road to climb, in one gigantic step, back to the peaks where I belonged.

He was right. I had asked for it.

My life had started not on a peak but on a plateau. (I knew the difference between peaks and plateaux, and even how to spell the French plural 'plateaux'. My governess Miss MacRae had not taught me much, but she was enthusiastic about geography, and could look up French plurals in a book.)

I was born at Strathlarrig Castle, above Loch Grannom, in Western Perthshire, in the Central Highlands of Scotland. It was the ancient home of my family. My Papa was Percival Charles Edward Douglas, 11th Earl of Larrig and Mount Douglas. I was his only child and heiress, and no girl in the world could have been luckier in her birth.

There must have been drab days and dismal days in my childhood; there must even have been ill-temper and punishment. But I do not remember them. I thought that if I died and went to heaven (which did not seem very likely) I did not want any other heaven than Strathlarrig.

The castle itself was very large and very beautiful. It compared well with the greatest neighbouring houses, the castles of Glendraco and Ravenburn. (It compared *very* well with Ravenburn, which had been built by a millionaire in 1830, as a monument to his millions.) It had a moat, in which there were wildflowers instead of water; it had a drawbridge which did not go up, and a portcullis which did not go down; it had inner and outer courtyards, and a central keep of awesome height; and four acres of roof, part stone, part steep-pitched slates from Snowdon. It had great rooms and small rooms, an infinity of rooms, and miles of passages, and a warren of cellars and a warren of attics, in all of which I played hide-and-seek with throngs of neighbouring children. It had fine gardens, and girdling them a fine park with two distinct herds of exotic deer, and girdling that the home farms and the tenant farms, and girdling them the big hills, deer forest and grouse moor, which fell in green cliffs, each side of the Larrig river, to the wooded bottoms of Loch Grannomside.

I was the only child of loving and indulgent parents. I had a loving and indulgent governess, my dear Miss MacRae. I was petted by the indoor servants and spoiled by the outdoor servants. I ran completely wild and I was completely happy.

I was not taught much by Miss MacRae, but I was taught everything I wanted to know by all the others. I had my own fat pony before my fourth birthday, and rode as often as I ran or walked or climbed. I had my own fishing rod before I was seven, and drove my own pony-phaeton before I was nine. Of course I was too young for these things: but I wanted them: so I was given them.

Even my most terrifying childhood memories were somehow joyous. When I was eight, I had a slender silver-grey pony called Gimcrack.

(My great-great-grandfather, the 8th Earl, went to Newmarket in 1766, and wrote to his Countess that he had cheered a beautiful, swift, delightful little grey racehorse called Gimcrack. The letter had been preserved, in an album in the library at Strathlarrig, and I read it. Of couse my own beautiful, swift, delightful little grey acquired the same name.) I was never supposed to ride without a groom beside me. Especially I was not allowed to ride Gimcrack without a groom, because he was excitable, and pulled hard. I found this restriction irksome and insulting. I was long off the leading-rein, and I was proud of my horsemanship and of my horse. Gimcrack could gallop like the wind, and jump like a stag. It was not what the grooms liked, or what their staid old horses liked. So, one day in June, just before my ninth birthday, I gave my groom the slip. It was gloriously easy. I jumped a wall which his horse refused. I heard the hoarse shouts of the poor groom behind me, but I screamed that I was run away with, and could not stop. Then I found that it was true. Gimcrack and I went a wild, pell-mell gallop down a long slope of the hillside, over a burn, and on and on and far away from anywhere. I would have been frightened, if I had allowed myself to be so silly. I made myself enjoy every hair-raising stride of that wild gallop. I lost my hat and my whip. I had no idea where we were going, or where we had got to. I held on to the pommel of my side-saddle, and clung for dear life, and stayed safely aboard Gimcrack—until a tinker rose like a grouse-bird from the heather, and Gimcrack shied and threw me off.

The next thing I knew, I was alone on the heather, with a sore head, in the darkness. I was cold. I had lost the coat of my habit. It had been stolen. There had been a gold locket round my neck on a chain. That was gone, too.

I started walking in the darkness. But I did not know which way to go, and I kept falling down, tripped by old heather, and my head hurt. I began to weep. I was furious with myself, and thankful that no one could see. I sat, hugging my knees, until daylight, thinking of the stories the crofter-folk told, about the little people and the kelpies and the evil spirits of the hills, and fighting a great battle, inside myself, against fright and further tears. I was *not* frightened. I was clear on the point.

They found me two hours after sunrise. Gimcrack had come home, with a swinging stirrup and reins about his knees, shinsore and sorry for himself. There had been a hue-and-cry and an all-night search.

Mamma and Papa were so thankful to see me safe in the morning, that there was no thought of punishment from them.

Miss MacRae thought there should have been. 'You were thoughtless and inconsiderate, Catriona,' she said. 'I think you must be forbidden to ride for a month.'

'I thought you would be glad to see me back,' I said, 'but you are sorry.'

'Oh *no*, dearest child,' cried Miss MacRae, appalled that I should think this of her. So there was no further thought of punishment from her.

Lachlan MacGibbon, the groom I had escaped, thought there should have been.

'Yon waur a verra, verra ill ploy, ma leddy,' he growled at me, when I went to the stables, next afternoon, to see how Gimcrack was. 'If ye waur the bairnie o' a croft or a fairm ye'd be whippit.'

'I came to help you clean the tack and the harness, Lachlan,' I said, 'as a way of saying sorry, you know. But if you think I should be whipped—'

'I didna just say that,' cried Lachlan. 'I'd be blithe for yer aid wi' the leathers.'

So we cleaned the tack together—I loved the smell of saddlesoap— and there was no further thought of punishment from him.

Fishing, I fell into burns times without number. Even Mamma exclaimed with dismay, from the sofa where her health obliged her to spend all her time, when I came dripping into the drawing room.

'You cannot stop me falling in, Mamma,' I said, 'because I cannot stop myself falling in. So wouldn't it be best if I was taught to swim?'

Mamma threw up her hands (but only a little way, because any vigorous movement exhausted her) at the audacity of this suggestion.

I began swimming lessons, from a famous athlete called Captain Barclay, two days later.

And this was a curious and renewed miracle about my childhood. Things that should have turned out wrong, by some magic turned out right. It was so when I was climbing on the roof, and the storm came.

Climbing on the roof would have been utterly forbidden, even by my gentle Papa. But I took good care that neither he nor anyone else knew that I did it. The oldest, medieval parts of the castle were roofed in stone, very rough and easy to grip, simple to climb in safety, and therefore uninteresting. New slate roofs covered the other parts. They were steep-pitched and smooth. The height from the ground was truly awesome. The courtyards were paved in granite. It did not do, when one was climbing, to think of a fall all the way down onto those flagstones. Once or twice, when a loose slate slipped under me, I had to scrabble and scramble for safety, and then I could come close to admitting to myself that I was frightened. Just for a moment, you understand: just for as long as there was a serious danger that I should fall. This was the lure of the roof. It was a challenge, of the sort I could never resist.

Well, one stuffy summer night, I slipped out of my bedroom window, careful not to wake Miss MacRae next door. (I would not wake anyone else—the nursery wing was far from the other bedrooms or any of the public rooms.) A down-pipe took me up to the guttering, the gutter took me over the battlements, and the slates rose into the darkness like a hillside from the leaded passage behind the battlements. Up I went, like a spider in my nightgown, to the ridge. I pulled myself onto the ridge, and sat astride it, my nightgown round my thighs, gripping the ridge with my legs as though I were a jockey riding a horse—riding the great original Gimcrack himself. I imagined riding in a race. I had a midnight daydream of riding the winner of the big race at Perth.

As I enjoyed the roaring of the crowd in my mind's ear, the air seemed to crackle round me, and the wind gust hotly from every direction. And then, as so often happens in the Highlands, the storm rushed down from the high tops, and hit at the castle like a housemaid hitting at a carpet on a clothesline. Rain whipped at me, and violent wind tried to pluck me from the ridge. The slates, running with water, were as slippery as rocks in a burn. My fingers grew numb in the cold rain. It was bottomlessly dark.

I struggled not to be frightened, but I knew that I must not stay where I was. I must contrive to get along the ridge to the shelter of a chimney. I knew exactly where the chimney was, although I could not see it in the teeming, screaming darkness. I started inching along the ridge, clinging desperately with knees and arms, fighting the wind and the driving rain.

Even that terrible journey, of twenty slippery and buffeted yards, is a joyful memory, because of what I found at the end.

I reached the chimney, and it did give me merciful shelter from the worst of the wind and the rain. I could breathe better, without rain filling my mouth and my nose, and grip better, at the rough stones of the chimney, and think better, without the immediate prospect of being dashed on the flagstones of the courtyard. I could grip better still, when my fingers found a gaping hole in the masonry of the chimney, where a block of granite had crumbled or fallen out. There was a lull in the wind, and I heard a small, distressed peeping sound from within the hole. I groped in with one hand, gripping hard at the stone with the other, and felt several fluffy balls, smaller than my childish fist. I counted them, with my fingertips. There were seven. They were young chicks, nestlings of a bird which had found the hole in the chimney.

One of the keepers had shot, two days before, a pair of white-owls in the park. My Papa was angry when he heard about it, because he loved all birds, and knew that white-owls ate all manner of mice and rats and vermin: but he was not angry long, because his mind went off onto something else, as it always did.

These were the chicks of the white-owls, left to starve. Five of the seven had starved; I felt, with my fingertips, the unmistakable slackness of tiny bodies in death. Two were alive, wriggling and peeping under my fingers, frightened and hungry.

I lifted them carefully out of the hole, and put them into the front of my nightgown. They wriggled against the bare skin of my chest; their feet and beaks tickled so that I almost screamed.

The storm went away as quickly as it had come. I climbed safely back to my bedroom, careful not to squash the chicks by leaning my chest on the slates.

I gave Miss MacRae, in the morning, an explanation which she believed for having a soaking-wet nightgown, and two white-owl chicks. I reared the chicks, with help from half the castle. One died, and I buried him under a white wooden cross in the rose-garden. The other thrived, and lived happily, very tame and shamefully greedy, until we left Strathlarrig and our downward slide began.

That is a good example of how things that might have ended badly turned out wonderfully well. It is a good example of the benevolent magic that looked after all my childhood.

Although many of the things I liked doing, I liked doing alone, such as fishing, I liked company too. I had many friends of my own age, or near it. Though Strathlarrig was set in glorious wild country, it was not really at all remote—not far from the houses of many lairds of Glendraco, and Loch Grannomside, and Loch Chinnside, and Glendoran, and convenient for the grim little town of Lochgrannomhead.

Besides enjoying the company of my friends, and playing hide-and-seek with them, I profited from them in unexpected ways. When I was five, I was shown by Tom Ravenburn how to climb into my own home by a little trapdoor into the coal-cellars. This secret was very useful to me, on various occasions over the next few years. I showed it to my greatest friend, Tom's sister Katie; and I tried to show it to her little twin brother and sister: but the twins were afraid of getting dirty. I was *never* deterred by the fear of getting dirty, or the fear of breaking my neck; I am afraid I was never deterred by the thought of the trouble I might give, or the anxiety I might cause. Draco once accused me of being thoughtless, but his grandmother the 'Dragon' (who terrified everybody but whom I adored) said that I had three score years and ten for thinking in, and I must enjoy being thoughtless while I could: and so I did.

Though I had many friends, I lost the best ones. Tom Ravenburn killed a man, and had to run away, and they said he was afterwards killed in Australia. His sister, my dear Katie, was sent a little mad by this disaster, and never saw anybody. Old General Gordon of Carnmore sold his property to an ironmaster, so his son Alistair went away with his wife and children; the children were a loss to me, and Mariota Gordon was a loss to Mamma, as they had been childhood friends. But these were small blots on a near-perfect world.

I was lucky in almost everything, but I was luckiest, perhaps, in the love of Mamma and Papa.

Mamma had been an invalid ever since she gave birth to me (which was why I was an only child) but she never lost the sweetness of her nature or of her smile. She never lost her beauty, either. Though she became plump, with her enforced idleness, she still had the rose-petal skin and golden hair and clear blue eyes of the paintings of her when she was a bride. In a sweet, true voice she sang old Scottish songs, to my Papa's accompaniment: but never for as long as everybody wanted, because she was very easily fatigued. For this reason, she did scarcely any embroidery, or reading, and would have been bored but for the number of people who came constantly to sit with her.

My Papa was as sweet-tempered as she, but he had always the buzzing energy of a honeybee, the enthusiasm of a ratting terrier. He was a clever man—people said he would have been a professor at a great university, if he had not been born an Earl—with an enormous range of interests. Indeed, he had too many interests, with the result that he jumped like a sand-fly from project to project, leaving a trail of half-finished inventions behind him.

At one time he developed a passion for ballooning, believing that balloons were the mode of transport of the future. He founded the Highland Balloon Freight and Transport Company, and invested enthusiastically in his own beautiful idea. For months the park at Strathlarrig was full of brilliantly coloured balloons, which frightened the deer; but the wind often blew in an inconvenient direction, and it seemed the balloons did not go high enough to clear the hills.

After he had broken his leg a second time, Papa fell out of love with balloons, and fell to inventing a new musical instrument called the Larriphone, something between a violoncello and a tuba, which you were to blow through a mouthpiece at the same time as you played the strings with a bow. He had several of these instruments made in Edinburgh, and commissioned special compositions from leading composers, and gave recitals. To me the consort of Larriphones sounded wonderful, and unlike anything else, but they never found a place in orchestras.

I was fascinated by Papa's inventions, and very proud of them, and furious that the world did not at once adopt his new mousetrap, his new steam-locomotive, his new telescope, his new miner's-lamp. Of course he encouraged my interest, and often let me help him. I remember the glorious day when we dismantled a grandfather clock, in order that Papa could install a new kind of chime he had invented, which was softer by night than by day. Pieces of the clock were spread all over the carpets in the drawing room; Mamma on her sofa, like a mermaid on an island in a sea of little bits of machinery, smiled lovingly and proudly at us both; but when the last screw had been unscrewed, Papa, whose brain was always active, had a sudden idea about a new kind of step-ladder for painters and plasterers, and trotted out to the estate joiner's shop behind the stables, and began drawing plans on the whitewashed wall of a byre. Weeks later, the clock was reassembled by a watchmaker from Lochgrannomhead: but some pieces were missing or bent, and it never worked well again. Nor was the step-ladder a success, although Papa took out a patent, and had hundreds made out of oak and iron. People admired the ladder, but it was too heavy to carry.

Papa said the world was not ready for most of his ideas, but he never lost his optimism. The world was getting more ready, as each day went by, and each new idea was better than any previous idea he had ever had.

I think my parents were completely happy in their lives, and in each other, and in me. No wonder my life as a child was as near heaven as any human life can be.

The first changes puzzled me, but did not greatly upset me. I accepted them as a young child accepts the mysterious happenings of the grown-up world. The deer disappeared from the park, and were replaced by cattle and sheep. 'Good grazing land,' said Papa, 'should be enjoyed by the useful, not the merely decorative.' This was after the winding-up of the Highland Balloon Freight and Transport Company. Then the formal gardens were let go, and the topiary yews were left unclipped, and the golden carp disappeared from the ponds, and the white peacocks from the lawns. 'Ostentatious and artificial,' said Papa, 'we are better without them.' That was after the failure of the Larriphone. Then the number of carriages in the coach-house was reduced from twelve to three, and the number of horses to two, and the number of coachmen to one. 'How could a sane man want more?' said Papa. That was after he made a bonfire of step-ladders.

Fired by Papa's example, I was also an inventor, and invented a new kind of slingshot, which threw stones with amazing force: but not with amazing accuracy: so I broke one of the stained-glass windows in the Castle chapel. It was boarded up, and thereafter there were pine planks where there had been St Christopher carrying the Christ-child over a sky-blue burn.

Men of business came more and more often to see Papa (he would never go to them, because he would not leave Mamma, and she could not endure the fatigues of a journey)—lawyers and bankers and brokers and trustees—men with tall black hats and solemn whiskers. There were long conferences, in Papa's business-room. Afterwards, Papa was glum. But always Mamma cheered him up, and soon he was busy and happy as ever.

And then, soon after my tenth birthday, the world turned upside down. We left Strathlarrig. The Castle and estate were let to a Mr Jenks, from England. We moved to a farmhouse near Lochgran-nomhead, with four servants, and one carriage, and a two-acre garden. There was no room there for my phaeton or my pony. There was no park to prowl, no cliff to climb, no burn to fish.

Papa and Mamma consoled one another, and prayer consoled them both. Papa threw himself into new inventions that would restore his fortunes, and Mamma smiled and applauded, and waited for more visitors than she received. Old Lady Draco still came; young Lady Ravenburn did not come.

My horizons had been limitless. Now I could reach out and touch the edges of my world.

'We shall be back,' said Papa. 'This is only a temporary arrangement. Jenks is a good fellow. He will look after Strathlarrig for us. Poor little Cat, poor Kitten, it's hardest on you, I know, but don't repine. We shall be back before you know it. We won't be in these quarters long.'

Nor were we. We moved after two years to a smaller house, with two servants only, and one old wagonette, and half an acre of dismal shrubbery. Miss MacRae left, in tears, and Papa concerned himself with my education. But he did not have very much time for it, as his head was so full of ideas for important new inventions.

'I am *never* unduly optimistic, you know,' he said to Mamma, 'but I do seriously believe that the world has been waiting for a portable commode for railway journeys.'

The last of Mamma's jewellery financed the manufacture of the Larrig Traveller's Companion.

'Of *course* I do not grudge a few trinkets, dearest,' she said. 'I am so happy that I have been able to help a little.'

'You shall have more and better jewels,' said Papa.

'I know,' said Mamma comfortably. 'I know all our prayers will be answered.'

And some of their prayers were answered. They prayed for courage, and they had courage. They prayed for one another's happiness, and they had that too.

Mr Jenks found Strathlarrig too expensive. The lawyers could not at once find a new tenant for so enormous a place. The loss of the rent was a serious matter. We moved house again.

Our third rented house was the first I really hated. We had one servant, a woman with grease on her forearms and hairs on her chin. Mamma could not entertain. Even she was ashamed to be seen by her old friends in her new parlour. I was growing towards womanhood, and people said I was a beauty, but I was ashamed to be seen by my old friends in my new clothes.

Papa had no such scruples. Never a dandy, he looked like a tinker, with frayed cuffs to his shirt, and darns in his coat, and dents in his hat. He bustled to and fro, more than ever like a terrier, trying to finance his new invention among the shopkeepers of Lochgrannomhead. They were not impressed with his steam-plough, although he calculated the profits they would make to eight places of decimals.

I tried not to be angry with Papa. Ah God, how hard I tried. I tried not to feel bitter and betrayed.

'Poor little Cat, poor Kitten,' said Papa. 'But it's only a temporary arrangement, you know. You shall have silk gowns and high-stepping horses. Everything will be back as it was, you'll see, as soon as people wake up to their own best interests.'

'Everything will be all right, little Pussy,' said Mamma, 'because Papa's newest idea cannot fail to be appreciated.'

But I was not a kitten or a little pussy, a contented pet purring by the fire-side. I was growing up and I was half mad with anger and helplessness and shame.

Papa was sent twenty guineas by a lawyer, some dividend or rent he was due. It came at a fortunate moment; it was a God-send. Papa bustled out and into the town, to buy some things we truly needed. He came back with a pot of exotic honey, a bottle of expensive French wine, and a silk shawl for Mamma. She shrieked with joy, and kissed him, and said that he spoiled her. I left them holding hands, like children, while he told her about a new idea he had had while he was walking home from the shops.

I ran out of the horrible little house before it suffocated me, and walked blindly, far and fast, out into the empty countryside. A carriage appeared. I hid behind a rowan-tree at the roadside, in case it should be anybody who knew me. It was. In the carriage was Georgina Campbell of Drumlaw, whom I had known all my life. She was a little older than I. She had left the schoolroom. She was soon to be presented at Holyrood, and to go to the balls and races. She wore a red silk gown, and a lovely little red hat with a white plume in it. The carriage was a spanking new Victoria, its brasswork and varnish gleaming. The horse was a beauty, a bright bay with a smooth, powerful action. The coachman was as smart as a pipe-major on parade. Georgina was rattling home to Drumlaw, to a comfortable house with excellent servants, to her own big bedroom with a wardrobe full of silk gowns, to a free and full life among her equals, to a father who held what he had.

The Campbells of Drumlaw had been a good deal flattered to be asked to Strathlarrig.

I did what I had never done, not once, since we left Strathlarrig. I threw myself on the ground, and burst into a passion of weeping, beating on the ground with my fists, cursing my fate and my father.

2

As I walked home, I fought and won another of my internal battles. Misery was childish and unhelpful. Tears were profitless, and made my eyes red. Rage was a waste of energy, and I would be needing all my energy: because, although I was only fifteen, I decided that I must take charge of the household.

Papa was too brilliant and too busy to be bothered with daily details. His eyes were on the stars, and so he did not see three-penny-bits on the ground. He was wonderful at calculating the most complex mathematical formulae, but they disabled his brain for stretching fifteen shillings to cover our food for a week. He trusted the most palpably dishonest shopkeepers, because he believed the best of everyone; he swallowed the most obviously false stories, because he could not imagine that anyone would try to deceive him; he knew everything would come right, because he prayed, and knew that his prayers would be answered. All that was best about him, made him the worst of all possible managers. All that I loved most about him, was what most infuriated me.

And Mamma? Dearest Mamma could not manage an egg into an egg-cup. She not only lacked all talent for practical matters, she lacked any experience of them. She had never made a decision in her life. Papa decided even what colour of gown she should wear, and always had.

I made myself think objectively about my beloved parents. It is not an easy thing for an ignorant child of fifteen to do. It is not a proper thing for one so young to do. I found it painful. I felt treacherous. But I forced myself to be old far beyond my years, and to think of my parents as children. Children they were. They needed looking after. I was the only person who could do it. It was as simple as that. There would be no more tears or rages, then, no more bitterness or despair.

It was a good resolution, that one. A saint could not have kept it. I was far from being a saint.

Dr McPhee had been to see Mamma, and he was drinking tea with Papa when I got home. Dr McPhee did not seem to be enjoying the tea. Papa had made it, as it was Morag's afternoon off. He treated tea-making as something between a scientific challenge and a nursery game. (He loved both scientific challenges and nursery games.) He treated laying and lighting the parlour fire in the same way, and making up Mamma's bed, and drawing up the household accounts. The results were always interesting and unusual.

Dr McPhee was a little bristling man like a terrier, with unruly black hair turning to grey; he had a rapid, irritable manner which concealed a very kind heart. He came to see Mamma at least once a week. He was her only regular visitor. I did not know when Papa had last paid him. I was quite sure that Papa did not know either. Dreamers, I thought, have other victims beside themselves.

Dr McPhee might not be enjoying his tea, but he was enjoying his conversation with Papa. Any intelligent man must have done so. It was a pity Papa saw so few intelligent men, since he had removed himself entirely from society.

The two of them were in the parlour. Mamma was still upstairs, in her poky bedroom, where Dr McPhee had examined her. I foraged for scraps of cake or biscuits in the kitchen, for we had had a frugal luncheon, and my violent walk had made me ravenous; but Morag had stolen every morsel of food there was.

I could hear Papa's melodious, almost fluting, voice, along the little dark passage, and Dr McPhee's brusque contributions.

They talked about a thousand things whenever they met, those two clever men starved of the conversation of clever men. That day, they had somehow got onto the subject of breeding and training animals.

'You'll take the case of the thoroughbred racehorse, Lord Larrig,' Dr McPhee was saying. 'Not a beastie with which I am personally well acquaint, but one the subject of copious and meticulous record, and therefore an excellent example for an academic appraisal of the matters we are discussing.'

'My grandfather tried to breed racehorses at Strathlarrig,' said Papa, 'but the climate is too harsh. I myself would prefer to see races held between steam locomotives or balloons, to guide us in the designs of the future. Racehorses have no function except to race, whereas balloons . . .'

He sighed. There was still a soft spot in Papa's heart for balloons.

'You cannot breed a balloon, by one model out of another,' said Dr

McPhee, with the strangled snort he used for a laugh. 'The point I am making is of general application among living creatures, but I am citing the thoroughbred racehorse because of the plentiful and exact information the creature has collected about itself. From dubious motives, no doubt—the evil of gambling. But there's many a useful by-product from an ill activity.'

'As when,' said Papa, 'I was laid up with a broken leg, and in that uncongenial enforced idleness, had leisure to give intensive study to the problems of a new kind of musical instrument. The problems, you will understand, are artistic as well as technical, a combination as complex as it is fascinating.'

Papa liked hearing what other people had to say, but he did not like them to go on for too long. In conversation, as in life, he jumped from subject to subject. It was as though each new topic was a room with doors leading in a dozen fascinating directions.

Dr McPhee, by contrast, was like a badger, who sank his teeth into the subject before him, and never let go, no matter what distractions Papa waved in his face.

'The thoroughbred racehorse,' said the doctor doggedly, 'any given individual example of the breed, possesses the sum of the qualities of its parents. It inherits perhaps colour and conformation from the dam, and impetuosity and a certain wildness of disposition, let us say, from the sire. Now, the question I put to you is, what effect will training and experience have on those inherited qualities? Let us take the case of a high-bred filly, who inherits great beauty, great abilities, great courage, but who inherits at the same time a streak of—let us call it enthusiasm, a streak of perversity and obstinacy. This filly, let us hypothesise, has been allowed to run wild. Has been, not to put too fine a point on it, grossly indulged by a handler with more kindness than commonsense. Then let us suppose that this pampered, high-bred young female creature is subjected to increasing indignity and suffering. Is compelled to eat indifferent hay, and prevented from running with the other yearlings, and feels the metaphorical if not the literal lash of the whip. What then?'

'She will kick,' said Papa, for once keeping close to the conversation, and for once giving an apposite reply.

'She will kick,' repeated Dr McPhee.

It was at this moment that I realised, with an almost overpowering shock, that Dr McPhee was not talking about horses at all. Papa was, but not the doctor. He was trying, tactfully and indirectly, to warn Papa about the future. My future. He was talking about me.

'If this filly's courage fails her,' Dr McPhee went on, 'her heart will break from despair. But, from her breeding, we may guess that that will not happen. We may guess that her courage will hold. If it does, she will be a wild and a dangerous character. She will shy and buck and bolt. She will kick and bite. What has happened to her is overlaid, so to put it, on what she is by nature and heredity, and the result is as explosive as the mixture of chemicals in a bomb.'

'Chemistry,' said Papa, 'is an area of study to which I have not heretofore had time to devote sufficient attention . . .'

I had no chance to kick, when I took over the reins of the household.

It made no difference to Mamma—she had never held any reins. Papa was delighted to have more time for his serious work.

We managed a little better. I persuaded Papa to give me a fixed sum weekly, and never to give me less. It was almost all the money he got from the lawyers who had taken charge of his affairs. I drew up careful accounts, trying to add up correctly. I gave myself headaches, poring over columns of figures, and remembering how many pence went to a shilling. I apportioned the money between the rent, the wages of the servant, the outlay on food, Mamma's medicines (she needed one or two medicines, but her happiness required a dozen) and other absolute necessities.

I tried to leave a little over, each week, for luxuries, and to save a little against calamity. It was impossible. There was none to spare.

Morag and Papa had shared the marketing between them. It was hard to say which did it worse. If Morag cheated us, the shopkeepers cheated Papa. I embarked upon it, shyly at first, not liking to haggle with the iron-faced shopkeepers of Lochgrannomhead, furious with shame at showing how we scraped and scrabbled for pennies: but becoming harder and more brazen, and striking all the bargains I could. I found that a high imperious air sometimes saved me from being cheated by the market wives—the horrible slatterns who had taken advantage of Papa's gentleness. Such an air accorded oddly with my wretched clothes. More often, with the fat pasty men in the shops, the butchers and bakers and fishmongers, a smile and a fluttering of my childish eyelids knocked pence off the prices.

I would sometimes wake up in the night, and blush hotly all over to think how I had ogled some elderly tradesman, and saved a sixpence—I, who had once lifted a finger and acquired a pony-phaeton . . . but the sixpences were saved, and spent, and saved again by the same means, and carefully spent, and so life went on, and we were not starved or thrown into the street.

It was satisfying at first, to prove to myself how well I could manage the affairs of a household. It was another challenge. It became a grinding and humiliating labour, unchanging, each week identical.

Often I glimpsed the girls I had known in other days, who had been driven into the town from their fathers' country places. They were laughing and dressed in silks and buying expensive trifles, shawls and fans and pearl buttons, and exotic fruit and candies. I hid in the doorways of shops, until they were safely by.

I saw Elspeth Gordon, with her parents. They had gone abroad, when her grandfather sold Carnmore Castle: it seemed they were back. I was sure that Mariota Gordon, Elspeth's mother, would come to see Mamma. But she never did. Elspeth never came to see me, either. Elspeth was exactly the same age as I. Soon she would be out of the schoolroom, and flirting with cheerful young gentlemen. I had been out of the schoolroom for years, and I had as much chance of meeting any gentleman as of finding the Sovereign Touchstone amongst Papa's new chemicals.

Papa was besotted about this new field of scientific enquiry. He equipped a shed as a laboratory (Dr McPhee found him a few retorts and tubes of glass, and sold him some chemicals for a few pence) and spent happy hours making appalling smells. His clothes became shabbier than ever, stained with acids and reeking of chemicals.

He invented a new fuel, superior to coal, for railway engines and the boilers of factories. One day, when the problem of its vapours was resolved, it would be a household fuel, too. He was certain, of course, that his fortune was made. He talked of nothing else for weeks. The problem was to finance the large-scale manufacture of Larritherm. He could not sell Strathlarrig—castle or estate—because it was entailed on me. There was nothing else left for him to sell.

What he could do, was to commute part of his tiny income into a lump sum. (The income was so tiny, because of the burden of mortgages.)

There was a solicitor in Lochgrannomhead called John Macgregor, a small sharp-faced man with a sharp red nose and sharp red eyes. He was not one of Papa's regular lawyers, and I was surprised to find them in deep conference on several successive days. A paper was to be signed and witnessed. The effect was, that Papa had a fistful of money at once, and John Macgregor had the rents of some of the Strathlarrig farms.

'It is providential,' said Papa. 'I never knew that such an arrangement could be made, or I would have made it long ago. I am infinitely grateful to Macgregor. Larritherm will be patented, and we shall float a company for its massive commercial exploitation. We shall benefit humanity, and at the same time recover everything, everything, which . . .'

'How wonderful it is, dearest,' said Mamma, 'to make such great profits from something so truly useful. Virtue *is* rewarded, as we always knew it would be.'

'And in no time at all,' said Papa, 'I will repay Macgregor, and recover control of those farms, as well as of everything else. And then, my dear, you shall be back in your home, with rings on your fingers and maids at your call. And you, little Cat, will be Empress of Strathlarrig again, with gaze-hounds and spaniels and horses and carriages, and soon you shall be presented at Court, and we shall give a ball for you at Strathlarrig—the very grandest and gayest ball that ever was seen!'

'Yes, Papa,' I said, 'but are you sure it is wise? This artificial coal you have invented—'

'Larritherm is not artificial coal, Kitten. It is an entirely new and original composition. It burns hotter than coal. I have calculated that half a ton of Larritherm will heat as much water to boiling point as a ton, or almost a ton, of old-fashioned coal.'

'There, Pussy!' said Mamma. 'Only fancy—*half a ton* of Papa's invention . . . *Such* a quantity of boiling water. . .'

'If it is three times as expensive to make Larritherm as to dig out coal,' I said slowly, frowning as I tried to do the mental arithmetic, 'then it is still cheaper to use twice as much coal.'

'Pooh,' said Papa. 'Manufacture on a really large scale will bring down the price, naturally. Macgregor agrees with me about that, and he's a shrewd enough fellow.'

'Do the other lawyers agree? The proper lawyers?'

'They're not chemists, little Cat. How should they know about such things?'

'Is Mr Macgregor a chemist?'

'He is in my confidence. I have explained the whole to him. That is why he is obliging me with a hundred and thirty sovereigns.'

'Do you trust Mr Macgregor, Papa?'

'Of course I do!' cried Papa, much astonished at my question. 'Do you not? Why do you not? How can you not? He is a professional man, and acts according to professional standards and ethics. He is an honourable man, a religious man, a family man—in short, of course I trust him!'

'You must not get into the way of mistrusting people, Pussy,' said Mamma. 'It is horrid.'

Well, I tried to dissuade Papa.

I said he was reducing our income by a third, and we could barely live, even as we now lived, on the whole.

He said that Larritherm would carry us, on a wave of wealth, back to Strathlarrig.

He would not have it that Macgregor had the face of a ferret and the reputation of a fox.

He would not have it that his darling new fuel was far, far too expensive ever to take the place of one lump of coal, even if it burned as well as he said it did.

He burned some in the grate in the parlour, to convince me of its merit. It did burn. It glowed reluctantly for a short time, and went out. Papa talked airily about circumambient temperatures. It smelled abominable. Papa explained about ducts and fans and ventilators.

'Ventilators, Pussy,' echoed Mamma. 'For myself, I find the smell rather pleasing than otherwise, as soon as one has got used to it. But, in any case, there will be ventilators!'

I strove with them, like Jacob with two angels. I strove with myself at the same time, to keep my temper. I was aghast at the prospect of trying to manage on what Macgregor was leaving us. I knew the value of Larritherm to the nearest penny. It was not as much as a penny.

'We won't be able to live in this house,' I said. 'Even this horrible little house.'

'We will not need to!' said Papa triumphantly.

'We will go home to Strathlarrig,' said Mamma.

She smiled at Papa, proudly and comfortably, and he stretched out and took her hand.

That afternoon, in Macgregor's office, Papa signed away a third of our income.

That night, in bed, I decided to run away.

Next morning, at breakfast-time, Papa was bubbling and hissing with enthusiasm, louder than the kettle on the hob. Mamma patted his hand, whenever he held it still enough for her to do so.

They were Babes in the Wood. They had to be looked after. I had to look after them.

I decided not to run away.

I began instead enquiring for a cottage to rent, at the price I calculated we could afford.

Papa's magnificent new capital was not quite enough, it seemed, to finance the commercial development of Larritherm.

He called on Macgregor again.

When he came I strove again, with all my might and main, to stop this renewed folly.

Even at the time, I found it an extraordinary situation—a fifteen-year-old girl, with not much education, and no experience of the world beyond squalid haggling in shops, and no friends, talking like a governess to two middle-aged people, an Earl and Countess!—taking the part of sanity and commonsense, maturity, caution, prudence and providence, against whim and nursery daydream and the quest for fairy gold.

Mamma supported Papa, comfortably certain that this time—*this* time—our fortunes were restored.

'All that is required,' said Papa, 'is a little time—a little courage—and a little more capital. We have the time. God has granted us the courage. Macgregor is providing the capital.'

'Everything thought of,' said Mamma happily. 'A solution to each problem.'

I lost the battle with them, and I lost the battle with myself. Papa was unshakably determined to sign Macgregor's second paper; and I lost my temper.

I did not scream, but spoke quietly and slowly. I remember the sound of my own voice in my ears, unfamiliar in its bleak flatness.

'Haven't you done enough to me?' I said to Papa. 'You have proved a hundred times that you are incapable of inventing a teacup. If you were honest, you would admit it to yourself. But you deliberately lie to yourself and to Mamma and to me, pretending that you can do something useful, when you have to be helped to tie your shoelaces.

You are not clever, but half crazy. You are the most selfish man who ever lived, because you indulge yourself and amuse yourself, and cheerfully ruin my whole life. You say you love me. What a fine way you have of showing it. Look at this room. Look at my clothes. I would not mind giving my life to looking after a man, but I am sick and tired of playing nursemaid to a selfish and thoughtless imbecile. I will not forgive you, for what you have done to me. If you were sane and honest, you would not forgive yourself. But you are not sane and you are honest and you are not a man. You are like a silly little spoiled child, playing with expensive toys which I have paid for. *Which I have paid for.* If I knew how to curse, I would curse you.'

The bleak voice stopped. I found I had no more to say. There was silence in the ugly little parlour.

Papa was looking at me with a face of most abject misery. Mamma was crying softly.

I could not bear Papa's face, or Mamma's tears. I ran out of the room, and threw myself on my bed, and cried my own tears—only my second storm of tears—tears of shame and rage and bitterness, and terror of the penniless future.

I sat on a footstool by Mamma's sofa. I was aghast at myself.

'You see, my dearest Pussy,' Mamma said, 'people are as they are, and if you love them, you love them as they are. If Papa were a grim man of business, we might live more richly, but would we love him as we do? When I married Papa eighteen years ago, I swore that I would love, honour and obey him. I do, I always have, I always will. "For richer, for poorer, in sickness and in health." Those words mean exactly what they say, you know. It is not a polite form, it is a sacrament. I undertook to make Papa happy. I made that the object of my life, when I married him, because that is what marriage is. He is happy doing what he does, hoping as he does, being what he is. You can see that as well as I can. Well, dearest child, if *that* is how he is to be happy . . . you see? What are a few jewels and servants, weighed against his happiness? What sort of wife would I be, if I preferred silk gowns to his happiness?'

'Yes, Mamma,' I said, 'but. . . .'

'And then again, you know, dearest Pussy, he does *not* delude himself that he has been successful in his ideas or his investments. He is ashamed, so ashamed, of his failure. He is so ashamed to have dragged us down to this. What good will it do, if I reproach him? I will tell him nothing he does not know, quite well, for himself. Will *that* make him happy? Will *that* get us home to Strathlarrig? Oh dear . . .' Mamma paused. I saw that she was gently weeping again. She went on, shakily, 'Have you ever seen anything to match his courage? When everything is in ruins about him, he continues to strive and to hope, he continues to work, harder than ever, for our sake. . . .'

I buried my head in Mamma's lap, shaken by sobs of contrition. They were better tears than my other tears.

I knew that I loved them both, dearly and deeply and permanently.

And in part of my mind I knew that every word I had said was true.

I was doing things no young girl should do. I was not doing things every young girl should do. In some ways I had already grown up, in others I had not started growing. Part of me was middle-aged, part infant.

Looking back, I suppose I was a sort of deformed creature, a monster. Yet this monster dwelt within a shell which was far from deformed. People had always said I was beautiful, and I had always believed them, because it is a delightful thing to believe. Nobody now said so, because I saw nobody except market stall-holders and dour shopkeepers, who were not given to compliments. But there was a little grubby looking-glass in my little grubby bedroom, and in that I saw that I was beautiful, not quite in the ordinary way, but in a way of my own. I fancied myself a princess disguised as a beggar-maid. Really I was a beggar-maid disguised as a beggar-maid.

My face was my fortune. Much good it did me, when no one saw it.

In the fulness of time—and the less time the better—I must find and ensnare and marry a very rich man. It was my only hope of survival, and my parents' only hope. It was an absolute necessity. It was an absolute impossibility. I had as much chance of meeting a rich man, or any gentleman, as Papa had of inventing a perpetual-motion machine.

I knew nothing whatever of social rules, forms, machinery, procedures; we had left all that behind us when we left Strathlarrig, when I was ten. My ignorance allowed me to make preposterous plans, for falling into the path of this young millionaire duke or that. I composed the conversations between us, and sketched out, on his behalf, the ardent way that he courted me.

All fifteen-year-old girls daydream. There are few, I think, whose daydreams turn always about money.

I was a monster indeed. I must have been detestable to live with.

The lawyers came, Papa's real lawyers, from Perth. Their hats seemed taller and their whiskers more solemn than ever. I heard murmuring voices through the parlour door—a sombre monotone, like the lowest register of the Larriphone, punctuated by the expressive fluting notes of Papa's voice.

Papa wore a lop-sided smile when the lawyers had left.

'It is remarkable how things work out,' he said, with a heartrending attempt at heartiness. 'One thing that we have always longed for, but never had time for, is travel. Foreign travel, my dear! New sights and sounds and faces, Kitten! We shall all benefit immeasurably. I am truly excited at the prospect.'

Mamma looked at him with happy anticipation. What new treat did her wonderful husband have in store for her?

'Mr Murdoch and Mr Patterson are not *very* pleased at the arrangements I have made with Macgregor,' said Papa. 'Of course it is a kind of jealousy. They think I should have had no dealings with any lawyer except themselves. A small-minded attiude, and all too characteristic of a certain stamp of professional man . . . No no, I must be fair. They did formulate cogent arguments . . . At any rate, they pressed upon me the desirability of—of a visit abroad. A somewhat prolonged visit. We can find quarters in Dieppe or Boulogne, and live far cheaper than here. The amusing part is, Murdoch and Patterson put this suggestion to me as a deplorable necessity, little thinking how warmly we shall welcome the chance to widen our horizons and enrich our experience.'

Mamma clapped her hands, like a child at a party. 'I have not been to France since I was a young girl,' she cried. 'How I shall love to see it again!'

'And we shall be spared the horrid embarrassment,' I said, thinking of the number of times I had hidden from the people I once knew.

'What embarrassment?' said Papa, who had never felt any.

We removed to Dieppe in the spring of 1860. I passed my sixteenth birthday listening to a funny little band in a pretty little park.

Papa acquired a cotton jacket and a broad-brimmed hat, which he thought the suitable clothes for an exiled gentleman. He divided his time between inventions and practising his French. He spoke with great fluency, with much fluttering of his hands in the Gallic fashion, but the local people were not well enough educated to understand a single word he said.

Mamma simply changed one sofa for another; the solitude of one bleak little parlour for another.

Remittances arrived monthly, for Papa, from the lawyers. My great struggle was to get my hands on the money before Papa had spent it all—not on himself, never on himself, but on scientific toys, or useless gifts for Mamma and me.

In spite of the occasional efforts of my governess Miss MacRae, I arrived not speaking a word of French. I picked it up quickly, in the market and parks and port. I made friends. I was aware of male admiration, which was pleasant, and of female envy, which was far from unpleasant.

I could dress better in France. I could laugh, and enjoy myself. I could listen to graceful compliments in French from happy young men and roguish old men and tubby middle-aged men in gorgeous uniforms. It was all tawdry enough—a very narrow and limited provincial life—but it was heaven after Lochgrannomhead. Best of all, by far best of all, was that I did not have to dodge into doorways to avoid my one-time friends. The French were used to exiles like us, and another impoverished *milord,* more or less, made no great impression on them.

I was happier in Dieppe than I had been for six years. I made new plans. They were good plans.

It did not do. Mamma grew homesick. She became listless, and more easily fatigued than ever. The little French doctor tugged at his beard, and Papa grew more and more worried. Mamma's smiles grew forced; her chatter dried up. She could not get used to the food, or to the sound of foreign voices from the kitchen. She hid it as long as she could, but misery was making her ill.

We had to go home.

'Please, dear God,' I prayed with passion, 'let them go anywhere but Lochgrannomhead. Let them go to the South-West or the North-East or the Borders or anywhere in England, but not where everybody knows us and laughs at us. . .'

But to Lochgrannomhead we returned: because it was where Mamma felt at home.

Gravely, regretfully, Mr Murdoch and Mr Patterson found a house for us.

It was very fortunate, and very clever of them. They found a far better house than Papa could afford, let at a peppercorn rent.

'It is ridiculous,' said Papa. 'It makes one despair of human nature, except that one should *never* despair of an imperfect but perfectable creature, made in the Divine image, and inhabited by the Holy Ghost. . .'

'It is a truly lovely house,' said Mamma, 'and I am sure we shall all be very happy here. What a fine bedroom for you, dearest Pussy! And a drawing room where I can entertain my friends!'

There Mamma deceived herself. When old Lady Draco grew too old, she had no friends.

'The ridiculous part,' said Papa, 'is that we are to become a kind of living advertisement. Have you ever in your life heard of anything so preposterous? This house is one of several built by a Mr McGrouther, a speculative builder, it appears, from Glasgow or thereabouts. The houses are all of a pattern—a very good pattern too, in my estimation— which enables him to build them more cheaply. The methods of mass-production, applied to domestic architecture—fascinating, is it not? I am, for one, more than gratified to be taking my part, in a meas- ure, in so useful a revolution. . . At any rate, Mr McGrouther is com- mendably anxious to trumpet the virtues of his design, and so to at- tract people to buy and inhabit his admirable houses. To this end, he is anxious to be able to state, as an indisputable fact—really, this part is almost too ludicrous to describe—to state that his houses are *as lived in by the Earl of Larrig*. Did you ever in your life hear of such a thing?'

'Oh God,' I said. 'Will he put advertisements in all the newspapers?'

'Of course!' said Papa, delighted at the thought.

We had been laughed at by one small town. Now we should be derided by the whole of Scotland.

Myrtle Lodge was mass-produced, indeed. The phrase 'jerry- builder' might have been coined for Mr McGrouther. If our Dieppe doors rattled in their frames, our Myrtle Lodge doors either would not close, or would not open, so much had the wood warped, and so badly had they been made. When you crossed a room, the whole house shook. When you dropped a pin, the whole house heard. Drafts whis- tled through cracks, and slates fell off the roof. It was a year old, when we moved into it, and had stood empty for a year, because nobody wanted to buy it.

There was a plot of ground about it, in which a garden had not yet been made. It was full of broken bottles, the remnants of wrecked carriages, and limbs of derelict furniture.

The house was on the edge of the town, close to the old main road to Crianlarich. On one side, in a sort of long shed like a byre, were camped navvies who were making a new road. They were paid on Saturday nights. We got no sleep then, and our windows rattled with songs and oaths. On the other side was a livery-stable, with the most despondent horses I ever saw, and the most vicious horse-flies I ever felt.

'It is wonderfully convenient,' said Papa, 'to have horses, an infinity of excellent horses, available for hire on our very doorstep.'

'And we shall all feel so much safer,' said Mamma, 'with those good men beside us. No marauders! No tinkers! No bandits!'

They were enchanted with Mrytle Lodge, with everything about it.

At least, I had some reason to suspect that Mamma *pretended* to be enchanted with it, in order not to seem to reproach Papa even by the smallest implication. The effect was the same. The effect on Papa was certainly the same. The effect on me shows what sort of a person I was then—prematurely old and cynical, yet hardly out of the cradle. I thought: it is *silly* to be so blindly devoted to someone. I do not think so now, but that is what I thought then.

I celebrated my sixteenth birthday listening to a band in a bandstand in a park. I celebrated my seventeenth birthday listening to navvies in a stupor in a cowbyre.

We had no contact with the great, but we had news of them.

We had news about the Gordons of Carnmore—or once upon a time of Carnmore. I had seen Elspeth Gordon before we went abroad, and had thought that they must have come home. They had, indeed, but not to Carnmore Castle. They had taken some other house, nearby. I thought it strange, that they should choose to live close to their lost ancestral home. It was strange in us, too. But of course, the Gordons had not lost all their money. If they could not live in their old home, they could hold up their heads.

'Perhaps,' said Mamma vaguely, 'they have come to buy back Carnmore from . . . who was it bought Carnmore, dearest?'

'Sir James Lithgow,' said Papa.

It turned out that he was no longer Sir James Lithgow, but had been created the 1st Lord Carnmore, on account of having made so much money. It further turned out that he was no longer alive, but dead, and had been succeeded in title and property by his son. Young Lord Carnmore was said to be charming, accomplished, a wit, a good sportsman, an ornament to the county.

'Just the sort of gentleman you should meet, Pussy,' said Mamma wistfully.

I agreed.

Then we heard that Neil Draco, whom I had known all my childhood, was marrying a Miss Christina Drummond, of whom we had never heard. We were all asked to the wedding at Glendraco, for the sake of ancient friendship. Mamma could not go. I would not go. I could not have dressed well enough to hand round the tea-cups: and I had no clear idea of how to behave at such a function.

Later that year, another childhood friend was arrested and tried for murder. That was Tom Ravenburn, whose sister was sent mad by his disgrace. But it turned out she was neither mad, nor his sister, and they were married at Christmastide. We were all asked to that wedding, too, but we could not or would not go.

I might still have been in Dieppe, for all I saw of anybody.

For a thousand reasons, I at least should have attended those weddings, gorgeous festivals in the life of my own countryside, merry celebrations among my childhood friends. For a thousand reasons, my attendance was out of the question.

Mamma brooded about this, and about my approaching eighteenth birthday. She brooded about young Lord Carnmore, and young Lancelot Gordon, and other young men whom we had once known. She spoke vaguely of Holyrood, and the Perth Meeting, and the Rannoch Ball.

'Pish,' said Papa. 'The purest flummery. The future will have no time for such extravagant rubbish.'

He looked at me, when he said this, with a flicker of uneasiness in his eyes. He had not forgotten my outburst. He never would forget it.

For once, Mamma took a decision of her own, and wrote to her Cousin Madeleine, the Viscountess Crondall.

'Madeleine has daughters of her own,' said Mamma. 'One, I think, of just my Pussy's age. She will like, I daresay, to bring out Pussy with her own girl.'

Cousin Madeleine did not like.

She drove a great distance to inspect me, bringing Hilda, the daughter of my age. Cousin Madeleine had the most expressive sniff I had ever heard. Hilda had the smallest eyes and the largest bosom I had ever seen. We all had tea together, in the room Mamma had hoped to make a *salon*. The conversation was stilted and the atmosphere strained. I found Cousin Madeleine's eyes on me, and in them an expression of suspicion and hostility. I found Hilda's eyes on me, and in them an expression of the purest amazement.

It happened that, after tea, mother and daughter were left alone for a moment. Naturally they discussed what was in all our minds. They did not know how thin were the walls of Myrtle Lodge.

'I hope Catriona *will* come to stay with us, Mamma,' said Hilda, to my surprise. 'She is so beautiful, and so strange.'

'Those are just exactly the two reasons why she will *not* come to stay with us, Hilda,' said Cousin Madeleine.

I wondered, afterwards, which was the more important reason. Sometimes I wonder still.

In the year that we were away, there were changes in Lochgrannomhead, too—the sort of changes that you do not notice if you are there while they are happening, but that strike you if you come back after an interval, like a child growing two inches.

There were raw new houses round the edge of the town—none quite as raw as Myrtle Lodge, but many nearly as ugly.

Several shops had changed hands, after bankruptcies or deaths or retirements. There were half-a-dozen shopkeepers who did not know us at all. One was a pharmacist, Thomas Haddow, a man like a bull with a shop like the cave of the Demon King.

Papa pressed his nose against Haddow's window, like a hungry child outside a pastry-cook's. His mind was surging towards chemistry again, and Haddow had all the miraculous ingredients he wanted.

'I have worked out the formula on paper,' Papa said.

'For what, dearest?' asked Mamma, with eager interest.

'Larridyne,' said Papa impressively. 'It is more than a new medicine —it is a new concept in medicaments. It will revolutionise the treatment of a dozen diseases—a score!'

'What does Dr McPhee think of Larridyne?' I asked.

'I have not discussed it with McPhee. He is an excellent fellow in many ways, but not of an adventurous mentality. He is blinkered, you know, by his professional training. He cannot comprehend the larger vision! My plan is to formulate Larridyne, make a series of clinical experiments among the poor, and announce my findings at a public meeting which I shall call in Edinburgh.'

'Fancy!' said Mamma. 'Edinburgh!'

I was not as worried as I would once have been. Papa dutifully handed me the money I needed for the housekeeping, and it left him only pennies for his amusements.

I was surprised that he continued to haunt Haddow's shop, and to closet himself in his new laboratory (a coal shed) and make more terrible smells than ever.

I was still more surprised when Thomas Haddow, himself, called at Myrtle Lodge one January afternoon.

Mamma was resting upstairs, in her bed. Papa was in the coal shed, secret and silent. Our one servant Jennie was out. I received Mr Haddow alone.

He came into the parlour, holding his hat in front of him. He seemed to fill the room with his great bulk and his great voice. He looked far more solid and durable than any of the gimcrack furniture in the room. His hands were like sides of beef, in size and colour; I could not imagine how he made little pills, or filled small medicine bottles with tinctures.

'I'll beig yer leddyship's pairdon for siccan intrushon,' he boomed, 'bu' I'll no' be mad' a fu' o' by the Duk o' Cromarty hissel'.'

'I am sure nobody could make a fool of you, Mr Haddow,' I said, feeling nervous, because he could have swallowed me at a gulp, and looked in a mood to do so. I tried not to show my nervousness, but smiled as nicely as I could.

'Ay! Ay! The auld yin hae pu'd the wul ower ma een! Ay! I believit an Airl. Wha'd no' believe a beltit Airl o' the Realm? Sae I gi'ed him his desairs—fi' puns wairth! Yon's ma listie—bide an' speir! Bide an' speir!'

Mr Haddow thrust a paper under my nose. The paper was covered in black, crabbed handwriting. An enormous forefinger jabbed at the items.

'Fower drams o' sperrits o' camphor! Ye see ut? Ye see ut? Six grammes o'sulphate o'maircury! Ye see ut?'

'But,' I said, 'that is impossible, Mr Haddow. How did my father pay—'

'He didna'! No' a cowrie hae he peddit!'

'But he took away—'

'He tuk awa' fi' wairth! I didna fret nor fash. An Airl, ma mannie, says I tae masel', hae a bushel o' golden guineas ahint his hatband—'

'Good gracious,' I said, 'you gave him credit?'

'Wae's me! I gi'ed him credit! Yon waur two muns syne, yer led-dyship, an' I canna affaird, an' I willna affaird, tae shalder siccan awfu' bairden!'

His voice rose from a boom to a bellow. His face was dark with in-dignation, and twisted with self-pity.

'The chiels o' the toon,' he said, controlling the violence of his rage and grief, 'hae telt me wha' a ful I med o' masel'. But I'll no' stand sic-can bairden, yer leddyship! Fi' puns! 'Tis no' gentle in his Lairdship tae sairve a puir mon sae.'

Five pounds! It was an awesome sum of money for us, for me. I was used to dealing in pence, and sometimes grandly in shillings, in my household accounts. (I was well used, by now, to calculating how many of the one went into the other.) Five pounds!

Mr Haddow was owed it. Mr Haddow wanted it. Mr Haddow would make an almighty commotion if he did not get it. He could not get it. We did not have it.

I stared at Mr Haddow, in utter consternation. He stared at me. The trouble was, I thought, that he hated to be made a fool of. Like all Scottish tradesmen, he prided himself on his canniness. His pride had been hurt by the mockery of the townsfolk. Well, his pocket had been hurt, too. He would go to the law. We would have the bailiffs in—moon-faced men, in billycock hats, who would carry away our few poor sticks of furniture.

Mr Haddow would be entirely within his rights.

Everybody in Lochgrannomhead would know about it. Everybody in Perthshire, everybody in Scotland, everybody in the three king-doms, would know that the 11th Earl of Larrig and Mount Douglas had had the bailiffs in, and lost his bed and his dining table.

Which would be the greater, the pity or the mirth?

Mr Haddow stood, his hat in his hands as though he expected alms, staring at me implacably. He meant to have his rights. I never saw such determination on a face, except my own.

This was a challenge beside which all other challenges shrank into simple little puzzles for children.

Children. Childhood. I had mastered a trick in my childhood, which I used sparingly but with invariable success. I was not given to tears which I had not summoned, thinking them poor-spirited and profitless, and hating the weakness which produced them: but I was sometimes given to summoning tears. I had escaped many lessons from dear Miss MacRae, by sobbing that I was tired or miserable.

I summoned tears. I sobbed softly, with a copious flow of water down each cheek. My eyes blurred by tears, I kept a watch on Mr Haddow's face.

It was full of dismay and contrition. He was a soft-hearted man, I saw, for all his bulk and his anger.

I hiccupped at last that he should be paid the moment we had the money. He almost patted my shoulder, I think. He went away dismayed at his own harshness, unmanned by my tears, content to wait for his silver.

My tears dried up the moment he shut the door behind him.

I felt a mixture of triumph and abject shame. I had taken advantage of a kind-hearted man, by playing the helpless child I was not. I had acted, cynically, a humiliating and most uncongenial role.

But I had won. At least, I had won time.

It became evident that there had been colloquies amongst the tradesmen of Lochgrannomhead. A dozen had put their heads together, and found that they had all given credit to Papa. They all came, singly or in twos and threes. Papa hid when they approached, and never emerged until they had gone. Mamma quailed, and retreated to her bed. It was always left to me to deal with them.

I dealt with them. I sobbed, stammered, and brokenly promised payment when we could—the very moment we could.

The total amount was sixty-eight pounds and eleven shillings—a gigantic, a shattering figure by the standards of my housekeeping. I suppose, at Strathlarrig, it would have gone in a morning.

At least no tradesman in Lochgrannomhead would ever again give credit to Papa.

'How do you mean to pay, Papa?' I asked him, trying to keep the sick anger out of my voice.

'With the first profits of Larridyne, to be sure,' said Papa.

He avoided my eye when he spoke. He had never done so before. He was like a boy caught stealing apples.

'I so wish,' said Mamma, 'that I could attend the public meeting in Edinburgh, dearest, when you announce the discovery to the world.'

I was aghast, as never before. Papa had never been actually bankrupted, but now it seemed a serious possibility.

When the tradesmen called a second time, and a third, all dozen together, it became a certainty.

Once again we were saved, by Providence and those admirable lawyers. They found a tenant for Strathlarrig, which had stood empty for so long except for caretakers.

He was called Sir Richard Grant. Papa was told all about him by Mr Murdoch and Mr Patterson, so that he would know he had a suitable tenant. This was courteous, but quite unnecessary—for a few pounds a month, Papa would have let his castle to the Wild Man of Borneo.

It seemed the Grants were baronets of ancient creation—one of them had carried a slop-pail, or carved a chicken, for King James the First and Sixth—with a still more ancient estate in Lanarkshire. The whole of that estate turned out to be not farm-land, but earth and turf on top of coal. The two results of this were, that the Grants were enormously rich, and they had to find a new place to live.

Sir Richard had recently inherited. He was twenty-eight, and unmarried. I began to be interested in a chornicle which, up until now, had been quite boring.

He was well spoken of by everybody. He came to the tenancy with recommendations from the Duke of Cromarty, the Earl of Draco, and other respectable grandees.

I thought perhaps the story was becoming boring again.

He was paying an excellent rent (which he could well afford) and could be relied upon to look after the castle, the estate and the people.

'Only twenty-eight,' said Mamma. 'And a bachelor.'

She looked at me, and I looked at her, and the same thought was in both our minds.

I had as much chance of ensnaring Sir Richard Grant, as of Larridyne curing a whooping-cough.

Sir Richard took up residence in Strathlarrig in the middle of February—a miserable season for a move. We knew this by a letter from the lawyers. We did not go to see him settle in. We did not see him at all.

Almost immediately, a letter arrived for Papa, by the hand of a groom, on the embossed Strathlarrig writing-paper.

Dear Lord Larrig,

I am sorry to trouble you with my domestic concerns, but a matter has arisen on which I can only be advised by you.

You will remember Hamish McCallum, tenant of a small farm called Easter Dalgarth. Mr Murdoch has advised me that McCallum's tenancy ought not to be renewed, as he is years behindhand with his rent, not through ill luck but through idleness and dishonesty, has been guilty of habitual negligence and bad husbandry, and is an inveterate poacher both of the river and of the preserves. I have inspected the steading and the farmhouse, and what I have seen goes far to bear out Mr Murdoch's account.

McCallum himself, however, swears to me that he had your personal Assurance, during the Summer of 1854, that his tenancy was secure during his lifetime. There appears to be nothing on paper concerning this.

I am disposed to take Mr Murdoch's advice regarding McCallum, but if you did give your word to the tenant, then I must regard it as binding upon me.

May I propose, as the method least troublesome to yourself, that I give myself the honour of calling upon Lady Larrig and yourself in the course of the next few days? I shall beg half-an-hour of your time, in order to discuss McCallum and one or two further matters of similar personal character on which I shall value your guidance.

May I trouble you to tell my groom if this is agreeable to you, and to indicate the day which would be least inconvenient for my call?

Believe me, dear Lord Larrig,

yours very sincerely,

Richard Grant.

'McCallum,' said Papa, 'McCallum. I remember the name. And the farm, of course. But how can I be expected to remember, after a gap of seven years, what I may or may not have said to the fellow?'

'Sir Richard can't come here,' I said.

'But, my dear—' Papa began.

'Sir Richard can't come here,' I repeated violently.

He would see the rickety little villa, the cheap furniture, the curtains with torn linings and the carpets with bare patches.

He might easily see a dozen importunate Lochgrannomhead tradesmen: because, of course, the whole town knew Strathlarrig had been let, and the creditors would be smelling their silver.

'You must go to the castle, Papa,' I said.

'Oh no, my dear,' said Papa. 'Going, and talking, and returning, I should be away for a whole day! I cannot spare a whole day away from my laboratory! Besides, your mother might be needing me.'

Meanwhile, Sir Richard's groom was still waiting outside the house, very smart in drab breeches and top-boots and a white neck-cloth with a pin. He stood by the head of a tall bay horse. The leather and brass of the tack was gleaming; the horse was gleaming, in spite of the season of the year. The groom was staring at the house and at the derelict garden about it, at the dirty paint and the drifts of dirty snow. There was not much expression in his face, but what there was suggested a bad smell. It was not hard to read his thoughts.

'I can receive Grant in this room, or perhaps in the dining room,' said Papa uncertainly.

'I will not have him come here,' I said.

Before they could say any more, I went out to talk to the groom. I told him Papa would call on Sir Richard Grant the next day, at three o'clock in the afternoon. I thought that, if he was committed, Papa could be made to go, and we should be spared the humiliation of an inspection by our new tenant.

But like many very gentle people, Papa had a streak of astonishing obstinacy. (It is something, alas, that I have inherited from him, but without the gentleness.) When it came to the point, he would *not* go to Strathlarrig. He was immersed in a new experiment; Mamma could not be left. He would send to the Castle, and ask Sir Richard to call at Myrtle Lodge.

'I will go in your place,' I said. 'I will tell him you have forgotten what you said to Hamish McCallum, and answer any other questions he has.'

'But, dearest child—' wailed Mamma.

'I will not have him come here,' I said, for the tenth time.

I hired a phaeton from the livery stable. They were prepared to trust me for the reckoning, because they knew Strathlarrig had been let.

The horse was young and raw-boned, with a wild eye. The harness was patched and stitched, and the reins felt like pieces of wire, so long was it since they had seen saddle-soap. The phaeton was deep in ancient grime, and stuffing was coming out of the cushions.

I had not driven for years, but I had not forgotten how to do it. At least, I hoped I had not.

The gaunt young horse went well, although he had a tendency to shy, in spite of blinkers. I knew that if he started to bolt, I would not be able to hold him: so I made very sure he did not bolt. We covered the eleven miles to Strathlarrig in excellent time. I enjoyed the drive, although it was bitterly cold, and my fingers were entirely numb and my nose felt like a lump of ice. It was heaven to be sitting again, even in such a vehicle, behind a fast trotter, even one of such dubious character. I felt enormously grateful to Sir Richard Grant, who had made this expedition possible with his rent, as well as making it necessary with his problems.

I came down from the low hills of the lochside to the mouth of the river Larrig, and then up the river, by the valley road, towards the castle. This was all Strathlarrig land—farms by the river, then sheep-walk and rough grazing, then grouse-moor and deer-forest. I felt a strange mixture of emotions, seeing the familiar landmarks: the little hump-backed Bridge of Groy, the white steading of Mualichmore, the new plantation of pheasant preserve, the long pool in the river, called Rory's Pool, where I had caught my first salmon at the age of eight.

Seven years, and nothing had changed. Seven years of drab, humiliating exile from all this that I loved so passionately. I was filled with homesickness. I wanted my empire back. I wanted my life back, my freedom and my friends. All the yearnings which I had managed to tread down, came flooding back into my mind; and as each new bend in the road revealed some unforgotten friend, knives twisted in my heart. The trees and rocks shouted greetings to me. All this was *mine*, and I had been cheated of it.

We rounded the spur of Creag an Imrich, and there was the castle before us. Snow covered the gardens. There was ice in the ruts of the road. The trees were bare. Many of the windows of the castle were curtained or shuttered, as though only a little of it was in use. It looked unwelcoming and sad. But my heart leapt. I would have screamed a greeting to my home, if I had not thought it would make the horse bolt.

The groom who came to the horse's head was, by chance, the one who had come with the letter. He looked at my carriage as he had looked at Myrtle Lodge—pity and disgust and astonishment were not quite perfectly hidden behind his well-trained mask.

He looked from the carriage to me with a flicker of pure astonishment. In his world, young girls did not transact confidential business with their fathers' tenants, nor drive by themselves eleven miles in freezing February weather to pay calls at castles. They did not in my world, either, or anybody else's world. It was unheard of. Well, there is a time to begin everything.

He should have seen me with the Lochgrannomhead shopkeepers.

The great hall was not quite as I remembered it. There were no suits of armour, which I thought a great loss. Perhaps Sir Richard Grant did not like armour, or his servants the labour of cleaning it. It was a sort of desecration, that it should have been taken away. And the huge oaken chairs, like choir-stalls in a cathedral, had been replaced by other furniture. More comfortable, perhaps, but *wrong*. Sir Richard was taking unwarrantable liberties with a place he had simply rented.

The small drawing room to which the butler led me was not in the least as I remembered it. It was a warm, sunny little room, hung in yellow silk. A fire burned in the same steel grate, but everything else was different—carpets, furniture, pictures. This surprised and upset me. I had expected everything to be as familiar inside the castle as outside.

The butler, who looked like a mute at a funeral, said that Sir Richard had been told of my arrival, and would be with me directly. I nodded. He left me, prowling silently out of the room as though not to offend the dead.

I took off my gloves. I saw that one had split, and would have to be darned as the other had already been darned. I hid the toes of my cheap and elderly boots under the hem of my skirt.

I warmed my hands at the fire, and tried to rub life back into my fingers.

I looked round the room disconsolately. There was nothing familiar in it—not one old friend to remind me and welcome me. The new furniture was very elegant, and the new pictures were charming enough, but they were not what I expected or what I wanted. I felt lost and forlorn among these bright strangers.

When I saw myself against the beautiful furniture, I felt desperately shabby. My clothes matched the disreputable old phaeton I had arrived in. They matched Myrtle Lodge and its squalid surroundings. They did not match a small drawing room in a millionaire's castle.

The door opened, and a man stood with his hand on the knob.

'Lady Catriona? I am so sorry to have kept you waiting. When they said you had come, I thought there must have been a mistake. I hope my fire has warmed you, after what must have been a very cold drive.'

He was unpleasantly surprised to see me. That was obvious in his face and in his voice.

I blinked at him. The warmth after the cold (I insist that it was only the warmth after the cold) had caused a blurring of my eyes and a pricking of tears under my lids.

Sir Richard Grant was tall—six foot and two or three inches; slim, but with broad shoulders; his hair was thick and black, with a slight wave; he was clean shaven; his features were striking, though slightly irregular—his nose seemed to have been broken, and there was a cleft not quite central in his chin; his eyes were grey, wide set under a tall brow, with heavy straight black eyebrows; he wore riding boots and a black coat—he was dressed almost exactly as his groom was dressed; his expression was solemn, perhaps disapproving, certainly very much surprised; his voice was pleasant enough, and pleasantly deep, but his tone was constrained, as though he deplored the conversation he was obliged to have.

He was in my house, which he had changed and spoiled.

I thought: he disapproves of talking business with a girl. He despises my clothes. He feels pitying contempt for Papa and all of us. He is a pompous booby.

He said, 'Will you sit down?'

I thought: if I sit down, I shall reveal my deplorable boots. I can stand by the fire, on the excuse of wanting to warm my hands. Then I thought: why should I care what he thinks of my boots? Let him dare criticise my boots, or anything about me. He can afford good boots because he had lucky ancestors. He deserves no credit for his boots or for usurping my place in my home.

I sat down, defiantly revealing the scuffed and patched toes of my boots.

I saw him glance at them, and look away. The distaste on his face was more marked than ever. A saint would have begun to feel angry.

I said, as calmly and coldly as I could, 'In the matter of Hamish McCallum, I am sorry to say that my father cannot remember making any assurance about the tenancy.'

'I had expected to hear so from his own lips.'

'He could not get away. He is, um, preoccupied, and very busy with important work.'

'I understand.'

'No, you cannot possibly understand. He is engaged in scientific work which—'

'I assure you, I understand perfectly.'

He did understand. He understood very well. My blood boiled.

It was absurd that Papa had not come. He could perfectly well leave Mamma for a few hours, and his scientific experiments were childish tomfoolery. It was permitted to *me* to admit these things to myself; but how dared Sir Richard say them, even by implication?

'Your father cannot remember making the assurance to McCallum,' said Sir Richard, frowning. 'But he cannot specifically remember not doing so?'

'No, of course not.'

'Then I am obliged to give McCallum the benefit of the doubt. That is vexatious, but mandatory on me.'

His tone blamed Papa for the vexation. I thought this monstrously unfair. How could anyone remember what he might have said seven years before, when his mind was full of inventions?

'Perhaps in the business room—' I began.

'The lawyers, naturally, have all the papers your father left in the business room. They have, naturally, been through them. Well, I need trouble you no further in the matter.'

'You said in your letter that there were other questions—'

'For discussion with Lord Larrig, yes. When it is convenient for him to receive me, or to call here, I shall hope to consult him.'

'But I have come all this way specially so that—'

'I believe I need trouble you no further, Lady Catriona. I am grateful for your kindness in coming here, and will not detain you. I must now beg you to excuse me. Before you go, may I tell them to bring you some hot tea or coffee? Or hot broth, if you prefer?'

'No, thank you,' I said, having some difficulty in bringing out the 'thank you'.

He would not discuss anything with me. He would not waste his time. I was a girl, an ignorant child, knowing nothing, not worth listening to. A business conversation between us was not only purposeless, it was improper. Besides, I was dowdy and repulsive, a shameful tattiebogle on his expensive furniture.

'Where did all our furniture and pictures go?' I asked suddenly. 'Why is everything new? Was ours not good enough for you?'

He looked at me with astonishment as evident as the groom's.

'The contents of the castle were all sold seven years ago,' he said.

I was silenced. I might have known that Papa would realise any money he could, by selling whatever could be carried away. I might have known, but the thought had never crossed my mind.

I turned my face away from Sir Richard Grant, so that he should not see the dismay in it.

He could not wait for me to be gone. I obliged him, and left at once, to his most evident relief.

I drove away without a backward glance, adding up his enormities in my mind. He had 'understood perfectly' that Papa was too busy to visit him—and the tone in which he said so was full of patronising contempt. His face had shown his distaste at talking to me about anything, and his disgust at my clothes and boots. He disdained to consult me, because he thought I was not worth consulting. He was living where I should have been living, enjoying all the things that were mine.

All he had was good luck. All I had was bad luck. How dared he despise me, when he had nothing to be proud of except money he had not earned?

He was a prig, a purse-proud parvenu, a rude and humourless boor. Even his boots were too shiny.

What a pity that a million pounds should be wasted on such a stick.

I felt passionate indignation at the cavalier way I had been treated —I, the heiress of the very place where I had been insulted and dismissed. Absorbed in my rage, I drove carelessly. I did not hold that wild young horse as hard as he needed to be held. Also, my fingers were numb with cold again.

The horse broke from his trot into a canter. I hauled at the reins with all my strength, but he was away, and he had a mouth like iron. Then, I think, the furious rattling of the old phaeton further alarmed him. He began to gallop. I remember screaming, clinging, still trying to control him. The phaeton bounced like a stone on a scree. Trees and walls rushed by. I passed a man by the roadside; I heard a shout, but we hurtled on. The horse's feet skidded on the icy puddles, so that I began to wonder, in an idiotic way, if he would fall first, or the phaeton disintegrate, or the whole bounce off the road into the river.

The horse sped round a corner. The nearside wheels of the phaeton struck a milestone. There was a crash. I had a sensation of flying through the air. That is all I remember.

3

I found I was lying on my back, with a face hanging like a moon two feet above my own. I was shaken, and bruised all over; my head ached, and I felt a little sick. I was lying on snow-powdered heather at the side of the road. My head was pillowed on something soft, and a rug covered me.

The face above me was silhouetted against the steely February sky. I could not all at once see it clear.

'You should lie still a little longer, I think,' said a light, pleasant voice from the sky, from the head above me. 'Then let us see if you can move.'

I put a hand to my aching head, and sat up slowly. A strong arm behind my shoulders lifted me and supported me, which was a great comfort.

I looked round dazedly. My disreputable phaeton and my wild young horse had been transformed, by some miracle I could not yet grapple with, into a smart closed carriage with a pair of spanking greys, at whose head stood a cockaded groom, while a fat coachman stood by with a respectful and anxious face.

'My carriage, at your service,' said the pleasant voice. 'The remnants of your own are half way to Lochgrannomhead by now, if your horse has kept his footing.'

The owner of the voice was partly behind me, owing to his supporting my shoulders when I sat up. I twisted my head to look at him. This was a mistake. I groaned, with a weakness that annoyed me, and closed my eyes for a minute.

Presently I was able to inspect him. He was a man of middle height and slender build, perhaps thirty years of age, with a handsome, open face that belonged to the open air, blue eyes like my own, and, something startling in a man, hair as guinea-gold as my own, with a similar tendency to curls. He was extremely well dressed. I did not think he should have been kneeling in the dirt of the roadside in such trousers, nor have dropped his silk hat onto a whin bush.

'The strength of your pulse gave me grounds for optimism about your condition,' he said. 'I have not ventured to make a more extensive medical examination. Can you move your limbs?'

I tried to do so—each arm, then each leg. They moved stiffly, but in a normal fashion.

'They seem to work,' I said dubiously. 'I will stand up in a moment.'

'I think you should, when you can,' he said, 'before you freeze to death.'

'Yes. Is this your rug, over me?'

'Fortunately we were carrying several.'

'Oh! . . . Here is another, which you gave me as a pillow . . . Thank you very much. They will be all dirty, like your trousers . . .'

I was talking nonsense, because of the bang on my head.

It did not discompose my rescuer, who smiled. He had a very broad, sweet smile. He said, 'A flake of snow will do neither my rugs nor my trousers irreparable damage. I pray that your fall has done *you* no irreparable damage. If not, allow me to say that you are a very re-silient young lady, as well as a very beautiful one. Your descent from the carriage, while sudden, was extremely graceful, a fact which I doubt if you fully appreciated at the time. Really you flew through the air like a swallow, but the impact of your reunion with the earth must have been quite violent. Fortunately, you chose this patch of heather for your arrival. Also fortunately, we were close by.'

He continued to chatter cheerfully, while I gathered my strength and my wits.

Presently he helped me to my feet. My head swam, and I staggered; but his arm about my shoulders held me up. It occurred to me that he was (like myself) much stronger than he looked. It was infinitely com-forting to feel that sturdy support. Usually I hated weakness in my-self, and hated needing help, but now I was very glad of help, and es-pecially his help.

He said I was very beautiful. I thought he was beautiful too.

'Do you think we can adventure the ten paces to the carriage?' he said. 'Lean on me as much as you must.'

'But where—?'

'My plan, with which I hope you will agree, is to go at once to Dr McPhee. Or, if you prefer, some other medical man known to you. You may feel all right, and you may look very much more than all right, but you did take a devastating tumble, and I think a doctor should satisfy himself that, when you bounced, you left no vital part behind.'

'Oh, no! I mean, yes! I know Dr McPhee. But it is a great nuisance for you—'

'It is a great pleasure. That is unfortunately put. I should say, the one redeeming aspect of an episode otherwise deplorable is that it gives me the opportunity of assisting you.'

Once I was used to standing up, I found I could walk quite well. My head ached, but it was no longer swimming. My legs felt sore, but they were up to my weight. The stranger helped me into the carriage, and I sank back gratefully on the cushions.

The coachman handed something in through the window, before he climbed back onto his box. It was my hat, which had fallen off. My rescuer inspected it, grinned cheerfully, and put it on my lap.

It had been a cheap and shoddy hat, at its best and newest. Now it was a battered ruin. That might have concealed its original nastiness: but its state had the unfortunate effect of making it the more obvious that this was a dreadful little hat, bought cheap from a dreadful little shop.

I looked down at myself, at the rest of myself, and I was aghast at what I saw.

He noticed my expression, and I was sure he read it accurately. Everybody always did. I never cared to conceal my feelings, and was incapable of doing so.

'Other ladies,' he said, 'would look desperately woebegone and tattered, after such a mishap as yours. You do look a *little* tattered—we cannot deny a *little* damage—but not at all woebegone. Tell me, if the question is not impertinent, do you meet all disasters with the same extraordinary fortitude?'

'Well, I try to,' I said. 'It is silly to moan.'

He looked at me with an expression I knew a little and liked very much. I had enjoyed it, among the clerks and half-pay officers in Dieppe. He looked at me with frank admiration.

The carriage started, and we went at a sedate pace towards Lochgrannomhead.

We talked, of course. He did not ask me who I was. It did not occur to me to ask him who he was—which shows, I think, that I was still not quite myself, or I would have been extremely curious. I had never seen him before. The door of his carriage was crested, but I did not know the arms. He was handsome and kind and amusing, and his turn-out declared he was rich. I must have been quite stunned still, not to ask myself, and him, who he was.

I liked it that he did not pretend that I was not tattered and dishevelled after my accident. He even *announced* that I was tattered, made a joke of it, and turned the whole into a charming compliment.

Naturally enough, I found myself mentally comparing the two gentlemen I had met, both for the first time, that afternoon.

This stranger showed a frank friendliness, a considerate kindliness, a respect and an ease of manner which made him delightful company, even for a bedraggled female with cheap, torn clothes and a cheap, battered hat, with her hair coming down, and splits in her gloves. For all he knew, I was a governess or a chambermaid. My clothes must have suggested so. But he treated me like a queen with whom he was on friendly terms.

Sir Richard Grant, who knew exactly who I was, treated me like a tiresome back-street urchin.

He told me of other journeys he had made, on horseback or wheels, or by train. He had been all over France and Italy, looking at the buildings and pictures, and ruins, and Alps, and riding after extraordinary French deer-hounds in huge forests, and fishing for trout in little icy streams in the Pyrenees. By his account, he had the most amusing adventures, and been most lucky in all the charming people he had met. I thought the people he met were the lucky ones.

'I have been to Dieppe,' I said, not wishing to seem entirely insular.

'Ah, oui? Et vous avez joissi de votre séjour à cette ville, que je trouve sympathique mais un peu étroite?'

'Etroite, peut-être,' I said, 'mais bien plus libre pour moi que la vie que je passe ici.'

'Bravo! I should say, brava! It is utterly extraordinary that, while returning from a dreary and conventional luncheon, I should find a ravishing young lady insensible on the roadside, and strange to the point of incredibility that she should number fluent French among her accomplishments.'

'It is my only accomplishment,' I told him, 'except adding up shillings and pence.'

He looked a little startled at this. I did not blame him. I had said much more than I meant, as I usually did. He did not press the matter.

I was already in a position to see that this was one of the nicest things about him. He saw that I was shabby and sad. He must have guessed that I had much to hide, to be ashamed of: that my family had fallen on evil days, and slid from a high place to a low one. Therefore, he asked me nothing. That, I thought, was what was meant by truly gentlemanlike behaviour. He must have been curious about me, especially since he found me beautiful. He must have assumed I had been visiting Strathlarrig, as that road led to no other gentleman's house. That in itself was odd enough. Yet he asked me nothing, in case finding answers to his questions should give me embarrassment or distress.

Sir Richard Grant had stared at my boots, and turned away in disgust.

Under the cordial influence of conversation and laughter, I felt much better after a few miles. I felt sufficiently myself, to feel what I might have felt before, which was a vivid curiosity of my own about my rescuer. Who was he, with his crested carriage and his smart servants, his luncheon parties and his foreign adventures, his good humour and his beautiful manners, his bright blue eyes and bright gold hair?

I could not ask questions, without laying myself open to answering questions. I did not want the stranger to know who I was, until I could contrive to look as I should, without having to apologise for anything, to explain away my clothes and our house and furniture. I hoped we should be better acquainted, but not until the beggarmaid looked a little more like a princess.

He astonished me again.

He said, 'There is something I should like to say to you, my anonymous nymph of the roadside. I hope I can find words to do so, without sounding pert or pompous.'

I thought he would find good words. He did so.

He said, 'I have sat inches away from you for nearly thirty minutes, and have had neither desire nor ability to take my eyes off you during all that time. Am I verging on pertness?'

'Well,' I said, 'yes, perhaps, but I am not offended yet, and at least you are not being pompous.'

'Not offended *yet*. That is reassuring, but not entirely. It implies a doubt about what follows. A doubt I share. Now, my inspection—involuntary, but wholly pleasurable—my inspection of your face and person has of necessity included a glance at your *toilette*.'

'Oh dear.'

'About which I wish to make two points. *Primo*, though you add shillings and pence, you are manifestly not the architect of your own fortunes. How could you be? Misfortune may be yours, mismanagement is not. If you have suffered and suffer still, it is through no fault of yours. Incidentally, as far as I can see, you *have* no fault, but I am perhaps being premature in allowing myself that aside.'

'No,' I said, and wanted to bite off my tongue.

He smiled. I felt myself smiling back.

My behaviour was thoroughly unseemly. I knew nothing of social rules, but I was pretty sure I was breaking most of them. I had never flirted with a gentleman (only with a few Frenchmen, whom I did not take seriously, when I was *very* young) and I was not quite sure what flirting consisted of: but I suspected that I was doing it, with a complete stranger, travelling most improperly alone with that stranger in a carriage. Pish, I said to myself, using Papa's nearest approach to an oath. What had I to do with the rules the respectable made for each other? I had been pushed out of their world. I would make my own rules, or adopt those of my new friend.

His rules allowed smiling. So, feeling the smile on my face, I let it stay there. Probably I could not have extinguished it, even if I had wished to do so.

'Allow me to make my second point,' he said, his own broad smile remaining happily on his face. 'You can safely feel immune from the effects of clothes. You do not need to be made elegant. Other women rely on silks and velvets of artfully chosen colours, and on whalebone and tailoring of still greater artifice. Not you. I do not say that silks would not become you, only that you do not need them. You could outshine any drawing room, any ballroom in the realm, in a tinker's second-best coat.'

I could think of no reply to this, except 'Thank you'. So I said, 'Thank you.'

He laughed, and gave a little bow. There was, I thought, no derision in his laugh.

Well, he had been as kind as he knew how, in what he said. But he was thinking of me in a way I did not want him to think of me. There was sympathy in his voice. I did not want sympathy. It was too close to pity. The last thing I wanted was his pity.

I wanted to impress him. I was very clear that I wanted to impress him. I think this was natural, if not very admirable. He was handsome and amusing and kind. He was widely travelled and experienced. He had the evident trappings of wealth, and the easy confidence I was sure depended on wealth. With all these things he impressed me. I wanted to impress him, quite as much, in return.

I had extensive experience of impressing the Lochgrannomhead shopkeepers, and a little experience of impressing the petit-bourgeois gallants of Dieppe. I did not think either would serve me very well with my rescuer. I thought I must take my cue from him. What impressed me about him, must impress him about me.

So—as to handsomeness, we seemed already to have scored that point. He had said more than once that I was beautiful, in different ways, each more delightful than the last.

As to being amusing? Well, I had more and more answered his chatter with my own, and he had laughed at me as much as I at him. It was not a form of conversation I was used to. It was not heard at Myrtle Lodge, nor in the streets of the town. I had been constrained and uneasy when I first entered the carriage, owing to the strangeness of my situation: but in his company I had gradually relaxed: I had felt myself being fed with confidence, like a berry fattening and reddening in the sun. I was having my first lesson in talking freely to an attractive man of my own class, and I found it easier and easier, pleasanter and more pleasant.

I thought we had scored that point, too.

As to being kind? It was a great point, in my opinion of him. I could not prove my kindness, as he had proved his, until opportunity arose. But, meanwhile, I could smile, as his social rules allowed, and show the warmth of my disposition, and the amiability of my character. Smile I did, most strenuously, though it might lay me open to a charge of saucy flirting.

As to being widely travelled and experienced, I could claim only poor little Dieppe, and a good knowledge of conversational French. He did seem impressed by this. It would have to be enough.

There remained the trappings of wealth, and the easy confidence they gave.

I turned away from him for a moment (though I was regretful to do so) and stared out at the harsh wintry landscape. I was thinking hard. This was a new and peculiar challenge, which called for new and most peculiar methods.

I took a deep breath, my resolution formed, and turned to face him. 'You may be wondering, sir,' I said, 'why I was driving along from Strathlarrig, dressed as a milliner or a—a pastrycook.'

'If there had been such a question in my mind,' he said gravely, 'it will remain in my mind.'

'I think I should explain, because you have been so kind. Well—I was obliged, for confidential reasons, to visit, um, a farmer called Hamish McCallum, at a place called—called Easter Dalgarth. He is a farmer, you know. And a poacher.'

'Do you often call on poachers, Miss . . . ?'

'Haddow,' I said, having made another important decision. 'Esther Haddow.'

'My name is Lithgow. Alexander Lithgow.'

'How do you do, Mr Lithgow?'

'How do you do, Miss Haddow?'

I was sorry he was only a Mister. But it was not a fatal drawback, and as far as I could see it was his only drawback.

'It was necessary,' I went on, thinking quickly as I spoke, 'not to enrage the man McCallum, or fill him with resentment, by arriving at his farmhouse in a carriage with grooms and footmen and so forth, and wearing silk gowns and jewels and suchlike . . .'

'Ah! You were in disguise!'

'In a way. Not precisely. I was not wearing a false beard.'

'I am glad of that, Miss Haddow.'

'In any case, it would have fallen off, when the phaeton hit the milestone.'

'Perfectly true. An entirely valid observation.'

'So, you see, that is why I was driving that odd carriage, and wearing these odd clothes.'

'Easter Dalgarth, from the road you were on, is on the Strathlarrig estate?'

'I believe it is. Yes, to be sure it is.'

'And your host is a tenant of Lord Larrig?'

'Yes, of course. Well, a tenant of his tenant.'

'You are connected with Lord Larrig? A relative, perhaps?'

'Yes,' I said, glad to return to the truth.

'I have heard it said, hereabouts, that there are members of that family remarkable for their beauty. I am glad to have the report confirmed, by the evidence of my own eyes. Since you have been so frank, Miss Haddow, can you bring yourself to enlighten me on a point which, I confess, has me as much intrigued as baffled?'

'Yes,' I said dubiously. I was ready for some questions, but not many.

'Why were you obliged to visit, disguised albeit not in a false beard, a crofter or whatnot in the hills above Strathlarrig?'

'Because,' I said, 'there was an idea that Lord Larrig had promised the man a perpetual tenancy, and another farmer wants the farm, to whom I owe a favour, which is not such a very great matter, only he gave me the use of a—a pony some time ago, and I feel myself indebted, which I dislike and disapprove of . . . Oh. I have got myself into a muddle.'

'I can untangle the knot, or even cut it, Miss Haddow. You were trying to help a friend. You have answered my question in terms which, if I may say so, cause me the minimum of surprise.'

I had explained away my clothes and my vehicle. In doing so, I had convinced him that I was as kind as himself. I did not like that. It was not what I had meant. The pretended kindness had somehow appeared in the story, without my wishing for it. I did not mind lying about my clothes, but I did not like lying about myself. I think a kind of pride was involved. I think I was oddly constituted.

'You must please not think me better than I am,' I began, to put right the lie I had told.

'You must please not think yourself worse than you are,' he replied softly. 'Or we shall begin to disagree, perhaps violently, which would be the greatest pity.'

He smiled suddenly. I had to accept that his opinion of me was formed, and that it was a good opinion. I had impressed him, though I had travelled no further than Dieppe.

'Voilà que nous arrivons à la ville,' I said, in a spirit of the purest showing off.

'Et alors il nous faut chercher le bon médecin, pour nous assurer que vous n'avez cassé ni la tête ni autrechose.'

We rattled into the town, and up to the doctor's gaunt grey house in the Kirk Square.

The doctor was out, but a young maidservant said he was expected back immediately. She curtseyed to me, which very few people did. She knew who I was, of course.

I realised, with a sick feeling, what anybody with any commonsense would have known all along—that I was fou to have given myself a false name in a place where everybody knew me, and where I was sure to be addressed by my real name.

We waited in the small parlour in which Dr McPhee sat people to wait (where I had waited a thousand times, while he wrote out prescriptions for Mamma) and discussed the grim pictures on the walls. Mr Lithgow made me laugh so hard that my headache began to return.

A different servant came in, and said that the doctor was back and would see me at once. By chance, she did not use my name. They were a silent lot in that household, except for the doctor, who could talk without stopping for an hour, except to Papa, who contrived to stop him; perhaps his talking so much gave the others no chance, and so, over the years, they lost the habit of speech.

Dr McPhee concealed, as always, his kindness and concern under his brusque, badger-hound manner. He said I had broken nothing, but I was very foolish and very lucky, and also very strong and healthy, but a blow on the head was always fraught with possible danger, and I must take to my bed for two full days, with the room darkened, and neither read nor sew nor attempt the household accounts.

'I will look in this evening,' he said, 'to make sure my orders are complied with. I've kenned you too long to trust either your obedience or your good sense.'

'Yes,' I said submissively. 'And, um, although this may sound odd, will you very kindly *not* tell Mr Lithgow who I am?'

'Mr Lithgow, is it?'

'Yes, of course. So he told me.'

'Ay. In that case, who am I to miscall your benefactor?'

Usually I walked from Myrtle Lodge to the doctor's, and back again. I wanted to do so now, in order to hide the house from Mr Lithgow. But the doctor would not hear of it, and Mr Lithgow would not hear of it, and I felt so very bruised and shaky that I was not very sure, myself, that I could have walked so far.

We re-entered the carriage, and a minute or two took us to my detestable home.

I planned another ingenious fable, to explain the house away. I planned to say that I was staying for a week with an old servant, as a kindness, who had been installed in the villa. But I had not the energy to tell this story, or any other. Suddenly, as Mr Lithgow helped me from his carriage to our door, I was smitten by overwhelming fatigue and weakness, and my knees trembled, and I almost fainted: and he carried me bodily into the house.

I learned afterwards that he and Papa, between them, got me up the narrow stairs to my bedroom, and that Jennie the servant put me to bed, with some help from Mamma.

I came to myself in the morning, feeling battered but myself and in one piece.

I lay quiet for the next two days, content to do so for the first time in my life. Mr Lithgow filled most of my thoughts. Sir Richard Grant, all unwelcome, made me angry from time to time. I wondered vaguely where the delicious fruits could have come from, that were piled in little baskets by my bedside.

I came downstairs, with Dr McPhee's permission, feeling stiff but hungry and healthy.

I blinked in astonishment at the parlour. Someone, in a Perthshire February, had found armfuls of gorgeous flowers. I blinked at Mamma. She had a new, fleecy shawl over her shoulders.

'Lord Carnmore,' said Mamma, 'has called twice a day for the last two days. Such a delightful young man, and very deeply concerned about you, dearest Pussy. He and Papa have become the greatest friends. And generous! Did you ever in your life see such beautiful flowers?'

'Lord Carnmore?' I stammered. 'But we do not know him. We have never met him. Why should he suddenly . . .'

Mamma looked at me blankly. I looked at her, equally blankly.

Lithgow. Sir Something Lithgow had bought Carnmore, and become Lord Carnmore. He had been succeeded by his son, a young man, said to be amusing and travelled and a sportsman . . .

I had had daydreams, years before, of falling in the way of a millionaire duke. Well, he was not quite a duke, but I had fallen, in the most literal sense, in the way of a rich young lord.

Who knew all about me. Who knew I had lied to him. Who knew my circumstances—as anyone must, who took one look at Myrtle Lodge and at Papa.

I was filled with crawling shame. Mine had been such a petty lie, and it was found out so instantly. I had tried to make myself seem richer than I was, and kinder than I was. At best, I should have from Lord Carnmore the pity I had not wanted. At worst, I would disgust him as I disgusted Sir Richard Grant. But for better reasons. I *deserved* Carnmore's disgust.

I was angry with myself. I resolved, ever after, to tell the truth. My reason was not a good or moral one. It was simply, that it was so disagreeable being found out in a lie.

The very first thing I had to do, was to explain to the livery stable about the phaeton, and ask if the horse had got home, and find out how he was. They should not have given me such a horse, but still I felt guilty, because if I had been concentrating he would not have bolted.

I was nervous about my reception at the livery stable. To my astonishment, I was greeted by bows and smiles.

I was to take what horses I liked, what vehicles I liked, whenever I liked. I was not to worry about the reckoning. The wrecked phaeton had been paid for. The slight injury to the horse had been more than paid for.

Lord Carnmore had been to the stable, going straight from Papa, the afternoon of my accident.

As I crossed the rough ground to our house, I saw the gigantic Thomas Haddow, the outraged pharmacist whose name I had borrowed. He was crossing from the road with a large wooden box. He looked at peace with the world, and greeted me as respectfully as he could, apologising for not being able to pull his hat off.

Lord Carnmore had paid the debt. He had paid all Papa's debts in Lochgrannomhead. Mr Haddow was delivering chemicals to Papa, which Lord Carnmore was paying for.

This was too much. This was generosity run mad. Papa should have had more pride. It was abject in him, to accept such copious charity from a man twenty years his junior.

I saw Papa, bustling happily into his laboratory, on the brink of world-shaking achievements, a man without a care. He was not abject. Stained and reeking with Mr Haddow's chemicals, he was completely happy.

Seeing him so, Mamma was completely happy.

What view, then, was I to take?

I knew what view to take, after I had spoken to Papa.

'You must not misunderstand the position, little Cat,' said Papa happily. 'Of course I could not accept the young fellow's charity. That would be unthinkable. But this is a business relationship—purely a business relationship. Carnmore sees fit to invest in some ideas of mine, in return for a percentage of the share capital when we float the companies to exploit them. An entirely normal undertaking. Nothing more usual. All that is unusual is the vision he displays—a far cry, I may say, from the short-sighted, self-destructive obscurantism of many of the people I have approached . . . Of course, Carnmore has made a very good bargain for himself. Too good, many people might think. The shares of my companies he will one day own are quite disproportionate to the investment he is making now. His father was an iron-master, a pretty hard-headed customer, I imagine. Like father, like son. He won't be a loser, be sure of that. Still, beggars can't be choosers, and I made the undertaking he required. Then again, when the time does come, I shall be indifferent to a few thousand guineas here or there.'

In order to make Papa happy, and end his worries, Carnmore had deliberately laid himself open to serious reproach.

I thought this was more generous than all the money he had given.

That afternoon, the carriage I knew stopped at the door, with the coachman and groom I knew. There was nobody in it. I tried to hide my extreme disappointment.

His Lordship's compliments, and he has no use for his carriage this afternoon, which is obliged to wait uselessly in Lochgrannomhead, while his Lordship has a business conference with the gentlemen in charge of building the new roads. Horses and men would rather be active than stand idle, and Lady Catriona will be doing them, and his Lordship, a favour, if she will use the carriage for two or three hours, to take her where she likes.

Once again, charity was dressed up in a false beard; in granting a favour, Carnmore pretended to be asking for one.

I accepted the offer, in the spirit in which I hoped it was meant.

It was a glorious day, one of those brilliant February days, when a white sun glares at the snowdrifts at the side of the road, and kindles the frost in the twigs of the trees, and silvers the shining unbroken snow on the big hills. If one took a deep breath, it seemed to freeze one's lungs, but the air was like wine, iced white wine, of the sort Papa once drank with his salmon at Strathlarrig . . .

I came back to find Carnmore in the parlour with Mamma. He had walked to the house, to pick up his carriage. Mamma and he were very deep in talk, like old friends. In that horrid parlour, Carnmore looked like a creature from another planet. His hair looked like polished precious metal, in the pale afternoon sunlight. He was very well dressed. He shamed the chair he was sitting on. He shamed the whole house. He shamed me.

Papa came into the room, just as I did, by the other door. He was carrying a tray with tea-things, as it was Jennie's afternoon off. The teapot was cracked, and the cups did not match. Papa himself looked like an old-clothes-man after a storm.

I would have been mortified, but Carnmore gave me no chance to feel anything but delight that he was there. He jumped to his feet when I came in, and hurried across the room (it was not far to go) with his hand outstretched. His face was lit up by his smile; it seemed to light up the whole room, more brightly than the sun.

He took my hand, and held it for a moment, and said, 'I do not have to ask if you are recovered, Lady Catriona. You look like . . .'

'Like what?' I said, in what I hoped was not an arch voice.

'Like a fully recovered young lady.'

'And that is entirely thanks to you, Lord Carnmore,' said Mamma.

'No question of that,' said Papa, putting down his tea-tray. He misjudged the height of the table, so that the tray landed on it with a crash, and tea spilled out of the mouth of the pot, and the tray was swimming with it.

Carnmore drank a cup of tea. I saw him avoid the chip in the cup which Papa had given him. Either he enjoyed Papa's tea, or he was a good actor. I thought again how truly a gentleman he was.

We could not pretend to him any more. Our life was stripped bare in front of him. Mamma and Papa were incapable of pretence, and I was very bad at it, but even if we had been consummate liars, Carnmore could see our whole situation.

And he had sat with Mamma for an hour, during each of the two previous days, captivating her completely with his gentleness and good humour. And he had sat with Papa for an hour, on each of those days, hearing about chemical formulae and mechanical contrivances, and 'investing' in Papa's inventions.

Twenty minutes later, I walked out with him to his carriage. It was Mamma's suggestion that I should. I was a little embarrassed, not by the suggestion, but by the way she made it.

'Why did you call yourself Mr Lithgow?' I asked abruptly, as soon as we were out of the house.

'Because you said you were Miss—what was it? Haddow?'

'That was because . . . But how did you know it was not true?'

'You might as well have said you were the Empress of China, or the under stillroom maid at the Lochgrannomhead Hotel.'

'That is what I was dressed like. That is what I am still dressed like.'

'I told you two days ago how little that influenced my attitude to you. How did I know? How could I not know? Since I came back to Scotland, I have often heard you mentioned.'

'Good gracious. Who by? I mean, by whom?'

'The people who were once your familiars, none of whom have forgotten you, although none seem to have seen you for many years.'

'I suppose you can understand that.'

'Oh yes. Deplore, but understand.'

'What do people say about me—about us?'

'That your father has more enthusiasm than good fortune, your mother more kindness than good health, and you—'

'And I?'

'More beauty than is good for anybody.'

'Oh . . . Is that possible?'

'No. It is the voice of envy.'

'Anyone who envies me,' I said, 'must be very mad.'

'Oh no. Oh *no*. May I call on you tomorrow? Just to see how you are, you know.'

'Mamma will be very pleased to see you.'

'And you?'

He smiled as he spoke. I felt myself smiling back. I did not answer him aloud. I did not need to.

He did not call every day during the next three weeks. There were three whole days when he did not come at all! They seemed extremely empty days. He sent a carriage when he could not come himself, to take me for a drive if I liked. I did like, indeed.

In the carriage, the second time it came, lay an amazingly luxurious fur cape and hat and muff—such things as I had had as a young child, but never touched since then. His lordship's compliments, said the coachman, and he begged me to accept them. They were objects he happened to have by him, and they were, of course, no use whatever to himself. It was better for such things to be used, or moth got at them. As he hated waste, he would esteem it a favour, et cetera et cetera.

I did him the favour he asked, and wore the furs.

When he called, Mamma was a little obvious about leaving us alone together. Her manners were not as good as his. No doubt, through long disuse, they had become rusty. But the result was, that we *were* alone together, far more often, and for far longer periods, than if Mamma had been a conventional hostess, or a mother with conventional ideas about chaperonage.

At the beginning of April, Carnmore suggested that Mamma and I—Papa too, if he could spare the time—should call on him at his castle. He would send a carriage which had good springs and deep cushions, so that Mamma should not be shaken.

Mamma was determined that she could not make such a dangerous and exhausting expedition. But she was determined that I should go. Of course this was impossible. I could call alone on Sir Richard Grant, because he was living in my house, and I was Papa's representative. I could *not* call alone on Lord Carnmore. It seemed I could not call on him at all. It was a hideous shame.

Dr. McPhee intervened. This was, I am sure, Carnmore's idea. The doctor said that if she kept warm, and did not exhaust herself when she arrived, sightseeing all over the castle and its policies, Mamma would get nothing but benefit from an outing.

The castle was breathtaking. I had visited it as a young child, when the Gordons still lived there: but not since. It was transformed by the wealth and taste of its new owners. By the standards of Strathlarrig (to say nothing of the standards of Myrtle Lodge) it was unbelievably luxurious. But the luxury was neither vulgar nor out of keeping. Nothing was showy. Things were for use rather than display.

Most of the improvements had been made by old Lord Carnmore, but some, very recently, by the young Lord. They included things I had never seen, or even heard of. For example, the bathrooms had hot running water, heated by a great distant boiler, coming from taps set above the baths. The pipes carrying the hot water were not buried into the wall, under the plaster, but ran through the passages and bedrooms, so disguised as to be almost invisible, warming the air of the castle to a comfortable level. A steam-engine in a vault behind the kitchens both pumped water from the wells, and pumped it up through the pipes, even to the highest floors of the castle.

'I wish Papa had invented something like this,' I said.

'He has worked in more important spheres,' said Carnmore gravely, which pleased Mamma.

I was fascinated by the ingenuity of these arrangements, and I loved the comfort they gave. But what struck me most was the beauty of Carnmore, which as a child I had not had the wit to appreciate. Its setting was splendid, and the views from its windows magnificent. Most of it was very ancient. It was quite small—a quarter the size of Strathlarrig—yet it had a grandeur and dignity which many greater buildings lack.

The rugs on the floors glowed like lamps with rich, dark colours. There were three tapestries in the dining room, two hunting scenes and a battle, which were as dainty in detail as miniature paintings. There was a long gallery of pictures, mostly Italian, which I knew I would need more education to understand.

Some of the armour in the hall had come from Strathlarrig. Of course Lord Carnmore had too much delicacy to mention the fact: but Mamma recognised the pieces.

The servants were numerous and pleasant. A few of them had come from Strathlarrig, too. One old kitchen-maid burst into tears when she curtseyed to Mamma.

'We will inspect the stables on a warmer day,' said Carnmore.

A fortnight later, Carnmore called, and asked for an interview with Papa.

He had not made any passionate advances to me—or at least, if he had, they were so subtle and tactful that I did not know they were passionate advances. He had not given me any presents, except the furs. He was not supposed to do so, by the rules, until he had spoken to Papa. I thought they were silly rules.

He *had* had several intimate conversations with Mamma, which she would not tell me about. She spoke about him often, however, in terms of the warmest approval. As far as I was concerned, he did not need an ally to plead his cause. But he had one.

I heard some of his conversation with Papa, through the paper-thin walls of Myrtle Lodge, although I tried to try not to.

The subject of the conversation surprised me, at first. Carnmore said that Papa should have much better workrooms and laboratories. 'A coal-shed for *your* experiments, Lord Larrig? I venture to suggest that the world would benefit more, and sooner, if you had a well-lit and commodious place of work, with room to store your equipment and tools, with room for a desk where you may make your calulations . . .'

'Perfectly true, my dear fellow. You can have—no layman can have—any idea of the degree to which inadequate premises hamper a man of science.'

'Since you have done me the honour of allowing me to invest some trifling sums in some of your projects, Lord Larrig, and since I therefore feel in a measure involved, with a financial stake, and since you have convinced me of the immense potential value of the work you are pursuing, it seems to me that commonsense, business sense, obliges me to suggest other premises for you, and to protect my investment with a minor further investment to this end.'

Carnmore was offering to rehouse us. I thought Papa would accept. He did.

There was a substantial converted farmhouse on the Carnmore estate. Lord Carnmore took Papa to see it. Papa came back in raptures. He was vague about the details of the house, but lyrical about the outbuildings, in which he could establish his work. There were things to be done to the house, which would be ready by the end of the summer.

'Carnmore is a sensible fellow,' said Papa. 'He will get a larger and a speedier return on his investment, when I have the space and facilities I need.'

While these arrangements were being made, Papa gave Carnmore permission to pay his addresses to me.

Carnmore was now allowed to make passionate advances to me, and he was allowed to give me expensive presents. He made the fullest use of both opportunities.

The first time he kissed me on the lips, his own were as gentle as the wings of a moth. The second time, I sensed an ardour to which I did not know how to respond. The third time, there was a sort of delightful violence about his kiss, which was the most exciting thing I had ever experienced.

Words went with these and his other actions. I could not imagine that anyone had ever spoken such beautiful words before. It was all completely new to me, and I liked it very much.

Of all the presents he gave me, the best was a horse, the first I had had of my own since we left Strathlarrig. Of course there were no stables at Myrtle Lodge, and I would not entrust my beauty to the livery-stables next door. It had to live at Carnmore. To ride it, I had to go to Carnmore. When I went there, it was not to spend all the time in the stable or in the saddle.

I got to know the castle well. I passionately loved its comfort and its beauty. When I came back in the evening to Myrtle Lodge, I passionately hated its meanness and ugliness.

Things moved quickly, but not too quickly for me.

One blowing, springlike day in late April, we rode together, Alexander Carnmore and I, up the hill behind the castle to a point he wanted me to see. A long circuit behind and up the hill took us back towards the castle, and almost to the lip of a cliff. He dismounted there, and lifted me off my lovely Clinker. I was excited to feel the pressure of his hands through my habit, and to be aware of his strength.

The groom that followed held our horses, while we walked down a little defile to a natural belvedere of springy turf, which overhung the valley below. And there was Carnmore Castle, ancient, grey, gaunt, grand, like a toy beneath us.

I gasped with astonished delight, and marked the towers I was getting to know so well, and the gardens and stables and steadings, and the glint of the burn, and the first beginnings of palest green in the trees.

'Do you like it, Pussy?' he asked softly, using as he sometimes did the name my mother had made for me.

'Yes, Sandy,' I said, in a funny little voice, because I thought he was going to give it to me.

'It is yours,' he said, 'but I am afraid there is a string attached. I go with the gift.'

Mamma agreed with me that evening that I was truly in love with Carnmore.

The engagement was announced. The wedding was to be on Midsummer Day, my eighteenth birthday. I was delirious with happiness.

In the normal way, the father of the bride is altogether responsible for the wedding and its feast. He makes all the arrangements, and pays all the bills.

Somehow, this time, without anything being said, there was a different arrangement.

'I wonder why the Gordons have refused their invitation?' I said, looking through a great pile of acceptances in the library at Carnmore.

Sandy shrugged. 'They don't like my being here. They are, or were, the Gordons of Carnmore. They think they should be living here. They think I'm an intruder in their ancestral home.'

'But your father bought it from General Gordon. They have nothing to complain of.'

'People are not always reasonable, about such things as ancestral homes. Especially in the Highlands of Scotland.'

'How silly. I would like to see them again.'

'I'm afraid you won't, not as friends, not if you bear my name. But perhaps it's not worth it? The friendship of the Gordons is more important?'

I laughed and kissed him. I was coming to do so quite easily and naturally.

I was measured for a huge wardrobe of clothes. I began to wear a few of them, which had been made quickly, but most were to await my arrival at Carnmore as its mistress.

How the days dragged! And a day in a house like Myrtle Lodge drags most slow of all.

Dr McPhee came as usual to see Mamma. Afterwards he had a cup of tea as usual with Papa.

I was not interested in hearing their conversation. I was in a happy dream of my new home, my new clothes, my new dignity. After our marriage, we were to spend a day or two at Carnmore. Then Sandy was taking me abroad. It would be much unlike my other foreign travels. I had plenty to dream about.

Sandy had mentioned racehorses, and visits to Newmarket and Ascot; great house parties in Norfolk, for the very best pheasant shooting; weeks on the Isle of Wight, with the yachts of the Royal Yacht Squadron. Golden horizons expanded in every direction; I gazed at them with joyful impatience.

But Dr McPhee's brusque voice cut through the walls of Myrtle Lodge like his lancet through a wet newspaper.

'Do you really,' he was saying, 'do you really know anything about your prospective son-in-law, Lord Larrig?'

'A delightful fellow,' said Papa, 'combining generosity with vision, good manners with good sense, and—'

'And a good reputation with a bad one.'

'Bad? Bad? Bad? What the deuce are you talking about?'

'I don't just know. It's not something for which I can personally vouch. I know him very little. Notionally, I have been his physician for three years, but I've never been required to attend him because there's been nothing wrong with him.'

'Just so. There is nothing wrong with him.'

'So a lot of people will say, hereabouts and further afield. But there's an old friend of mine, a fellow student of ancient days, with whom I keep in correspondence. He's in London now, a fashionable physician with a very wide acquaintance. Young Carnmore has been in London a good deal—'

'Of course he has. Every young man should. The great world. Politics. The House of Lords. I myself, if I had the time, could contribute some ideas to the debates in that chamber which . . . In the matter of patent laws, for example, there is an inequity about which . . . And then, in the matter of the fuel used by railway locomotives . . .'

Papa wanted to jump like a harvest-mite from subject to subject; Dr McPhee had his badger's grip on what he wanted to talk about.

'My friend has heard some disquieting rumours about Carnmore.'

'Pish,' said Papa. 'The mutterings of the envious.'

'That is possible. But my friend knows that Lady Larrig, Lady Catriona and yourself are among my patients, and he thought it his duty to apprise me, so that I might apprise you.'

'Pish, pish.'

'You will not listen, my lord, because Carnmore has promised you—'

'I say pish to your scurrilous rubbish, McPhee.'

Dr McPhee never called Papa 'my lord' unless he was angry. Papa never called the doctor 'McPhee' unless he was angry.

Neither was as angry as I was. Mischievous women and jealous men had whispered their London poison about my Carnmore; some fawning fashionable doctor, with flapping ears and a busy pen, had gleefully sent their lies to Scotland. Now Dr McPhee was trying to destroy my happiness.

Pish, indeed.

My engagement ring arrived at last, delayed because it had been specially made for me to Sandy's own design. It almost hurt my eyes, to look at the gems in full sunlight.

The kiss he gave me, when he put the ring on my finger, had something savage about it. He made me think of a desperate clansman of the old times, ravishing a girl from a lowland village. It was exciting, and a little frightening. I lamented my ignorance, which Mamma did nothing to dispel.

But I would know soon enough all there was to be known. I allowed myself to be *very* curious. I contemplated the future with a sort of delightful alarm.

I was *not* frightened. I still forbade myself to be frightened of anything. But I was only seventeen: though, when the day came, I should be eighteen.

I did not want advice—just some simple, basic information, of which I had absolutely none.

Nothing would induce Mamma to say a word on any 'nasty' subject. The only person to whom I could have turned was Dr McPhee. I would not turn to him, now or ever again, because he was treacherous and underhand and mischievous.

In the second week of June, a fortnight before the wedding, a carriage I did not know stopped at the gate of Myrtle Lodge.

We had had a few callers, since my betrothal was announced. People had come to offer congratulations and gifts. Mamma had expected the Gordons, but they never came. I wondered idly who had such a very smart brougham, and, with a more vivid curiosity, what gift I was being brought.

To my utter astonishment, Sir Richard Grant jumped down and strode towards the house.

Of course he had come, I thought, for some urgent business with Papa: some other matter like that of Hamish McCallum. Being the kind of man he was, he would not have the courtesy to send a letter in advance, but simply arrived, not caring if his visit was welcome or convenient.

It was not welcome to Papa, who was absorbed in contriving a new oil-lamp for carriages. It was not welcome to me.

I heard him say to Jennie, at the door, 'Is Lady Catriona at home?'

'Ay, sir.'

'May I beg the favour of a few words with her? I have an urgent and private communication to give her.'

That was my gift, was it? An urgent communication from Sir Richard Grant? What on earth could it be? Advice about getting better boots?

Jennie came fluttering into the parlour, where I had been sitting in a haze of opulent visions. I thought wryly that, in a sort of hard and mannerless way, Sir Richard was a fine figure of a man, and Jennie was terribly susceptible.

I did not want him to see the parlour. I did not want him to see me in the parlour in my own deplorable home. I did not want him to despise me even more than he did. I did not want to give him that satisfaction. I did not want to talk to him.

'I am not at home,' I said to Jennie.

Even as she fluttered out, Sir Richard stood in the doorway, his tall hat in his hand and a savage frown on his face.

'I must beg you to hear me, Lady Catriona,' he said.

'How dare you?' I flared. 'Do you burst into the presence of ladies, in Lanarkshire?'

'Only,' he said, his frown no less savage, 'when absolutely and categorically obliged to do so.'

'Show Sir Richard to the door, Jennie,' I said.

'I know my way to the door, Lady Catriona,' he said, to point his contempt of our horrid little house. To Jennie he said, 'Please leave us.'

'When you have finished giving orders to other people's servants,' I said, very angry indeed, 'you will allow me to go out and order your coachman to drive into the loch.'

'I understand your resentment of this intrusion. When you have heard me you will, I believe, understand that I am required to make it.'

'What is required of you, Sir Richard, is an apology and a withdrawal.'

'I shall make both, but neither until you have heard me.'

'We are not physically strong enough to eject you by force, so your extraordinary behaviour—'

'Is occasioned by an extraordinary situation.'

He glared at Jennie as though he would beat her over the head with a chair. She gulped, glanced at me despairingly, and scuttled out of the room.

Sir Richard closed the door behind her, and turned to face me. He looked as though he would beat *me* over the head with a chair.

He said slowly, 'If this visit is distasteful to you, allow me to assure you that it is a thousand times more distasteful to me.'

Oh yes, I thought—it must indeed be odious for so rich and proud a man to visit a hovel.

'Every instinct,' Sir Richard went on, 'combined to persuade me that my calling here would be unwelcome to you for a dozen reasons. And I knew that what I had to say would make it the more unwelcome, a thousandfold. I have been very sorely tempted to—to mind my own business. But conscience will not permit such an evasion. I should have come here before, said what I have to say to you when your betrothal to Lord Carnmore was first made known to me. I postponed coming here, in the faint hope that the betrothal might be broken off by one party or the other, an outcome which would have spared me the intensely disagreeable task which conscience has given me.'

I had already been much surprised; I was beginning to feel still more surprised. I was already very angry; I was beginning to feel still angrier.

'I came here with extreme reluctance,' said Sir Richard. 'I forced my company on you with still greater reluctance. But I could not forgive myself if I allowed you to go on as you are going, in ignorance of—of where you are going.'

'I am going to Carnmore,' I said.

'Yes.'

'I am not inclined to listen to—'

'Of course you are not! But your eyes are closed and must be opened. I wish to God that someone other than myself could open them, but no one in this county, I think, knows what I wish I did not know.'

'I repeat that I will not listen—'

'I repeat that you must listen—you must be made to hear. This is no pleasure to me, Lady Catriona. I have never done anything I so much detested as to face you with—what you must face. I will be brief.'

'Good,' I said rudely. 'I am very busy.'

'I was in London for several months, the year before last. I knew Carnmore slightly, and some friends of his well. He was there, as he is here, generous and popular. But certain people, as I discovered to my surprise, went out of their way to avoid him. There were certain houses to which he was not admitted. There is a club, of which I am a member, for which he was blackballed by no fewer than four members who knew—things not generally known about him. Listen! I can see by your face that you are angry and incredulous. Believe me, I do not blame you. Be as angry as you wish. I beg you not to be incredulous. I beg you to hear me out.'

Beg? He? He would not have known how to beg. I knew. I had become expert. He was hectoring me in my own house, and I did not believe a word he was saying. Of course Sandy had not been blackballed from membership of a club. The idea was ludicrous. Any club would welcome him. Any house would welcome his visits. If anybody avoided him, it was because his excellence shamed their own wretchedness.

'When drunk,' said Sir Richard, seeming to have to force himself to tell his monstrous lies, 'Carnmore seriously injured, half killed, a woman of the streets whom he had brought back to his lodgings. She survived, but lost the sight of one eye and the use of one arm. The affair was hushed up with great difficulty and at great expense. The woman was bought off, and did not proceed with the complaint she was about to make, without which the Metropolitan Police could not take proceedings. His father heard, and paid, and the shock brought on the heart attack from which he died.'

'I do not believe—' I began, now in a towering rage.

'Silence!' Sir Richard barked.

I was so astonished by this supreme rudeness that I gaped at him, and was silent.

'The episode I have described was not isolated. It was one of several, only the most serious. Carnmore was compelled to leave London, or he would be in prison now. That is why he travelled abroad. What he may have done there I do not know—'

'You do not know,' I repeated, keeping my voice low with the most titanic effort, so that Mamma should not be frightened by my screaming. 'You do not know anything. These are—' What was Papa's phrase? —'these are the mutterings of the envious. I do not understand your motives in telling me these dirty lies, but I suppose you are jealous of a better and more popular and more attractive man than yourself, and I suppose it amuses you to try to make me miserable. Well, you will not succeed, and the only person who comes badly out of this is you.'

'I am not amusing myself,' said Sir Richard grimly. 'I can think of no way of spending a morning which I should not prefer. I do not care what you take my motives to be, but I entreat you to accept that what I say is true, known by me beyond any doubt to be true, known by others to be true, who would bear me out—'

'Bear you out?' I said. His words gave me an idea. 'I know someone who will bear you out.'

'Dr McPhee? He and I have—'

'No,' I said. 'Someone else.'

Before he could stop me, I jumped up out of my chair and ran from the room. I ran out of the house, to the barrack next door where camped the road-making navvies. There were three lounging in the sunshine, with pipes in their mouths and caps on the backs of their heads, outside the barrack. I knew them vaguely by sight. They knew me.

'I need your help at once, ' I panted to them. 'All of you. To throw out of my house a man who—a beast who has been insulting me.'

They were delighted. They had seen Sir Richard's carriage. They had probably seen him go to the house. They would feel bitter resentment of such a man, expensively idle while they broke their backs for pennies. They were commanded, by me, to do violence to him. They could come to no trouble. They were doing their duty, saving a noble damsel from a bully. Of course they were delighted.

They were great hulking fellows, in huge boots and dusty clothes. They grinned, and growled, and knocked out their pipes, and followed me to Myrtle Lodge.

They tugged off their caps when they came indoors. They stood aside for me to precede them. They had better manners than Sir Richard Grant.

I led them into the parlour. Sir Richard was standing by the empty fireplace, looking solemn.

'There he is,' I said to my army. 'Take hold of him and throw him out of my house. If he struggles, you must hit him.'

I glimpsed, as I spoke, my own face in the looking-glass over the fireplace. I had never seen myself white and trembling with anger before. I hardly recognised that chalky mask with narrowed eyes and a clenched mouth.

'Wad ye offer, ma mannie?' growled the biggest navvy: and the three of them laid hands on Sir Richard.

I thought he would struggle. I hoped there would be a glorious and bloody battle. I did not care how much furniture was smashed—Sandy would replace it.

To my keen disappointment, he allowed himself to be marched unceremoniously out of the house. I thought contemptuously: he is a coward, as well as everything else.

The navvies were disappointed, too. They had hoped for better things. To assuage their disappointment, they picked him up and threw him, in the direction of the road and his carriage. The day was fine, but it had rained heavily in the night, and there was a large puddle of liquid mud. It was there that Sir Richard landed heavily, on his face.

He got up stiffly. His front, which I could not see, must have been covered with mud. He limped to his carriage. His coachman appeared from the other side, having seen nothing of this. The coachman exclaimed, calling something I could not catch about his master's condition.

Sir Richard climbed into his carriage, without looking back. I did not see his face again. I imagined, and devoutly hoped, that it was plastered with mud, to pay for the mud he had tried to plaster on Sandy.

I laughed as he drove away. I meant him to hear me. He must have heard me.

My navvies would not accept a penny for what they had done. I wanted to kiss each of them.

Midsummer Day dawned glorious. I had known it would. My eighteenth birthday: my wedding day: I was in a daze of happiness and hope.

Papa made himself look as smart as he could. Mamma twittered like a happy canary-bird.

The ceremony was in the Episcopalian Church in Lochgrannomhead, a raw new building of purple brick, with lurid stained glass windows and a tesselated floor in squares of mauve and yellow. To me, that day, it was the most beautiful place in the world; and I was the most beautiful girl, in my white wedding gown with the enormous hooped skirt, and the rope of pearls Sandy had given me looped round the veil on my head; and Sandy was the most beautiful man.

There was a huge luncheon afterwards, in the Lochgrannomhead Hotel, and all my old friends were there. Except the Gordons. Sir Richard Grant did not attend.

I had not expected my husband to have that bottle of brandy in the carriage.

4

He stood in the middle of my lovely bedroom, rocking on his feet, holding his bottle by the neck, his hair on end. There was brandy on his chin and on his shirt-front and on his breath. His face was grey and shining with sweat. His mouth was half open and his eyes half closed.

He suddenly shouted a string of obscenities, in a voice so slurred I could scarcely understand it. I knew the words, which I should not have known, because of the drunken navvies in the barrack by Myrtle Lodge.

Lucidity once again returned to him. His eyes opened and his voice cleared.

He said, quietly and reasonably, 'I wonder if you know the law, dear little Pussy? Do you know law? I know law. Law says, you're my pro-property. An' all your property is mine, too. You know what that means? You mus' do everything I say. Everything. An' everything of yours is mine. Everything. Mine. Like the castle. Not this one. That one. Your father's castle. Mine.'

He laughed. His laughter gusted the smell of brandy into my face.

'I like owning castles,' he said. 'My grandfather, he didn't own a castle. He didn't own anything. He lived in a room in the Saltmarket, in Glasgow. One room, with thir-thirty people in it. My father remembered. They slept on straw. My father told me. He didn't like it. So he went away, an' made a mill-million pounds. Your father didn't make a million pounds. He lost a million pounds. My father was a better man than your father. Wasn't he? Answer me, you little bitch.'

'Yes,' I said.

'Yes. Ye-e-es.' He imitated my voice, in a high, affected falsetto.

He relapsed into mumbling, and drank deep from his bottle.

He said clearly, 'My father made a million pounds, and sent me to Eton to be a gentleman. Thass what I am. A gentleman. A lord an' a gentleman. I knew boys at Eton. Lots of boys. I knew hun-hundreds of boys. They were lords and gentlemen. They said I wasn't a gentleman. They saw my father, when he came to see me. They laughed at him. Because he spoke—because he came from Glasgow, and still spoke . . . They called me "Gorbals", all the boys did. The dear little Eton boys, the noblemen and gentlemen. They laughed at my father's accent, and called me "Gorbals".'

The unforgotten bitterness rang in his voice. His face was twisted with it.

He staggered to a chair, and sat in it heavily. He reeked of brandy. I stood looking at him, which was all I could do. My one hope now was that he would drink himself insensible before . . .

It seemed likely, as he drank deep again.

'I went to Oxford,' he said, as though chatting to a stranger at a party. 'Nice place. I liked Oxsh-Oxford. I was happy there. Until. One day. I heard. A man. I thought was my friend.'

His voice was clear enough, but he seemed to have difficulty in getting the words out of his mouth, so they came at intervals, like pebbles dropped in twos and threes.

'I thought. My friend. Heard him say. Lithgow. Good fellow. To borrow money from. Likes lending money. Buys friendship. But you can't. Can't make a friend of Lithgow. First gen-generation gennle-man. Slum-child. Glasgow slums. Stinks of the Glasgow slums, Lithgow does.'

He paused, frowning, looking inwards. He was tasting the bitter flavour of his memories.

He suddenly screamed, 'God damn them all to hell!'

I stood like a stone. What else was I to do?

He began to speak more cheerfully, more connectedly. He said, 'Had women, lots of women. Bought them. Had plenty of money. Not much fun, though. Other fellows liked it. They borrowed money from me to pay for their women. I never really saw the point of it all. I never got ex-excited. Then I found I liked it if I hurt them. The more I hurt them, the more I liked it. They didn't like it, but I did. It didn't matter if they liked it or not. I paid them. I only hurt women I despised. Whores. I paid them.'

Sir Richard Grant's story flooded back into my mind. I almost cried out with the shock of it. It was true. Every word of it was true.

I had refused to believe it, because I was determined to disbelieve it. I wanted so desperately to disbelieve it. I yearned so avidly for all that Carnmore could give me. I was stupid and dishonest and greedy. But I was not then eighteen years old, and I was sick of penury . . .

And Dr McPhee's London friend—that report was true, too, and Dr McPhee was right to speak as he did to Papa. Papa had refused to listen to him, because Carnmore was offering him his heart's desire, as he was offering me mine. Papa truly thought I would be happy with Carnmore. He was determined to think so.

'I still,' said my husband thickly, 'I still only hurt women I despise. Whores. You're a whore. Lady Catriona Douglas. Lady Carnmore. You're a whore. Your mother's a whore and your father's a whore. It's true, isn't it? Whole family of whores. I paid them. I paid your mother an' your father an' you. When I first met you I despised you. You know that? You didn't know that, did you? I despised you. You know why? You don't know why, do you? You said you had fine clo's an' carriages an' servants. You were lying. You were pretending to be as rich as me. But you're not, are you? You thought you were deceiving me. But you weren't. I knew you were lying. I knew why. I saw then you were a whore. I despised you. I still do. I despised your parents, the first time I saw them. Stupid. Poor. Do anything for me, for money. Whores. Only wanted my money. Whores. Whole family of whores. Mother, father, daughter, all whores. All for sale. Ari-aristo-cratic whores. All for sale. So I bought you. You know that, don't you? You were for sale, so I bought you, darling little Pussy.'

He made 'Pussy' the most vicious word he had yet used.

'I bought,' he went on huskily, 'I bought your mother and your father, and I bought you. Pussy. Kitten. I bought you. So now I can hurt you. I like it when I hurt them. It's no—no good, if I don't hurt them. I can hurt you, if I want to, 'cause I bought you. Take off my shoes.'

I looked at him, startled.

'Take off my shoes, you whore!' he screamed.

He drank deep, and thrust his feet along the floor towards me. I prayed that the brandy would disable him quickly, quickly. Meanwhile, it seemed perilous not to obey.

I fought down my disgust at going near him, touching him. I knelt down in front of his chair. I untied the laces of his left shoe, and tried to pull it off. It was tight, and resisted me. He raised his right foot, and planted it on my breast, and pushed violently. I was thrown over backwards, holding his left shoe, my breast bruised and hurt by his shod right foot. I hit my head as I fell backwards, on the foot of another chair. The foot was sharp, and bronze ball-and-claw. It hurt my head. I cried out. I felt tears in my eyes, from the pain, as I struggled back to my knees.

He laughed.

I began to undo the laces of his right shoe. But before I could pull the shoe off, he raised his foot again, and planted it on my breast, in the same place, and pushed violently, so that I fell backwards again, and hit my head on the foot of the same chair.

It was his new game.

I struggled to my feet, my head and breast hurting, tears in my eyes.

'Take my shoe off, whore,' he said loudly, waving his foot in the air.

I prayed to God that the brandy might knock him unconscious soon. I knelt before him, and a third time he pushed me over backwards with his foot. He laughed.

We played this game a dozen times. Each time, he laughed. Each time, he drank from his bottle.

I forced myself not to cry or to cringe. If he saw that he was hurting me, hurting me enough to excite him . . .

He tired of his game, and I pulled his right shoe off.

'Socks,' he said.

Shuddering with disgust at contact with his skin, I drew off his silk socks.

'Kiss my feet,' he said.

I was revolted. I could not do it. Though I was at his mercy, I could not and would not. Whore I might be. Bought I might be, and my whole family with me. I could not and would not kiss this monster's disgusting foot.

I shook my head, dumbly.

He slapped me. I did not cry out, but the stinging blow brought more tears to my eyes. He laughed when he saw them. He took a handful of my hair, and pushed my head down. He pushed my face down to his feet on the floor. His hand in my hair, pulling and twisting, was agony. I could not check my tears. I kissed his feet. My tears fell on his bare feet.

This seemed to satisfy him, for the time. He lay back and closed his eyes. He looked ill and wretched. His mouth was hanging open and his breathing was harsh. I thought he was unconscious from the brandy. I waited, silent, watching him. He did not move. His breathing was heavy but regular. I was sure he was in the drunken stupor I had prayed for.

I tiptoed to the door. He had locked it, but the key was in the lock. I tried to turn it softly. It made a loud click. I looked back at him, aghast. He stirred and mumbled. He did not open his eyes. I opened the door and slipped out into the luxurious corridor.

As I began to close the door, gently as could be, there was a bellow from the room.

'Whore! Whore!'

I ran like the wind down the corridor, to the head of the great stair-case. There was a light burning in the hall below, a single oil-lamp. By it, I could see the startled upturned faces of two menservants.

'Puss-Puss-Puss, come here! Kitty-Kitty-Kitty!' bellowed my husband, from the open door of my bedroom.

I fled down the stairs, in my fur-trimmed silken gown.

'Sht-stop her an' bring her back,' screamed Carnmore.

They stopped me and brought me back. They did not look me in the face. They were both footmen, known to me a little, called James and Henry. They were tall men, strong, young, neither more than twenty-five years of age.

They were loyal to Carnmore, or frightened of him, or dependent on him.

'For the love of God, let me go,' I said to them, unable now to check the downfall of tears.

They could not let me go, or they would not. My husband was enti-tled, by every law, to have me dragged back to him. They were obliged to obey him. They did not reply to my begging. They did not look at me or at each other or at their master, as they dragged me back to my master in my bedroom. They had each a hold of one of my arms. In struggling, I hurt only my arms.

Soon I would be hurt enough to excite and delight my husband.

They shut the door on me, and he locked it. This time, he pocketed the key.

'Little Pussy tried to run away,' he said softly. 'Naughty Pussy. Ungra-ungrateful Pussy, after all I've given her. Needs pun-punish-ment. Less think of con-condign punishment.'

He frowned in thought. He went unsteadily, absently, over to the fireplace. He poked at the glowing coals. He left the poker, carelessly, among the red-hot coals.

He looked at me owlishly. He was dribbling a little, from an open mouth.

He said, 'Thash a pretty gown. Too pretty for naughty Pussycat. Take it off.'

I hesitated. My hesitation pulled a trigger in him, and set off an explosion of violent rage. His face worked, like the face of a spoiled child in a tantrum. He rushed at me, and seized hold of the silk, and pulled it off me. He ripped the gown to pieces. He threw me onto the bed. He tore at my undergarments, rending them, tearing them off me. When I struggled he slapped me so hard across the face that I fell back almost stunned. He himself seemed infinitely powerful, lent by anger and brandy an inhuman strength.

When he had stripped me naked, I tried to cover my nakedness with my hands. He slapped me again, across the face and across my breast. I saw the red mark left by his fingers, livid on my breast.

'Ha ha,' was all he said.

And then, almost more startling than anything that had gone before, he was once again lucid and reasonable.

'We have had trouble,' he said, 'with beef-bullocks.'

I lay helpless on the bed, stark naked, looking up at him in utter astonishment.

'They stray,' he said. 'We cannot fence in the whole hillside. They stray off into other herds. One bullock looksh—looks mush like another. So how do we i-identify them? Ha ha! You know, don't you? We brand them.'

A sickening idea came to me. I writhed at the thought.

He pulled off his jacket and waistcoat and tie, and dropped them on a chair.

'You're a naughty little Pussy, always trying to run away,' he continued sadly. 'Might get losht. Nobody would know you were mine. Might lose you. Don't want that. I bought you. Don't want to lose you, not yet. Want some val-value for my money. So I'd better brand you. On the rump, you know. Like a beef-bullock. Little calf. Swee' lil calf.'

He went over to the fireplace. He had not left the poker there carelessly. The tip was red hot. The handle was too hot to hold. He touched it, and recoiled with an oath. He wrapped a handkerchief round it. He lifted it from the fire, and crossed the room to my bed.

'On the rump,' he said thoughtfully. 'Turn over.'

Never in my life had I been in such utter despair. I was completely helpless.

Worst of all, worst of all, the branding-iron would hurt me enough to excite his perverted lust. I was sure of it. 'I only like it if I hurt them. The more I hurt them, the more I like it.' He would hurt me very badly, and he would like that very much. There was a red glitter in his eyes, hotter and more horrible than the red-hot steel itself.

When he picked up the poker, he put down his bottle. It was on the mantelpiece, gross and incongruous among the dainty knick-knacks.

I jumped off the bed, on the far side from him. He gave a shout, and lurched round the bed after me. I sped to the fireplace, and picked up the bottle by the neck. I thought, idiotically: what a pity—it is still a quarter full. It will be wasted.

He came at me, brandishing the poker like a sword.

He lunged at me with the poker, just as I swung the bottle with all my strength at his head. The poker grazed my ribs, as I struck. I felt the searing pain, for a split second: and in the same split second, the bottle exploded on his head, and he slumped to the floor at my feet.

His hair was full of broken glass and blood and brandy.

My first thought was that I had committed murder. Would they hang me? Or would I spend my life in prison? I did not mind. The scaffold was better than this dainty padded bedroom. Rats in a prison cell were better company than this creature on the floor.

He stirred and mumbled. I almost shrieked with surprise. I felt—it is extraordinary to remember—but I felt a pang of regret that he was alive, as sharp as the pain of the burn in my side.

I stood over him, ready to hit him again with his own poker. But, though he was alive, he was in a stupor now, from the blow with the bottle and from the brandy that had been in the bottle.

If his head needed attention, it could get it later. That was the very least of my concerns.

I was trembling violently. I was sobbing uncontrollably. I was unable to think of anything, except the narrowness of my escape from torture and defilement, and the depth of the trouble I was in.

I was in a pit I had dug for myself.

I looked round the lovely room, trying helplessly to concentrate, to think clearly. I saw my reflection in the great gold-framed looking glass. The sight gave me a shock—the slim white body, topped with wildly tousled yellow hair. I had forgotten I was naked. It was, perhaps, the first thing to deal with.

Well, that was no problem. I had dozens of gowns to choose from . . . Gowns? I could not escape in a gorgeous hooped gown, or lie hidden, or evade search and capture.

I wanted a young boy's clothes. There were none here. A man's clothes, then. His clothes.

I gritted my teeth, and set myself to pulling off his trousers. It was most awkward. I did not want to touch him. Above all, I did not want to startle him back into consciousness. Very slowly, very gently, I undid all the buttons I could find, and eased the trousers inch by inch downwards from his hips and off his legs.

Dubiously, I stepped into the trousers myself. They felt most odd. They were absurdly long. They reeked of spilled brandy.

I could do nothing about the brandy, but I could cure the length. I had been given, among all my birthday and wedding presents, some little gold embroidery scissors. They were the only scissors in the room. I hacked away at the legs of the smart black trousers, so that they came only to my feet. They ballooned about my hips and legs, but they were the right length, and when supported by braces they stayed up, instead of falling disgracefully to my ankles.

In the pocket of the trousers was the key of the room.

I looked at myself dubiously, still naked from the waist up. I knew that I should have a shirt, his shirt. That meant pulling it over his head, over the mess of spirit and blood and glass in his hair. I felt sick at the thought, and sick when I tried to do it. I railed at my own weakness—but I decided to do without a shirt. Instead, I chopped the skirt from a chemise of my own, with my faithful embroidery scissors. The effect was grotesque, but decent.

I cut off my hair. I almost cried with regret as those heavy masses of wavy gold fell from my head onto the pillow-case which I had spread to catch them. It was difficult, hacking with little scissors at the back of my own head. But, in the end, I found I had a short, wildly-uneven yellow thatch, and I hardly recognised myself.

My face, unfamiliar without its usual golden frame of hair, looked very pinched and solemn. I thought I looked like an unhappy young boy.

I burned my hair in the fire. I was careful to burn every scrap. Shorn locks would show that I had cut it off, and give Carnmore some help in looking for me. It hissed, and crinkled, and shrivelled, and flared with little coloured flames. I thought: this is better than Papa's chemistry. This experiment works.

His waistcoat and coat were on the chair where he had dropped them. I put them on, and examined myself again. I folded back the cuffs of the coat, which covered the tips of my fingers. I cut the cuffs off, where the folds were, with the little scissors. The scissors were blunted and bent by now, so my cuts were very ragged. The stiff masculine material enveloped me, hiding my bosom and the whole female shape of my body. I did look like a boy—a boy in his father's clothes, crudely cut down for him.

I could do nothing about shoes. Any of my own would give me away. His were twice too big for my feet. Well, I had sometimes gone barefoot as a child.

I felt in the pockets of coat and waistcoat. I found five gold sovereigns, and a gold watch. I left them there. I thought they would be useful. I had no compunction about taking them.

I looked at the jewels in the jewel-box on my dressing table. Every piece there he had given me. They were a king's ransom, to me. My hand stretched out to the jewel-box, but fell back to my side. Those I could not take: I would not.

I pulled off my wedding-ring. It came off easily, having been on that finger for twelve short hours. I stood for a moment, frowning. I thought that if I left it, he might find it, and it would be a clue for him. If I took it, it might give me away to someone. I opened one of the great windows, and threw the ring as far as I could into the night sky.

A gust of wind battered at me through the open window, carrying a flail of cold rain. I shivered. Yet I knew I was fortunate in the night. If I once got clear away from the castle, a thousand men could search all night without finding me, without seeing me in the dense darkness, or hearing me in the thrash of wind and rain. A windless moonlit night— a proper romantic midsummer night—would have made things far more difficult for me.

Not that they were easy, I thought, remembering the footmen in the hall.

I could not leave by the window. There was a sheer drop of smooth stone, without any drainpipe or creeper, to the paving below. I thought of cutting the sheets from the bed into strips, knotting them together, and climbing down this rope. It was possible. I had gone down ropes from windows as a child, at Strathlarrig, and almost been punished for risking my neck. But it would take too long. The sleeping beauty on the floor would not sleep forever. He would come to life with a bad headache, and in a very ugly temper.

If I were still there . . .

I unlocked the door. I opened it, very slowly, and peeped out into the corridor. The big chandeliers had been snuffed; there was a single tall candle in a glass bell at the head of the stairs. There was no sound, except the slash of rain against a window at the end of the corridor, and the boom of the wind in some chimney.

I closed the door, as softly as I could. I locked it from the outside, and put the key in my pocket. There would be a spare key. The housekeeper was sure to have one. But I thought the locked door might gain me a little time.

I tiptoed to the head of the main stairs, the carpet soft under my bare feet. I peeped over the balustrade, down into the great hall. The single lamp still burned, near the huge front door. Up against the door itself had been placed a chair. A man sat in it, a servant. He might be asleep, but he would wake if I went that way.

It was as though the household had expected me to try to run away, and was organised to prevent it.

Leaving the main stairway, I walked along passages towards the back stairs, reached through a baize-covered door. The door was locked. I could not get to the back parts of the castle. I ran, silent on my bare feet, to the floor above, and to the floor above that. On each floor, there were doors into the back passages. They were all locked. I had to go down the main stairs. There was no other way.

I did so, like a mouse, keeping low. My hair might be short, but it would be brightly visible in the lamplight, unless I kept my head in deep shadow, or out of the line of sight of any watchers. Of course I should have taken some dark scarf or shawl from my cupboards, to cover my head. But I had not thought. And no power on earth would have induced me back into my bedroom.

I crept down the stairs, and crouched by the newel-post at the foot. My masculine clothes felt stiff and clumsy, and seemed to make a terrible rustling noise wherever I moved. I was thankful for the slashing rain on the windows each side of the front door.

My head on the stair-carpet, I peeped out from the newel-post, and looked all round the hall. I could see no other watcher. Doors opened off the hall into some of the rooms of the castle—the principal drawing-room, a smaller saloon, and the library. I did not know if those doors were locked at night. I could not imagine why they should be, but many households had old and careful rules, especially where treasures were kept. Carnmore was full of treasures . . .

The suits of armour were threatening and ghastly in the lamplight. They were like evil sentries, prison guards, mailed warders. But I could hide amongst them, if I could get to them. I might be protected by armour that had been brought out of Strathlarrig.

From the foot of the stairs, twenty feet of bare marble stretched in every direction. The man with his back to the front door commanded every square inch of this empty floor. If he were to open his eyes, as I crossed to the nearest hiding-place . . .

I was not ashamed to be frightened of what might happen to me, if I was caught and dragged back once again to Carnmore. He had sought to punish me with a red-hot poker, simply for trying to run away. What would he think the right punishment, for breaking his head with a bottle?

What would his servants think, of the new Lady Carnmore who did that to her Lord?

I stared in perplexity at the watcher with his back to the door, trying to make out if he were awake or asleep. I could not even be sure whether his eyes were closed. The lamp was beside and a little in front of him, a large unshaded oil-lamp on a small table. The effect was that his face was part lit, part shadowed, like the face in the Rembrandt painting (sold by Papa) in the library at Strathlarrig; the effect was that his eyes might be tight shut, or wide and alert and staring at me, and I could not tell which.

The only way to be sure he was asleep was to wait and watch. If he were awake he would move, eventually, though it was no more than a finger. I had learned this as a child, escaping from the nursery when Miss MacRae dropped off—or, sometimes, pretended to drop off, in order to catch me escaping. That might be the door-keeper's strategy. I had to wait.

But I dared not wait. Every second that rushed by, gave Carnmore time to come to his senses, to beat at the locked bedroom door and scream for his servants. There would be bright lights everywhere, eyes everywhere, armies all over the castle who knew the castle far better than I did. It was no place for me to play hide-and-seek with fifty hunters.

I had to cross the hall, get into one of the rooms that opened off it, and climb out of a window. I had to go now.

I gulped, and crossed my fingers. I prayed, 'Please God, let that man be asleep.' I slid round the newel-post, keeping in a crouching position. I sped across twenty yards of bare marble, to the nearest suit of armour. The marble floor felt cold and wet to my bare feet. My baggy trousers rustled scratchily. I crept behind a great gaunt black suit of armour, and peeped out, under the knight's arm, at the watcher.

He made a sudden movement, raising a hand from his lap to his face. He rubbed his face. I heard him grunt and yawn. There was a lull in the furious wind, and in the sudden silence his yawn was loud in the hall. He sat up sharply in his chair, and looked round. He was wide awake. I could see his eyes now; the lamplight gave them a kind of inhuman glitter. He was staring straight at my armour. I thought he was staring at me. I thought the bottoms of my stiff baggy trousers must be sticking out each side of the narrow steel legs of the armour. I thought he saw them. I thought I was caught.

He yawned again, and stood up. He was stiff, from sleeping in an upright wooden chair. He began to stroll round the hall. I did not think he was searching, but wandering aimlessly, stretching his legs. He crossed towards the suit of armour nearest the foot of the stairs—the one I was hiding behind. His face was in darkness as he approached me, because the lamp was behind him. He was a big, heavy man with a hard look. His footsteps rang loudly on the marble floor, over the renewed thrash of rain on the windows. He came right up to my suit of armour, as though to talk to it, as though to talk to me. He was taller and bigger than the suit of armour. I crouched behind, trying to keep my hands from trembling, trying to quiet my breathing and the thudding of my heart in my throat.

He raised a hand to the visor of the helmet. His hand was inches from my head. He made an adjustment to the position of the visor, and stepped back to examine it critically. He strolled to the next suit of armour, on the other side of the fireplace. I circled round my own suit, keeping it between myself and him.

I had played this game as a child, dodging round trees or rocks or tables, hiding from Mamma or Miss MacRae. I was not playing now for childish stakes.

It struck me that if any other servant came into the hall, or onto the landing above, I must be seen at once. I prayed desperately that no other servant was awake and watching. I prayed that the big man would go back to sleep by the door.

He showed no signs of doing so. He had slept enough. He was wakeful and bored. He strolled round the hall, looking absently at the armour, the great dark pictures, and the mounted heads of stags.

And the minutes ticked by. And Carnmore would wake up and begin to shout.

He went back at last to his chair by the door. He settled himself into it, with a gusty sigh. I heard the chair creak. I could not see if he closed his eyes.

I trembled with indecision. I did not dare stay where I was, a moment longer than I had to, for fear of the hue-and-cry that must come. I did not dare go to the shelter of the next suit of armour, until I was more sure that his eyes were closed.

I could not tell about his eyes. I had to take the risk. I took it.

He did not move. He made no sound.

I crouched behind the second suit of armour, and then the third and fourth, and so approached the door of the great drawing room. Then I had six yards of bare marble to cross, and there was nothing to hide behind anywhere near the door. The shadowed face of the watcher was half turned towards me.

I cursed the stupid trembling of my knees, and the suffocating thudding of my heart.

I went to the door, my chin on my shoulder, ready to run and hide if the man made any movement. He made none. I reached the door, and grasped the handle.

The door was locked.

The door of the small saloon was locked, also. The door into the back part of the castle was locked. I fought despair. I was sure the door of the library would be locked—obviously, it was the rule of the house that all these doors were locked.

I tried to make a new plan, crouched trembling behind armour. I could climb up inside the chimney from the great hall fireplace, perhaps. I could hide there until the search had died down. Or I could go up, all the way up to the chimney-stack at the top. Then what? Fly? Or I could come out of the chimney into some upstairs room. And then what? My last state would be no better than my first.

The hall was full of weapons, swords and halberds arranged in panoplies on the walls. I could reach down a sword from the wall, kill the watcher by the door, let myself out . . .

Kill a sleeping man, in cold blood? A servant, who was simply doing what he was told?

Well, if it must be it must. I could think of absolutely nothing else. I can barely believe that I truly planned to kill a sleeping man with a sword. Still a scaffold seemed better than my bedroom, and prison rats than my husband.

I crept to the fireplace, over which hung an armoury of swords. I climbed onto the heavy brass fender, and reached upwards. The tips of my fingers just grazed the hilt of the lowest sword. I could not reach it. There was no mantelpiece I could climb onto—only the gaping cave of the ancient fireplace. There was no furniture I could move —only oak chests too heavy for me even to drag.

I fought against tears of despair. I lost. I wept with terror at what I faced.

And then there came that which I most dreaded—a banshee scream, unearthly loud, from upstairs—again and again, like some hellish trumpet, louder by far than any noise of the storm.

Almost at once there were answering shouts, and the sound of running feet.

The doorkeeper sprang up out of his chair. He started at a run across the hall, towards the stairs.

I thought: I can get out of the front door, after all.

The man stopped, turned, stared at the front door. He ran back to it. He took the massive key out of the lock, and carried it with him up the stairs.

I could see that there were lights on the landing above. There were more screams of the purest rage from the bedroom.

I ran to the door of the library, in the tiny hope that, of all the doors, it might be unlocked.

It was.

I had a moment of amazement. There were precious manuscripts and pictures in the library, and an antique globe of great rarity, and some very unusual printed books. Then I remembered that the windows of the library gave onto a courtyard, not onto the outside world like the windows of the other rooms; perhaps they thought no robber could get so far. The courtyard itself was impregnable.

This gave me hideous problems: but they were problems for later. At least I was out of the great bare spaces of the hall.

I slipped into the utter blackness of the library, and closed the door softly behind me. There was a gigantic click, but no louder than the slam of my heart.

I had been into the library only once. It was no place for an active illiterate like myself. I could not remember, in my excitement and confusion, where anything was. I groped away from the door, trying to visualise a hiding-place. There was a smell of old leather, and of beeswax polish. It was very quiet, as the windows giving onto the courtyard were sheltered from the storm. I heard the ponderous ticking of a clock, and beyond that the thumping feet and calls of servants, and, a long way off, the screaming of a madman in a fury.

My groping hands felt the edges of tables, chairs, the great globe in the centre of the room. On the tables I felt candlesticks, papers under paperweights, folios and albums. It was the blackest darkness I had ever known. There was no chink of light below the door or through its keyhole. I supposed the windows were shuttered as well as curtained. I stubbed my bare toes against the foot of a chair, and almost cried out with the pain. In staggering, I knocked over a candlestick. It fell with a crash I thought must be heard all over the castle. I stood still, palpitating, listening. Doors were banging and people calling. There were footsteps in the hall, many footsteps.

Imperatively I had to find somewhere to hide. Where? A cupboard? Was there a cupboard? Any searcher would look first in a cupboard. Where, then?

My groping fingertips met a thin, curved wooden railing, that rose at a steep angle from waist height. I could not imagine what this might be, until I remembered the library ladder. This was a lovely old piece of work, a little spiral stairway of brass and mahogany, which could be pushed on castors to any part of the shelves. It would not hide a spider.

Searchers would rush in with oil-lamps and candles. They would look behind things, and under things. Would they raise their eyes to the ceiling?

Would they light the great central chandelier?

The door of the library burst open. A manservant in shirtsleeves hurried in, holding a candlestick, with his palm shielding the flame. Light washed in from the hall, which was full of lamps and full of people.

Almost before I realised it, I was up at the top of the ladder, close up to the cornice above the topmost shelf of books. This top shelf was made for big volumes, but it was not full of them. My desperate fingers felt books lying flat, and some small books. I thought there might be room for me to lie along the shelf, that it might be just deep enough and high enough. I thanked God I was slim and active.

Two other servants, a man and a woman, had come into the library after the first. One had an oil-lamp, one a candle. They searched noisily and thoroughly, looking under every chair and table, and in the big cupboards between the windows.

Like an eel, I wriggled from the top of the ladder onto the topmost bookshelf, and tried to plaster myself against the back of the shelf. I was lying half on top of books. The dust of old books filled my nostrils, and I had to fight to stop myself sneezing. I could not move a finger, once I was wedged into the bookshelf. I could see the wavering lights of the searchers, and hear their mutterings and heavy breathing.

The oil-lamp was waved at the ladder. But not quite at the top of the ladder. Nobody expected a ladyship to be lying in a bookcase. I seemed to die, as the halo of lamplight swam towards me: and to come to life when it dipped away.

I do not know how long I lay miserably on the bookshelf, dust in my nose, the edges of books digging into my breast and hips, my burned rib paining me, and my head where I had hit it on the bedroom chair-leg, and where he had seized his handful of my hair. I do know that I was never for one single moment alone. Servants came in and out, with lamps or candles. Everything was searched three and four and a dozen times—except my topmost bookshelf. Always, when a party of servants went out, one stayed behind, or another came in.

They moved the ladder, in order to search the top of the cupboards.

My husband came in. I could not see him. I heard him. I was so astonished that I nearly fell off the shelf. His voice was sober, reasonable, not loud. He had gone upstairs a rabid animal; he had come downstairs a rational gentleman. I thought he must be extraordinarily healthy, to recover so completely and so quickly. The thought gave me no joy.

'Her ladyship has had some kind of seizure,' I heard him saying, with a sort of worried sadness. 'It is most necessary that she should be found, in case she does herself an injury. Has every herd been knocked up? Every hand on the farm?'

'Ay, ma Lord,' said a voice I did not know. 'There's fufty sairchin' the policies.'

A seizure, indeed. I wished I had had strength to hit harder with the bottle.

Carnmore went away, but still one or more servants stayed. I was so miserably cramped, that I was not sure I would be able to climb down, or to walk when I got to the floor. If I ever got the chance to get there. Daylight must be coming. The curtains would be drawn back, and the shutters opened. Sunlight would stream in, as I had seen it in this room a fortnight before, glaring at every shelf of books, glaring at my hair and face.

And then I was left alone. The library door was shut. I heard, this time, the key turn in the lock. I was in pitch darkness again.

Cramp was screaming in my leg and foot, and my left arm had gone to sleep because I had been lying on it. I was a long way from the floor. To this day I do not know how I climbed down from my shelf, without falling, with a cramped leg and numbed arm.

I groped my way to the nearest window, sensation coming back with violent pins-and-needles to my arm, my cramped leg hardly able to support me.

My dread now was that it was daylight.

I hauled back a curtain, the rings thundering along the curtain-rod. I unbarred a shutter, the bar falling with a clang like a gong. The shutters had bolts also, which I had great difficulty pulling back in the dark. I pinched a finger savagely, between two pieces of metal I could not see. I swung a shutter open. It seemed to screech as loud as Carnmore's screams. Each of these awful noises, I thought, was like to bring a regiment of servants charging into the library. But the door stayed closed.

It was still dark outside, and as wildly stormy as ever.

Suddenly there was a mechanical whirr behind me, and a great *bong*. I was so startled that I bit my tongue, to add to my discomforts. The bong was twice repeated. It was the library clock. It was only three o'clock. My ordeal had seemed endless, and dawn imminent: but I had two or three hours of darkness still.

I opened the window. Though it was enormous, the sash slid easily upwards, and could have been raised with a finger, because of new weights on new sash-cords in a new frame. All such details of the castle had been seen to by the Carnmores, father and son. It was nice that their efforts helped my escape.

I leaned out of the window into the wild wet darkness. My face was at once full of rain. There were hurricane-lamps on hooks in the courtyard, but they lit little except the rain that streamed down about them.

Looking left, I could just make out the high west side of the castle chapel, all dark, which formed one side of the courtyard. Opposite were the estate offices, into which I had never set foot, with a light in the window. To my right was the great gate in the curtain wall.

The gate might be watched. I thought it likely not, as nobody would dream that I could climb it. It was more than twenty feet high, enormous oak, crested with evil spikes. I could not climb it. No one on earth could have climbed it, without a ladder. But I could leave that way, even so.

The paving-stones of the courtyard were some twelve feet below me. That was no problem. Though I was out of practice at dropping from windowsills, I had once been expert at it. It is not a thing you forget how to do.

I could see no one in the courtyard. No one would willingly stand sentry out of doors in such weather.

I climbed onto the windowsill, sat on it, twisted until I lay on my stomach. My head and shoulders were inside the library and my legs hanging down the outside wall. I edged myself outwards, so that more and more of me was hanging out over the stones. I took my weight on my hands, and lowered myself to the full length of my arms. I did not like the thought of losing my grip on the wet stone. I let myself drop. When I reached the ground, I did not remain upright, but bent my legs, as a cat does, to take the shock of the fall. It *was* rather a shock, and hurt my bare feet. I slipped and fell as I landed, but without damage.

I was immediately soaking wet. The rain felt very cold, though it was Midsummer Night. The flagstones were cold and slippery to my feet. My hair was saturated by the rain.

I did not like leaving the library window open, unshuttered, uncurtained. It might be seen any second from inside, if anyone came back into the room. It would be seen at the first peep of dawn.

Well, did it matter if they knew how I had got away, so I was clear away?

'Hey, wha's there?' shouted a voice.

A lantern swung. I was not alone in the courtyard. I had been seen. But I could not have been more than glimpsed, by dim lantern-light, in that rain. I could not have been recognised.

I called out, ''Tis Jaikie Bogle frae the sculldoonerie, sairchin' for her leddyship!' I spoke in the shrill whine I had learned, long ago, from playmates I was *not* supposed to have.

There was an answering grunt. The man did not ask what the 'sculldoonerie' was. This was as well. I had no idea. It was a word I had found myself inventing. If I had said 'boiler-room' or 'still-room' or such, the other might have known that there was no Jaikie Bogle there.

I was glad to find that my wits were not addled by my adventures or by the rain, but working as quick as was needful. I crept towards the gate, keeping well away from the lanterns. I was congratulating myself on my cleverness—when I felt a hand on the collar of my coat.

'There's no' a Jaikie Bogle in the cassel,' said a voice hoarse with suspicion.

I was not so very clever.

A lantern swung. I tried to wriggle away from the imprisoning hand on my neck. I was held fast. The lantern and my face were coming closer together. This was discovery. This was utter disaster.

I raised a bare foot, and kicked at the lantern. I felt the hot glass and metal for an instant, then saw the lantern fly away from the hand that held it, and crash to the flagstones. The surprise made my captor loose his grip. I tore myself away from him. I ran a few strides.

Where? My man was shouting names. Others would come to his call, more men, more lanterns. I could not hide in the courtyard. There was nowhere to hide. I hated the idea of going back into the castle, but it was the right thing to do.

I sped in through the door of the estate office. I had a confused impression of desks, stools, stacks of boxes, a single oil-lamp on a bracket, an inner door, and one startled face ten yards from me, at the other end of the long room. I swept the lamp off its bracket. It crashed and exploded, plunging the room into darkness. I ran to the inner door, bumping into furniture, stubbing my bare toes again, hardly feeling these accidents. I felt wildly excited and very frightened. I was taking an appalling gamble—but it was all I could do. I opened the inner door, then violently slammed it shut. I dropped to my knees, and on all fours crept like a mouse back towards the outer door.

The man I had glimpsed *must* think I had gone by the inner door. The hue-and-cry must be inside the castle.

'Dougal! Wattie! Brang's a licht, for Goad's sake, mon!'

Feet thumped outside. Two men with lanterns crashed into the office.

'Ay, yon road, intil the lairders—'

The hunt surged inwards, to larders and sculleries and kitchens.

Other men had run into the courtyard from other doors—doors I did not know, had never seen, doors leading I knew not where. There were many more lights. But the men dazzled each other, and confused each other with shouting. None thought I could have got clear away from the castle; none thought I would ever get clear away, because of the height of the great locked gate.

I crept to the side of the gate, unseen. On the way, my foot touched something soft. I picked it up. I blessed it. It was a Highland bonnet, a Tam-o'-Shanter, very wet. I crammed it on my head. It felt like a cold pudding, and came down over my face like a soft coal-scuttle.

The gate was hung between two great square granite pillars, which stood out by almost a yard from the curtain wall. On the side nearer the library, the wall stretched away smooth and featureless to the corner of the courtyard. A ladder would have been as needful there as on the gate itself. But on the other side there was a sort of buttress, the full height of the wall, a yard from the pillar. So there was an embrasure, between buttress and pillar, like a three-sided chimney.

Now, when I was a child at Strathlarrig, I made a particular pet of a herd called Jock McBurney. His special merit was his skill at climbing rocks, which he taught me. There was a place in particular he showed me, a twenty-foot cleft in a cliff called the Pope's Chimney (Heaven knows why); the rock was sheer and smooth, but could be climbed easily, if one knew how. Jock taught me how. You were to place the soles of your feet against one side of the chimney, and your back and the palms of your hands against the other side, and hold yourself so, pressing to keep in position. It was then simple to move one foot at a time, and one hand at a time, and one's back, and so go up the chimney. Jock McBurney put a rope round my waist, and stood at the top of the chimney, so that even if I slipped I would not fall. I did not slip. Jock forbade me utterly to attempt the climb without him and without the rope. Of course I ignored this rule. Herds did not give *me* orders.

There was no important difference between the Pope's Chimney at Strathlarrig, and the gap between buttress and gate-pillar at Carnmore. Except that I had never attempted to climb rocks in pitch darkness, or in torrential rain and a gale-force wind. I hoped these things would not make much difference.

They made a large difference.

I had an agonising climb up that chimney, my feet and hands and back always in the greatest danger of slipping on the wet stone. All were very sore, and I guessed bleeding, by the time I was half way up.

There were still people surging about in the courtyard, and many lights in the castle windows I could see. I was fairly well hidden in my chimney; but not from a man who came close with a lantern. Several did, to make sure the gate was safely locked and barred. But they did not explore the chimney. They did not know it could be climbed. They had not had the benefit of Jock McBurney's friendship.

If the middle of the chimney was bad, the top was worse. The wind tried to pluck me away, and the rain to wash me away. My clothes were torn, and heavy as lead with water. I crawled over the top, clinging with every fingernail and toenail, and started down the matching chimney on the other side.

I was far more exposed to the weather. The outer chimney was shallower. *But* I was outside Carnmore! No walls, no doors, no locks, lay between me and freedom.

I was desperate to hurry, but I could not. To fall and break a leg now, to lie helpless until they found me by daylight . . .

My husband would like me with a broken leg, if the pain was bad enough . . .

I reached the ground at last. It was muddy, running with wet mud. It sloped steeply into the old moat. The grass was slippery with the wet. I could not keep my footing, but rolled down into the moat. It was not filled, but it was not dry. It made no difference to my state.

I climbed up out of the moat, sliding and slipping on the wet steep bank. I was beside the new carriage-drive which old Lord Carnmore had made. I could not get lost. The carriage-drive came at last to a road, which led straight to Lochgrannomhead. I started down the drive, hurrying, running as long as I could run, walking fast when I could run no more, then running again. I slipped and tripped and fell, often and often. It was terribly unimportant, except that it slowed me up. Every minute was putting distance between myself and that abominable bedroom, that extraordinary mixture of men to whom, fifteen hours before, I had been bound eternally with hoops of gold.

I rejoiced at my freedom. I sang snatches of wild music into the teeth of the wind. I never once looked back. The future was full of problems—all the old problems, and a horde of new ones—but I was free.

There was never any doubt about where I should go. There was only one place where I could go. Papa would hide me from Carnmore, somehow. We could flee abroad again, or go anywhere, far, silent, safe. I would tell him a little of what had happened, and he would protect me.

It was a long weary road to Lochgrannomhead. I was bottomlessly tired. Worse, the sky began to pale in the east. I must go careful in daylight, and keep myself completely hidden.

It was still teeming with rain. Grey tatters of clouds, instead of black, raced across the sky.

I began to see a few herds, with their plaids over their heads, and carters with their faces deep in their upturned collars. They did not see me, for I lay in ditches until they passed.

When the light had strengthened enough for me to inspect myself, I wondered if this furtiveness was necessary. My ludicrous baggy trousers and coat were caked with wet mud, and torn in a dozen places. My legs were mud-caked to the knee, in spite of trousers, and my arms to the elbow, in spite of sleeves. I imagined my face was in the same state. The great wet pudding of my bonnet clung all round my face, hiding my hair and brow and ears.

I looked at Carnmore's gold watch, which I suddenly remembered. It had stopped at half-past-three. I had broken it during my climb. Well, Papa could sell it for a hatful of guineas.

The gold sovereigns were still safe in the pocket of the waistcoat.

When I reached the edge of Lochgrannomhead, I was almost too tired to walk. My feet were bleeding, as well as caked in mud. My clothes felt too heavy to carry. I almost decided to go through the middle of Lochgrannomhead, the quickest way to Myrtle Lodge. No one would see me.

But I fetched a circuit, that added half an hour to my journey. Having got so far, it would be supreme folly to take one unnecessary risk.

I neared my home. The navvies were astir in their barrack, and I smelled frying bacon. That made me realise that, as well as being exhausted, I was ravenously hungry. I had not eaten since the previous midday. I had taken—God knew I had taken—an extravagant amount of hard exercise. The smell of frying bacon would have been more than I could bear, but that I knew I should have what breakfast I wanted, the moment I was safe in Myrtle Lodge.

I rounded the corner of the navvies' barrack, creeping, careful not to be seen. I came into view of my home. My heart almost burst with thankfulness.

A carriage I knew was waiting in the road by the house. I had ridden in it so often. A coachman I knew sat huddled in his greatcoat on the box. A groom I knew stood despondently by the heads of horses I knew.

He was here. He was with Papa. He had beaten me to it.

5

'Oh dear,' said Mamma, in an uncertain voice that sounded full of tears, 'oh dear! Poor, poor Alexander! How ashamed I feel! How distressed and worried you must be! How *could* my wicked Pussy have been so wilful, so ungrateful . . .'

Mamma was up, early as it was. This was unheard of. Only for Carnmore would she have come downstairs before eight o'clock.

They were all three in the parlour. I was hiding in the little passage outside, which led to the dining room and kitchen. It was dark where I crouched, sore and exhausted and muddy and bleeding. I should not be seen, if any of them came out of the parlour into the passage. I could hear very well. The walls of Myrtle Lodge had not become more like the walls of Carnmore Castle.

'It is not as though,' fluted Papa, 'Catriona had not been brought up in accordance with strict religious and moral principles. Which renders it the stranger, the more deeply upsetting—'

'To some extent,' came the gentle, reasonable voice of my husband, 'in some measure, I blame myself—'

'I cannot allow you to accept a blame which is, alas, to be laid at the door of that headstrong child!' cried Papa.

'She was not, I think,' said Carnmore slowly, 'quite prepared for the —intimacies of the married state. I was—I think I may be forgiven for being—fervent. I am very deeply attached to my wife, ardent in my devotion to her, and . . . I have said enough. The very last thing I would wish to do is to distress you, Lady Larrig. Suffice it to say that in—what I have touched on—I hope without offence—'

'No tittle of offence!' said Papa. 'Not a jot!'

'Therein,' said Carnmore, 'may lie the explanation of conduct which —well, I can admit to *you*, who love her as I do, that my wife has wounded me very deeply. Of course I forgive her. I will forgive her utterly, and from the bottom of my heart, if only she will come back to me. That is my dearest, my only wish. I want my little wife back.

We shall make a fresh start. And—I swear that, if adoration and consideration can make her happy—'

'Of course you will make her happy, Alexander!' cried Mamma. 'We have always known that you would!'

'I beg and pray for the chance to prove you right, Ma'am.'

'We pledge ourselves to give you that chance,' said Papa solemnly.

'Yes,' said Carnmore. 'Of course, one does not wish—one would not dream of insisting on the point—but this—defiance, this disappearance —does more than cause pain to myself and, I dare guess, to you also—'

'Pain, indeed, Carnmore!' said Papa. 'Pain and mortification and acute embarrassment!'

'Yes. Of so much I made sure—so much I felt safe in assuming, on the basis of the unfailing goodwill you have been so very kind as to show me, since I first had the honour of making myself known to you. Unfortunately, as I say, there is more at issue than the pain Catriona has caused all of us.'

'She is your wife,' wailed Mamma.

'She is my wife, in the eyes of God and of the law. She is legally obliged to bear me company, to dwell under my roof. I venture to believe that she is morally so obliged—'

'By gratitude, if nothing else!' said Papa.

'One might indeed have hoped so. Meanwhile, the law is most clear and specific on this issue. It is, I do not need to remind you, the absolute legal obligation of every person to endeavour to persuade—to compel, if need be—my errant bride to return to the hearth where she will be as lovingly protected, as fondly indulged, as an adoring husband can contrive.'

'We are alive to our duty in this regard,' said Papa. 'Have no fear that we will not faithfully perform it, if ever the occasion arises.'

'We should hope to persuade,' said Mamma uncertainly, 'but, if advice and entreaty fails—'

'She shall be brought back to you,' said Papa.

'Meanwhile,' said Carnmore, after a pause, 'I find myself in a difficulty. A number of related difficulties.'

'If we can be of any assistance, in any way—' began Papa eagerly.

'Yes. As you know, I have made some substantial investments in your work, Lord Larrig, and defrayed certain expenses which you had previously contracted. Further, I am in the course of preparing premises for you in which, we all trust, your scientific work may proceed more rapidly and valuably.'

'Yes, yes! It is kind of you. It is more than kind—it is wise.'

'It is, of course, to a father-in-law, to a trusted and intimate family connection, that I make these—gestures. It is with an—if I may without presumption so express myself—it is with an ally that I have been dealing, and hope to continue to deal.'

'I hope so, too,' said Papa, most obviously meaning what he said.

'I have said enough. Too much, perhaps. I may rely on your help, then, in using your very best endeavours to return to me the wayward little wife whom I love and esteem so deeply?'

They chorused that he could rely on them.

He had given them, in equal parts, husbandly love, and the awful majesty of the law, and threats.

I was too numb with exhaustion, and distracted by my aches and pains, to think clearly: but in a confused way I wondered which most firmly made my parents his allies—love, or the law, or his threats?

I might have been heartsick at their treachery. But I was not. He had been so kind to them. He had seemed so gentle to me. He seemed now hurt, puzzled, adoring, desperate to get me back, prepared to forgive completely if only I would return to his—to his protection.

And without his friendship, what did they face? Bankruptcy, ruin, ridicule. They knew it, as well as he. He had shown them the pot of gold at the end of the rainbow; they were in no hurry to turn their backs on it.

Every man, woman and child in the kingdom was legally obliged to return me to my husband. If Papa had refused to do so, Papa would have been a lawbreaker, a felon.

'I shall move heaven and earth,' came Carnmore's pleasant voice through the parlour wall, 'to find my bride, my lost love.'

'You will succeed, Alexander,' said Mamma, 'if our prayers are answered. But should you exert yourself, with that poor head?'

'To go through a low doorway in the dark,' said Carnmore, with the smile in his voice that I knew so well and had liked so well, 'is to court a headache. Fortunately I no longer have one. I never do have one, for more than a minute or two.'

'Miraculous!' said Papa.

'No. Temperance, and a thick skull. This bandage makes my trifling injury look far more dramatic than it is.'

I crept away towards the kitchen. I could do no good here. It was more dangerous for me than anywhere else, except Carnmore itself.

Jennie was in the scullery, banging at the breakfast pots in the sink.

I knew I could cross the kitchen without her seeing me, if I went under the table.

I was wrong. She came out of the scullery, just as I crept beneath the table.

'Och, ye ill laddie,' she screeched.

She seized a broom, and rattled it at me under the table, as though I were a thieving cat. I took hold of the head of the broom, and pulled it out of her hands, to throw her off balance. I sprang out from under the table, and scrambled out of the kitchen window. I had left it open, when I came in by it. It was a mercy that Jennie had not shut it. She disliked open windows, even in June.

I fell to the muddy ground outside the window, followed by Jennie's screams. Though I was too tired and sore to walk, I ran.

'Wull ye coallar yon wee cateran, sirs?' screamed Jennie to Carnmore's servants.

The coachman was on his box-seat, and not built for running. The groom let go of the horses' heads, and gave chase for a few strides. But the coachman shouted to him to come back. I turned a corner, out of their sight, and collapsed into a ditch.

It was as muddy as every other ditch I had met, in the previous six hours.

Normally, I knew I could have outrun that groom or any other liveried servant, booted and heavy-coated and unused to running. But not just then. I was too tired and footsore. It was lucky—terribly lucky—that the coachman had called him back. I supposed the horses were restive because of the rain, and needed their heads held if they were to stand still.

I had been saved from Carnmore by Carnmore's impatient horses.

This thought went round and round in my head, affording me some sort of obscure satisfaction. Then my head began to swim. I suppose it was fatigue and hunger. It may have been shock, at hearing my parents swear to return me to my husband. I could not have stood up. I did not have energy to try.

My last thought was that neither Jennie, nor Carnmore's men, had recognised me.

I opened my eyes to find the rain ceased, the wind dropped, and the sun high in the sky. I supposed I had slept four or five hours. I felt better, but abominably stiff, and above all ravenously hungry.

I had never in my life felt so hungry. I had never had a hunger that could not be speedily and plentifully satisfied. The food at Myrtle

Lodge had been nasty, but never short. We had not starved. There had been dainties aplenty, after Carnmore took us all under his wing. I was starving now. I felt I would have committed murder for one raw potato.

I knew I had to make a plan. Since my parents were my enemies, I had to go elsewhere, get other help. Go where? Get whom? Every man's hand was against me. It had to be so, by law. The thing was too difficult for me to think of, until I had eaten. I could not think, I could scarcely exert myself in any way, until I had eaten.

Could I steal food? The wives in the market were dreadfully alert, with eyes in the backs of their heads. But steal? Why steal? I suddenly remembered the five golden sovereigns in my waistcoat, yesterday part of a gentleman's wedding suit. I could buy food for an army, in the Lochgrannomhead market; I could even buy enough food to satisfy my own gnawing hunger.

I limped towards the market. Though I had gone the same route so very many times, with morning-bonnet and shopping basket, I was in no fear of being recognised. Nobody knew my face better than Jennie, and Carnmore's coachman and groom were pretty familiar with it. I felt wonderfully refreshed by my sleep, though I needed more than four hours, and though I was exceedingly stiff.

I thought the soles of my feet would soon become toughened.

Hobbling somewhat, I planned what I should buy. A loaf of bread, a pound of salted butter, a pot of jam, maybe a honeycomb, a bag of sweet cakes and ginger biscuits, a punnet of fresh-picked strawberries —with five sovereigns in my waistcoat pocket, I could be more liberal in my ideas than when I did the family marketing for Myrtle Lodge. I could buy an armful of things which I could eat without the effort of cooking. But, I thought, why should I restrict myself? Cooking was no great problem. Often and often as a child in the hills about Strathlarrig, I had been Bonnie Prince Charlie hiding out in the heather, before Flora Macdonald took him over the sea to Skye. Then I had made campfires, and cooked mutton-chops on a spit, and pretended to enjoy the mixture of raw flesh and charcoal. The herds and gillies and keepers had taught me these useful attainments. There was much to be said for a childhood like mine.

I thought of a mutton-chop—two or three or four mutton-chops— browning on the pointed end of a stick, over a fire of thorn and hazel. My mind's ear heard the sizzle, my mind's nose smelled the intoxicating aroma. I almost wept with hunger at the thought.

Food pushed out of my mind all thought of Carnmore, of my parents, of the future. For all my stiffness and the state of my feet, I found myself almost running towards the marketplace.

The very first stall I came to was Mirren McGibbon's. She was selling a big baking of fresh oatcakes. Oatcakes and honey! The thought was enough to make me sob like a puppy. I stared at the heaps of oatcakes, pale-brown in colour, crumbly in texture, and tasted in my mind the stiff heather-honey spread to a depth of half-an-inch.

Somebody else was staring at the oatcakes, too. He was a boy of unguessable age, with a pinched underfed face, stiff carrot-red hair which had been cut by someone with bad scissors and bad eyesight, an ancient and disgraceful pair of trousers which had once belonged to a big man, but had been cut down, by those same scissors, to the length of his spindly legs, held up by a piece of frayed rope, and a coat also far, far too big for him, patched and darned and tattered and filthy, and a battered billycock hat stolen from a tattiebogle. He had no shirt or shoes or socks. There was on his face, as he stared at the oatcakes, an expression of the most passionate desire.

In fact, he looked very much like me.

I saw Mirren McGibbon glance suspiciously in his direction. No wonder. What he was, and what he wanted, were blindingly obvious. She was a big, heavy woman, with a reputation for sharpness even in that place of shrewd bargainers. I had bought biscuits and baps from her times without number—a very few at a time, as befitted the Myrtle Lodge budget.

She glanced suspiciously at me, as well as at the hungry boy. Of course, she thought we were two of a kind. I laughed inwardly to picture her astonishment when I fished a gold sovereign out of my pocket.

I felt a strong fellow-feeling for the boy. I pitied him. He looked as though his life had been hard, and was hard still. His face was very young and very old at the same time. I supposed that he would be deeply ignorant about some things, and deeply learned about others—that he would not know most of the things he ought to know, and know much of what he should not know.

Like myself, again.

I limped over to him, and murmured, 'Ye'll wush an aitcake, laddie?'

'Ay,' he said softly, glancing at me and then back at the market-stall.

I saw that his eyes were of a very pale green. I saw that there was a new, livid bruise on his cheek, and that his lip had been cut.

'Ye ettlin' tae tak' a muckle han'fu'?' he whispered. 'Ye'll nae dae sic-can ploy. Yon auld weef is a bluidy sleith-hoon'. I ettled masel', a whilie syne, an' I ken. *But—*' he suddenly grinned—a broad, joyful grin, that must have hurt his split lip—'*but* I ken a sta' awa' ahint yon ither pairt . . .'

'We'll bide here,' I said.

He raised his gingery eyebrows almost into his scarlet thatch of hair. I noticed then how pitifully thin was his neck, how bony the shirtless and grimy chest under the dreadful coat.

I winked at him. I had scarcely ever winked at anybody in my life before—certainly not since my childhood among the herds and game-keepers—but it was one of my accomplishments.

He gave a sort of strangled giggle. Though he was hurt and hungry, he got some amusement out of life. He was someone I could learn from.

I marched, with as much dignity as I could muster on my painful feet, up to Mirren McGibbon behind her oatcakes.

'I'll tak' a pun o' yer aitcakes, Mistress,' I said boldly.

'No' while the een bide in ma haid,' said Mirren sourly.

'I hae the siller,' I told her.

'Ay, like, if ye stale it.'

I opened my mouth to deny this charge. Then I remembered that I had stolen it. Well, that was no business of hers. I fished in my waist-coat pocket, and triumphantly held up a sovereign.

'I'll hae a pun,' I said, 'if ye'll gie's the change.'

Quick as a snake, her arm shot out from behind her oatcakes, and her big bony fingers took hold of my ear. I gave a screech, more of surprise than pain. I tried to pull away, but she held me fast. I thought she would pull my ear off, or stretch it to twice its size. I screeched again, this time more from pain than from surprise.

'Whaur's the polis?' shouted Mirren. 'Tak' hauld o' this laddie! Ye ne'er cam' by a pace o'gauld honest!'

In a flash a sense of my folly came over me. I was an urchin—a muddy, bare-footed boy in pauper's clothes. How could such a crea-ture have a gold sovereign, unless he had stolen it?

My disguise was too good.

And now the other market wives were crowding round—women of all ages and sizes, but one in their grimness. A sickening memory came to me, of a ring of Strathlarrig keepers closing in on a wildcat. The poor cornered beast tried to break free between them, but one caught it as it passed with a club, and broke its back. I had been totally on the side of the wildcat; at that moment, I passionately hated my friends the keepers.

These scowling market women would not break my back with clubs. But I would be handed over to the County Police. My sex would be discovered within two minutes, and my identity within five.

And then I should pay—God in Heaven how I should pay—for that blow with the brandy-bottle.

Mirren McGibbon still had hold of my ear. The circle of remorseless wives closed round me. There were men, too, at the back of the crowd, drawn by the fun of catching a hungry little thief.

Ah God, why had I brandished that damning coin? To surprise Mirren McGibbon, to impress the ragged boy, to buy a handful of oatcakes, I had got myself into this toil.

Someone had run to fetch a Constable of the County Police. I knew the Station, a solid yellow building hard by the market place. The Constable would not be long. He was not long. I saw a whiskered face below a blue helmet, pushing importantly through the crowd.

If I had had a knife, I think I would have tried to stab myself.

Suddenly there was an appalling crash—the sound of a thousand plates breaking on the cobblestones. A man and a woman in the crowd at the same moment wailed—it was their stall, I knew it well, I had bought 'seconds' there, imperfect pieces of china, to replace the things Papa and Jennie broke. The stall-holders began to struggle back through the crowd towards the ruin. There was another crash—another plank table dislodged from its trestles. I wondered numbly what had crashed—jam-jars, pie-dishes, tumblers. A third stall crashed, some distance off. They had all been left unguarded, because of the sport of my arrest.

The crowd now pushed two ways, some towards me, some outwards, to look at the damage, to protect their own stalls, to catch the mischief-maker.

It was the red-haired boy. Of course it was. It must be.

There was shouting and confusion all round me, enough to addle the senses. The crowd jostled against Mirren McGibbon's stall, so that her neat piles of oat-cakes tumbled. She screamed with outrage. Her grip of my ear relaxed. I pulled away from her. Then I did what I had done so often in a crowd of grownups, at the races and the Highland games and the country fairs—I dropped on all fours and scuttled among their legs, like a rabbit, so that they could not see me, or tell where I had gone. My toes and fingers were trodden on. I scarcely felt it. I blessed my smallness, and the briskness with which I could wriggle among legs.

I got clear of the crowd, and ran. Then fifty people saw me. They set up a shout, and boots pounded after me. I heard a whistle. It was not that of the Constable. It was the special shrill whistle made by two fingers in the mouth. The red-haired boy. It must be. Following the whistle, I raced up an alley I did not know, between the old houses of the quarter. I turned a corner. I was out of anyone's sight— for a second. There was no sign of the boy. I sprinted on, stiffness forgotten.

I came to a dead end—a wall of grey stone, thirty feet high, with not so much as a window. The boots and shouts were loud in pursuit.

'Whisht,' said a voice by my feet.

A thatch of red hair was just visible behind a grating in the bottom of a house-wall. Hands lifted the grating clear. The gap it left was small but it was big enough for me. I dropped on my face in the alley, and wriggled through. My preserver put the grating back, just as the crowd pounded up the alley to its end.

We crouched out of sight, in the disused coal-cellar served by the grating.

'The laddie didna gang this raud, ye ful,' said a deep angry voice.

'Ay! I spied him!'

'He'll be intil a hoose!' cried a third voice.

'Like. Constable Cairns s'all speir o' the wives.'

There were ponderous knockings on doors, official questions, shrill denials. No one had seen a young lad in a dirty black suit of clothes, a thief, a villain.

The tumult died down. The alley began to empty. We did not dare to look out, but we could hear all that went on.

'Yon waur a kelpie,' quavered the voice of an old wife.

'Havers!'

'Ay, ay. Nae laddie borran o' wumman spens awa' intil thin air.'

'A kelpie wi' a gauld piece?'

'Ay, ay. 'Twas fairy gauld.'

'Havers!'

The red-haired boy giggled, and I turned to face him.

'Thank you,' I said.

He shrugged and grinned.

I put out my hand. He took it awkwardly, as though he had never shaken hands before.

'Hou dae they ca' ye?' he asked after a moment.

'Jaikie Bogle,' I said, for I had liked the name when I invented it.

'Jaikiebogle? Losh, yon's a lang nem.'

'No, it's two names. Jaikie, and Bogle.'

'Yer speech is verra queer.'

So it was, I realised. In my thankfulness, I had forgotten to speak broad.

'Twa nems,' he went on, marvelling. 'Ah thocht folks haed bu' yin.'

'Hae ye but yin?'

'Ay. They ca' me Benjie.'

His own speech was not quite like any I had ever heard—not the whine of the poorest crofter children, nor the broad talk of town or countryside. He had only one name, and thought it was usual. He had never shaken hands.

'Whaur are ye frae, Benjie?' I asked. 'Whaur dae ye bide?'

'Guid kens. Ah bide whaur ah lays ma heid.'

'On yer lane?'

'Nay! The clan haulds—the clan aye haulds.'

Clan? But he had only one name. And he lived where he laid his head.

If I had not been so tired, and lately so very frightened, I would have realised long before what came to me now. He was a tinker—one of the wandering brotherhood of thieves and beggars who were the terror of Godfearing households.

'Whaur's the clan the noo?' I asked him.

'Ah dinna ken. Ah ren awa', syne Murdo bashit ma face wi' a but.'

'Murdo?'

'Ay, owr chief. A skeely basher wi' a but, is Murdo. A maun feend Murdo. Ah maun gae back.'

'Why?'

He shrugged. The gesture was hardly visible in the great loose folds of his tattered coat.

''Tes ma clan. Ah hae nae ither folks. An'—' he grinned again—'ah bided on ma lane twa-three nichts, an' ah didna leek it.'

'Hungry?'

'Ay, a wee. When a graw a fu' mon, ah'll mebbe streek off on ma lane.'

'How auld are ye, Benjie?'

'Ah dinna ken. Whiles they ca's fowertin, whiles fuftin.'

It might be so, I thought. His skinny body looked nearer ten or eleven, but that was because of the grinding poverty and misery of his life. His ugly little face was almost wizened, like that of an old dwarf.

'Wherefo' did ye save me?' I asked him suddenly.

'Yon gauld. Ah cudna stan' the thoct o' it gaun tae the polis.'

'Do ye want it? Ye s'all hae it, for savin' me.'

'Nay, nay! It maun gae tae the clan, tae Murdo!'

'But—'

'An' ye maun gae wi's tae Murdo.'

'But I don't want—'

'Ay, ye maun gae wi's.'

He glanced at me, looking almost apologetic, and drew out a horrid knife from his pocket. It had a rough bone handle and a six-inch blade.

'But Murdo bashit ye!' I said.

'Ay. 'Tes his richt. He's owr chief.'

'Ye ren awa'!'

'Ah maun ren hame. He'll be blithe tae spy yon gauld, wull Murdo. "Hey, sirs!" Murdo wull say, wull Murdo, "Hey, sirs! Benjie's a guid laddie, wi' gault tae his breeches." Gi's the gauld, mannie.'

I hesitated. He gestured with the knife. It looked very sharp. He looked as though he could use it, and had used it. I handed him one gold sovereign. I was careful that the other four should not clink together in my waistcoat pocket.

Benjie nodded, and unexpectedly grinned at me again, with the greatest friendliness. He did not put away his knife. He held it where I could see it. I was a long way from understanding him.

I said, 'But ye dinna ken whaur Murdo bides.'

'Och, he'll no' be faur. There's muckle hooses hereaboots he'll mebbe veesit.'

'But ye dinna ken wha' raud he tuk.'

'There's tinker-folk ahint the wud, owr the glen. They're no' a clan lik' owr clan, but they'll ken fine whaur Murdo's gaun. We'll bide here tull dairk. Dinna ettle to ren, mannie, or . . .'

He gestured with his knife. I thought he meant it. I thought he could use it, and would use it.

Could I tackle him, disarm him, perhaps knock him unconscious, and escape on my own in the dark? He was the same height as I, but surely I was stronger and quicker in movement. Was I? He had upset three of the big market-stalls, before anyone realised what was happening; he had escaped down this alley and through the grating, before anyone saw him. He might be skinny, but it seemed he was very tough and quick.

And he was used to fighting, the vicious tinker fighting with knives. And he had saved me.

And—the greatest point of all—I would be better hidden in a tinker party than in any other place in Scotland.

'I'll gae wi' ye tae Murdo,' I said submissively.

He nodded. There had never been any doubt in his mind but that I would come.

I slept for a time, on the coal-dusty stone floor of the cellar. I did not mind the hardness of the stone—I could have slept on a bed of nails. What woke me was hunger. It was almost past bearing.

Benjie was just as hungry. He was more used to it.

I asked him how he knew about the grating that could be moved, in this particular alley. He said he had run down this alley, and whistled for me to follow, just because of the loose grating. All the tinkers of his clan and others knew bolt-holes of this kind, in every town they visited. Often they made them themselves, for future use in emergencies.

What had seemed a miracle was very easily explained. I understood how tinkers survived, when every hand was against them.

As it was against me. More hands than ever. I had been safe in my disguise. But now I was known, in my disguise, as a thief, to fifty market woman, *and* a Constable of the County Police. Not all would believe I was a kelpie. Not the police.

I had to explain myself to Benjie.

He looked at my clothes with a knowing eye, and felt the cloth with a knowing finger. Tattered as he himself was, he had stolen clothes for his seniors in the clan. He knew I wore good cloth, new, though it was torn and muddy. I tried to make my speech as rough as his, but from time to time I slipped, and surprised him. He knew I was not one of his ilk. I came of the 'ithers', the respectable world, however low I had sunk. This was clear to him, little as he knew about the ways of the 'ithers'. It made him curious and suspicious.

I was very ingenious. I said I had been a page-boy in a big house, recently dismissed for theft. I had taken the clothes of an upper servant. The sovereign was the reason I was dismissed. They knew I had stolen it, but they did not get it back, because I had hidden it.

He was quite convinced by all this. Why not? It was a thoroughly convincing story.

What great house was it, where I had been employed?

I hesitated before answering. Well, what house? It had to be one I knew, and it had to be big. There was only one big house I knew well, as well as a page-boy would have known it. Not Carnmore. Only Strathlarrig.

Benjie nodded. He had heard of Strathlarrig. This put the seal on my story. I dozed off again, content that I had given myself a credible background.

We spent the day so, lying or sitting on the stone, amidst ancient coal-dust. I was too thankful to be free of Carnmore to be depressed about my state. Besides, I was where I was, and I could go nowhere else, and I was what I was, and I could be no one else, so there was no use in moaning.

We talked a good deal. I tried to imitate Benjie's speech, his strange accent and some of the strange words he used. I was quick at mimicry (which was how I had learned to speak French so easily) and by evening I was sure I would be taken for a tinker, by sound as well as by sight.

I did not learn much of Benjie's life. I was highly curious about it, since it seemed I was to share it, but he had no skill in describing it to me. This was because he took it all for granted, and could not understand that what was ordinary and boring to him, was strange and interesting to me.

In his turn, he was curious about life among the 'ithers'. I was surprised by the things that interested him. He had seen cooking-ranges, and plates and forks, and beds and armchairs, when he begged at the back door of a farmhouse, or helped to rob one; and he was quite puzzled about the purpose of these things. He hardly believed me when I told him that most of the world sat on chairs, round a table, to eat its meals, and put its food on china plates, and carried it to its mouth on silver forks. He thought this a most complicated and laborious way of going about the business of eating.

He had never tasted tea or coffee. But he had been used to drinking stolen whisky since his earliest childhood. No doubt that had stunted his growth.

I found that half the words of everyday speech were unknown to him—napkin, saucer, omnibus, footman, pencil, shoelace, comb—these and a thousand other ordinary things had played no part in his life, so he had no names for them. He could not picture a school or a dominie, a kirk or a minister. He knew that books existed, but not what they were for. It was not only that he could not read or write; it was that he had never seen the operations of reading and writing, and could not imagine how black marks on white paper could have the meaning of words. But he knew far more than I about the workings of the County Police and the Sheriffs' Courts.

When I used words strange to him, he made me repeat them, and took care to understand what they meant. He remembered them. He used them, later, carefully, glancing to me to see if he had got them right.

I found it very extraordinary that the day after my wedding, the day after my eighteenth birthday, I should be spending my time teaching English to a tinker-lad in a coal-cellar.

At the same time, he taught me words, or I picked them up from him, which I had never heard before—his names for different kinds of camps, and knives, and methods of poaching and thieving, and meat-stews. (How we did keep coming back to food!) I guessed that most of these tinker words were blasphemous or obscene. I adopted them with relish. They were to be part of my disguise, and I was charmed by their novelty. They would not go into written letters—I cannot imagine how those weird sounds could be spelled—and I think the page would catch fire from a thunderbolt if I did try to write them down.

Well, the day passed. I dozed when I could. Benjie did not once relax his vigilance, that I saw. He often grinned, and sometimes giggled, but he never let go of his knife. I thought we were becoming friends, but I was certainly still his prisoner.

We could not see the sky from our grating, but we could see the sunshine in the alley. After the wildness of the night, the day turned fair. Darkness was a long time coming, because of the season of the year. It was very late, I thought, when Benjie murmured that we should go.

We wriggled out of the opening like two lizards. Benjie carefully replaced the grating, against another moment of need. We crept through the empty streets of Lochgrannomhead, hiding from the few late-owls we saw. Benjie led me out of the town, and along the loch-side road. I was so hungry now that I was past hunger. But I had slept enough, and although I was very stiff at first, I was soon happy to be active and moving.

Two miles from the town, we went through a wood in the broad, flattish glen of the River Grannom. Benjie seemed to see as well by dark as by day. He never once went wrong, and hardly stumbled. Beyond the wood was farmland, but unfarmed, because of some old legal squabble. I had never explored this part, which was ugly and untidy and bore a bad reputation.

Tinkers were camped in the shelter of a ruined steading. They had no roof, but they had yard-high walls as a break for the wind and for prying eyes.

Benjie gave the cry of a whaup, a little wrong. A sort of barking answered him. He and I went across waste land to the ruins. It was full of thistles and whin, and unkind to bare feet. Benjie gestured me to go in through the gap which had once been a door. I could see him quite well in the thin midsummer darkness; I could see that he gestured not with his hand but with his knife-blade.

I went in. Benjie followed close behind. I saw the glow of a fire near burned out, and dark figures crouched round it. I could just make out other people, stretched on the ground. There were women and children, as well as men—perhaps fifteen in all.

There was a question from the fireside, barked in a rough voice. I could not understand a word of it, but only that it was a question, from the speaker's voice going up at the end.

Benjie answered, in his strange shrill voice. I could not understand a word of his answer, except the name Murdo.

There was more talk, in which others joined. I made out a familiar word or two—'raud', 'nicht', 'wud', but no more. I thought these tinkers were telling Benjie where Murdo was to be found. They were neither friendly nor unfriendly. They did not ask us to join them. They did not offer us food or drink. I thought they were suspicious of Benjie. They would tell him where his chief had gone, but he was not one of their group, and they would not have more contact than they must with him or his companion.

I was being rejected by tinkers, because I was a tinker of still lower rank.

I stood inconspicuously, far from the fire. No one paid any attention to me, except Benjie. I saw, in the dim firelight, the glint of his eyes, as he kept me under his eyes. I saw that he blocked the doorway, in case I had any idea of running away. I saw the red gleam of the firelight on his knife-blade.

I was not frightened of these people. They must have been peaceable tinkers, to be camped so near a town. They must have justified the name, by which so many of their lawless kin were also named—they must actually have mended cooking-pots for the people of Lochgrannomhead. Their speech was rough and strange, a foreign tongue, like Benjie's. But Benjie was not their brother. He was of Murdo's clan, a different kind of tinker and a worse.

After ten minutes we set off.

'They're no' ower freen'ly, yon stirp,' said Benjie, as we struck up the hillside going away from the loch.

He spoke, to me, as normally as he could. Almost he spoke two languages—he was almost like the many country people who spoke the Gaelic and the ordinary Scotch, usually with the Gaelic as their mother-tongue, and the one they thought in. He knew that his tinker-talk was no good to me, 'yin o' the ithers'. He talked more freely and fluently to his own kind, in his own tongue.

What tongue was it, I wondered, stupid with hunger and fatigue, as we climbed the rough ground in darkness which was scarcely darkness. It was nothing like the Gaelic. I knew the sound of that, although I only understood a few words. I had heard of people called Gipsies—Egyptians—Romanies—and wondered if the tinker-folk traced to them. But Benjie's carrot hair did not suggest Gipsy, I thought—they were surely a blackavised people, very southern and swarthy in their colouring.

We climbed and climbed, over the shoulder of a hill, and began to descend, always going inland away from the loch. I had no idea of our direction. There was no moon. The night was dry but cloudy. I was utterly lost. Benjie seemed to have the instinct of a homing pigeon, or of a swallow that travels from Italy to Perthshire in the spring, coming accurately to the very place he means. I laboured along, thankful for grass and heather under my bare feet, instead of stony roads.

I had felt better for being on the move. I had got past the worst pangs of hunger. Now I followed Benjie like a walking doll, seeming to put one foot in front of the other like a piece of clumsy machinery, like some useless invention of Papa's. I felt I could go on for ever; I felt I could not go another yard.

I was going deeper and deeper into hiding from Carnmore, and all the formidable allies of Carnmore. I thought that if I were dead, my corpse would still be walking behind Benjie, to get further away from Carnmore.

Into this strange grey state of mind, of utter fatigue and hunger, came a curious memory. I remembered a lesson with gentle Miss MacRae, my governess at Strathlarrig. Lessons in that sunny schoolroom, with kind servants and loving parents and sunshine and freedom and happiness, were a far, far cry from my present state. Perhaps that is why I remembered them.

'After the Forty-Five,' I heard Miss MacRae's soft voice, 'the defeat of Bonnie Prince Charlie, some of the little clans that had supported him were quite destroyed! It was a dreadful thing, dear. I do not mean that they were all put to the sword, much as Butcher Cumberland would have liked that solution to his problems. But they were proscribed. That is a new word for you, dear, I think? You shall write it down, and remember it. Though how often you will require to use it, nowadays . . . At any rate, there were many small Highland clans which had been most *admirably* loyal to the Young Pretender, and their punishment was, that they simply ceased to exist! Yes! They were chased off their lands, and robbed of their names, and driven into a life of . . .' Miss MacRae paused impressively, 'a life of vagabondage! That is another new word for you, I fancy, and you must write it down in your word-book. And these vagabonds, these *waifs* of a storm which they had not called up, took to the hills and the heather, and slept in dingles and ditches, and starved, and poached, and stole, and begged . . .'

'And got put to the sword?' I suggested hopefully.

'No, dear. At least, not all. And people say their descendants survive as—'

'Bandits?'

'Tinkers, dear. Which is almost the same thing . . .'

This quirkish memory awoke other memories, of my golden childhood—scrapes and adventures, happiness and safety, love and laughter. I did not think about the years between, as I plodded after Benjie, or of the previous night, just twenty four hours before . . . at least, I tried to keep out of my mind the detestable pictures which kept trying to invade it. I let myself think about my childhood. I told myself I was reliving my childhood, tramping barefoot across the empty uplands. I was living the games, the make-believe and dreams, of my childhood, a vagabond and fugitive, like the great Montrose, like Rob Roy Macgregor, like Prince Charles Edward himself. Benjie was my playmate, the first I had had since I was ten.

A playmate with a knife in his hand.

I did not know how far we walked, or how long we were walking. It was still dark when we came to a burn, and, following its course upstream, up a narrow glen, came to another ruined steading. Benjie gave his whaup's call again, but was answered this time by the bark of a raven.

I thought that he was identifying himself by his call, as well as giving warning of our approach: and the answering call told him to come on.

Murdo's clan? My new home? What would become of me now? I trembled a little, then cursed my own weakness, and tried to follow Benjie manfully towards the steading.

A little short of the ruin, Benjie stopped, and gestured to me to stop. He seemed from his hesitation, a great deal more nervous about approaching his own clan, than he had been when he went up to those others. Though I was almost past thought, I thought this told me something about Murdo.

There was a question called from within the steading, in a voice I took to be a woman's—a sort of harsh drone, like that of an old wife selling haddies or apples in the streets. The only word I could understand was 'Benjie'. The owner of the name replied, with an unmistakable quaver in his voice. The woman droned some kind of command. Benjie at once bundled me forward, and we went together through a collapsed doorway into the ruined steading.

The scene was much like that other camp, except that there were no women or children. But I could not make that out. I had heard a woman speak.

By the remains of a fire a man was getting to his feet. Others remained sitting or squatting. I counted nine in all. I counted them repeatedly, which was almost all my numbed brain was capable of. The man who stood up was very tall (whisky did not stunt all these people), and I could just see a mane of black hair and a great black beard, a plaid over his shoulders, and jackboots on his feet. I supposed, my brain moving as slow as treacle, that the boots had been stolen from the corpse of a murdered soldier.

He spoke: and his was the womanish voice. It was startling, that that high fishwife drone should come from such a tall man with such a heavy beard. He jabbered at Benjie. Benjie stepped forward, cringing from the blow he seemed to expect to receive. He was right. The tall man hit him suddenly with the flat of his hand. Benjie wailed and went sprawling. The tall man kicked him as he lay, somewhere about the face.

I heard a scream. I realised that it was I who had screamed, to see a skinny boy so treated by a grown man. It was a scream of rage, as well as of fear and horror. Much good it did me. I felt a stinging blow on the side of the head, and was sent sprawling to the ground beside Benjie.

Whimpering, the boy held up my golden sovereign, in the glow of the fire, showing Murdo what he had. The bearded man took it, bit it, and dropped it into some fold of his own clothes. He screeched some questions at Benjie, who pointed at me. Murdo then screeched at me. I could not understand what he said, beyond the word 'gauld'.

Rough hands took hold of me, and pulled me up onto my knees. My arms were twisted behind my back, painfully. Murdo leaned down, and went through my pockets. He found the other four sovereigns, and the broken gold watch. He chattered with satisfaction. While he searched me, his face was close to mine, and I felt his breath on my face. I smelled it. It reeked of I know not what—carrion, whisky, death.

I was in an acute terror lest, when he plunged his fingers into my waistcoat pockets, he should feel my breasts under my clothes, and realise I was a woman. My mind reeled at the thought of what might happen then—must happen then—a solitary girl, accounted beautiful, fallen into the den of womanless cut-throats.

I was saved by his haste, by his greed for gold, by his joy at finding it: and by the excellent stiff serge of Carnmore's wedding suit.

The coins and the watch disappeared into Murdo's pockets. There was a growl of satisfaction from the other men. They were content that he should hold the booty. Perhaps they trusted him to share it, or to spend it on their behalf.

Murdo jabbered at Benjie, asking evident questions. Benjie replied with growing confidence. I heard the name 'Strathlarrig' mentioned a dozen times.

Murdo turned to me. I was still held, kneeling, by the fire, where he could see me. He lowered his face close to mine. I could not recoil from the reek of his breath, because of the arms pinioning mine behind me.

'Ye ken Strathlarrig Cassel,' he said slowly, in an accent even thicker than Benjie's.

'Ay,' I said, attempting the shrill whining note I had been learning all day. I repeated the story I had told Benjie—that I had been a page-boy, dismissed for theft. I embroidered it a little. I said that the Housekeeper had dismissed me, not Sir Richard Grant, who would hardly know me. I said that I was an orphan, with no family to go to, except an aunt who was so strict, that she would not have me in her house after my disgrace.

'Ye kens rauds intil the cassel,' said Murdo, searching for words that did not come easy to him. 'No' dowers, bu' wee rauds, tae cam' intil the cassel douce, the nicht. A soople laddie maun ken siccan rauds, hey?'

A road into the castle that could be taken secretly by night—the way an active boy might learn of, to get into trouble, or out of trouble.

I hesitated. I did know such a road. It was a trapdoor, which led into a coal-cellar. Because it was invisible, it had no locks nor bolts. Tom Ravenburn had showed it to me, when I was very young.

I was to be a guide, to show these desperate thieves into my own home.

'Hey, laddie, hey?' shrilled Murdo, in that weird womanish voice. He took out a knife like Benjie's, but three times the size, and with the point drew a circle on my waistcoat. There was a growl from the men about us. Murdo would cut my stomach out, if I did not tell of a road. They all knew it. I knew it.

'Ah ken siccan raud,' I quavered. (I did not have to put the quaver into my voice. To my own disgust, it was there, whether I wanted it or not.)

'Ay?' said Murdo, grinning like a dog-fox.

'Ower wee for a muckle mon.'

'Ach! Ye'll gae intil the hoose, an' cam' till anither dower. Ye'll apen yon dower. Ye'll no' ettle tae ren, wi' Benjie ahint ye wi' a kneef. Hey, Benjie?'

'Ay, Murdo,' said Benjie, with a sort of cringing eagerness.

Presently my arms were released. I collapsed on the ground, and lay where I fell. I was in the midst of them all. I could not have gone a yard without being seized, even had I had the strength to go a yard.

There was talk all round me for a long time, of which I understood a few words. They were discussing the burglary which I would make possible. They seemed to need no sleep, or to have slept all day. Murdo's shrill voice broke in often, cursing some other to silence.

I had thought myself past thought, and past hunger. But I found my brain painfully alive, although my limbs were almost powerless. And I found that I was hungrier than ever. I knew Benjie was in the same state—he had been as ravenous as I, in the morning, and had had no more to eat than I. I thought he did not mention this to Murdo, for fear of another blow and kick.

I would look for a chance to escape from Murdo's band, every moment until I was actually inside Strathlarrig. Once in the castle, I would look for a chance to escape from Benjie. I knew I could hide from an army, on my own ground, in the attics and cellars, and the little winding passages of the oldest parts. Beyond that I could not look. But I found myself trying, shifting sleepless on the ground with the voices droning above me. I made a glorious plan: I would work and beg my way down to the Border, and all the way down England to the South Coast, and somehow over to France: and there, with my knowledge of French, start a new life as a . . . that river could be crossed when I came to it.

No no, I furiously reminded myself—I could not go so far from my parents, who needed me even though they had betrayed me.

I held an exhausted debate in my mind, quite useless and idiotic, against the rumble and screeching of the voices. It changed at last into a troubled dream, in which Carnmore, with a smashed skull, forced me at knifepoint through a trapdoor into my bridal bedroom . . .

I woke to movements and voices, broad daylight, a crackling fire, and the smell of cooking meat. I sat up stiffly, rubbing my eyes with my knuckles, then looking blearily round. The first thing I saw was Benjie, tousled and sleepy-eyed, sitting up just as I was. At that moment he looked very young, like an ordinary little boy, like the little boys I had played with in the sunshine at Strathlarrig . . .

He looked at the meat, which was on a spit over the fire. He sniffed. He looked at me, and grinned broadly. I felt myself grinning back. Why not? I was alive, and like to be fed. That was enough for the moment. The next hour and the next day and the next year must be met as they came.

A man began to cut pieces off the roasting meat, with a knife like Murdo's. I saw that the meat was a haunch of venison. I wondered whose red-deer it was, poached in June. Probably it was a calving hind, the easiest to catch at that time of year. It should choke me, to eat the meat of a beast that ought to be protected. I did not think it would.

The man who was hacking up the venison threw a piece to Benjie, who caught it and at once began gnawing at it. He held the slab of half-cooked meat in his fingers, and his cheeks and chin were immediately covered with grease. The man threw me a piece. I tried to catch it, but fumbled. The meat fell upon the ground beside me, and when I picked it up was grimed with the dust of the ground. That should have choked me, too. Covering my face with grease should have disgusted me. Well, I doubt if a piece of venison has ever been eaten so quickly or so completely: or dirty fingers licked so thoroughly afterwards.

I asked Benjie when we were to go to Strathlarrig. He shrugged and frowned and gestured warningly. I understood that I was to ask no questions. I asked none. I said nothing and did nothing all day, but sat or sprawled in the sunshine, in that dingy ruin.

Murdo returned from some expedition when the sun was high in the heaven. I was interested to see him by daylight, though I was careful not to stare at him too openly. I thought he was about forty, with a hard, thin face and black eyes. He had stringy, muscular arms, matted with black hair. I guessed he had black hair all over his body, like an animal. He moved with a sort of grace which was as surprising as his voice; I thought he would be a swift runner and skilful climber, and a very dangerous fighter. He looked a man without any softness, incapable of pity, incapable of love.

Of the rest of the party, Benjie was the only boy. The others ranged in age, perhaps, from twenty to fifty; but it was not easy to be sure, because of their dirty beards and the grime on their faces. They paid me no attention, for which I was thankful. I wondered at their bringing a lad like Benjie with them on what was obviously a thieving and poaching expedition. I guessed that his size was his value. He could be put through small openings, and then open doors for the men.

Murdo stared at me when he had eaten some meat. His eyes were as hard as pebbles. I was uneasy under that stare. I wondered if he suspected . . . anything. I stared back, as a point of pride. He spat, and turned away. I felt a small stab of satisfaction, that I had out-stared the dreadful Murdo. It was my only satisfaction, all that day, except an occasional grin, of great friendliness, from Benjie.

There was good peaty water in the burn near the steading. Some of the tinkers drank it. None washed in it. I longed to scrub some of the filth from my face and arms and feet, but I knew that such a thing would be a grave mistake. My hands, for example, were hidden by grime as though by black worsted gloves; clean, they would not have looked like a page-boy's hands, still less a tinker-lad's. However I might itch with dirt, or even crawl with vermin, I must leave it so.

When idle, the tinkers simply lay in a sort of waking stupor. They had nothing else to do, when they were not actually stealing or travelling. I caught the trick of it.

I renewed the debate in my mind: whether I should run away to England and even to France, or stay to keep watch over my parents. Old memories flooded back to me, of love and gentleness, of old, shared, private family jokes; recent memories, too, of helplessness, childishness, mismanagement. I did not see how I could do anything for them, while I was a fugitive. I did not see how I could stop being a fugitive, while Carnmore was alive. But I grew more and more certain that I could *not* desert them completely.

I owed them too much. I loved them too much. They needed me too much. At the very least, I must keep a sort of eye on them, when I was free to do so.

That night was not the night of the robbery. For some reason, Murdo was not ready. Benjie would not tell me the reason. I thought he did not know it, but was ashamed to admit to me that he did not.

We passed another day exactly like the one before. I grew better and better at lying in a waking stupor, digesting half-cooked venison, watching the sun wheel and sink.

And then, as that second sun went down, I was aware of a kind of suppressed excitement in the camp. Knives were sharpened on pieces of stone. Murdo jabbered long at some of his men. They looked obedient and gleeful. He spoke sharply to Benjie, looking at me. Benjie nodded. Like the others, he sharpened his knife. He did not grin at me again, but came and squatted beside me, as though I must be continually under his hand until the business was done.

Murdo questioned me closely about the trap-door—where it was, how it could be approached, what noise it would make: and then about the door which, when we were once inside, Benjie and I would open to the men. I told him the exact truth. In answer to more questions, I said there was a watchdog at the steading of the home farm, but none by the castle itself. I said there was no outdoor sentry, but a watchman patrolling indoors. It was so in my childhood. I hoped it was still true. I did not want to betray Strathlarrig, but I could see no profit in lying to Murdo. If I lied, Murdo must find me out, and his anger was armed with a sharp-pointed knife.

We moved when it was almost full dark. From the lie of the country about the camp, I knew more or less where we were, and I thought we had some six miles to cover before we reached Strathlarrig. I supposed the journey would take three hours, as there was some rough ground, though no high hill. Whether this guess was right or not, I cannot tell. It might have been two hours or six that I stumbled along with Benjie one pace behind me—always one pace behind me, and his breath on the back of my neck—in the midst of the single file of Murdo's army. Murdo himself led, I think, and set a sharp pace. It did not trouble any of the others. I, who had always so prided myself on my strength and endurance and fleetness of foot—I alone laboured for breath, and felt all the old aches return to my legs and flanks.

The place where Carnmore had burned me gave me discomfort too.

Then we came down into the broad glen of the Larrig River. It was all familiar ground to me now, by night as well as by day. It was familiar to Murdo, too. He did not slacken speed. But all speech ceased, and the file of men hurried towards the castle in dead silence.

We passed the place where I had had my accident, and Carnmore rescued me, and my troubles began . . .

Then the high, spiky bulk of the castle rose up before us,. blacker against the blackness. There was an almost inaudible growl from the men. This was their victim. They thought the castle must be full of treasures. For all I knew, they were right.

I wondered if I should be given a share. I wondered what I would do with it, if I was.

We went more stealthily up through the policies. I prowled as silent as any. I knew Benjie's knife-point was inches from the small of my back. We went up to the very wall of the castle, which towered above us like a cliff in the darkness. No lights were showing anywhere. There was no sound.

I showed Murdo the door which Benjie and I could open—a small back kitchen door. It had bolts and chain, but no lock. At least, it had had none, a fact often useful to me in my childhood. Then I led Benjie and one of the men to the trap-door which Tom Ravenburn had shown me a dozen years before.

It was reached by a climb over iron railings, and lay behind a low wall which extended, for the eye, the masonry of a terrace. No one would have guessed of its existence. It was not used (or had not been, in Papa's time) because there was another trap-door for coal, more convenient for the wagons to reach. This unused little one was covered in moss, almost invisible even by day unless you knew just where to look.

I breathed a prayer, when I groped in the moss with my fingertips.

Murdo would not take kindly to marching all night on a fool's errand.

Even at that tense moment, it struck me how extraordinary it was that I should be praying for success in helping a band of thieves into my family's house.

I felt the oaken edges of the trap-door, let into a frame of stone. And then my fingers found the iron ring by which it could be lifted, let into a socket in the wood. I scraped away the moss with my finger-nails, prised up the ring, and lifted the trap-door clear of the opening. It was light, because it was so small. In a moment I had it out, and lying on the stone beside the opening.

The man who had come with us took something from his clothes. I could just make out in the darkness that it was a coil of thin rope. I saw it ended in a loop. The man put the loop over my head, and drew it tight. It was not choking me, but with a harder pull it would have done so.

I understood. I was to go down into the coal-cellar first. But I could not run away in the darkness, without hanging myself. Murdo and his men were very careful.

I hoped very hard that the man who held the rope would pay it out faithfully as I went down.

It was a squeeze for me to get down through the opening. My hips and shoulders were narrow, but they were broader than when I was eight, and my stiff loose clothes hampered me. My bare toes found the rough wood of the old ladder which went down the wall into the cellar. I went down it slowly, not quite sure of the rungs. I was sure no one had used the ladder, in the last ten years, and the cellar was damp. But the rungs were sound. Soon my feet met the ancient stone of the floor.

It was bottomlessly dark. All I could see was the paler square of the opening directly above me. Then that was blotted out, as Benjie started to follow me down.

I was inside Strathlarrig—my Strathlarrig. I gulped at the thought.

I was not alone. Benjie was beside me. He had come down the ladder like a monkey. He now held the end of the cord, which had me leashed like a setting-dog. He also had his knife. I could not see it, but I was keenly aware of it.

I led Benjie up out of the cellars, and into the back passages by the kitchens. It was still utterly dark, but, though I had not set foot in these warrens for eight years, I remembered every yard.

We heard nothing. Strathlarrig was asleep.

We came to the little under-servants' door, and I groped in the dark for the bolts. They moved easily enough, and the chain likewise. The door had a latch, instead of a handle. It was impossible to open it silently, but I tried.

And then I smelled the reek of Murdo's breath on my face, and the little stone passage was full of silent men.

I led them to the dining room, for the silver I supposed would be there. (What worried me was, that I had to pretend that I knew Sir Richard Grant's arrangements. I devoutly hoped they were the same as Papa's arrangements. *He* had kept a lot of silver in the dining room, at least until he went in for balloons. After that, there was scarcely any silver . . .)

Sir Richard did as Papa had done. A candle was lit, and the little flame danced on candlesticks, salvers, chafing-dishes, figurines, on the sideboard and on the great table. A sack appeared, unwrapped from someone's waist. Into it the treasures began to disappear. All was done in silence. All that could be heard was the chink of silver and gold in the sack, and then in a second sack.

I stood watching my father's tenant being robbed of a king's ransom. I felt the rope snug round my neck. I could see Benjie's knife-blade in the candlelight. The whole scene is etched on my memory with the most startling clarity—the candle, held up by Murdo himself; its light, softly illuminating the tattered, bearded men who moved so silently and worked so deftly; the shadows they cast on the wall, gigantic and weird.

What happened then happened so quickly, that I was confused at the time, and have been confused ever since.

I know that the great door of the dining room suddenly opened. Light flooded into the room, from an oil-lamp in a man's hand. I recognized the solemn butler, in shirt-sleeves and slippers. He was alone. Murdo spun round to face him. Murdo's own candle lit his face. The oil-lamp lit it. The butler looked full into Murdo's bright-lit face. He might know no other face in the room, but he would know that one.

Before I could blink, Murdo's knife was in his hand, and was deep in the butler's breast. The butler crumpled at Murdo's feet. His lamp crashed beside him, and went out. Murdo stabbed him as he lay, in the breast and in the neck, again and again. He wiped his blade at last on the butler's shirt. He never once let go of his candle. One hand was enough for murder. All this was done in utter silence.

The other men were frozen into immobility. Murdo hissed at them. They went back to work, as though nothing had happened.

Murdo shut the door. He looked slowly round the room. He nodded with satisfaction at seeing the second sack filled, and silver going into a third. His eyes came to my face.

I had seen murder done. Sick with horror, I stood like a statue. He raised his candle, so that the light fell full on my face. My feelings must have shown there. I was not of his clan. I was an outsider. Those others, his followers, would be loyal to him, out of terror if nothing else. That breed would stick together, and if need be hang together. I was not of the breed. They were guilty with him. I had been forced here. I could save myself from all trouble, by telling what I had seen. I could hang Murdo, by telling what I had seen.

All this flashed into my head. If I could see it, so could Murdo. See it he did. He murmured something to Benjie. I felt the cord tighten round my neck. Murdo came catlike towards me, holding the knife.

6

I would have screamed. I tried to scream. A scream might bring other servants, armed men. I might be dead, but Murdo could be caught, with the victims of his knife at his feet. I was wise and right to try to scream: but that is not why I did try. It was pure terror that filled my lungs for a scream.

I could not scream, for the tightness of the noose round my neck. I was almost throttled by it. The idiot thought flashed into my head that I was like to die of the rope before I died of the knife.

Murdo stood so close to me that I felt and smelled his breath on my face. He held the candle high with his left hand. He raised the knife with his right.

I was rigid with terror, and still fighting to scream. With one hand I was uselessly trying to loosen the throttling noose about my neck; the other I raised towards Murdo, in an instinctive effort to ward off the knife.

Murdo's face, lit as bright as my own by the candle-flame, showed no expression of any kind—not anger, not impatience, not glee. He was bringing no emotion to the task of killing me. He neither liked it nor disliked it.

So we stood, for a split second that seemed an hour. Murdo's men stood motionless about me, Benjie behind me, Murdo before me.

Then two things, utterly surprising, happened at the same moment.

Something which came from nowhere knocked the candle out of Murdo's hand. And the rope went slack about my neck. The room was in pitch darkness. There was a hiss of fury from Murdo. I think he lunged towards me in the dark, knowing well where I was, and unaware that I was no longer held motionless by the rope. But as he lunged, a hand pushed me sideways. Taken by surprise, I staggered, tripped over my own bare feet, and fell. I think the fall saved my life, taking me so suddenly away from the point of Murdo's knife. Someone dropped to the floor beside me. I knew that it was Benjie, although I could not see an inch in front of my face in the dark. I felt his hand under my armpit, pulling me across the floor towards the door. I crawled after him, at the same time pulling the noose of rope from my neck. I kept hold of the rope, from an instinct that it was all I had that might be of use to us. All about us was a kind of stifled pandemonium, a whispered fury of searching for a light and for me.

Murdo's voice, in a harsh whisper that cut through the other noise, said, 'Benjie!'

Benjie had put out the candle. He had whipped it out of Murdo's hand with the free end of the rope. Murdo knew it. If they found a light before we found the door, Benjie would join me in a puddle of blood on the floor.

Providentially, it seemed the candle had been whisked far away by the rope's end. It was under something, in some corner. They could not find it.

Two grown men could never, I think, have crawled even as far as we did, undetected, half the length of the great dining room, even in the pitch darkness and the confusion. But for a skinny urchin and a small woman it was possible. We made small targets for their boots and groping hands, and we moved as fast and quiet as lizards.

As I crawled beside Benjie, my groping hands found a bundle of clothes on the floor, and on the clothes a hot wetness. With a sickening shock I realised I was pawing the body of the dead butler, and his blood was all over my hand. I almost cried out. It would have been the last sound I ever made. I fought to keep silent, and to control the trembling of my knees.

Murdo's harsh whisper now was cursing his men into silence and into stillness. Absolute silence fell. Benjie and I froze, lest any movement gave us away. Murdo gave orders. I could not well understand all that he said, but I understood soon enough what his plan was. A man was to guard the door. Three others were to guard the windows, one to each. That left five, including Murdo himself, who would go in line, like beaters in the old deer-hunts, from one end of the room to the other. They would grope every inch of the way; they would leave no unexplored inch between them, between the pieces of furniture, under and above the furniture, so that we must be found.

I was in despair. Murdo was no fool. He had to kill me. To do so he had to find me. He had no light. He was going by far the best way about finding me. I did not see how he could fail.

The tinkers moved about the room, taking up the positions Murdo had ordered, bumping into the furniture and into each other in the

dark, cursing softly and often stumbling. Under cover of this confusion, Benjie and I could move and even whisper.

Benjie whispered only, 'Wae!'—because he had acted involuntarily,
and now faced the dreadful consequences.

Moving with the greatest caution, my hands once again found the
crumpled and blood-daubed body of the poor murdered butler. An
idea came to me, that promised a tiny chance of salvation. An idea so
ghoulish that, the moment it came to me, I recoiled from it. I knelt,
trembling, Benjie's hand on my arm, the rope in a bundle held to my
breast.

Murdo's men were at their stations now—one by the door, one by
each window in case we should try to escape that way, five in a line at
one end of the room. The five began to move slowly forwards, as
Murdo commanded them. And, as he commanded them, I was sure
that their hands swept over every inch of the carpet, about and under
and over every piece of furniture, disciplined and methodical. The
line of five became six, as the man at the door joined it. This was after
Murdo was satisfied that we were not near the door, and could not get
near the door.

We could crawl further from them, away into a far corner of the
room. That would postpone my death for a few minutes, and Benjie's
too, no doubt. It would do no more.

My idea for escaping still filled me with horror. But it still offered
the one thin chance I could see.

I found Benjie's ear, and whispered, 'Here's the dead body. Hide
underneath it.'

I heard Benjie give a sharp intake of breath. I knew how he felt, I
thought. Like me, he was struck by the horror of burrowing beneath a
fresh-murdered bleeding corpse. Like me, he saw that it offered a
fragment of a hope of safety.

The line of men advanced on us, inexorably, a foot at a time. I
heard fingers brushing backward and forward over the carpet, and
heavy breathing. I believed I smelled a waft of Murdo's rancid breath.

Benjie and I lay side by side, as close as lovers, and very slowly and
cautiously pulled on top of the two of us the big limp body of the
butler.

Even the faintest, the briefest gleam of light would have revealed
an extra hand or foot to the body, a tuft of yellow or red hair, the improbable contour of a body lifted a little clear of the floor by two

small bodies beneath it. Hands, in the darkness, might find the same oddities.

I tried to still my trembling and silence my breathing. A trembling and breathing corpse would make us a frail hiding place.

I felt the blood of the murdered man on my hand and on my cheek. I thought that, if his soul were looking down and could see, he would understand the impious use we were putting his body to.

I felt Benjie's hand, trembling as mine was trembling. There was some comfort in that, so neither of us trembled too much.

Nearer and nearer came the methodical sweeping of the searchers' hands, the shuffle of their knees on the carpet, their laboured breathing.

Very close. There was a man almost on top of us. There was a hissed exclamation. The voice—unmistakable even in a whisper—was Murdo's. The body above us shook, as Murdo groped and prodded. Fingers came within inches of my face, buried under the shoulder of the corpse. Murdo muttered, and crawled on.

With one accord, Benjie and I lay as motionless as our dead rescuer, until the searchers had moved on a yard and two yards and three. Then I felt the pressure of his fingers on mine. I understood. Slowly, slowly, we lifted the corpse off ourselves, and rolled away from beneath it. On hands and knees we inched towards the door. My finger-tips found a hinge, then the heavy mahogany of the door, then the handle.

They would hear us open the door. Let them hear. They would not find us, once we were out of the room.

As I slowly twisted the great ornate brass door-handle, there was a metallic booming from some distance away, loud, urgent. It was the alarum-gong which hung in the entrance-hall, beaten in ancient days to summon the castle to the battlements, beaten in modern times to give warning of fire or accident.

In a moment the castle would be full of lights and running men.

My heart flamed with relief. In a moment, Benjie and I would be safe, among friends.

Instantly it sank again into despair. Friends? They would find out who I was, and send me back to Carnmore. Better Murdo's knife than that.

I opened the door a crack. There was no light near in the passage, but through the high archway into the hall I could see a moving glimmer of light. I opened the door and slipped through, pulling Benjie after me. We sped along the passage, away from the hall, back into the warren of larders and sculleries and pantries. Benjie followed, trusting me because he thought I had been a page-boy in the castle. Where? There were lights and shouts ahead, lights and shouts behind.

I was jumping from the frying-pan into the fire.

As though to remind me of the future, the burn Carnmore had given me with his poker over the ribs suddenly began to pain me. I had not thought of it, since I went through the trapdoor into Strathlarrig.

I led Benjie, running hard, into the maze of little unused passages behind the kitchens. There was no light here. Even I became confused. But I found at last the refuge I was seeking—a place where I had hidden as a child, from my lessons with Miss MacRae, or to frighten and tease Papa, or for no reason. It was a cupboard behind a larder behind a stillroom, all three long unused, all replaced by more convenient cupboards and larders and stillrooms. No one would have guessed that the cupboard existed. It had a supply of air through a grating high in one wall. It would serve.

Once in the cupboard, we were far from the life of the castle, or from life of any kind, except mice or beetles which scratched faintly in the walls. We were like those mice or beetles ourselves—undetected, undetectable, safe until we starved.

Questions gibbered at me, as soon as I collapsed in a corner of the ink-black cupboard. Had Murdo and his men got away? By the windows? With their sacks of gold and silver? Had there been a battle between tinkers and castle servants? How many more were dead? Who had sounded the alarm, and how had he known to do so? What had brought the butler to the dining room? Why came he alone?

I asked myself all these and a score of other questions, huddled with Benjie in the cupboard, exhausted and filthy, with blood as well as mud on my clothes. There were no answers. Benjie knew no more than I.

I asked myself: what is to become of me? There was no answer.

And at last I asked myself the question that should have been the very first, that should have been uppermost in my mind. Why had Benjie saved my life, at the risk of his own? And what was to become of him?

Distressed, I said, 'The clan, Benjie—the clan is all you have—'

'Hey? Yer speech is awfu' queer.'

I remembered to broaden my voice; and asked him again why he had done what he had done, and what he would do now.

I felt him shrug in the dark. He did not know why he had done it. Or, perhaps, he had an inkling why, but he had not words to explain. 'Generosity, self-sacrifice' did not come into the vocabulary of Murdo's clan. Benjie could not recognise nor name such emotions, even when he saw them in himself.

He was a little aghast at what he had done, at the toil he had got himself into. Murdo would not forgive. I did not think Benjie quite regretted it: but he fervently wished he could have saved my life without cutting himself off from the only folk he knew, without laying himself open to Murdo's anger.

The hours went by. We did not know how many hours. Life was timeless, in that little cupboard. There was no daylight in our musty refuge. There was no sound, except our own low voices, and the scratching of the creatures in the walls.

Benjie still had his knife. I still had the rope. Otherwise neither of us had anything at all, except our shocking clothes.

I thought about my state and about Benjie's.

If Murdo and his men had been taken, they would swing for the death of the butler. Then Benjie would be friendless: but at least not in daily terror of the punishment Murdo would have for him. But if Murdo had escaped . . . As to myself, if Murdo was free, he must try to find me and kill me. One word from me to a Procurator Fiscal, and Murdo would be hunted down like a stray dog with the dumb-madness, and given the same treatment. He *must* find and kill me. Well, I could make myself safe from him—and find myself alone with Carnmore, behind locked doors. If I invoked the help of the law, of my friends, of my family, that would happen as sure as sunrise. And the folk of Lochgrannomhead had seen me, and would know the face and clothes of Jaikie Bogle the thief, if not of the Lady Carnmore. The face and clothes of Benjie, too, likely.

Benjie thought I was a young boy, of maybe twelve or thirteen years of age. He had made himself responsible for me, to the point of destroying his own life. I saw that I must make myself responsible for him. I could do no less. I was grown up, or so they said. God help me, I was a married woman. I knew a little bit of the ways of a little bit of the world. But I did not see how I could help either of us. I did not see how we were to survive, or where things would end for us. I was not sure that, for me, survival held out such very great attractions: except that my parents still needed me, in their helpless muddling progress from day to hopeless day: and I thought Benjie needed me, in his utter loneliness, cast out by outcasts.

We slept on and off. We were very hungry. We could steal food from the kitchen, but not yet. Benjie's face, in sleep, looked terribly pinched and haggard.

Well, we were both still alive, and we were both still free, and that was the most that could be said of either of us. I could see no future that held anything better. We must try to stay alive. We must try to stay free. That would be the best possible. No other hope could be entertained. There was no other hope.

After an unguessable number of hours, we crept stiffly out of the cupboard, and through the larder, and through the stillroom. We peeped through a door into a damp corridor of black stone. Through a little window below ground level we saw a sprinkling of stars.

With Benjie's hand on my shoulder, I groped my way towards the kitchens. I was alert for any sight or sound of the nightwatchman that I was sure Sir Richard Grant would have—tonight, even if he had never had one before. There might be prowling dogs also—many of the largest houses had them, indoors as well as out. Again and again in the blackness, I stubbed my bare toes most painfully on steps I had forgotten, and once I almost stunned myself, by hitting my forehead on a door which had always stood open during my childhood, but was now shut.

We came at last to the great kitchen, where a single oil-lamp on a bracket cast a warm, dim light. We crept in, nervous as field-mice. Benjie looked round in amazement. He had hardly ever seen the inside of a kitchen before, and certainly never one the size of a bowling-green, with scrubbed tables, and a range like a steam locomotive, and coppers and kettles as big as bathtubs hanging from hooks, and doors opening into game-larders and vegetable-stores and ice-houses, so that it was all more like a village than a single department of a single household.

A big clock, ticking ponderously, said that it was nearly three in the morning. This was good luck. It might have been almost dawn, or barely dinner time, for all we had known.

Where would there be food that was cooked and ready for our use? I stared round, puzzled, trying to remember the arrangements of old Mrs Cairnie, Mamma's cook. It came to me that everything was different. Sir Richard Grant had changed everything round, or perhaps his predecessor Mr Jenks. Well, no doubt they had made it more convenient; the kitchen maids in the old days had been forever complaining. For years it had been in Papa's mind to redesign the kitchens on modern principles, but there were always more pressing calls on his time . . .

I began opening doors and peering into cupboards and lifting lids and sniffing. I found huge racks of raw vegetables, and carcases of sheep and pigs and poultry, and sacks of flour, and barrels of lentils and rice, and limitless shelves of preserves and pickles. Surely somewhere there must be a side of beef or a leg of mutton, cut into, half eaten, waiting to be minced or served cold?

This next door? Surely ten years ago it had led to another larder? Surely I remembered shelves, behind this very door, with cold turkeys and cold duck and cold gammon and vegetable pies and tarts and trifles . . . Almost whimpering with hunger at the thought of all these things, I softly opened the door.

I screamed. There was no rope round my neck to stop me. The door led not to a larder, but into a corridor. There was a light in the corridor. It was a lantern, in the hand of a tall man in a Highland bonnet. He was hardly two yards from the door, approaching it. Pushing the door open, I almost fell into his arms.

I sprang away from him, and fled to the far end of the kitchen. Benjie ran to my side, looking frightened. The watchman came in.

'Och, wha' hae we here?' he rumbled. 'Ye ill caterans, ye thievin' diels, we'll hae the laird the noo an' the polis the morn. Heuch! Ye bided douce whiles yer frien's ren awa', hey? A verra ill ploy, ma laddies! A—verra—ill—ploy.'

He moved quickly for a big man. And he carried a cudgel in his other hand.

Benjie and I fled round the end of one of the ten-foot-long scrubbed pine tables, where the maids chopped vegetables and filleted fish. Then began a wild game of catch-as-catch-can, the watchman darting this way and the two of us dancing that way, till he turned and hurled himself at us, and we skipped away again and round the table to safety.

It could go on all night. But the night must end. And any moment another person might come.

On a dresser at the end of the kitchen stood a brass hand-bell as big as a bucket, with a handle two feet long. The watchman glanced from us to the bell, and then back to us. It was horribly obvious what was in his mind. He had thought to catch us on his own, without rousing the rest of the castle, which would earn him the gratitude of the other servants as well as the praise of his master. But now he had tired of our game, and would summon help. He lunged round the table, sending us flying to the far end, bringing himself to within a few feet of the bell. He gave a sort of triumphant snarl, put down his lantern, and picked up the bell.

Benjie smote me on the arm, and made a gesture of pushing above the table. By a miracle—because my mind was working terribly slowly—I understood him. Together, we pushed at the end of the table with all our might. It slid with a scream over the polished stone floor, and caught the watchman on the thighs, at the very moment that he raised the bell to ring it. Watchman, cudgel, bell and lantern crashed to the floor. The lantern exploded; lantern and bell made a monstrous noise when they fell.

Benjie and I sped out through the nearest door, which was the one I had opened into the passage. Though I had made that mistake, I now knew exactly where we were. When we turned a corner, we were at the bottom of a narrow flight of back-stairs. Once we were on the stairs, all was blackness again.

The watchman must have been on his feet in a twinkling. We could hear the crashing jangle of the big hand-bell, seeming as loud as the great gong in the hall. But because he had been on the floor, startled, he had perhaps not seen which way we went. No one would think we had gone upstairs, because no one in his senses would rush into a trap by running upstairs in a strange house.

The stairs turned a corner, at a small landing. An archway opened to a passage. There were lights at the end of the passage. That was bad luck. Above, the stairs were narrow and spiral, snaking up inside a small tower. Upper servants had lived in that tower. Did they still? Had they heard the bell? They did; they had; doubly alert, no doubt, after the bloody atrocity of the previous night. There was movement in the tower above us.

We came to a little narrow window on the stairs, once used, I had been told, for shooting arrows and pouring oil. It had been leaded and glazed in recent times, and could be opened. I opened it, groping for the catch in the dark. I hooked the noose of the rope, from which I had never been parted, over a projecting stone which my desperate fingertips found. I threw the free end of the rope out of the window.

None of this could Benjie see. I had no idea how near the end of the rope would come to the ground.

'Follow's doon the rope, Benjie,' I whispered. 'Quick, laddie.'

He gave a sort of whimper, the first I had heard from him. (I hoped he had heard as few from me.) Indeed it was a horrid prospect, to go from pitch-darkness inside into pitch-darkness outside, far above the ground, and then to trust a thin rope of uncertain length . . .

A broken back, a broken neck, were better than being caught and sent back to Carnmore.

I squeezed feet first through the window, found the rope with my toes, and went down quickly, not hand over hand but sliding, bumping painfully against the rough stone of the tower, burning my hands on the rope. I saw the ground below me in the starlight. I could not tell how far down it was. It seemed to be rough grass, as I remembered the ground hereabouts. My bare feet, gripping the rope, found that they had no rope to grip. I had come to the end. I lowered myself by my hands to the very end of the rope. I had hurt my hands by sliding down the rope, and I could hardly support my weight with them. I straightened my arms, lowering myself as far as I could. I had no real idea how far the ground was. I let myself drop, not ready to but unable to hold the rope another second. I seemed to fall on and on, and to hit the ground with a smack which jarred every bone in my body, knocked the wind out of my lungs, and caused me to bite my tongue.

I could see Benjie coming down the rope, in the starlight. He came down more slowly than I. Perhaps he had never climbed up or down a rope before. There were lights in the tower. I prayed that no one would see that the little window was open, that no one would see our rope.

Benjie came to the end of the rope. He clung. I heard again his frightened whimper. I knew he was not easily frightened, but this was all strange to him.

'Cam doon as far as ye can,' I called to him softly.

'Wae, wae,' he murmured from above me.

He lowered himself a little more, struggling on the rope. He did not know how to grip the rope with his legs. He was exhausted and insecure. He gave a little wail, and let himself fall. I tried to catch him, to break his fall, but he fell more heavily and awkwardly than I. He gave a thin yelp of pain.

He hauled himself to his feet, with my help, crying with the pain. I was aghast at the thought that he had broken his leg. What would I do then? Take him to Dr McPhee, and at the same time give myself up to my husband?

I told him to stand on his good leg, with his hands on my shoulders to support himself. I knelt, and felt his injured leg. There was no break in thigh or calf. His ankle was sound. He gasped with pain when I felt his knee. He had wrenched or sprained it—perhaps broken it. Well, with four broken knees between us we must get away from this place, well away, and before dawn.

The journey that followed was exhausting for me and agony for Benjie. He tried not to cry with pain. I think he was as ashamed as I would have been, to show such weakness to a younger lad. Skinny and underfed as he was, his weight bore very heavily on me. My legs and back were screaming with the strain he put upon them. I was near tears myself, but I fought and beat them.

I think his need of me gave me a strength I could never otherwise have had. I prayed it would be so in the days ahead of us.

We rested on a tussock of old heather. I began to laugh, which amazed me as much as it amazed Benjie. I could not tell him that I was struck by the sudden maniac quality of my life—that I should be obliged to escape, twice within a week, from my husband's castle and then my father's castle.

Dawn approached. I had known more or less where we were. At the first glimmerings of pallor in the east, I knew exactly. And now my childish games were of use to us once more, for I remembered a little cleft between rocks so choked with whins that it became a sort of cave.

We could hide there, during the perilous hours of daylight. When darkness came, we could see how things were with us—with our hunger, and Benjie's knee, and the rest.

It was no good trying to plan beyond finding somewhere safe for the day.

We crawled through the whins into the cleft. The thorns caught at our clothes and skin, so that I saw in the strengthening daylight red lines scored on Benjie's face and hands, and here and there a seeping drip of blood: and on my own face the same, no doubt, to join the blood of the butler dried upon my sleeve and cheek.

Benjie collapsed with a groan. I examined his knee as soon as there was light to do so. I was sure he had broken nothing, but it was a bad wrench. It should be bound up, and kept damp and cool (I knew well

about sprains, having twisted my limbs so often in childish escapades).
What should I bind it up in? The remnants of the chemise which was
my shirt? That must increase the risk that my sex would be discovered, if I was again caught, searched, manhandled. In the end I took
off my tattered and filthy coat—so smart and fashionable such a short
time earlier—and with Benjie's knife cut part of the lining out of it. I
tore the lining into strips, and tied up Benjie's knee. About cooling
water I could do nothing, until dark. There was no burn or lochan
near—not even a peat-hag. There was nowhere I could get water without the near-certainty of being seen.

Benjie understood. He showed me he was grateful for the little I
could do for him, though he lacked words to say so.

That day was trying. To our hunger was added a raging thirst, for
the day was fine and the sun very hot. I was bruised and sore; my
burned ribs hurt, and my rope-burned hands. That was nothing to
what Benjie underwent, with the unceasing pain of his knee.

There was a burn near—tantalisingly near—the Allt a 'Ghlinne, which
ran down into the Larrig at a place called Magachan. I knew every
yard of that burn, which tumbled down the face of the hill, and had
peat-brown pools under baby waterfalls where little trout could be
caught with a worm. At the nearest point, the burn was a bare
quarter-mile from our refuge. But it was a quarter-mile of steep,
smooth hillside, partly heather, mostly grass, without rocks or any
trees, on which a beetle could have been seen from a long way away,
from up or down the banks of the Larrig, and from a huge area of the
hillside opposite. My black clothes, dirty as they were, would have
been noticed on that pale grass whether I crawled or ran, even by a
man who was not searching for us. And every man was searching for
us. All day, whenever I peeped out through the screen of whins, I saw
horsemen and carts and carriages on the road that ran alongside the
river, and herds and keepers on the hill. This was because of the band
of tinkers that had burgled the castle, and the murder they had done.
The whole countryside, it seemed, was alive with searchers, looking
for Murdo and his men, looking for Benjie and me. The tinkers had
maybe escaped without being clearly seen; but Benjie and I had been
most clearly seen, by the nightwatchman, and could be most clearly
described. I could not think of getting water until night.

Nor food.

We had not eaten for two days and two nights, and our need for
food was imperative. I was weak for lack of it, and Benjie's case was

worse than mine, because he was a boy and still growing. I did not think I could go far; but I did not need to go far—only down to the meeting of the burn with the river, less than a mile, where the farm at Magachan lay.

Magachan was one of the smallest farms on the Strathlarrig estate, but it was tenanted by one of the kindest couples, Donald and Eppie Doig, who in my childhood fed me a hundred times with baps and braxy ham and milk fresh from their single cow. They had a dog called Ranter, also my friend, a collie with a wild blue eye. The farmhouse had four rooms, of which one, the overstuffed parlour, was used only on the Sabbath, when Donald read aloud to his children from one of the three books in the house—the Collected Sermons of the Reverend Doctor Ulysses Montgomerie. Eating, sewing, the studies of the children, conversation with neighbours, all the life of the family went on in the farm kitchen; when they were all there, it was as crowded as a cattle-pen at Lochgrannomhead market. Though strict with their own, the Doigs were terribly indulgent with me. More than once they told fibs to get me out of trouble, in spite of their Free Kirk convictions. I was their 'wee leddyship', and once Donald said that I was 'the licht o' owr een'.

I thought I could trust the Doigs, and I hoped I could trust Ranter. All day it was in my mind to go there, reveal myself to them, tell them my story, throw myself on their mercy, and beg for shelter for Benjie and myself in the steading. I was sure that, in fact, we should have beds in the farmhouse: for was I not their little ladyship, and the light of their eyes? It would only be until Benjie's knee was well, and he and I could shift for ourselves. It would not be fair to stay longer. The expense of feeding two extra mouths could be no small matter to the Doigs; and if they were found out by Sir Richard Grant's men to have harboured us, they faced dreadful trouble, and probably eviction.

I was sure—almost sure—of a welcome from the Doigs. But I could not reach the farm by daylight. There was flat bottomground all round it, before the hillside rose smooth as a tilted billiard-table. Far away, beyond the steading, in a meadow by the big river, I saw a man cutting hay with a scythe. I supposed it was Donald. I could not stalk up to him. On that bare ground I would have shown like a cockroach on a tablecloth.

The going down of the sun was a relief, and with darkness I could safely go to the burn. I unbandaged Benjie's knee—it was swollen to the size of one of Papa's balloons—and took the strips of stuff to the burnside. Before anything else I drank deep from the cold, peaty water. I was sorely tempted to scrub the filth from my face and hands, but this would still have been a very bad idea. I wanted to take a quantity of water back to Benjie, for him to drink, but we had nothing in which I could carry so much as a teaspoonful. Benjie had lost his ancient billycock hat when he fell from the rope at Strathlarrig. Thirsty as he was, he could not himself have gone ten yards over the steep ground between the crevice and the burn, even with my help. It was amazing that we had got as far as we had, the previous night. Fear had driven us, as thirst could not. Besides, Benjie's knee was far more swollen now.

Benjie was glad of the cold wet bandage. I hoped it would reduce the swelling. I could not guess how soon he would be able to walk.

As I made to leave him again, he clutched at my arm.

'Ye'll no' bide awa lang, Jaikiebogle?' he said, a little shrill note of anxiety in his voice.

'I dinna ken. I canna tell, mon. If there's folk in the fairm, I'll mebbe tak' a whilie tae feend the vittles we're needin'.'

'Ay . . . There's beasties an' kelpies tae the hull, ye ken . . . Ah'm no' blithe tae bide on ma lane.'

'Ye'll no' be afeared, Benjie lad!' I said heartily.

'Nay! Nay!' he said, trying to sound brave.

Though he had been a thief and an outlaw all his life, Benjie was in many ways only a very little boy. He had never spent a night alone on the hill, as I had at half his age. I did not blame him for being frightened. He had always had the clan round him, by night and by day, except when he ran away before, and then he was safe in a town. I half believed in the beasties and kelpies myself, as I had spent my childhood among the herds and crofters and old wives, who totally believed in them.

But, as for myself, I was more frightened of being frightened than I was of the kelpies: and more frightened of other things, too.

I gave Benjie what courage I could—which was good for my own courage—and set off carefully down the steep hill in the starlight. The night was not at all dark, though there was no moon. It never is quite dark, in the Highlands in midsummer. I had to go gentle, in case searchers were still afoot. Also, the dry hill grass was slippery, and the thought of my spraining an ankle also was too horrid to contemplate. At best, Benjie and I would starve to death, and at worst, if I were found and caught . . .

The ground became steeper, before it flattened by the farm and the river. I had difficulty keeping my footing. I did not want to go too slow, or the Doigs would be long abed, and drowned in exhausted sleep; I did not want to leave poor Benjie longer than I need. But I dared not go fast over the steep ground in the dark. The best way to travel was one I had used so often in my childhood, going down steep slopes in unsuitable clothes—I went down on my behind, in which position I could exactly regulate my speed, and keep in perfect control of my descent.

A light breeze blew up from the south, up the glen from the distant loch. I sniffed it, breathing deeply, and it refreshed me, for that strong hill air would almost do instead of food and drink. I thought I smelled heather, whin, lime-trees, and little wild-flowers.

I smelled something else. It was as I slid gently by a big rock that stuck up out of the hillside a few yards off. This new smell made me flatten myself on the grass on my face, still as a stone, and try to sink into the hard ground; it made my heart thud painfully in my throat.

It was a smell of whisky and carrion and dirt. It was the smell of Murdo.

Then, on the breeze, I heard a murmur of voices, hardly above a whisper. The tinkers were out. Why? To rob a poor little farm like Magachan? To rob Strathlarrig again, or recover sacks of silver they had been obliged to drop? To look for Benjie? To look for me? To poach young grouse or calving hinds, or fresh-run salmon in the Larrig?

Lying with my face pressed into the hard dry grass, I thought that it could not be me they were out looking for. They must suppose that, since I had run away, I was far away. They could not know that Benjie had wrenched his knee, and allowed us to come only a little distance; they could not know that Benjie and I had stayed together. They would be looking out for me, always, wherever they went, because I could hang them all: but they would not expect me to be here.

Not expect me, no. But if they found me . . .

I was sure I could slide down, on my face, so quiet and so flat to the ground that at ten yards distance they would never know I had been by. I was downwind of them, so that even in the quiet night there was small risk of any little rustle reaching them.

I began to move, inch by inch, making no more sound than that of a hand softly stroking a piece of tweed. All was well, I thought. All was very well. When the time came to climb up again, perhaps Murdo and his men would be gone.

And then I heard murmuring voices below me. More of them were hidden in a patch of broken ground, which showed dark against the pale starlit grass, twenty yards downhill from where I lay.

And then there was a low whistle, further still down the hillside, directly between me and Magachan. The whistle was answered from the rocks. The whole band must be out—all nine—strung in a line down the hillside. They must have crept there from above, while I was bandaging Benjie's knee in the crevice. It was a miracle of luck that I had not blundered into them on my way back from the burn— that they had not sought our crevice as a resting place. They were not moving now. They were in position, waiting. For what? I puzzled at the strangeness of the thing, gripping at the grass with my bare toes so as not to slide down into their arms.

The answer when it came was so obvious that, had I not been so tired and hungry, it must have struck me at once. One or two of the band were not with the rest, but far away upwind, gently driving deer towards the cordon formed by the rest. Coming downwind on the deer, very slow and gentle, those others would let their scent be blown along the face of the hill. The hinds would scent it, and move uneasily downwind and away. They would not panic, but simply move, a yard or two at a time, with their calves, alert but not seriously frightened, aware of some oddity upwind of them, unaware of the cordon downwind, of the knives and spears waiting for them.

The new calves would be only a month old or a week old, at this season. They would be easy to kill.

I thought it was insanely rash of Murdo to bring his men back almost to the policies of Strathlarrig Castle—to bring all their necks almost into the noose. Murdo was not insane. He was clever and careful. His being here, then, showed two things. First, they were confident of outwitting and outrunning Sir Richard Grant's keepers. From what I had seen of them, I thought they were right. They would melt away with their carcases without a soul the wiser. Second, it meant that they had not been seen, by anyone in the castle except the one man they killed, on the night of the robbery and murder. Though they might be caught poaching, they could not be accused of the other.

Except by me.

They would be on the lookout for any moving thing, this hunting night, alert as wildcats, quick as weasels. Hare was good flesh, fox was good pelt. They would kill first, then look to see what they had killed. Murdo would be content to find that they had killed me, in mistake for a badger or a wild sheep . . .

I had got to where I was unseen, unheard, because the eyes and ears and whole attention of the tinkers were concentrated in the other direction, southwards, upwind; they were looking and listening for deer, not urchin boys or murder-witnesses. But how long could my luck hold? I had only to lose my grip of the slippery grass for a second, and slide a few feet: I had only to set a pebble rolling, so that it knocked into a rock. Out would come six or seven or eight long knives, or blades lashed to the ends of shafts.

I was almost mad with hunger. I was thirsty again, after crawling with my face in dry grass. I was weary and sore. I thought of the welcome and sanctuary that awaited me, without doubt, at Magachan. I thought of Benjie lonely and frightened and in pain, in the crevice behind the whin-bushes. I had to move. I hardly dared to move. Dared I stay where I was? It was possible that at any second I might be seen, a dark shape, against the pale ground, in the thin darkness. It would not be dark for ever. The tinkers would be away at the first peep of dawn, if they did not finish their business long before that. And at the first peep of dawn they would see me. They could not fail to. They could not fail to see me if, their bloody affairs finished, the men to my right came along the hill towards me, or the men below came up the hill towards me.

Could I jump to my feet and run like a hare up the hill? I would take them by surprise—I would give myself a flying start. But their eyes would be as well used to the darkness as mine—better, likely, as the business of their lives was done in darkness. They might not lose sight of me before they were running after me faster than I could run. If I hid in the crevice where Benjie was, they were like to find both of us, Benjie as well as me. I could not do that to him. To cut and run was sorely tempting, but it was no good.

All I could do was to crawl to my left, across the face of the hill, downwind, away from them, over some hundreds of yards of utterly smooth, bare, steep-sloping grass. It was a horrid prospect. Crawling along or up the hill was more exhausting than sliding down, because active physical effort had to be made, to achieve each inch, with knees and elbows. Crawling so made more noise, too—the rustle of arms and legs over the dry grass, instead of a smooth slide over it. My clothes—Carnmore's stiff serge wedding suit—rustled more loudly over the grass, because of its thickness and stiffness, because of the excellence of the cloth, than any other clothes I could imagine.

If I were to go, there was no sense in delaying. I did not want to go. I stared wretchedly at the great sweep of pale grass in the starlight, and thought with despair of crawling, a great black shape, all across its face, inch by exhausting inch. I hardly dared to go. I dared not stay. I started.

Dear knows how long I crawled. My face was soon pouring with sweat, in spite of the cool night breeze, because of the effort, and because of my thick serge clothes. Dust and grass-seeds stuck to my cheeks, and worked into my eyes and mouth. Every second I was waiting for an exclamation, a whistle, the sound of running feet. My progress was terribly slow. It had to be, for silence, and because a movement registers in the corner of a man's eye. The great sweep of grass ended in rocks and heather—sanctuary, a darker colour, cover— an illimitable distance away. All that distance had to be crawled. I seemed, after dear knows how long, to have reduced that distance not at all. I think I began to suffer a sort of delirium, from hunger and fatigue: and I became certain that the hillside was elastic, stretching away from me as I advanced over it, so that however far I crawled, I had still the same distance to crawl. This thought brought angry tears to my eyes, at which I became angrier.

Long and long I crawled, sweating and weeping, and at last allowed myself to go a little faster, being further from the eyes and ears of the tinkers. But I dared not rise even to my hands and knees. I still wormed flat along the ground.

Then, coming down the wind, I heard sharp voices—movement—a ring of steel. The deer had come to the shambles. The tinkers would be busy killing what beasts they could catch, and cutting them up so they could carry them. In the starlight I saw a dozen hinds, with baby calves, streaming away up the hill. Now I could run. I jumped to my feet, and raced towards the heather.

I heard the call of a whaup, far behind me. It was no whaup. Had I been seen? Terror gave wings to my heels, and new strength to my rubbery legs. I was thirty yards, twenty, ten, from the blessed sanctuary of tumbled rocks and heather, when my left foot twisted below me as I ran, and I felt a shocking pain in it, and my leg collapsed under me, and I fell, and rolled. Clutching at the grasses, I managed to stop myself, and crawled the remaining yards to the edge of the grass. Whatever had happened to my ankle, I could still crawl. Soon I was deep in tangles of old heather, tussocks two feet high and more, dark like my clothes. I looked back. I could see nothing. I could hear nothing.

I began to think I was safe. I could go down in safety now to the foot of the hill. Somehow, sprained ankle or no, I could drag myself to the farmhouse of Magachan. The tinkers would not be thereabouts. Even if they had seen me, they would not expect their runaway to knock at a decent door.

And then, to my utter dismay, I found that I could not move. Not at once. I had to rest. I did not sleep, but I went into a sort of swoon, without losing consciousness. I could see and hear and even to a small extent think, but I could hardly move so much as a finger. I cursed my weakness—but even my curses were feeble.

I heard the tinkers. They were all about me. It seemed to me that I smelled the special reek of Murdo. They had seen me, though they could hardly have known that it was me they saw. They could not search a hillside of heather, with rock above and bracken below, in the dark, without hounds; they could not wait for daylight, burdened with the carcases of stolen deer. They could not guess that another fugitive had sprained an ankle, and lay now no more than five yards into the heather.

Boots brushed through the stiff tendrils of old heather a man's length from my head. I recognised, beyond doubt, the special scent of Murdo. I lay as still as death, my face almost in a mud-hole, feeling not far from death. The rotting smell of the mud was perfume to the stink of Murdo.

A whaup's call summoned the men together, and I heard them go uphill towards their own distant sanctuary.

For a long moment, thankfulness filled my mind. It was pushed out by another thought: how was I to go even the short way to Magachan, when I seemed too weak to move, and certainly could not walk? Then a third thought drove out this one in its turn: wherever I went, as long as I looked like Jaikie Bogle, in crowded streets or on the most remote hilltops, I risked being seen by one or other of Murdo's tinkers; and the moment I was seen, the whole murderous pack would be after me. This as long as I lived, as long as any of them were alive. I must go always with my chin on my shoulder. I could never be free of instant danger, while I looked like Jaikie Bogle.

And then, if I looked like Catriona, the Baroness Carnmore . . .

Benjie's face came before my mind's eye, pinched with hunger and the pain of his knee. I tried to stand. I could stand, but I could not walk. A stick might have made it possible, but there are no sticks on a Highland hillside. I had to go on hands and knees. It was possible. It was better than my serpent crawl. My ankle hurt me, but it was not past bearing. I was no longer in danger of swooning. I was driven forward by my own hunger, by the prospect of the Doigs' farm kitchen, by the thought of Benjie.

I came down from the hill, and onto the little infertile fields of Magachan. Hope, hunger, the thought of Benjie, dragged me across the fields towards the farmhouse. I crawled past barn and byre. There were no lights in the farmhouse. There was no sound from anywhere. I was at the very end of my strength. I could hardly support my weight on my hands and knees. Indeed, more than once, I half collapsed. I neared the single little door of the farmhouse. I yearned passionately towards it, towards the comfort and sanctuary inside. I pictured the wooden settle where I had so often perched as a child, the range, the dangling joints of salted meat and loops of sausages, the brine-tub of pickled fish, the warm lamp and the warm welcome . . .

I had utterly lost track of time. I supposed it was midnight. It was unkind to rouse, so late at night, folk who worked as hard as the Doigs. But the devil drove. I glanced up at the sky, stupid with fatigue, as though I could tell from the position of the stars what hour it was. What I saw was a faint milkiness over the hills to the east.

Dawn. In one way it was better. The Doigs would soon be afoot. They did not waste a moment of daylight—they could not afford to do so. But though I ate and drank enough for two or ten, I could not get back to Benjie until night fell again. Certainly I could not ask Donald Doig to go, and convict himself in public of harbouring fugitive criminals. What would Benjie think, how would he fare, alone for the whole of a long summer day, after a lonely night? Poor boy, I thought numbly, poor Benjie.

I stirred myself to crawl the last few feet to the door, when a black-and-white shape burst suddenly out of a byre, and barked at me furiously.

'Ranter,' I said softly, 'here, Ranter.'

'Bob!' screamed a woman's voice from inside the farmhouse. 'Be stull, ye auld ful!'

Bob? Who was Bob? What was Bob?

A window of the house glowed as a lamp was lit. The door opened. A man stepped out, with unlaced boots, and a plaid held round his half-dressed person. He was a big red man with a short beard. I had never seen him before. He carried a bull's-eye lantern. He held it up, shouting at the dog. He saw me.

'Guid Goad,' he said, 'wha's yon wee bairnie? Bob wull no' hairm ye, laddie. Whisht, Bob! Stan' tae yer pins, laddie.'

'I canna,' I said.

'Och, puir wee bairn. Losh, ye're a braw sicht, black as the pit o' pairdeeshon—'

'Where's Donald Doig?' I asked, as straight and brave as I could.

'Donald, is't? Och, Donald deed a whilie syne.'

'And—Eppie?'

'Awa tae bide wi' her guidsire intil Glendraco. Ye'll ken the Doigs, laddie?'

'Ay,' I said, and collapsed once again on the hard muddy ground, in a fury of barking from the collie.

There were no Doigs here, but strangers: no Ranter, but a stranger. I might have guessed it would be so, after so long. The thought had never crossed my mind.

I raised myself, painfully, in time to see a woman come out of the farmhouse, carrying a candle in a glass, and clad in a greasy wrap. She thrust her candle near my face, bending double to stare at me. She was a scrawny, hard-faced woman. The harshness of her voice was in the greatest contrast to the gentleness of her man's.

She screeched that I was the thief Lachlan Pringle had seen. Small, a young lad, with yellow hair and blue eyes, very dirty, in a very dirty oversized black suit. Lachlan Pringle, I understood through a fog of despair, was the Strathlarrig nightwatchman. All the servants and tenants of the estate had been given descriptions of the thieving tinker lads. Anyone who saw them was to bring them at once to the castle, or to send at once to the castle.

Rumbling unhappily, the farmer had to agree with his wife. She was most obviously right.

She leaned down, and seized my ear. She tried to pull me to my feet. I cried out with the pain of my ear and of my ankle. She let go of my ear, to give me a powerful slap over it. I collapsed on the ground again, with the force of the blow and the weakness of the ankle.

God-fearing farmer-folk treated me just as tinkers did.

The man, gentler, half dragged and half carried me into the kitchen. I looked round drably. It was all much as I remembered it—neater, perhaps, with no sign of children living there.

Perhaps if the wife had had children, she would have been kinder to a runaway tinker lad.

I sat on the settle (the dear familiar settle) under the button-hard eye of the wife, while the farmer went up-river to the castle. She would give me nothing to eat, saying that I had stolen food from the mouths of honest men. She would give me nothing to drink, saying that thirst was one of the punishments the Good Lord had devised for sinners in perdition, and I would do well to try a foretaste of my eternal state.

The sun rose, and climbed the sky.

I wondered what Benjie was thinking.

The farmer came back at last, with the nightwatchman I knew, and with a small man in neat clothes whom I took to be a factor or manager.

The watchman took one look at me, and nodded decisively.

'Ye're certain positive, Pringle?' said the neat man.

'Ay,' said Lachlan Pringle. He was certain positive.

'Whaur's yon ither laddie?' the farmer asked me.

'I dinna ken,' I said in a tinker whine. 'He ren yin raud, Ah ren anither.'

There was a sort of debate, which I was almost too tired to take in, about what should be done with me. The farmer was for letting me go, with a piece of bread and a smack on the head. Lachlan Pringle was for letting me go after a sound beating. The factor said I must be taken to Lochgrannomhead, to the Procurator Fiscal, in case I could throw any light on the murder of the butler. The wife agreed, but said I should be whipped before they took me.

I was not whipped in body, but I was flayed in mind.

In the middle of the morning, a man came with a small cart. I was dragged out of the farmhouse, and bundled into the back of the cart. Lachlan Pringle climbed in beside me. He was my gaoler, until I was in gaol. He was the witness against me. We drove off towards Lochgrannomhead.

The last thing I saw of Magachan was the hard, virtuous face of the wife.

The first thing I saw of Lochgrannomhead was one of Murdo's tinkers.

It was at the edge of the town, beside one of the roads into the town. (The other end, I thanked God, from Myrtle Lodge and my parents.) I had no more than a glimpse, of a thin bearded face in the

gap of a tumbledown wall. I knew the face. It was the man who had
thrown me my first lump of half-burned venison, which I had dropped
in the dust. He saw me. I caught the look on his face. There could be
no mistaking it. Even in the stupid state I was in, I saw that he saw
me. I knew he would follow, and then run to report to Murdo.

We went to the Sheriff Court, a new building like a small grey fort.
The driver asked for the Procurator Fiscal. He was directed to a house
in the Kirk Square. We went to the Square. I saw Dr McPhee in the
distance, coming out of his house with a black bag. We stopped at the
front of a tall building. Part of it, I knew, was a solicitor's office, the
office of a Mr Craigie. Mr Craigie was the Procurator Fiscal. I had
never been inside the building, and I did not know Mr Craigie even
by sight. I had moved in humbler circles in Lochgrannomhead.

By Mr Craigie's house two carriages were waiting. The nearer had a
coachman on the box, and a groom at the heads of the pair. I looked
at it indifferently, blankly . . . and then I recognised it. I knew carriage, horses, coachman, groom. I knew the crest on the door.

My husband was inside with the Procurator Fiscal.

7

People were going to and fro in the Kirk Square, wives to the market, carters, labouring men, women with fish or vegetables to sell to the houses of the square. I saw several faces I knew. They were not likely to recognise me.

But they recognised Jaikie Bogle.

'Hey, sirs!' sang out a voice like a bugle, from a market-woman built like a horse. She was staring at me fixedly from the pavement, not six feet away. 'Hey, sirs! Yon's the laddie tuk a sackfu' o' Mirren McGibbon's atecakes! Polis, hey! Stop thief! Grip the laddie, sirs!'

'He's grippit, Mistress,' said Lachlan Pringle calmly.

But by this time a sort of hue and cry had been set up by all the riffraff and loungers in the square, who were for pulling me out of the cart and dragging me to the Police Station. Lachlan Pringle and the carter had almost to fight to the Procurator Fiscal's door, while the street women shouted at me, and shook their red fists, and plucked at my clothes and hair.

Jaikie Bogle was easily recognised, it seemed. That would make things easy for Murdo's men.

We went inside the house, into a long narrow hallway with stairs rising from the far end. There was plenty of light in the hallway, from the fanlight over the door and from a window on the stairs. A clerk came out of a door by the foot of the stairs. He and Lachlan Pringle greeted each other as old friends. The clerk said the Procurator Fiscal was engaged with Lord Carnmore and with Mr and Mrs Gordon of Inverdoran.

I was not too bowed down with despair to be astonished by this. I knew how much the Gordons hated and resented Carnmore. Yet they were under the same roof as Carnmore. I was under the same roof as Carnmore. We would not go up to the Procurator Fiscal's office until he came down. He would pass us in the hallway. The hall was hardly wider than a passage—hardly five feet wide. He would pass within a yard of me. He must.

He did.

A man came down the stairs. Though he was silhouetted against the staircase window, I knew him instantly. How should I not? He stumbled on the stairs. Was he drunk? Could he be, at noon? Would he be, having a meeting with the Procurator Fiscal?

I tried to hide myself behind the big figure of Lachlan Pringle, but the way my captor was holding me made this impossible. The watchman held me in front of him, a hand gripping my collar. It was as though he was deliberately thrusting me under Carnmore's eye. I could not move my feet, because I could not put any weight on my sprained ankle.

Carnmore came to the foot of the stairs, and strode along the hallway towards the front door. His face came into the light from the fanlight over the door—bright morning sunlight, streaming in, illuminating his face as though he were making an entrance onto a stage. His face was very pale, and set hard. But his mouth twitched. His eyes stared straight before him. They looked sightless, glazed. I knew that look. He was not drunk, but angry. He was blind with rage. Something had happened upstairs to infuriate him. He turned his head to look blankly at Lachlan Pringle and myself. He brushed past the clerk, who bleated something to him which he ignored, or did not hear. He brushed past me. His arm brushed against my coat—his own wedding coat. He did not smell of liquor, but of the fresh-scented spirit which he put on his hair. I found that I was trembling violently, to find myself so near him. It was an incredible, a desperate experience. It was worse than being the same distance from Murdo, from Murdo's knife.

Carnmore looked at me, but he did not see me. He brushed against me, but he did not know me. It was because he was blind with anger. In his normal, cool, perceptive state he would have looked at me curiously—who would not?—a little filthy barefooted prisoner of the law, an object of interest and maybe pity. He would have seen and known me. No amount of mud, no cropping of hair, would have disguised me from *his* eye.

I did not understand his rage, but I thanked God for it.

He passed on, and opened the door. I watched him, out of the corner of my eye. With his hand on the doorknob he stopped. He made a visible effort to calm himself. The blindness left his eyes and the tautness his face. He even contrived a slight smile. He went down the steps, into the crowd of loafers who still waited there, a normal and cheerful man.

'His lordship's a wee bit fashed,' said the clerk with a wink to Lachlan Pringle.

'Ay, like.'

'There's a ceevil action tae be brocht in the Sheriff Coort, by a tenant who clems a breach o' contract, eveecshun in breach o' contract o'tenancy.'

'Yon's an awfu' ploy,' said Lachlan Pringle, 'yon eveecshun o' puir fairmers.'

'Ay, forby it's no' legal when there's a vaalid contract.'

'Sir Richard Grant wull no' eveect a settin' tenant, wi' or wi'oot contract.'

'Sir Richard's a guid laird, the toon kens tha'.'

'Ay, better than the auld ful Larrig. Carnmore is no' ettlin' tae eveect the Gordons?'

'No no, mon. They bide at Inverdoran the noo. 'Tis they are supportin' the tenant, wi' the advocate's fee an' a' an' a'.'

'Verra guid.'

'Ay, verra guid. The puir folk waur tenants o' their ane kin, lang syne, ye ken. The Procurator Fiscal ca'd a bit conference the day, tae pershued Carnmore tae re-instet the tenant, an' save the fashment o' the coort hearin'. He spake tae Carnmore lak' a dominie tae a sully bairn, did owr Mr Craigie.'

'Ye waur in the rum, Tam?'

'No. The dowr hae a braw muckle keyhole.'

Lachlan Pringle laughed.

'Carnmore is no' accustomit tae siccan lectorin',' said Tam. 'He didna like it.'

Another clerk called from above. The thieving boy was to be brought up. Lachlan Pringle helped me upstairs, to a broad landing full of sunlight. A door opened. A tall black-avised man like a hoodie-crow ushered out two people. They were the Gordons—Alistair and Mariota, Carnmore's enemies, she the childhood friend of Mamma. I recognised them at once, but I hardly saw them. I was furiously planning how I should deal with the new situation.

The Gordons were not blind with anger. They did look curiously at the young prisoner, the villainous urchin. They had plenty of light with which to do so, and plenty of time in which to do so, because Mr

Craigie, in a hoodie-crow voice to match his appearance, was delivering a long and stately farewell.

Lachlan Pringle hauled me into the room at last. I looked round, with a sort of numb curiosity. It was the first solicitor's office I had ever been in. It had an air of gloom, even though it was full of sun, with dusty deed-boxes from floor to ceiling, and a great black desk like a coffin on a hearse.

When he saw that it pained me to stand, Mr Craigie made me sit down. But he spread a newspaper over the chair before I did so.

Lachlan Pringle's manner became solemn and important. He described finding me and Benjie in the kitchen at Strathlarrig at three in the morning, and then my capture by the folk of Magachan. He suggested I might be involved with the band of robbers who had murdered John Jardine, the butler, the night before. But for this possibility, he said, I would have been whipped, fed, and sent on my way.

The Procurator Fiscal said he had been quite right to bring me. 'As my duty is in all cases of violent or suspicious death,' he said, 'I am investigating the shocking death of John Jardine, in preparation for the prosecution of the perpetrators in the Sheriff Court.' He turned his crow's beak towards me, and asked my name.

'Jaikie Bogle.'

'John?'

'Ah dinna ken. 'Tes aye Jaikie.'

'Age?'

'Ah dinna ken.'

'Where are you from?'

'Ah dinna ken.'

'Your family? Father? Mother?'

'Ah dinna ken.'

I spoke in the tinker whine I had learned from Benjie. I made myself out a little simple-minded. I was an orphan. I had run away from an orphanage because they beat me. I did not know what the orphanage was called, or where it lay. I went about the country, begging for bread. I had got the clothes I wore off a tattiebogle in a cornfield, I did not know where the cornfield was. I had met another lad, here in this town, in the marketplace. We had stayed together for a few days, for company. We had climbed into a castle two nights before, through a trapdoor the other lad knew of, because we were very hungry. We did not take anything. We could not find anything. We did no harm. We ran away when we were seen. The other lad ran one way and I ran another. I was going to beg for food at a farmhouse, but instead I was collared. I meant no harm at the farmhouse. I was nearly dead from hunger, or I would not have tried to steal food from the big castle.

Mr Craigie rang a bell for his clerk. Lachlan Pringle's friend came. He was given silver from the Procurator Fiscal's pocket, and told to go out to the market to buy food for me.

While this was going on, I was tempted to tell all the truth about Murdo. That would take one knife away from my neck. But I foresaw giving evidence in the Sheriff Court—scrubbed and smartened for the occasion—and it was entirely obvious that my sex and identity must be discovered. As things were, I still had the tinkers to avoid, but there seemed to be a chance—just a chance—that this kindly hoodie-crow behind the desk would let me run free.

So I said we had been miles away from the big castle, the night before we were found there. We had been in this town, hiding in a cellar the other lad knew of. We had tried to beg food in the town, but had failed. I did not know why we had gone to the big castle, which was a weary way to walk. But the other lad was older and wiser than I, and he said we should go, because he knew a way in by a trapdoor. Maybe he had an idea we would meet people there, friends who would feed us. But we did not see any friends, or anybody at all, except the big man who had brought me to this place in a cart.

I stuck to this story. Mr Craigie cawed and croaked at me for a long time, but I insisted that we had seen nobody, and that we had been a long and weary march from the castle on the night the man was killed.

The clerk came back with cakes and oatcakes and baps and crusty bread and butter and honey and jam and cheese. I was taken away into another room, a little dusty cubicle beside the office. As I crossed the landing, half carried by Lachlan Pringle, I saw to my great surprise that the Gordons were still there. My raging desire for food, now that there was food for me, so filled my mind that I did not stop to wonder at the Gordons spending all morning in a frowsty office. The clerk spread a newspaper over the chair in the cubicle. I was given a knife and a plate, a jug of milk, and locked in.

Food totally engrossed me. I thought of nothing but eating. Until I had eaten, I could think of nothing else. I was in a terror lest my meal should be interrupted before I had finished. I might be dragged away, leaving uneaten oatcakes! The idea was so awful that I gobbled like a savage, like Jaikie Bogle.

I had almost finished before I thought of Benjie. As soon as I was free, I would go and find him, with food. As soon as I could walk, at any rate. I was very worried about him, now that my stomach was full and I could think about other things.

I licked the honey off my fingers, and wiped them on the seat of my trousers. There was not a crumb left to eat, or a drop of milk to drink. There was no sound from outside. The door of the cubicle was still locked. I did not try to think about the future, beyond making vague plans to feed and help Benjie.

Now that I was replete, sleep began to creep over me, overmasteringly. I could not hold my eyelids up. I did not try. I sank back in the chair, and felt myself drowning in a warm soup of sleep.

A voice woke me. I opened my eyes, gummily, and rubbed them with my filthy knuckles. I looked round dazedly, not knowing at all where I was. I must have been very deeply asleep: I must have been very tired. Slowly consciousness and memory came back. The door of the cubicle was open. Through the door, out of the cubicle, went a smartly dressed woman, a lady. It was Mrs Gordon. She had come into the cubicle while I slept. Still stupid with sleep, I wondered why.

Lachlan Pringle came for me, and took me back into Mr Craigie's big office. Both the Gordons were there, standing by the desk, while Mr Craigie sat behind it. Alistair Gordon was about fifty, a man of medium height, plump, with long soft whiskers going from brown to grey; he had a round, placid face, and little grey eyes, and a pink bald spot in the midst of soft greying hair. He was neatly dressed in a pale-coloured suit with a spotted neckcloth, and he carried a broad-brimmed Panama hat. Mariota Gordon was a few years younger—Mamma's age—and striking where her husband was comfortable and commonplace. She was an inch taller than he was, with a big bonnet and a silk dress that rustled like wrapping-paper whenever she moved. Her hair was black, her eyes a kind of gold, her cheekbones high, her chin narrow and jutting. I remembered hearing that she was said to be a very good manager; she looked it, and looked as though she would enjoy it.

Both the Gordons smiled at me—he kindly, she coolly—when Lachlan Pringle hauled me back into the room, and sat me down on the chair protected by the newspaper.

'Well, lad,' came the harsh voice of the lawyer, 'you're feeling better, I fancy, with half the market under your ribs?'

I nodded, wondering very hard what was going to happen next.

'I've been asking myself what to do with you, and by the book the answer is clear. We can't have vagrant boys running about the countryside, and breaking into the houses of law-abiding folk. You'll understand that one day, if you don't understand it now. We can't have it, d'you hear? And we won't. Forby, there's yourself to be considered. You don't seem an evil laddie. But you're on the road to evil—theft, burglary, poaching, and one day a householder struck down, like poor John Jardine at Strathlarrig. Go on as you are, laddie, and you'll end in prison for certain and on the gallows likely. I can't condemn you to that. The law won't permit me and my own conscience won't permit me. My duty is to commit you to the Boys' Orphanage at Butterbridge. They'll clean you up and dress you up and feed you up. They'll teach you to read and write, and do your sums if you've a bent that way. They'll teach you a trade. Maybe a carpenter. How would you like to be a carpenter, making good wages and a credit to the community, eh?'

I suppose my face showed my utter despair.

Stripped and scrubbed, the moment I arrived. Everything discovered. Carnmore.

'Well,' said the hoodie-crow behind the desk, 'that prospect is not so terrible as you seem to think. However, there is an alternative.'

I suppose my face showed a blaze of sudden hope.

I should not have let my face show anything. In my character, I should not have understood the words he was saying. But, even under a layer of mud, my face was always as transparent as a windowpane.

'Mr and Mrs Gordon here have taken pity on you. They need a willing young lad in their stables, they say, and they'll take a chance with you. You'll be fed and clothed and cared for. Now listen to me well, laddie.'

He looked at me gravely. I stared back.

'You're to behave yourself. You're to show yourself grateful. You're to work hard and learn. You're to be obedient and respectful. You understand me?'

I nodded.

'And you're not to run away. Above all else, you are *not* to run away.'

'He won't,' said Mrs Gordon unexpectedly.

'I've no doubt he'll try, ma'am,' said Mr Craigie. 'Vagrancy is the way of life of a lad like this—the only life he's known.'

'A full belly and a soft bed ought to reconcile him to our ways,' said Mr Gordon.

'Yes, sir, they ought. But I must warn you that in accepting responsibility for young Bogle you are doing exactly that, in law and in conscience.'

'We'll do at least as much for him as the orphanage would,' said Mrs Gordon.

'That includes keeping him on the premises, ma'am.'

'Yes. We faithfully undertake to do that.'

'He'll be needing—for some while he'll be needing, in my experience —constant surveillance. Leave him on his lone, and one day he'll cut and run as sure as Easter. In that event the responsibility will be yours.'

'We accept it.'

'It's very good of you, ma'am, sir. Very good indeed.'

'Don't make too much of it,' she said. 'It's not precisely unheard of. A number of families we know, who can afford it, have taken unfortunate young boys like this into their households.'

'Ay, ma'am, that is so, and some live to regret it.'

'I can't deny that.'

'I pray you'll not be among them.'

'We all pray so. Pringle, will you report all this to Sir Richard Grant when he returns from Glasgow tomorrow?'

'Ay, mem.'

'I do hope he'll approve of what we're doing.'

'Och, he wull, mem.'

'Tell him also that he will be welcome at Inverdoran as soon as he finds it convenient to call.'

'Ay, mem.'

Lachlan Pringle took his leave with painful formality from Mr Craigie and the Gordons. As he passed me, on his way out, he gave me a gentle buffet on the shoulder, and an encouraging grin. I was touched that he was pleased that things had worked out so happily for me.

'Well,' said Mrs Gordon, 'we must be getting back to Inverdoran with our new stable-boy.'

'Yes,' said Mr Craigie. 'But before you go, ma'am, there's a bit I think I should say. I've been thinking during the morning, and I believe we should all make a wee bit allowance for Lord Carnmore, just at this time.'

'Make allowance for his evictions?'

'No indeed, not in a case where a contract of tenancy is being illegally abrogated. I mean with regard to—the intemperance of his reaction to my remarks theretowards. You know he was married a few days ago.'

'Yes. We did not attend the ceremony.'

'Lady Carnmore has been ill, very ill seemingly, from the moment of the wedding. Confined to her room, to her sickbed. That is a dreadful thing for a bridegroom, ma'am—a distraction which maybe explains, if it does not excuse, the—the tricky mood we saw him in this morning.'

'It must be disagreeable for her, too,' said Mrs Gordon, who seemed less than heartbroken to hear of my 'illness'. I found this surprising, as she had known my family in better days. She went on, lightly, 'Worrying for her parents, too, I imagine?'

'No doubt.'

'How are they, Mr Craigie? Do you hear reports of them?'

'I am not in touch with Lord Larrig. I know Dr McPhee sees them regularly.'

'Does he see Lady Carnmore?'

'I understand he has not been called to Carnmore. They have another medical adviser, no doubt.'

'The more fools they.'

'You'll take the laddie with you in your carriage, ma'am?'

'Yes, why not?'

'I was thinking of the seats.'

'They can be sponged, I suppose. There are more important things than the seats of carriages. This poor boy's future is one of them. Come along to your new home, Jaikie.'

So I went with them to their carriage, hobbling between Mr Gordon and the Procurator Fiscal's clerk.

The crowd round the door had long gone about its business. But, as they lifted me into the carriage, I glimpsed one face I knew. A face with a black beard, and wild black hair, with pebble-hard eyes staring in my direction. Had he been nearer, I would have smelled the reek of his breath.

He saw me into the carriage, and he saw the carriage and its owners. He saw us rattle round the square and away.

The carriage was a brougham, with a pair of small, tubby horses. It was not as elegant as any of Carnmore's carriages, nor were the horses as good as any of his, nor was the coachman as smart as any of his servants. I was happy to be in the ordinary carriage of ordinary, kindly people. The Gordons sat side by side, on rather shabby leather cushions, facing the horses. I sat facing them, my bare toes dangling at their shins. There was hardly room for Mr Gordon's Panama hat, and Mrs Gordon's capacious bonnet, between the windows.

They asked me many questions as we went, with the greatest affability. Mrs Gordon in particular, who had seemed the cooler and remoter of the two, now laid herself out to make her new protégé feel comfortable. I told again the cloudy and incomplete story of Jaikie Bogle's previous life. I told of my meeting with Benjie in the marketplace, in case they compared notes with any of the market wives; I described him accurately, in case they compared notes with Lachlan Pringle. I told of our entering Strathlarrig by the old trapdoor for coal.

'But however did your friend know of that trapdoor?' asked Mrs Gordon.

'Ah dinna ken, mem.'

'I find that the oddest part of the story. How *could* a vagrant beggar-lad know of a thing like that?'

'Some pageboy told him, perhaps,' suggested her husband. 'Some young devil dismissed from the house.'

'I suppose that is possible . . .'

Mrs Gordon was a clever woman, I saw. She had put her finger on one of the very weak points in my story. She found others. She took off her gloves and, leaning forward, felt the serge of my sleeve between thumb and forefinger. I thought that, for all its filth and raggedness, she knew it was expensive material and practically brand new. Such stuff was never found on a scarecrow. I waited anxiously for her questions about the suit, but she asked me none. I guessed she saw that the chemise I wore as a shirt was made of silk. How on earth came an urchin like Jaikie Bogle by silk to his back? But she did not ask me about that, either.

It was not far from Lochgrannomhead to Inverdoran. The place was, indeed, too near the town. It was not where a family like the Gordons would have chosen to live, except that they apparently wanted to be as near as possible to their ancestral place: which I had always thought a perverse desire. The house was quite new, a solid, ugly, blackish building on low ground, and surrounded by low ground, with the Doran Burn running through the policies, and the loch not far away. Mrs Gordon told the coachman to go not to the front door of the house, but round to the stable yard. Mr Gordon seemed surprised, but his wife nodded briskly to him, as though to tell him to leave all the arrangements to her. I already had the impression that this was usual between them. To the stable yard we went—my new home. A groom opened the carriage door.

'Help the boy out, Angus,' Mrs Gordon ordered the groom. 'He has hurt his ankle and cannot walk.'

The groom's face was a picture of amazement, when he saw what he was to help out of his mistress's carriage. He lifted me to the ground, but he had an air of trying to do so without touching me. I did not greatly blame him. But he was much less gentle than Lachlan Pringle, whom I had knocked off his feet with a kitchen table.

'And now,' said Mrs Gordon, 'please find Robert Cochrane.'

The groom knuckled his forehead, glared at me with disgust, and trotted away to a coach-house.

I stood with one hand on a wheel of the brougham, so that I could take all my weight on my good leg. I looked round, intensely curious. The stables and coach-houses were in the normal quadrangle, with a big arch in one side for carriages and horses, and a little arch opposite for people on foot. I thought there were stalls or boxes for about twenty horses, and room for half-a-dozen carriages, with the usual tack-rooms and harness-rooms and feed-stores, and rooms above, I supposed, for the servants. It was all built in the same ugly blackish stone and the same heavy style as the house. It was not nearly as beautiful, nor as spick-and-span, as the stable yard at Carnmore; but it was much tidier than the stable yard at Strathlarrig in Papa's time.

Out of the coach-house, fetched by Angus the groom, came a fat man with an air of importance, wearing top boots and a canary waist-coat.

'That, Jaikie, is your master,' said Mrs Gordon to me. 'Mr Cochrane, our head coachman. You are to mind what he says, and learn what he teaches.'

I nodded. Robert Cochrane had a nice enough face.

'This desperate little object,' said Mrs Gordon to the coachman, 'is to work for you, Robbie, as soon as his ankle is better. Don't look so shocked, man—there's nothing the matter with him that a scrub and a change of clothes won't put right.'

Oh God, I thought, in renewed despair. Of course this must come, and all that follows from it.

'I want a word with you, Robbie,' said Mrs Gordon. 'Jaikie, do you sit here on this bucket until I call for you. Alistair, go indoors and tell them we shall be ready for luncheon in half an hour.'

As obedient as her servants, Mr Gordon trotted away through the smaller archway towards the house.

Robert Cochrane followed Mrs Gordon to the door of the coach-house. She talked to him long and earnestly, in a low voice. He or she often glanced at me as she talked. His bland, dignified coachman's face showed a little of the amazement I thought he must be feeling—even so well-trained a mask could not conceal all his surprise. I sat on the upturned bucket in the sunshine, while the undercoachman and the groom unharnessed the horses from the brougham, my bare toes tickled by straw on the cobbles of the yard.

Who would be set to scrub me? What would he do, when he saw my woman's body? What would I do, who could not run, who could not even walk?

After some quarter of an hour, Mrs Gordon strode out of the coach-house doorway and away across the stable yard. She waved to me as she went. I ducked my head, thinking it improper to wave back. Robert Cochrane the fat coachman rolled solemnly out into the sunshine. He called Angus the groom. Between them, they carried me into the coach-house, and up some narrow stairs. Angus seemed just as disinclined to touch me. They carried me into a room, bare-boarded, with a single barred window, where there was a flat enamelled tub and one rickety wooden chair. I was sat on the chair. Angus disappeared. He came back a minute later with a big rough towel, a bar of yellow soap the size of a brick, and a brush with a long handle that might have been used for scrubbing down the wall of a stable. He disappeared again, and returned with an armful of clothes.

'The bits o' a lad who was here in the stables,' said Robert Cochrane, 'brake his heid til a stane, puir fellie. They'll no' fit pairfect, but they'll sairve the day. Leave the stockin' frae yin fut, the ill fut, an' we'll hae a bandage ower it.'

Angus came back a third time, with two big stable buckets of hot water. He poured them into the tub, glared at me with resentment at the work I was causing him, and went out with a great clatter of empty buckets.

'Get on wi' it, Bogle,' said Robert Cochrane, 'an' we'll see a clean, respectable laddie as soon's ye can.'

He went out, and I heard a bolt thud into a door-post on the outside.

They were leaving me alone to scrub and dress myself. I was to be as private as a princess. Nothing could have been more unexpected, more blessedly welcome. It must be by Mrs Gordon's order. It was intensely thoughtful of her. I felt a surge of gratitude.

Well, the water was only just warm, and the soap was meant for the floor of an outhouse, and the brush had bristles like a stable besom; but that bath was the most glorious experience of my life. When I had finished, the water was almost black, but I was white. I hopped to the chair, and dried myself on the rough towel, and felt reborn.

I dressed in the clothes of the lad who had broken his head. Of course a boy's underclothes were quite unfamiliar to me, and designed for different needs, but I understood how they went, and they were not uncomfortable. I found I was to wear buff corduroy breeches, short boots over worsted stockings, a flannel shirt, and a short stiff jacket of some stuff which was like canvas. When I was dressed I felt like a postillion or a tiger; I would have liked a looking glass. Buttoned up, the stiffness of the jacket concealed my bosom; and I knew the slimness of my hips was boyish enough. I thought I would do.

Hazards remained. God knew, hazards remained.

I tried the door, but it was still locked. I hopped back to the chair. After a long time, heavy footsteps clumped to the door, and there was a knock.

'Bogle?' came the coachman's voice. 'Air ye clad?'

'Ay,' I called out.

The bolt shot back, and the door opened. In came a fussy elderly waiting-woman with a big stuff bag. She squatted creakily down in front of me, and looked at my puffy bare ankle. She clucked and crooned over it, and bandaged it with a cool and damped bandage. She was much gentler and more skilful than I had been, trying to do the same thing for poor Benjie.

'Pu' the stockin' ower the fut, but no' the but,' she told me. And then, when I had pulled the stocking over the bandage, she gave me a flannel slipper to wear until I could wear a boot.

I tried to thank her, in the language of Jaikie Bogle, but she clucked at me and creaked out. I thought that, though she was kind, her dignity did not allow her to be friendly with a stable-lad.

'Ye'll hae yin ither veesitor,' said the solemn Robert Cochrane: and in came a grinning man in an apron, with a pair of scissors.

'Hauld stull, laddie, an' we'll trim yer fleece,' said the newcomer, and began snipping at the ragged thatch on my head. As he snipped, he hissed, as a strapper hisses at a horse in the stable. I wondered how many manes and tails and fetlocks those scissors had trimmed. Ends of hair went itchily down inside my collar. The back of my neck felt cold. I was glad the man had not thought to use the kind of American mechanical clippers with which Carnmore's horses were made to look so smart.

'Ye'll du,' said my cheerful barber. 'A credit tae the establishment, eh, Mr Cochrane?'

'He's a bonny lad eneuch,' said the coachman, looking at me with solemn friendliness.

'Whaur s'al he bide the nicht? Wi' Angus an' the ithers?'

'No—the mustress says he's tae bide on his lane, in the wee rum ower the boiler.'

'There's a bed there?'

'There wull be a bed there, the nicht.'

'He's a favoured lad.'

'He desairves a change o' luck, mebbe. Forby, yon rum hae a dowr wi' a lock.'

'Ah. The renagate wull ren wi'oot a lock, eh?'

They both stared at me, as though at a specimen of an unheard of species. I stared back.

'Losh,' murmured the man with the scissors, 'sic a wee frail bairn tae hae passit siccan leef, wi'oot a ruf tae his heid or a plate tae his dunner.'

'Ay, it's no' easy tae credit. Weel, come awa', Bogle, an' set tae a bit o' dunner.'

They carried me downstairs, and in a room behind the coach-house fed me on a cut off a joint of boiled mutton, with pease-pudding and green stuff, and a pot of beer. I had never drunk beer before; I found the taste most peculiar.

I had not thought I could be hungry, after the quantity of stuff I had eaten in the lawyer's office; but I was. My glorious bath had given me a renewed and gigantic appetite. Angus was there, and three other grooms, and the undercoachman who had driven the brougham: but not Robert Cochrane, who went off to eat his dinner with his wife in his own quarters. The other grooms were middle-aged or elderly, neat in dress but coarse in manner, typical private grooms, not hostile to me but aloof, as befitted their higher station. (I was learning that servants are desperately concerned about their rank in their own world, and to unbend to me—the lowest of the low in the whole hierarchy—would have been far beneath their dignity.) Angus only, a much younger man, did have a hostile, resentful manner to me. He was still annoyed, perhaps, at having had to fetch and carry for a muddy waif from the hill.

I picked up a knife and fork, when my plate was put in front of me, and began to eat. As earlier in the day, I could think of nothing except food: but after a few beautiful mouthfuls, I felt eyes upon me, and glanced up, my mouth full of mutton. One of the older grooms, called Andrew, was looking at me with astonishment on his weather-beaten face.

What was I doing wrong?

I realised, with a jolt, that I was doing right, when I ought to have been doing wrong. How should Jaikie Bogle know how to use a knife and fork, like a Christian?

So I began to eat awkwardly, and rather messily, and pretended to handle my cutlery as though I had never used it before, but was imitating the method of the others. But the look of puzzlement remained on Andrew's face. I cursed myself and my greed, and resolved to be more careful—much, much more careful.

In the afternoon I could do nothing, so I did nothing, but sat on that same upturned bucket in the sunshine, with one foot in a carpet-slipper. I worried about Benjie; I worried about my parents; I tried not to worry about myself. I tried not to think of Murdo on one side of me, and Carnmore on the other.

A stocky, cobby horse was saddled and led away by one of the grooms; I heard them say it was for the laird, for Mr Gordon; he was off on horseback to visit a tenant. From the talk of the grooms, I understood he was an excellent landlord, as his father had been at Carnmore, and as Carnmore's father had been at Carnmore. The servants spoke with great freedom amongst each other, as I suppose servants always do about their masters. They talked of Mr Gordon with respect, but without awe. He did not inspire awe. Mrs Gordon did.

The Carnmore estate having been mentioned, its present lord was mentioned. He was not loved by the folk at Inverdoran, by the low no more than by the high. The grooms knew about his evictions of farmers and crofters, and they were angry. It did my heart good to hear him execrated.

Of course these servants knew far more about the great than the latter ever realised. So, listening to their endless monotonous chatter as they soaped leather and polished brass and mixed the evening feeds, I learned much about my new protectors. Master Lancelot was something of a milksop, I heard, idolised and overprotected by his mother all through his childhood. Miss Elspeth was more of a man than her brother, though not a beauty. The family was passionately anxious to recover the Carnmore estate. They had repeatedly made offers to Lord Carnmore, from the moment they came back to Scotland: but of course he refused to sell, and said he would always refuse. It was not so much, I gathered, that Mr Gordon wanted the estate for himself, as that Mrs Gordon wanted it for her son. The servants whole-heartedly supported their mistress. Only when the Gordons had recovered their own would the evictions and injustices cease, and things go on as they should. This theme ran through and through the conversation. The men kept returning to it. 'The auld folk sud come tae their ane.' Lord Carnmore was an outsider, a stranger. Even if he behaved well, he would command none of the fierce loyalty these Highlanders felt for the 'auld folk'.

Oddly enough, Sir Richard Grant could, although he was equally an outsider. Of course Strathlarrig was talked of, because of the murder of the butler. Papa was mentioned, with a sort of amused contempt which almost made me forget myself. Mr Jenks, the earlier tenant, was viewed with tolerant indifference. But Sir Richard was held in very high regard.

Carnmore's new wife was mentioned; I heard myself discussed. I felt my ears burning, as those of eavesdroppers are supposed to do; and, as eavesdroppers are supposed to, I heard no good of myself.

'She wed for the siller,' said the undercoachman.

'They say she's abed the noo, verra bad, wi' doctors an' a'.'

'It sairves her richt, tae hae contactit a maircenary marriage.'

'Yon's no' verra charitable, Andra.'

'She doesna desairve charity, mon.'

They were right: but that did not make it better listening for me.

A young maidservant came out into the yard, with a message about Miss Elspeth's pony. It was to be brought to the door of the house at eleven next morning. The girl was called Ina, it seemed. She was very pretty, as I could see Angus thought also. She had golden hair, very neat under her lace cap, and a slim trim figure, and small regular features. She was perhaps twenty. I understood she was Elspeth's own maid. Though taller than I, she looked much as I would have looked (before my hair was shorn) in the clothes of a lady's maid.

The older grooms teased Angus about her, after she had trotted away towards the house. He reddened and spat. I hoped Ina would do better than to marry Angus.

There was another meal at six o'clock—slabs of salt pork, with what I thought might be turnips or swedes, and with big chunks of home-made bread, with home-made butter and home-made cheese. I said nothing, during the meal; I tried not to be noticed. I tried to eat in a way that fitted Jaikie Bogle's background, yet not be so revolting that they would stare and comment.

The room itself was bleak and comfortless, furnished only with a deeply-stained pine table on rickety trestles, and half-a-dozen wooden chairs. There were bare boards on the floor, and the walls were white-washed. In one corner was a stove. I imagined that in winter, the men drew their chairs to it. If I were still there, I would be lucky to be allowed near it.

The food was not cooked anywhere in the stables, I learned, but brought from the kitchens of the house by a kitchen-boy. Consequently, nothing was ever quite hot, which was a cause of mild grumbling. It seemed that the servants' hall at Inverdoran was not large enough to hold the grooms and coachmen, as well as the indoor servants. (I compared this with my memory of the echoing vastness of the servants' hall at Strathlarrig, and the big, sunny housekeeper's room, and the butler's noble pantry, where I had often gone as a child for titbits, and to queen it among my vassals.) Robert Cochrane sometimes dined indoors, at the invitation of the housekeeper, but none of the others. I think this suited all parties. I remembered from my childhood that servants'-hall manners were formidably stiff and formal, and the free-and-easy ways of the grooms, as well as their language, might have been shockingly out of place. The arrangement certainly suited me. I was much better tucked away out of sight among these indifferent men, than struggling under the sharp eyes of a parcel of women upper-servants. I thought I would give myself away to them— by my hands, for example, and perhaps my movements—while the men chewed and chattered and belched, and seldom looked at me.

At about seven, Robert Cochrane came in. He gave Angus and the undercoachmen leave to go out, to the ale-house in the village a mile away, so they were in by eleven. He gave two of the others small tasks to do, to get things ready for the next day, when horses and carriages would be wanted. Andrew was left in charge of me.

It came to me that, except when I was bolted in the bathroom, I had been under somebody's eye from the moment of my arrival. I guessed I always would be. Well, the Gordons had undertaken not to let me run away.

That was very well, unless I was unmasked. It was very well, except for Benjie.

'The laddie wull wush tae gang tae his bed,' said Andrew, a little anxiously, to Robert Cochrane. He meant: he did not want to waste a whole evening watching me.

So I was helped to the boiler-room, where hot water was heated for the stables, and hauled up a kind of ladder to a little room over it, just by the main archway of the stable-yard.

If the grooms' dining room was bare, this little chamber was monastic. There was nothing in it, nothing at all, except a mattress on a bare wooden floor, with a single blanket. There was a single barred window, big for the room, but made so to match the others. The room was right under the roof, so that the ceiling sloped almost to the floor. No lath or plaster had been wasted on the ceiling—there were simply the bare joists, with the battens above them, and the slates above the battens.

The men nodded to me, and went away. I heard a key turn in the lock. It was still broad daylight. The mattress was stuffed with straw; it was full of lumps, and rustled when I touched it. I darkly suspected fleas, and all manner of creatures. Well, I had lain much harder, the previous nights, and Benjie was lying much harder.

I wanted to wash, but could not. I wanted night-clothes, but had none. I would have been glad of a book, or anything to occupy me, but there was nothing. I undressed to my shirt, and lay wakeful in the bright evening.

I do not know why, but I felt more forlorn than at any time since my escape from Carnmore. I had been hurt; now I was cared for. I had been very frightened; now I was safe. But I was miserable. I was even homesick for Myrtle Lodge. To my rage, I began to weep, silly, self-indulgent, helpless, useless tears, wetting my mattress and the sleeve of my flannel shirt.

I did not even have a handkerchief.

In the morning, they gave me some small crutches. Mrs Gordon had found them, I was told. Master Lancelot had hurt his leg, years before, and his mother had had the most elegant crutches made, which he did not at all need, and never used. I was able to hop easily about the stable-yard, and could be given work to do. I was set to polishing some steel chains, the sort that are used to hitch a pair of horses to the carriage-pole. They were very ancient and rusty chains, long out of use, and I rubbed and rubbed at the links, with white powder into which I spat, and a scrap of cloth. I felt very like a stable-boy, spitting into the polish and rubbing at the metal. Parts came shiny quite easily; parts were so deeply rutted with rust that I despaired of getting them smart. But I was glad to be doing something; and, doing something, I thought I was less conspicuous than when I was sitting idle.

There was always somebody by, to keep an eye on me.

Mrs Gordon came into the stable-yard in the middle of the morning, dressed for a walk. She saw me, and saw that I was busy, and looked pleased about that. She asked me if I had slept well, and eaten well.

'Ay, mem,' I whined, struggling to stand up.

She smiled, with none of the coolness I had seen in the lawyer's office. With the greatest kindness, she pushed me back onto the bench where I sat, and said I could jump to my feet when I had two good feet to jump to.

I was very touched: and after she had gone, I attacked the spots of rust with a new ferocity, so as to repay a little bit of the kindness I was being shown.

8

My ankle mended. I went after three days from two crutches to one stick, and after a week I was walking normally.

Though I was watched, there were moments when I thought I could have run away. I was sure I could run faster than fat Robert Cochrane, or the undercoachman, or any of the old grooms, though perhaps not Angus. But where should I run? And to do what? The thought of Benjie distressed and worried me: but his knee must have mended by now, as my ankle had; if he were still alive, he might be anywhere in Scotland.

I was still locked in at night. But I was given a nightshirt, and a wash-basin which I could fill at the pump in the stable-yard, and a toothbrush.

I settled painlessly into the routine of the stable-yard. There was not really so very much work to do. It was seldom that more than one carriage went out in a day; Elspeth called for her pony only once in my first week, Mr Gordon for his cob only two or three times. Lancelot was away, staying with friends; Mrs Gordon did not ride. Robert Cochrane invented tasks for me, like the cleaning of those ancient steel chains, but my labour was not truly needed. I had been given the place out of charity.

The only member of the family I saw regularly was the mistress. She came to the stables to give orders to Robert Cochrane, and to inspect my health and progress. She always had a kind word for me, though it was often a hurried one.

The other men took little notice of me. I was not bullied or teased. Angus, the youngest, was the one I liked least, not because he was cruel to me—he never looked at me, or spoke to me at all—but because he was impatient and heavy-handed with the horses. This only when he thought nobody else was looking. I had the impression that he disliked horses, that he was even a little frightened of them: and therefore, sensing this as all animals do, they were not as gentle and tractable with him as they were with the others and with me. I thought he should not have been a groom at all; I thought he thought so too.

I expected that someone would start to teach me to read and write. A master at the orphanage would have done so, as the Procurator Fiscal had said, and the Gordons were committed to doing no less for me than the orphanage would. The prospect was troubling. How quickly should I pretend to learn my letters? I did not want to seem too simple-minded, in case the Gordons changed their minds about keeping me; I did not want to seem amazingly clever, either, or an uncomfortable interest would be taken in my welfare. Above all, I did not want to give myself away, which I guessed would be all too easy. But this threat remained in the future. My schooling was never mentioned. I was surprised that Mrs Gordon was so remiss, when she seemed so conscientious and thoughtful about everything. I was thankful there was this gap in the completeness of her management.

One morning a fat pony was harnessed to the wagonette. It seemed that the family was going out for a picnic, and was to meet friends at some beauty-spot. Mr Gordon was to drive the wagonette himself. Of course, they would take a groom, to look after the pony while they ate or walked or talked, and perhaps a footman or a maid to help with the picnic.

As I helped old Andrew with the harness, I found myself wishing very hard that I might go out in the wagonette. For ten days I had been living entirely in the stable-yard, and its walls made a very narrow horizon.

To my huge surprise, Robert Cochrane said, 'Ye're tae gang wi' the wagonit, Bogle. Orders frae the mustress.'

I believe I gave a sort of squeak of astonishment. I scrubbed my stable-boy's hands under the pump, and dusted my boots with a rag, and put on the little round hat they had given to me (once worn by the boy who broke his head on a stone); and then I walked beside the undercoachman when he took the wagonette round to the front door of the big house. It was the first time I had seen the world outside the stable-yard since my disreputable arrival, mud-caked, bare-footed, in Jaikie Bogle's dreadful clothes. For the first time I properly saw the Inverdoran policies and park, and the details of the house itself. It all looked comfortable, well cared for, and drab. The garden was a dull garden. Big trees had been left too close to the house when the house was built, so I thought many of the rooms must be gloomy. Even the Doran Burn was a sluggish little water.

Hampers were loaded into the back of the wagonette. I saw the necks of bottles peeping from damp napkins in a basket. Then the family appeared at the top of the steps—Mr Gordon in tweed breeches, and a cotton jacket, and his broad-brimmed Panama hat; Mrs Gordon shrouded in a voluminous dust-coat, as though bound for a desert, and certain of sand-storms; and Elspeth.

I had not seen Elspeth before—not since I had glimpsed her in Lochgrannomhead, in the days when I had always hid from people I had once known, because I was ashamed of poverty. She took after her father, plump, round-faced, pink, with an amiable expression. She moved a little gracelessly, lumpily, as though she felt heavier than she was, and I did not think she was light. She was much more elaborately dressed than either of her parents, and she carried a tiny and very pretty parasol. She looked excited. I thought she was always pink —she had that kind of face—but that today she was pinker than usual. I wondered whom she expected to meet.

A footman followed the great ones down the steps, and handed Mrs Gordon and Miss Elspeth into the back of the wagonette. They sat facing each other, their feet among the hampers and bottles, on shabby cushions. Mr Gordon scrambled unaided onto the box-seat, and picked up the whip from its holder.

I supposed, of course, that either the undercoachman or the footman would get up beside the driver, and that I would cling to the back on the 'spoon' which was there for underlings like me. But the footman withdrew into the house; and the undercoachman still stood by the pony's head; and Mr Gordon gestured to me, with a smile.

'Up you get, Jaikie, look sharp,' he said, patting the cushion on the box beside him.

So I found myself beside the laird, as we trotted ponderously down the drive towards the lochside road.

The sun was very hot. We were not going fast enough, behind the one fat pony, for the movement of the air to be cooling. I felt my face growing scarlet. I envied Mr Gordon his cotton coat, much lighter than my stiff canvas jacket. But of course I could not take off my jacket, which was my servant's uniform: and I would not, because in shirtsleeves I would not look like any boy ever born.

Mr Gordon talked to me as we went, asking what Robert Cochrane was finding for me to do, and if the food was not better than what I had begged from farmhouse kitchens. It was difficult for me to concentrate on his kindly questions, and to give the proper answers of

Jaikie Bogle. This was partly because of the chatter of mother and daughter behind us, which was about their neighbours, nearly all of whom I had once known; it was partly because I wondered if I should see, peering between branches, a face I knew.

Surely I was safe with the Gordons. Murdo and his entire clan could attempt nothing while I was under the eye of the family. What, in any case, would Murdo now be thinking? He knew I had spent a morning at the Procurator Fiscal's. If I had described the murder, and the murderer, a description would have been issued, probably with the offer of a reward. Robert Cochrane would have heard news of anything of the kind, and discussed it at enormous length in the stable-yard. But I had heard no mention of description or reward. They continued to speculate about the mystery, producing all sorts of absurd theories. They said it was a crime that would never be solved, because nobody had seen it. Murdo had eyes and ears in Lochgrannomhead and in the countryside; he would know as much as I did. He would know that I had not named him or described him to the Procurator Fiscal. He would think I was frightened to do so—frightened of him, frightened of the results for myself, frightened of any involvement with law and courts and County Police. Therefore, I still had knowledge that could hang him. I was still a life-and-death threat to him. I would be so as long as we both lived, and wherever either of us went.

This is why I wondered if I should see a face I knew, and stared, without seeming to do so, at every spinney and hedgerow we passed on the road. That is why I gave distracted answers to Mr Gordon's kindly questions.

He did not seem annoyed, but smiled at me, and fell silent; and the waves of feminine chatter flowed over our heads from the back of the wagonette.

After two or three miles, going away from the town, we turned inland from the lochside road. We climbed a moderate hill, going along a deeply rutted track which was hard and bumpy in the dry midsummer weather, and would have been an impassable quagmire after heavy rain or in melting snow. It was not a place I knew. I could not imagine why the track had been made, or where it led.

The chatter behind seemed to sink in volume, but rise in excitement. I wanted to glance round, but of course that would have been highly improper. I did glance at Mr Gordon. He too had an expectant air.

Where on earth was this drab little path leading? There could be no great view, no grand woods, no deserted lochan, no rushing river or spectacular falls.

The ground flattened, and became stony. I was aware of Elspeth behind me, craning to look for something or someone. And then I understood what the track served, and why it was so deeply rutted. It ended by a quarry. Half an acre of ground had been gouged out, to a depth here of a few feet, there of twenty. But it was completely quiet and deserted. From the look of the ground about it, I did not think it had been worked for a long time.

Well, that explained the track, but not why we had come here, and not at all why the Gordons seemed so full of delighted anticipation.

Mr Gordon stopped the pony, and I jumped down and ran to its head. There was really no need to hold such a sleepy old animal, but I did so, to be busy and useful, and make a good impression on the Gordons.

Then Elspeth gave a squeak, and pointed over my head, and over the quarry, towards the big slow hillside beyond. I looked over my shoulder. I saw far away two horsemen, one on a big horse leading another on a smaller one. Master and servant, I supposed. The leader was too far away for me to recognise, but the Gordons knew who he was, because they were expecting him to come.

'I do think it so remarkable,' said Mrs Gordon, 'that a gentleman like Sir Richard should know about rocks and quarrying.'

'Not so very, my dear,' said Mr Gordon. 'He was brought up to have practical experience of all kinds of things—mining, and ironworks, and so forth, as well as horse-breeding and sport of all kinds.'

'I do not say it is not admirable,' said Mrs Gordon. 'I do not even say it is not gentlemanly. But I do say it is surprising.'

'But he told *me*, Mamma,' said Elspeth in a high, breathy voice, 'that since he inherited a vast amount of mineral wealth, like coal, I suppose—'

'And iron, and lead, and slates,' said her father.

'Yes, precisely—well, since he inherited all that, he felt obliged to—to understand how it was all dug up, you know, and what dangers were involved for the poor colliers, and how the mines could be made safer, which I think *very* admirable, and *very* gentlemanly—and also, he told me that the more he understood, the less anybody would be able to cheat him, which I think is *also* admirable, because he is removing temptation from people who might—who might otherwise give way to it, you know.'

'We're all delighted that Grant knows how to look after his own,' said Mr Gordon, almost laughing at Elspeth's tone of desperate earnestness.

'How slowly he is riding!' said Elspeth.

'Your eagerness to greet him is natural, dear,' said Mrs Gordon. 'Show it to us, by all means, but don't show it to him.'

'Oh! No! Of course not, Mamma! But I do not understand about this quarry. It is not ours, is it, Papa? Isn't it part of Ardno?'

'It is part of Ardno, and I can get a lease of it from old Ardno. He won't put up the capital necessary to work it. Hasn't got it, I daresay. I could, and will, if it's worth it—if I'm going to get a reasonable return on my investment.'

'You never will, Alistair,' said his wife.

'Financially, no, probably not. At any rate, that's where Grant is the man to advise us.'

'I suppose you'll drag him off, to stare at bits of stone,' said Elspeth.

'That *is* the purpose of our meeting here,' said her father mildly.

'One of the purposes,' said Mrs Gordon.

Mr Gordon scrambled down off his box, and helped the others out. Then he told Elspeth to stand by the pony's head (they were a practical, out-of-door family, well used to animals) while I was to help him unload the wagonette. Mrs Gordon meanwhile spread rugs on the ground. They did not mind in the least doing this sort of thing for themselves.

Sir Richard Grant rode up at last. I had forgotten how handsome he was, in a cold aloof superior way. He sat his horse well. From the time he had taken coming down the hillside, he did not seem as avid to meet the Gordons as they were to meet him, but he was cheerful enough. I had not seen him cheerful before. I had not seen him smile before. A smile improved him. He was quite different, wearing casual summer clothes and a smiling face, from the arrogant bully I had met at Strathlarrig, or the priggish lecturer I had had thrown into a puddle at Myrtle Lodge. Of course he was different. He was with rich people, whom he could respect, his equals.

His greeting to Elspeth was friendly—no more than friendly, but no less. He shook her hand, and smiled, and hoped she was as well as she looked. She made a desperate attempt to be as casual as he, but she was much more than friendly. I was glad to see that I was not the only hopelessly transparent female in Perthshire. I felt sorry for her. From the pony, to which I had returned, I saw her mother's stern and disapproving eye fixed on a blushing, stammering Elspeth; and I saw an embarrassed fading of Sir Richard's friendly smile, at this too-evident partiality.

To have too much dignity is pompous and tiresome, perhaps; but to have too little is a dreadful thing. I had never had much myself, so I knew.

The moment passed, and the four of them sat down on the rugs. Mr Gordon himself uncorked a bottle of wine.

Sir Richard's groom, with their two horses, came over to me and the pony. Between us we looked after the horses, and then looked after ourselves, with the basket of provisions that had been put in for us. The groom was called Rory Crauford—a little brown man like a monkey, about forty years old, who might once have been a jockey. He was delightful. He made me laugh so that I choked over my beer (I was growing used to the Inverdoran home-brewed beer) and nearly disgraced myself within sight of my masters. The picnic Rory Crauford and I ate was, as far as I could see, exactly the same as the one the Gordons were sharing with Sir Richard, except that they drank wine. That was typical of Mrs Gordon's arrangements.

In the intervals of Rory Crauford's drolleries, I heard scraps of conversation from the others.

Once again, I heard myself discussed.

'Had you not heard, Sir Richard?'

'No, I had heard nothing of this. I was obliged to go away just before the marriage, and only returned yesterday. You are the first people I have seen.'

'I'll wager your servants know about the chit's illness,' said Mr Gordon, 'and I'll wager they talk about it, in spite of the shocking tragedy in your house.'

'I don't doubt it. My servants gossip with your servants and with each other. But they do not gossip with me.'

'Very proper,' said Mrs Gordon, not sounding convinced that it was really so very dreadful to hear a good story from a groom. 'At any rate, the story is that Catriona was taken ill immediately after the wedding-breakfast, and has been confined to her bed ever since. And Carnmore has not sent for Dr McPhee.'

'But,' said Sir Richard, frowning, 'I happen to know that McPhee is Carnmore's doctor.'

'He is everybody's doctor. But not, it appears, Catriona's.'

'Has he never been the Larrigs' physician?'

'He has always been the Larrigs' physician.'

'Both hers and her husband's,' said Sir Richard, 'yet not summoned when she is taken ill.'

'I wonder what is wrong with her?' said Elspeth. 'Do you suppose it was the food at the wedding-breakfast?'

'Not unless everyone else has been extraordinarily secretive about their illnesses,' said Mr Gordon.

'I find this worrying,' said Sir Richard.

'Of course, we all do,' said Mrs Gordon.

'I, perhaps, even more than you.'

'From special knowledge?'

'You could call it so.'

'Of Carnmore, or of Catriona?' asked Mr Gordon.

'Of Carnmore. I know nothing of Lady Catriona except that she is very beautiful, and has almost too much spirit and courage.'

'So everyone has always said,' said Mrs Gordon. 'Of course, her upbringing was outrageous. But whenever did you meet her, Sir Richard? Nobody else ever clapped eyes on her, after her father threw away all his money, and then all his wife's, and then all his daughter's.'

'She came to Strathlarrig once, by herself in a carriage, to see me on a matter of business.'

'I find that almost incredible, even of Catriona,' said Mrs Gordon.

'So did I.'

'And verging on the improper.'

'So I thought.'

And so you showed, I said to myself, angry all over again at the cold brusqueness of his manner to me.

'In the event,' said Sir Richard, 'I was full of admiration.'

Admiration? I had filled him with admiration?

'She came because her father could not or would not,' Sir Richard went on, 'and she was determined that I should not see the depths to which her father's folly had brought them. I was slow to understand that, and ashamed that I had not understood it at once.'

'But to go alone, without even a servant, to call on you—'

'She had no servant. She had to come alone. At least, she felt she

had to. Consequently, I found myself obliged to receive Lady Catriona in a house that should have been full of *her* family, *their* servants, *their* furniture. It was embarrassing and uncomfortable for me.
Think what it must have been like for her.'

'Poor Catriona,' said Elspeth.

'Yes,' he agreed. 'Of course I tried to spare her embarrassment—'

'Of course,' said Mrs Gordon.

'By making the interview as brief and formal as possible. Acting, I
may say, against interest and inclination. I would have preferred to
ask her to dinner.'

'Good gracious!'

'I could not do so, naturally. That would have been grossly improper. I am not certain if I would have been deterred by the gross
impropriety of such an invitation, but it would have been cruel, I
think. To offer her hospitality in her own dining room—my silver and
glass standing where hers ought to have been—it must have rubbed
salt into what must already have been a painful wound.'

The Gordons nodded, believing Sir Richard. I found myself nod-
ding. I was beginning to believe him, too. I found myself revising my
harsh judgment on his behaviour that day.

I looked across at him, sitting on the ground in a position he managed to make graceful, the sun shining on his thick black hair and his
tanned face. But then again, but then again . . .

'You thought her beautiful?' said Elspeth, failing to keep a mortified
note out of her voice.

'Yes. Would it be possible not to?'

'We have not seen her since she grew up,' said Mr Gordon. 'She was
a lovely child.'

'She has fulfilled her promise, then,' said Sir Richard.

'She was a very spoiled and wilful child,' said Mrs Gordon.

'She may still be wilful, ma'am, but no one could call her spoiled. I
was lost in admiration for the—the dignity, the defiance, with which
she tacitly dared me to feel sorry for her.'

Lost in admiration? I wished I had known that at the time.

'I suppose Lord Carnmore has spoiled her,' said Mrs Gordon. 'He
can afford to.'

'I wonder,' said Sir Richard, 'what Carnmore has done to her.'

'That was the only time you have met Catriona, Grant?' said Mr
Gordon. 'That awkward occasion at Strathlarrig?'

'There was one other occasion,' he said shortly.

'Was your estimate of the child confirmed?'

'Of her beauty, yes. Of her spirit, yes.'

I expected him to tell them the dreadful story. But that was all he would say. He bore no malice. That is what utterly amazed me. He bore no malice.

I sat thinking idiotically: he is not only beautiful, in a gloriously stern and unsmiling way, but also kind and good.

When I thought he was being cruel to me, he was trying to be merciful. When I thought he was trying to ruin me, he was trying to save me.

Rory Crauford had been dozing, which was how I had heard so much of the conversation. Now he woke up, as cheery and chatty as ever: and I heard no more.

God knows, it was enough to be going on with.

Presently Mr Gordon took Sir Richard off to inspect the quarry, to the visible chagrin of Elspeth. Mother and daughter also decided to stroll. That is to say, Mrs Gordon decided. She seemed to me an active, impatient sort of lady, unwilling to sit doing nothing; I thought Elspeth would have preferred to sit doing nothing, except twirl her parasol in a manner likely to enchant Sir Richard.

Rory Crauford dozed again, after another tankard of Inverdoran beer.

I thought once again that I could have run away, if I had had anywhere to run to. But I realised that either Mr or Mrs Gordon kept me in sight. It seemed to be casual, a matter of chance, but it was not. Jaikie Bogle was not quite trusted yet. So I sat by the wagonette, with the three horses, and almost dozed myself.

I was startled into consciousness by a hoarse whisper, 'Hey!'

I sat up and looked round.

'Hey, Jaikiebogle!'

'Benjie!' I whispered, excited and delighted.

His thatch of carroty hair parted some tall fronds of bracken, five yards away. He was out of sight of all the others. A grin threatened to split his pinched, dirty little face.

I felt my answering grin creasing my own face—then realised that it might be seen by the Gordons, and perhaps understood. Only a ninny or a drunkard grins like a hound at a clump of bracken. So I dragged down the corners of my mouth, and tried to keep a solemn mask. I stood up, and strolled, ever so casually, over to the bracken where Benjie lay. I sat down beside his head. I turned myself away from the quarry and the carriage, so that although I was in full view, I could talk without being seen to talk.

'Losh, Jaikiebogle, ye're awfu' gran',' whispered Benjie.

'Ay. I'm a grum. Is yer puir leg mendit, Benjie?'

'Och, in twa-three days it waur mendit.'

We exchanged all our news in whispers. Benjie had joined a different band of tinkers, who had found him hobbling, very hungry, along the march between Strathlarrig and Inverdoran, and had taken him in. It was enough of a recommendation, apparently, that he had run away from Murdo's clan, for Murdo was feared and hated even by his own kind. Benjie had fallen on his feet. He said he was well fed, although from his face he did not look it. Murdo had gone away, into some other countryside, but Benjie was sure he had not gone far. He had left three or four men behind. That showed, as Benjie said, that he was within reach. Benjie had seen the men left behind. One was in Lochgrannomhead. One or two were usually by Inverdoran.

'Ay,' I said. 'Murdo kens whaur I bide.'

'Murdo kens a',' whispered Benjie. 'He maun kull ye, Jaikiebogle.'

I asked Benjie how he had found me.

''Tis a' the clash o' the toon,' he told me, 'a wee cateran wi' a yaller heid waur grippit an' carrit tae the Fisca'. An' folk saw ye gang awa' intil a carritch wi' the gran' folk.'

Of course, my whereabouts—Jaikie Bogle's whereabouts—were public knowledge. Benjie had come to seek me, out of friendship. He had not words to say so, exactly, but I understood what he left unsaid. Watching Inverdoran for a sight of me, he had seen Murdo's men watching. He did not think they had seen him, as he was small, and alone, and could wriggle like a slow-worm.

He could wriggle almost anywhere, and see and hear almost anything. He could carry a message. I had a truly excellent idea.

'Can ye gae tae the toon, tae Lochgrannomheid?' I asked him.

'Ay, certes.'

'Can ye feend a hoose ca'd Myrtle Lodge, on the raud tae Crianlarich?'

'Ay,' he said, more doubtfully.

'An auld fellie bides in yon hoose,' I said, and described Papa as he would seem to Benjie, without naming him.

I made sure that Benjie had taken in where the villa was, and what the occupant looked like. Then I gave him a message to give to Papa: 'Cat is hidden but safe.'

He repeated it, utterly puzzled, but willing to do this for me.

'Cat's a lassie,' I explained to Benjie. 'The auld yin's her sire. She ren awa' frae her mon, an' droppit oot o' sicht a whilie syne.'

'Ay . . . The auld yin wull be speirin', hey? What's s'all ah tell, Jaikiebogle?'

'Tell naethin'! Ye ken naethin'!'

Mr Gordon and Sir Richard Grant now approached the wagonette, strolling from one direction; and Mrs Gordon and Elspeth approached it, strolling from another. Rory Crauford woke up, rubbed his eyes, grinned at me, jumped to his feet, and became in a twinkling a deferential servant.

Benjie whispered a farewell, and said he would seek me again when the message was delivered. There was a tiny rustling in the bracken, and he was gone.

'Certainly the quarry is workable,' Sir Richard was saying to Mr Gordon. 'I should say you would lose a little money, but not much.'

'That is reassuring.'

'I understand. You will take up the lease, and work the quarry, pretending it is an investment. Your object is to provide employment for the poor wretches Carnmore is evicting.'

'I have a responsibility to them, an ancient responsibility, though they are no longer my tenants.'

'Not many people would see it so. Will you allow me to share a part of the investment?'

'That is very handsome, Grant, but you have no shadow of responsibility for those folk.'

'As a laird, no. As a neighbour, yes.'

They argued about it, each diminishing his own generosity, each saying that the other was needlessly generous.

Mrs Gordon arrived in time to hear the later part of the conversation. I thought she would have welcomed Sir Richard's contribution. I thought she and her husband would discuss it later, in private, and that she would win the argument. Well, it was reasonable. The Gordons were rich, but they were not as rich as their new neighbour.

I was busy with the harness of the pony when I heard Sir Richard say, 'So that is the young villain who tried to burgle my house?'

'That is he,' said Mrs Gordon. 'Jaikie, Sir Richard could prefer charges against you, but he is not going to do so.'

I touched my round groom's hat to Sir Richard. I almost felt like dropping a curtsey: which would have been an act of the wildest folly.

'A less villainous looking lad I've never seen,' said Sir Richard, smiling at me.

I had a momentary fear of his recognising me. He did stare at me with interest. I hoped I would not blush. It seemed horribly likely, as I stood self-consciously under his gaze. His face was amused and friendly.

I thought it a curious irony that he should show such different faces to Jaikie Bogle and Lady Catriona Douglas.

'My nightwatchman, Lachlan Pringle, tells me that you bowled him off his feet with a kitchen table,' Sir Richard said to me.

'Ay, sir,' I said in a strangled voice.

'He was annoyed at the time, but afterwards he rather admired you for it. And so do I.'

His smile was so warm that I felt myself beginning to smile back. It was impossible not to. I tried to discipline my features, which had never been amenable to discipline. I knew that I really was blushing now.

'The lad's a bit shy,' said Mr Gordon.

'A good fault,' said Sir Richard. 'What became of your friend, my lad?'

'I dinna ken, sir,' I gasped. 'He ren awa'.'

'A pity. You must be worried about him. If you do ever happen to see him, will you tell him to come to Strathlarrig and ask for me? Say I mean him no harm. Lachlan Pringle has forgiven him.'

'Whatever would you do with such a lad, Sir Richard?' said Mrs Gordon.

'What you have done, perhaps. That depends on the lad, on how he strikes me. Besides, I have questions for him. I do not like the thought of tinker-boys knowing secret ways into my house. I am anxious to find out how he came by knowledge of that trap-door, which I had no idea of myself.'

A plan I had been making in my mind disappeared like a feather in a gale. I had thought I would send Benjie to Strathlarrig, to be taken in and made respectable. (This shows how profoundly I was revising my opinion of Sir Richard Grant.) But of course he would have to answer questions. He would have to say that it was I, Jaikie Bogle, who knew of the trap-door. And then I would have to answer questions: and very likely my cake would be dough.

Wherever Benjie went, it must not be to Strathlarrig. Whoever he spoke to, it must not be Sir Richard Grant. For him that was a pity, perhaps. For me it was life or death.

I was deeply thankful that my parents would know—before the end of that same day, probably—that I was safe. I had racked my brains for a way to get a message to them, but I could think of none that did not seem certain to betray me. How could I ask the Gordons, or any servant of the Gordons, to go to Lord Larrig at Myrtle Lodge, and say that Lady Catriona—that Lady Carnmore—was safe and well? How could Jaikie Bogle know anything of her? How could I write and send a letter, when Jaikie Bogle could not write so much as his name? Whatever torment Mamma and Papa were going through, I could *not* risk exposure by reassuring them.

Now I had reassured them without risk of exposure. Benjie would simply repeat my message by tote, telling a man whose name he did not know that a girl he had never heard of was safe. Benjie would say no more, because he knew no more, however many questions Papa asked.

I lay that night on my straw mattress, congratulating myself on having seized the chance that Benjie offered.

Until a new thought struck me. The first person to whom my parents would pass on the message would be Carnmore. Obviously. My adoring husband, suffering as much agony as they. He might have guessed me dead, or hundreds of miles away; he might have guessed me hidden in the South of England, or in France, since he knew I spoke French. But now he would know I was alive and nearby. A tinker-lad had brought the message on foot. He could not have come many miles. Carnmore had perhaps relaxed his vigilance, suspecting it was labour lost. Now he and all his people would be alert as kestrels. If the Gordons took me out as a groom again, might not one of them see me? Sir Richard had not recognised me: but Carnmore would. He knew me so much better. And he would be expecting a disguise.

Next time he passed close to me, my face would not be covered in mud. He would not be blind with rage. He would know me. He would claim me, with the law and the Church and my own parents on his side. No power on earth could save me.

I wondered what I had done. I thought about it furiously, far into the night, from all sides of the question. I concluded at last that I had been right to send the message, for Mamma might be made really ill with worry about me. I had been right to send the message: but it was a dangerous game I was playing.

There were many visits to the quarry after that, since it was a new venture that needed much supervision. When the wagonette went, I went with it. Sir Richard was usually there. From remarks I overheard among the Gordons, I understood that he had been permitted to share the cost of the tools, the wages, the special carts and draught-horses, and so forth. Since he was there, Elspeth was there. Sir Richard remained always friendly to her. But I thought he was unhappy about it. He could not refuse to meet her, if he had an engagement with her father and she came too. But I thought he would rather not have met her so very often. Another man might have basked in her too-evident admiration. That was not his way, it seemed. I was glad it was not. More and more I liked and respected him, as the other servants did.

He liked me too, which I found so odd. He went out of his way to be kind to Jaikie Bogle, who had entered his home and knocked over his watchman. He spoke to me often, and sometimes at length. He asked me many of the questions the Procurator Fiscal had asked me, in case I could throw light on the murder of his poor butler. I did not like to lie to him. But of course my whole life at Inverdoran was a kind of lie.

I used to watch him, when he was busy at the quarry with Mr Gordon or one of the new workmen who had been engaged. He was often serious, but never stiff. The stiffness he had shown me at Strathlarrig was not at all his natural manner. He had something I admired, which was the trick of being friendly with a workman, yet without loss of dignity. Mr Gordon was a little too friendly, and he did lose dignity. Mrs Gordon did not lose dignity, but she was not often friendly (except to me, to whom she was very kind, when she had time). Elspeth had the unfortunate gift of not being friendly to servants, but not being dignified either—she inherited the wrong things from both her parents.

Looking at Sir Richard, as I so often did, I remembered my first impression of his slightly irregular handsomeness. Then his face had been overlaid by what I thought was arrogant coldness, odious conceit, contempt of poverty. I had not seen—had not allowed myself to see—what a delightful face he truly had. The conventional regularity of Carnmore's face—his prettiness, almost—struck me as insipid and commonplace beside the strength and humour of Sir Richard's.

And, of course, Sir Richard was a splendid figure of a man. As a boy, a servant, I could admire his physique quite openly, as I might admire any sportsman.

I did not think he was aware of my eyes on him. But I was sometimes aware of his eyes on me.

A dozen men were recruited to work the quarry, under a foreman whom Sir Richard found in another place. All the men except one were crofters whom Carnmore had evicted. Until I saw their number, and heard the story of each from Rory Crauford, I had had no idea that Carnmore was depopulating his estate on such a scale.

Of course, it was being done in other parts of Scotland, especially the West and the far North. Landowners wanted grouse-moor, deer-forest, sheep-walk, and hill grazing for their Highland cattle. I was brought up to believe it was cruel and wrong—which was one of the few good things about my education. It was terrible to see eleven able-bodied men, all married, all with children, who had been turned out of their homes by a single landlord. It was truly excellent that Mr Gordon and Sir Richard between them had saved these men—not their livelihoods only, but their dignity and self-respect too: for they were not getting charity, as far as they themselves could see: they were set to work hard for their bread, and could not know that the quarry was doomed to run at a loss.

The twelfth man was also an unfortunate, it seemed—a vagrant from no one knew whence, desperate for regular work and a settled life. I heard the foreman say to Sir Richard that the man was a risk, a doubtful quantity.

'Yes,' said Sir Richard. 'But we'll give him a fair trial.'

'Ye'd employ Judas Iscariot, Sir Richard, if ye thocht ye'd help him on his raud tae Grace.'

Sir Richard laughed.

Two days later I felt eyes upon me, from the depths of the quarry. I glanced in that direction, suddenly self-conscious, expecting to meet Sir Richard's friendly gaze. But it was the twelfth man, the outsider, who stared at me. When he saw that I saw him stare, he turned away, and plied his pick at the rock.

I did not recognise him. He was clean-shaven, which was unusual among those men, and had close-cropped brown hair like a soldier's. He wore the usual rough workmen's clothes. He seemed to hold himself aloof from the others—who, of course, all knew each other, while he was a stranger. When the foreman called an order to him, he looked sullen, but obeyed at once, as though determined to show himself worthy of his hire. Determined, at any rate, to keep the job and the regular wages.

I thought there was something a little familiar about the man's eyes. But I could not place them, or him. If I had ever seen him before, I did not know where or when. Nothing else about him was familiar. He had a distinctive face, too—a long, thin-lipped mouth, and a curiously square chin. Those features would not be easy to forget: but, if I had seen them, I had forgotten them.

A new horse came to the stables at Inverdoran—a young grey filly, who would one day pull a phaeton or a dog-cart. She arrived broken both to saddle and to harness, so they said, but she was still very nervous and inexperienced. She needed gentle and patient handling. She had just such handling, from Robert Cochrane, and old Andrew, and the others, and the farrier, and me. Sometimes she bucked, and sometimes tried to kick: but her kicks were nervous, not vicious. She did not try to bite, that I ever saw. Her ears flapped; often they were pricked, which is a sign of good temper. Her eye rolled with suspicion of things going on behind her back, but I did not think there was any vice in it. She was a problem, but a problem that could be solved. She needed time. She was worth taking the time over. I understood she had cost a lot of money. She looked expensive, with a small, elegant head, deep chest, delicate legs and little feet. Robert Cochrane said she was three-quarters thoroughbred, but her grand-dam was by a famous Hackney stallion from Norfolk. There were very few horses quite like her in Scotland, though I heard there were many to be seen in Hyde Park in London, where fashionable folk drove their phaetons. She was called Goosefeather, because of her grey coat.

One morning I was alone in the stable-yard with Angus, who after myself was by many years the youngest man there. Robert Cochrane had ordered him to clean out the manger in Goosefeather's loose-box, although she was still in there. She had fouled the manger, as horses sometimes do, especially if they are not very used to living in a stable. Angus did not seem anxious to go into the stable with Goosefeather. I did not think he had been near her until that day; one of the others had fed her, groomed her, led her out, harnessed her, and so forth. I had myself groomed her two or three times, being careful of her hind feet, but not having any trouble.

'Yon's a job for the laddie,' said Angus. 'For yince he can airn his siller.'

'Yon's a job for ye,' said Robert Cochrane firmly.

He saw Angus into the loose-box, before he himself went off with the brougham. What he did not see was that Angus came out of the box, and went back into it carrying a long cutting-whip. I did not like the look of that: but I thought he must have sense enough not to use a cutting-whip on a nervous filly in the stable.

I was sitting on an upturned bucket in the sunshine, polishing the brasses of the second-best harness. It was a job I quite enjoyed, although it made my fingers black, because the result was so visible and so splendid. (My hands were no longer anything like a lady's. I thought they never would be again. It seemed to me supremely unimportant.)

There was a thud, then a clang, from Goosefeather's loose-box. The thud, unmistakably, was a hind foot lashing out and catching the wall of the box. The clang was the water-bucket Angus had taken in there to scrub the manger. There was an oath: then the sharp crack of a whip on a horse's quarters—twice, thrice, four times. The horse screamed and lashed out again.

I jumped up and ran to the loose-box, shouting as I went, 'Stop that, you filthy bully!' I did not think to use the language of Jaikie Bogle. I did not think of anything. I was mad with anger at this treatment of the pretty little horse.

I heard the clatter of hoof-beats coming into the yard, just as I came to the open half-door of the box. I did not turn. I did not care. I did not think. I screamed at Angus again, telling him to stop. I saw that he had tied Goosefeather up very tight by the head to an iron ring in the wall. I saw the clear marks of his cutting-whip on the lovely grey of her quarters. The bucket had been kicked over, and all the water spilled. The filly was hurt and terrified, and lashing out, and trying to pull her head away from the wall. For the very first time, I saw her trying to bite.

I screamed at Angus a third time, saying I know not what. He twisted his head to look at me. His face was working with anger, and I could see that he was frightened, too. He threw a leg over the half-door, and jumped out into the yard. Before I knew what was happening, he knocked me down with his fist. I tumbled onto the cobbles of the yard, hurting my head and my back. He raised the whip. He was beside himself with anger, because I had seen him whip the filly, because I had seen him lose his temper, because I had seen him frightened.

Just before he brought the whip down on my face, he was himself knocked half across the stable-yard. It was as though he had been hit by a battering-ram. He had been hit by Sir Richard Grant, who had just ridden in, and jumped off his horse.

Sir Richard's own face was dark with anger. If his anger had been directed at me, I would have been frightened of that look.

He said, in a voice he was only just able to control, 'You miserable, cowardly bully.'

Reeling across the yard from the force of Sir Richard's blow to his jaw, Angus tripped and fell to his knees. He dropped the cutting-whip. He looked dazed. He stayed so, on his knees on the cobblestones, shaking his head, trembling.

Sir Richard had dropped his horse's reins. The tall black animal stood quietly. He took the reins again with one hand, and with the other pulled me to my feet.

'Are you hurt, Jaikie?' he said, the anger leaving his face and voice.

'Na, a's braw,' I said, remembering to speak as Jaikie should.

'You're a brave lad. You did well. The Gordons shall hear of this. They will be pleased and proud. I'm glad I arrived when I did.'

'Me tu,' I said, with deep feeling.

'Do you feel well enough to put my horse into a stable, Jaikie?'

'Ay, certes,' I said. 'S'al Ah tak' awa' the seddle an' breedle?'

'Thank you, yes, if you can manage them. You'll find him quite gentle.'

'Ay, Ah ken 'im fine. He's a guid auld lad, hey, auld laddie?'

'I'll see what I can do for that other unfortunate creature.'

'Tak' care, Sir Ruchard!'

He smiled and nodded. I did like his smile so much.

I led his horse, which was gentle and kindly as he said, into an empty loose-box. I took off the tackle quickly, and rubbed him down where he had sweated under the saddle, and saw that there was water in the trough. He could have hay or a hard feed later, if Sir Richard wanted: but what I wanted was to see how Sir Richard fared with Goosefeather.

He was faring well.

He had untied her head. He was stroking her neck, and murmuring to her words of no meaning but unmistakable in tone. He was telling her he was very sorry she had been hurt, and it would not happen again; he loved her; she would always be treated kindly; she must be good and quiet now, because she was among friends.

Sir Richard glanced up, and saw me at the half-door.

He said, 'Can you find me a handful of oats in a scoop, Jaikie?'

'Ay, sir,' I said, and ran to fetch them.

Running was not easy. My head ached and my back was sore. There was no sign of Angus.

It was only after a long time, during which he never stopped gentling and caressing and murmuring soothingly to the filly, that he was able to persuade her to snuffle at the scoop of oats. As soon as she did so, we knew that she was over the worst. Even then he would not leave her, but remained by her head, soothing her, stroking her nose and fondling her ears and patting her neck.

He spoke to me, as well as to her, as I leaned in over the half-door. 'Horses are not clever animals, in the way that a good dog is clever,' he said. 'But they have very good memories. They never forget a bad fright or a beating. I think this filly should be put in a different box, because this one will always have unpleasant associations for her. She should never be tied up short by the head. When the smith comes to shoe her, someone should hold her head, instead of tying her up. She must never be shown a whip, at least not a cutting-whip.'

'She s'udna glempse Angus, forby,' I said.

'Angus? The fellow who whipped her? You're quite right, Jaikie—he must keep his face away from her.'

Robert Cochrane came back presently, and Sir Richard spoke to him at length, while they both made much of Goosefeather. They glanced at me from time to time, as I sat on my upturned bucket, having returned to polishing the buckles and studs of the harness. Robert Cochrane looked round for Angus, too, but the groom had disappeared.

Angus was dismissed from the stables, as everyone expected, after what Sir Richard told the Gordons. He was not dismissed from Inverdoran, but given employment on the home farm. I was surprised at this. Robert Cochrane explained the reason to me. Angus's father had been a groom for old General Gordon at Carnmore, and had suffered a crippling injury from a kicking horse. Of course the Gordons had looked after him, and after his family. Angus had a kind of reason to be frightened of horses, and to lose his temper with them. He became a groom because it was what his father wanted. His new life as a hedger, ditcher, reaper, woodcutter would be rougher, and lower down in the scale of the working folk. I expected he would blame me for his demotion. I expected he would feel vindictive. I was right.

Lancelot Gordon came home. There was great joy and celebration. Though a boy, he was the ewe-lamb of the household. I scarcely saw him. It seemed he lived indoors, with books, unlike the rest of the family.

The grouse shooting started. There was a big party at Inverdoran, and several visiting horses and carriages. The wagonette and dogcarts were in constant use for the shooting and for picnics, so hours were long in the stable-yard. We entertained the visiting grooms, as the indoors servants entertained the visiting ladies'-maids and body-servants, and as the Gordons entertained their resplendent friends. The story was often told about me and Angus and Sir Richard and Goosefeather, so that I received more kindness and attention than a raw young stable-lad was used to. I was grateful for the kindness, but I could have spared the curious attention.

I was still, as it chanced, given a surprising amount of privacy, in the personal business of washing and dressing and sleeping. I was still locked in at night.

About the twentieth of August, a party was taken to have a great picnic at the quarry—everybody had to be shown the estate's new venture. A party of the indoor servants came, to set up tables on trestles and to serve the picnic, and a parcel of grooms and coachmen, including me.

I wandered a little away from my fellow servants, after we had eaten our own copious meal: I was grateful for their kindness and their rough good-fellowship, but I was not through and through a stable-lad, and it was needful for me sometimes to find silence, and to breathe sweet air that was not clouded with the grooms' black tobacco.

I heard a familiar whisper, from the tall bracken near the quarry: 'Jaikiebogle!'

Benjie had been away with his new clan, but they had returned to this countryside because there were nowhere richer pickings for the tinkers.

He had delivered my message to the 'auld yin' at Myrtle Lodge, and had been given a meal in the kitchen of the house.

'Yon waur an ill dunner,' he said.

It seemed my parents' catering was no better, in spite of Carnmore's charity.

He had not seen the lady of the house. He understood she was ill and abed.

Benjie chattered on, in his hoarse whisper, his carroty thatch just visible in the forest of bracken. I was in full sight of many people; I was careful not to show that I was talking to anyone. I was watched, but not closely.

Except by one pair of eyes—those of the one-time vagrant, the quarryman who was not an evicted Carnmore crofter, who had the odd square jaw and the thin-lipped mouth.

Benjie saw him. 'Ma Goad,' he said, his whisper startled and urgent. 'Yon's Kenzie, wi'oot the beard. Ah didna ken 'im a' yince. Ay, yon's Kenzie!'

'Kenzie?' I said, behind my hand, the odd name meaning nothing to me.

'Yin o' Murdo's. Ma Goad. He kens ye, Jaikiebogle.'

Those eyes *were* familiar. I had not recognised the rest of the face, because I had seen it covered by a tinker's rough brown beard.

Thereafter, I never wandered away from the rest of the servants. As far as I could, I kept myself surrounded by them. It was not always pleasant, but it was safe.

Sir Richard Grant called at Inverdoran once or twice a week throughout September. He had business of various kinds with Mr Gordon—the quarry, the legal tussle with Carnmore, in which he had also involved himself, and other things about which even Robert Cochrane was vague. I knew Mrs Gordon strenuously encouraged these visits (you cannot keep such things from servants, though you may think you can) and it was rumoured among us grooms that Sir Richard would one day offer for Elspeth. At our level, the match was warmly approved.

'No' like, no' like at a',' said old Andrew, 'yon greedy lassie wha weddit Carnmore.'

I did *not* approve of the match. I had to admit to myself that it was thoroughly suitable. Elspeth would be a dutiful and adoring wife, a competent manager like her mother, an efficient hostess; she would understand the life of a place like Strathlarrig; she would be concerned about the tenants and servants and their families. It was all marvellously suitable, and I was very much against it.

I was not sure, either, that the servants had the rights of it. Sir Richard did not come to Inverdoran because of Elspeth, I thought; he even came in spite of her. I was sure he sometimes came and went without seeing her. Perhaps being adored by Elspeth would become a habit with him, and he would slip by degrees into an engagement with her. The thought revolted me.

Usually Sir Richard rode over from Strathlarrig; sometimes he drove a dogcart, with or without my friend Rory Crauford. I used to look after his horse. I was glad to do so, and he seemed glad to have me do so. He gave me a shilling, each time, for the rubbing-down and watering; as September turned to October, I amassed a good store of shillings.

As well as taking a kindly interest in Jaikie Bogle, Sir Richard kept an eye on Goosefeather. Angus had undone the work of weeks. The filly developed a great dislike of harness, tried to rub off even a halter, bit at her stable door and at her manger and hay-rack, and usually tried to bolt when she was led out of her box to be exercised on the long rein. Robert Cochrane began to despair of her: but Mr Gordon wanted to persevere, because she was so beautiful, and had cost such a lot of money. Sir Richard followed this saga with interest. He always looked in on Goosefeather, talked to her, offered her a titbit, and asked me how she was behaving.

One day he exclaimed as he stopped by her box, and called me over to him. She had splintered one of the thin wooden bars of her hay-rack, probably by wrenching at it with her teeth. It was now highly dangerous—she could damage her mouth or her eye on that jagged point of wood.

Sir Richard was sufficiently intimate with the Gordons to take charge of such a situation without consulting anybody. Between us, he and I persuaded Goosefeather out of her loose-box, stopped her bolting, and put her in another box, where I gave her an armful of hay to occupy her mind. We went back to her original box. Sir Richard himself climbed onto the manger, in order to pull away the broken bar from the hay-rack. But the manger creaked dangerously, and began to wobble away from the wall. Sir Richard jumped down at once.

'It was only meant to stand the weight of a bucketful of oats or a bran-mash,' he said. 'But it will hold you, Jaikie. Do you know what you have to do?'

I nodded, and jumped up onto the manger. I stood on the edge, and reached up to the hay-rack. I took hold of the broken bar, and tried to pull it away from the rack. It was firmly nailed, and resisted me. Sir Richard stood by, to catch me in case I fell. I waggled and twisted the broken bar, to loosen the nail; I tried again, and it came away suddenly, taking me by surprise. I fell off the manger. Sir Richard caught me, in both his arms. I clutched at him. My arms naturally went round his neck. For a moment we were pressed together, and my cheek was pressed against his.

I felt a surge of joy and excitement. I felt a wave of something utterly new to me. I felt I had come home. I felt the strength of his arms round me, and I knew I wanted them there for ever. My arms were tight round his neck, and my face tight against his.

For a second we remained so, holding each other, clamped together, my feet clear of the ground.

Then he gave a wordless cry. It sounded like horror and disgust. He dropped me. He pushed me away from him. He almost ran out of the loose-box.

My legs would not support me, they trembled so violently with the strength of my new emotion. My head spun and my heart pounded in my throat. I sank down, so that I sat in the straw of the stable. My hands were shaking, and tears welled out of my eyes.

I had thought myself in love with Carnmore. But I did not then know what love felt like.

9

I crouched weeping in the straw in Goosefeather's loose-box, feeling as though I had been picked up by an eagle, and swept for a second into an undreamt heaven, and then dropped again.

In my confusion, in my excitement, in my misery, all became clear to me.

I had been in love with Sir Richard Grant for weeks.

Without realising it, I had come to depend completely on his visits to Inverdoran, to need his smiles and his kindness, to look forward to nothing else, to look back on nothing else. A life that ought to have been impossibly empty and tedious was full and fascinating to me—because he was occasionally part of it.

It came to me, with renewed astonishment, that some part of me had fallen in love with him when he came to Myrtle Lodge, to warn me against Carnmore. He was threatening my future—what I thought to be my future—more than he knew: and that, perhaps, was why I had had him ejected by the navvies, and that was why I was glad when they threw him in the puddle of mud.

It came to me that some deep-hidden part of me—some tiny part, wise amidst the folly of the rest of me—had fallen in love with him when I went to Strathlarrig.

Ah God, I thought, was ever such an irony? When I was Catriona Douglas, free and female, I had supposed I hated him. I had certainly done everything possible to make him hate me. Now that I knew I loved him, I was married to Carnmore. I was not free. And, as a result, I was not even female.

What if I confided in him, knowing that he was a man of honour, that he was to be trusted completely? Well, what? Was I to invite him to break the law, by hiding a wife from her husband? Was I to invite him to make adulterous love to me? I thought he was no lawbreaker. I was very sure he was no adulterer. He would recoil in disgust from the idea—

As he had recoiled in disgust from Jaikie Bogle.

Of course he had. A stable-lad, clinging to him amorously like a girl.

My canvas stable-boy's coat was as stiff as the sail of a fishing-smack. His coat was of soft tweedy stuff, but had some kind of lining, perhaps buckram, equally stiff. Between the two, there had been a sort of board between us when we clung together, so that he had not felt my breasts pressed into his chest. And my breasts were not so very large. . . Even when his arms were tightest about me, he still thought I was a boy.

Men did not passionately embrace boys. At least, I had never heard of such a thing. I could not imagine a man who would do so—a man who would want to do so.

And then whispers came back to me, from a dozen years before, even as I crouched sobbing on the floor. The incautious murmurs of grooms and herds, during my childhood. The mysterious rumoured sins of a certain tradesman in Lochgrannomhead, a chubby draper— the naughty insinuating looks of a new page-boy in our own household, who did not stay there long—the sort of shreds and wisps which fascinate a child because of their very oddity, because of the horrified whispers in which grown-ups mention them. For all I knew, there might be a great army of such as the chubby draper, such as the pretty page-boy. But Sir Richard Grant was not of their number.

Perhaps he thought I was!

Perhaps he thought I had clung to him harder than I need, longer than I need, after I was already safe from falling.

I sniffed, and gulped, and trembled, and realised that I had. I was just as immodest, being a girl, as I would have been if I had been a boy.

A sense of my immodesty swept over me, like a cold incoming tide: because I realised I had been longing to embrace Sir Richard for days, for weeks, without realising it—and when the nail pulled out of the hay-rack, and I found myself caught in his arms, no power on earth would have stopped mine from going round his dear neck, even though my feet had already been safe on the ground!

And the girl was a saucy boy. And she must go on being so.

Sir Richard's arms had been about me, as long as mine were about him, as tight as mine were about him. To stop me from falling. Only to stop me from falling? For a whole second, perhaps, after I was safe from falling?

I heard a clatter of hoofs in the stable-yard. Sir Richard was leaving. He had saddled and bridled his horse by himself. He had not wanted my help. He would not want it again. I should not again see his smile, or hear the kindness in his voice. I should have no more silver shillings from him. He would want no dealings, ever again, with the stable-lad whom he would rank with the long-ago simpering page-boy at Strathlarrig.

He would not want so much as to set an eye on a creature so abandoned and insidious as Jaikie Bogle. No decent man would. What, then? He would come no more to Inverdoran? Was that possible? He would come to the house, but no more to the stables? Was *that* possible? Would he allow himself to be so greatly inconvenienced—to be inconvenienced in the smallest degree—by one such as Jaikie Bogle? Why should he? He would come to Inverdoran, and to the stables, as soon as he was sure of not seeing me there. *That* was possible. A word to the Gordons, from him, would banish me. A warning. The merest hint. They liked and esteemed him; he was closely involved in some of their projects; and they had hopes—Mrs Gordon and Elspeth had hopes. . .

I would be sent to join Angus on the Home Farm, perhaps. More likely I would be sent back, with dark and disgusted hints, to the Procurator Fiscal; and from there I would go to the Boys' Orphanage; and there, when I slept and dressed in a room with a dozen others. . .

The others returned. Noon came, then evening. I waited for a summons.

Nothing was said to me. Sir Richard Grant had not demanded my dismissal, or warned anybody against me.

Life in the stable-yard was indeed tedious and even squalid, unredeemed by his visits, by his smile and his voice and his kindness. But I was still there. I was not on the farm or in the orphanage. I was in misery, but I was safe.

I was in misery, because love had come to me too late. There was one man in the world I wanted, and I could not have him. My greed and folly had put him out of my reach for ever. For ever! I might live to be a hundred, and I should not have my heart's desire. And it was my own fault.

The pit I had dug myself was deeper, deeper far, than ever I thought. I had put myself at the mercy of a drunken madman, my owner body and soul, because I wanted a few jewels and a big, warm house: because I wanted horses and carriages, servants and respect. I had condemned myself to the life of a fugitive beggar: then to a drab little servant's life. I had cut myself off from my parents, and from the whole world to which I belonged. I thought that was my punishment—the worst possible. It was not. There was more. Only now did I realise how much more. Only now did I feel the lash of my real punishment. I would not have the man I craved. Never, never, never, never, never. No other man would do. I did not want any other, ever. I knew this with utter certainty. There was only one for me, and I could not have him.

Day and night, every minute of every hour, I felt those powerful arms about me, and that face pressed against mine. I should not have realised, perhaps, the depth and power of my own feelings, but for those remembered arms, that remembered cheek. Those physical sensations had shown me to myself. A split-second of delirious happiness had made possible the sharpness of this misery.

Before, I had been a starveling in a world without meat. Now I knew there was meat—a banquet spread with the best of everything— forever just out of my reach. I had been shown it. I had tasted it. And instantly the furies snatched it away from me.

I had snatched it away from myself, when I married Carnmore for his money.

Robert Cochrane called me sharply to order. He said I had taken to daydreaming. He said I was no better than a great girl.

Looking at me closely, he said that I was pale and tired. Kind at bottom as always, he asked if I were eating and sleeping. Well, I was not sleeping. And I was not eating much, either, as old Andrew told him.

Robert Cochrane said he would send to the housekeeper for a physic. I believe he did so. A bottle arrived at the stables, full of blackish liquid with a fearful smell. I was to take a tablespoonful at bedtime. I had trouble pouring away the stuff, spoonful by spoonful, after my door was locked each night. Nothing out of a bottle would help what ailed me, except arsenic.

I never was tempted to that, even when, in the small hours of the morning, the sense of what I had thrown away turned a spade inside my heart. I was credited with spirit. I was proud of what I called my courage. Now was the time to show it.

But I was a very young girl in very great unhappiness, and though I managed to hide most of my tears, I could not stop them falling.

The weather held fine into the middle of October. Stags were coming down off the hill, shot by Mr Gordon's most energetic guests—though not by himself, as he was not built for deer-stalking, nor by Lancelot Gordon, who kept his nose in his books even in the glorious autumn. The heather had been a sea of purple; now the bracken was a sea of tawny gold. The nights were becoming cold, but, out of the wind, the midday sunshine was sometimes very hot.

The weather allowed the new quarry still to be worked, although in most seasons the track to it would have been impassable by now. One day Mr Gordon ordered the wagonette, to go up to the quarry for a last careful inspection before the winter. It was past the season for picnics, but Elspeth, they told me, was to go with her father. That made me guess that Sir Richard would be there. That made me wonder very hard if I should be there.

I was torn between a longing to see him and a dread of seeing him. I have heard that this is quite usual, among people who are hopelessly in love. God knew what my face would show, if I found myself near him. I did not think I should be able to control the twitching and working of my mouth; I might go scarlet, or chalk-white, or both, in circus patches; I should very likely weep.

I was to go, although Robert Cochrane was to go too.

Elspeth was, I thought, even less good at hiding her feelings than I. I did not know if Sir Richard had been recently at Inverdoran. I did not know if he had said anything to her, recently or at any time, to encourage the hopes she made so very evident. I did not think he would trifle with her. I did guess that she would build very high on anything at all that he said—interpreting a conventional politeness as an expression of particular regard, and inflating an enquiry after her health into little short of a protestation of love.

I knew about that building of cathedrals on chance remarks. I had done it myself.

He was there, indeed, tall as a tree on his tall black horse, his face as strong as a tree, and with the irregularity I loved so well, like the weathered bark of an oak. He jumped off his horse, when he saw the wagonette, and handed his reins to Rory Crauford. He started to stride towards us.

He saw me, holding onto the 'spoon' at the back, as a good groom should. He stopped dead. He coloured. I had never seen colour flood into his face before, or I think into any man's. It was a bright blush, like a girl's. The blood that suffused his face went as quick as it came, leaving behind an expression of disgust and wretchedness. I thought suddenly of the sea, as I remembered it on the north coast of France, and of the tide sucking outwards, and leaving a sad grey waste of sand and mud. That was how his face was, when he stared haggardly at the wagonette.

I do not think that Mr Gordon, or Elspeth, or Rory Crauford, or anybody else that was by, could have seen those expressions on his face. Though some knew him far better than I did, I knew him far better than they did, because I loved him. My love let me see—forced me to see—the disgust with which he looked at me, and his anguish at having touched—having befriended—so vicious a boy.

Stopping, Sir Richard made a pretence of adjusting the garter of his riding boot. That gave him a reason to come no nearer the wagonette, and a reason to turn away his face from us.

Mr Gordon jumped down, and helped Elspeth down, and walked towards Sir Richard. He called to Robert Cochrane to follow them, as the coachman could advise about the haulage of the stone. Sir Richard straightened as they approached. He glanced at the wagonette, to make sure, I thought, that it was coming no nearer. He had command of his face now, and of its colour.

I was startled that a little stable-lad could have so great an effect on a rich gentleman; even though that effect was visible only to the stable-lad.

I led the pony and the wagonette, and Rory Crauford the two Strathlarrig horses, to the patch of stringy hill grass where they could graze. Rory Crauford was as merry and friendly as ever.

'Och, laddie,' he said, looking at me with concern over his pipe-bowl, 'wha' ails ye?'

'Naethin', Muster Crauford. Ah'm as braw as aye.'

'Ye luk a wee bit seedy. Robert Cochrane s'ud hae gi'd ye a phessic.'

'He did tha'. It waur awfu', it reekit o' peet-hags. Ah drippit it awa' doon a dren. Ah culdna hauld siccan mextur tae ma belly.'

Even as I spoke, I was gazing at Sir Richard, without thinking to try to hide what I was feeling. I must have looked like a calf gawping at a trough of turnips. Rory Crauford glanced at my face, began to grin, and twisted his head to see what I stared at so hungrily.

He thought I was looking at Elspeth.

'Hey, laddie,' he gasped, 'ye're ettlin' tae wed the young leddy? I wush ye a' joy, bairnie, she's a bonny lassie eneuch, wi' a ruckle o' siller. Hoots toots, wull ye hae's tae the weddin'?'

I forced a smile, a very strained and self-conscious smile. Tears were pricking at my lids, because my love, who hated me, stood a dozen yards away. My unhappy smile made Rory Crauford think he was right. He burst out laughing. At the same time he patted my shoulder, to show me he meant me no ill by his teasing. Indeed I knew that, because I knew there was no ill-will in his whole body.

The others heard his laughter—the stags on the next forest would have heard it. They glanced in our direction. Robert Cochrane looked a little shocked; Elspeth looked only surprised; Mr Gordon was unable to stop himself smiling, in response to Rory Crauford's infectious laugh; Sir Richard's face was impenetrable. He turned away at once. He began talking earnestly to Mr Gordon, whose face changed as he listened, and who glanced towards me.

This was the end, then. I must be ready to run away. Inverdoran had served its turn.

I sauntered, casual as could be, over to the bank of bracken where Benjie hid when he came to the quarry. I waited there. There was no purpose in searching, or calling. If he was there, he would have seen me. He was not there. It had been a faint outside chance. He would have helped me to run away, before I was sent to the Procurator Fiscal, and the orphanage, and so back to Carnmore. Well, I must manage on my own.

And this time, the Gordons and the Inverdoran servants would be after me, as well as Carnmore and his people, and the Fiscal and the police, and my own parents, and Murdo and his clan. . .

Several of the workmen were busy in the quarry, whom I could see from where I stood by the bracken. One was the square-jawed, clean-shaven man whom Benjie had recognised. Kenzie, Murdo's man. He was there: and when the quarry was abandoned for the winter, some other work would be found for him. I would still be under Murdo's eye, even if I stayed at Inverdoran. And one day I would be under his hand.

Sir Richard called away Rory Crauford, and they rode away up the hill. I was surprised—I had expected one of the long quarry conferences. Mr Gordon looked surprised, too—he had clearly expected a longer meeting. And so had Elspeth.

For myself, I was once more torn. Part of me was devoutly thankful to see Sir Richard's broad shoulders receding up the hillside beside his small hunched groom; and part screamed inside my head that I wanted him to stay where I could look at him . . .

'Wa's up wi' ye an' Sir Ruchard, laddie?' Robert Cochrane asked me, when we were taking the wagonette back to the stable-yard.

'Naethin', Muster Cochrane,' I said, trying to look surprised and innocent.

'I didna hear a' he said tae the laird, but Gordon said; "Nae, nae, Grant, wee Bogle maun bide at Inverdoran. We hae a duty tae the bairn," says Gordon.'

'Sir Ruchard waur ettlin' tae hae me dismissit, Muster Cochrane?'

'Ay, or awa' frae the stables intil the hoose or the fairm. He doesna wush ye tae clash wi' ony o' his folk. Or the Inverdoran folk, eether; sae he adveesit the laird.'

'Ah'll no' gi' 'em the fever, Muster Cochrane.'

'Sae said the laird. "Bogle wull no' gi' owr folk the leproshy, Grant," says he. "I doot he wull," says Grant, "a kind o' leproshy." But the laird stud firm. "Wee Bogle bides tae Inverdoran," says he, "as we promissit the Procurator Fisca".'

Well, I could not truthfully blame Sir Richard. If I had been what he thought I was—and, dear God, what else was he to think?—I might have spread a kind of evil contagion, perhaps. That was how the herds and grooms had spoken, long ago in my childhood, when they whispered with a certain horrified glee about the draper and the page-boy. A contagion, yes, so they had called it: and when I had asked Miss MacRae what that meant, she had told me without realising what she was telling me. And Sir Richard called it a leprosy. It was his duty, perhaps, to have me removed to where I could do no harm. Or at least not that particular harm. It was neighbourly of him to warn the Gordons against me—as it had been neighbourly to warn me against Carnmore.

I could not in conscience blame him. But I did.

I was profoundly thankful that Mr Gordon stood firm by his promise to the Procurator Fiscal. I was profoundly grateful to him and to the rest of his family.

And the irony of it all struck me so hard that I began to laugh, even as I mucked out a loose-box with a pitchfork. Sir Richard was seeking to have me removed from my refuge—*because* he was convinced that I was an evil, perverted boy—*because* of that moment when he and I had had our arms about each other—which was *because* . . . and the chain went on, and on, and came at last to the point that he was seeking to send me, inadvertently, to a fate he could not guess at, against which he himself had warned me, *because* I had inadvertently disgusted him, *because* I loved him, which was *because* he was good and honourable, and *that* was exactly why he was trying to destroy me, although he did not know that that was what he was doing . . .

On and on and round and round went the chain, and it was a rare jest, the whole mad circle of it, and some cruel god must be laughing as hard as I, and probably in just such an eldritch, hysterical note—but the god's laughter would not be turning into racking sobs and a cataract of scalding tears, as mine did, causing old Andrew to stare in at me through the stable door with a face of wooden disapproval.

At eleven o'clock next morning (when I was still inclined to be watery-eyed) Rory Crauford walked two horses into the stable-yard. One was Sir Richard Grant's tall black, with an empty saddle. Sir Richard was calling on Mr Gordon. Rory Crauford said he was dressed as though for a banquet at Holyrood: but I was not sure that the dear little monkey-groom knew what was worn at Holyrood banquets.

At noon the message came to us that Sir Richard was joining the family for luncheon. Rory Crauford joined us. He and the horses were not called for until four.

It was a very long call for so busy a man as Sir Richard.

All the time I knew he was in the big house, not fifty yards away, my heart yearned towards it, and recoiled from it.

In the evening, the effective telegraph system of the servants tinkled the message from the house to the stables: Sir Richard had offered for Miss Elspeth.

There was great jubilation, and we all drank extra pots of beer.

I had no business to cry myself to sleep, when I was already and irrevocably married.

'Here's an unco' strange affair,' said Robert Cochrane, two days later, early in the afternoon. 'A letter tae Lord Carnmore. Tae be deliverit intil his lordship's ane hand, an' a reply tae be brocht hame.'

The astonishment was general.

'A letter frae the laird?' said old Andrew. 'The laird wullna enter the sam' hoose wi' yon Carnmore. He'll no' wreet yin waird tae siccan chiel.'

'Sae ye'd hae thocht,' agreed Robert Cochrane. 'But Ah hae the letter tae yon wee laither pooch, tae be deliverit intil Carnmore's hand. An' the reply tae be brocht the nicht, tae the hand o' the laird.'

'Is't wha' they ca' an olive-branch?'

'I doot it's nae siccan ting, Andra.'

''Tis verra strange.'

''Tis wairse. Forby, 'tis a breach wi' preecedent.'

A groom called James, a dull, steady man whom I had scarcely got to know in more than three months, was sent off on horseback with the letter in its pouch round his shoulder.

As always—and just as it would have been in the servants'-hall in the house—there was interminable speculation about that letter. All the men knew how bitterly the Gordons resented Carnmore's occupation of the place from which came his title; how greatly this resentment was increased by Carnmore's evictions; how hard they had tried to buy the place back; how firmly they had been rebuffed. Lancelot, apple of his mother's eye, would one day reign at Carnmore as his grandfather had—or Mrs Gordon would go near dying in the attempt. From the way the old grooms spoke, they would have died with her in the same cause. And I felt near as passionate about it, too, not only because of what I knew about Carnmore's soul, but also from the profoundest gratitude to the Gordons for their kindness to Jaikie Bogle.

Speculation about the letter extended into speculation about Carnmore's wife (a subject which had been rested for a welcome week or two). It was an ill ploy, they all once again said, to marry a man for his silver. But it was a sad and strange thing for a young bride to lie sick abed from Midsummer Day into the middle of October, with not a soul to see her but a doctor from a strange place.

I wondered what Sir Richard Grant thought about it.

The message that came back from Carnmore was verbal, not written. James delivered it to Mr Gordon, before he reported all that had happened to all the rest of us in the stable-yard at supper time.

He had delivered the pouch, as he had been ordered, personally into Carnmore's hand, at the gateway into the courtyard of the castle. Carnmore had read the letter with a strange expression on his face. James could not describe the expression. I could not imagine it—well as I knew all Carnmore's expressions—because I did not know what was in the letter. Like the others, I was sure it was not an olive-branch. Like them, I doubted if it could be another offer to repurchase the castle and estate, since that had been tried too often, and too often failed. It was not likely to be about the evictions, since all had said, and bitterly, on that sore subject, and a law-suit was pending still. It was not like to have any bearing on Elspeth's engagement to Sir Richard—Carnmore and the Gordons did not attend each other's family weddings, as I had cause to know. Well, then? God knew. So I could not guess what Carnmore's face might have been, from the various faces he had.

He read the letter again and again, James said, with first one strange expression and then another. For all his dourness, James had the gift of story-telling. He had us all on tenterhooks.

'On wi' ye, mon!' cried Robert Cochrane in exasperation.

'I maun tell it as it tuk place,' said James, maddeningly.

Tell it he did, slowly, with impressive silences.

First Carnmore said it was a lie, an impudent trick. James could not answer this, as he knew no more what was in the letter than the rest of us.

Then Carnmore fell to cursing most horribly. (That I could imagine. I had heard his oaths, his blasphemies, in my cushioned bedroom in his house.)

'"Ma Goad," creed Carnmore,' began James with relish.

'Whisht!' said Robert Cochrane. 'Here's a wee laddie ahint ye, James! Stop yer lugs, Bogle!'

We were not allowed to hear what oaths Carnmore used.

Recovering himself, Carnmore said he would come, at the time appointed, to the place appointed, which he knew. That message could be taken to Mr Gordon.

What was the time appointed? No one knew. What was the place appointed? No one knew.

It did not seem likely that I would be by, at this extraordinary rendezvous. But I must be ready to fly further and hide myself deeper than ever from any knife of Murdo's.

As in most establishments, the coachman or the head groom reported to the house each evening to get orders for the morrow. Sometimes a footman or a page-boy trotted out to the stables in the morning, with different or additional orders. This was almost always an aggravation, as horses had to be groomed and bridles or harness got ready in a hurry.

That evening, the orders were that the landau was wanted at eleven in the morning, with the top closed up if the weather looked bad, to take Miss Elspeth and Mr Lancelot to Strathlarrig. Fiancée was to take luncheon with fiancé, chaperoned by her brother. Robert Cochrane himself was to take them, with any groom he pleased except Jaikie Bogle.

That, I thought, was so that Sir Richard Grant should not be subjected to the infuriation of seeing me.

Also, the brougham was wanted at half-past eleven. The master and mistress had a business appointment. Willie the undercoachman was to take them, with any groom he pleased except Jaikie Bogle.

It crossed my mind—it crossed the minds of all the others—that the Gordons were away to meet Carnmore. In the light of this possibility, I was deeply thankful that I was not to come. But I wondered why I was not. Perhaps the Gordons thought the sight of me would enrage Carnmore, too.

There was no actual mention, in the orders, of Carnmore's arrival. Still none of us knew when he was to come, or where. I did not know what place to stay away from, or what hour to be alert.

On my straw mattress that night, I did not think every waking moment, and dream every sleeping moment, about Sir Richard Grant, as I had been doing. I thought about Carnmore also, and puzzled what the Gordons could be at, to arrange a meeting—if that was what they had arranged—with their most hated enemy. So, following my thoughts, Carnmore came into my dreams also, and I woke myself by the cry of despair and revulsion which his face in my dreams forced out of me.

A footman came to the stable-yard in the morning, just as we were finishing our porridge and eggs.

Bogle was to come at once to the house, just as he was, and report to Mrs McRibbie the housekeeper.

'Tae be meashurit for mair breeches?' suggested old Andrew.

The footman shrugged. He did not know why I was summoned. He did not care. But he was impatient to take me. I thought his own breakfast had been interrupted.

I went with him, utterly puzzled: and for the first time in my life set foot inside Inverdoran House. I did not like it. It was as dark as I had supposed, with the big trees too near the windows. It was the darker because of the gloomy paints and papers Mrs Gordon had chosen. As in many Scottish houses, there was tartan everywhere, too much tartan, as though the Gordons were preparing to raise a regiment of Highlanders, and dress them in kilt and plaid. Though large, the house had none of the gigantic magnificence of Strathlarrig; certainly it had none of the fascinating antiquity of Carnmore. The inside was drab, like the outside. No wonder the family wanted to move. The wonder was that they had ever gone there. So I thought, as I trotted behind the footman towards the housekeeper's room, trying not to let my mind dwell on whatever hazards awaited me.

Andrew's theory did seem a good one. I had had no new clothes since my arrival, only those left behind by the boy who had broken his head. There were two or three of everything, but with winter coming I did need more. I dreaded being measured for them. My jacket must come off, and a tape-measure go about my bosom . . .

The housekeeper's room was a good deal brighter than the halls and passages I had seen, with chintz to the chairs and a small coal fire to the grate. A big bright picture of the Queen hung over the fireplace, and on the mantelpiece was an infinity of shells and china ornaments.

I had never seen Mrs McRibbie. Housekeepers do not come to stable-yards. She seemed to me what a very young maidservant might imagine, when she had a nightmare about a dragon of a housekeeper. She was big and square, with a big square red face, and grey hair drawn back as hard and smooth as a polished gravestone, and little hard grey eyes, and the suspicion of a grey moustache. She was dressed with great magnificence in black. Standing by the fire, she towered over me as—as Sir Richard Grant had done.

'Sae,' she said, in a voice like a man's, 'this is the yin that s'al bring puir Master Lancelot tae his ane.'

I blinked at her, more completely puzzled than ever.

The footman went out, but, before he shut the door behind him, Mrs Gordon came through it.

'Ah,' she said briskly, 'the child is here. Are we ready, Mrs McRibbie?'

'Ay, mem. What s'al we du aboot the hair?'

'A shawl tied to conceal the hair, but tied well back from the face.'

'It willna luk verra smart, mem.'

'It need not.' She laughed briefly. The laugh did not get as far as her eyes. She looked determined and a little excited, as I imagined a gambler might look before making a dangerous and final wager.

She turned to me at last, and looked me up and down with a slight smile. There was something so cold about her smile that it frightened me more than a scowl would have done. When I had first seen her at close quarters, in the Procurator Fiscal's office in Lochgrannomhead, I had thought her smile cool. Then I had found it grown warm. Now it was as cold as the ice on a puddle on a January hilltop.

'Off with those clothes, child,' she said.

I gaped at her. It was absolutely the last thing I expected her to say.

'Quick, child. Don't keep me standing here waiting. We have time enough but not time to spare. Do you want me to get in a man to strip you?'

'Ye ken . . .?' I began, hardly able to speak in my astonishment and dismay.

'Don't bother to put on that idiotic voice. The time for that is past.'

'You know . . .?' I started again, still having great difficulty in talking.

'Yes of course. Why do you suppose you've been allowed to live like a nun? Bath in private, bedroom private—all very annoying for Robert Cochrane. He never saw the purpose or the justice of it. He's a comfortingly stupid man, or the reason might have occurred to him. He knows nothing, of course. Nor shall he know. That's why he's gone to Strathlarrig. Now for goodness' sake take those clothes off, and let's see if these others will fit you.'

I did not want to strip in front of them. But I less wanted a man brought in to strip me. I was sure, by Mrs Gordon's eye, that she would carry out her threat, if I delayed. So with numbed fingers I began to undo the manly buttons and buckles of my coat and shirt and breeches. I had become so very used to them, in more than three months! My mind was spinning with shock. Because I trembled and fumbled, Mrs Gordon began to help me, with efficient, impatient hands. It was she, more than I, who pulled my clothes off: so that I stood naked as a baby in front of the fire in the bright, fussy housekeeper's room.

'She's bonny,' said Mrs McRibbie, staring at me appraisingly.

I was embarrassed and annoyed to be stared at so by a servant.

'You are impertinent,' I said. 'Give me some clothes.'

Perhaps it was not a wise remark. I had taken a dislike to Mrs McRibbie.

'Ha!' said Mrs Gordon. 'The spirit of the stable-boy departs with the breeches. The daughter of a thousand earls returns, albeit somewhat underdressed.'

'The daughter of . . .'

'It's that mole by your eye, you know. Exactly like your mother's. If I hadn't happened to see that, through the mud on your nice little face, I would never have guessed you weren't a thieving tinker-boy. But once I saw it, of course, I saw the rest.'

Naked as I was, daughter of a thousand earls as she said I was, I sat down suddenly in a chintzy upright chair. My legs would not support me, as I took in what I was hearing.

She had recognised me by my mole, the one placed as Mamma's was, the one they said was just like the patch of a society beauty of Queen Anne's day . . . Seeing that, she saw the rest, my face altogether, my feminine body in spite of the filthy baggy clothes I wore, the remnants of Carnmore's wedding suit . . .

'Put these on, child, and be decent,' said Mariota Gordon impatiently, pulling from a cupboard stockings and underclothes.

I struggled to dress myself, fumbling, my hands trembling. I found it most extraordinary to feel my legs in skirts, to feel silk next to my skin, for the first time since Midsummer Night.

I remembered a moment in the carriage, when we had driven away from the office in Lochgrannomhead. She had felt the cloth of my coat, and looked at the silk of my shirt. Any doubt she had had, she had resolved.

She was a clever woman.

'Why?' I said suddenly, and I think more violently than I intended. 'You'll see.'

'Was it charity, as you pretended?'

'I am charitable to my own. I have no obligation to you.'

She was using me. How I should soon know. From the first moment, she had picked me up as a useful tool for some task, some project. She had let me think I was hiding in safety in the stables at Inverdoran, hoodwinking them all. It was I who was hoodwinked. She was keeping me on ice, like a piece of salmon, until I was ready to be served. Today I was to be served.

They always said she was a good manager.

No wonder I had had no lessons in reading and writing. She knew very well I had no need of them.

No wonder I had not been fitted for more groom's or stable-boy's clothes. She knew very well I would have no need of them.

No wonder I had not been dismissed, to the farm or the Fiscal or the orphanage. She had need of me.

They shook out a silk dress between them, when I stood ready in the chemise. It was a bright pale blue, a pretty colour, a colour that suited me because it matched my eyes.

I was thinking like a girl again.

'Colour's right,' said Mrs Gordon with a sort of sour satisfaction, echoing the thought that was in my head at that moment. 'I hope the size is. This was made for another girl, but she's much like you.'

'Near eneuch, mem,' said Mrs McRibbie, as though she would have grudged me a gown that fitted too perfectly.

'Yes, we're not trying to marry the child.'

This made Mrs McRibbie smile—a hard, brief stretching of that hard face. It did not make me smile. I did not know what it meant.

I was like a log, a puppet, a baby, being prodded and fiddled into the dress, unable to do anything for myself, still suffocating with amazement.

And very angry about the way I had been duped, at the way I was being made use of as though I were a spade or a dog-cart, at the gratitude I had wasted on this cold, greedy, selfish woman. I knew she was those things, because I had once been them myself.

As well as angry, I was very puzzled and alarmed about her plans.

'Shoes?' said Mrs Gordon.

'Here, mem. They fit the ither lassie.'

They were dainty enough slippers, in white silk, a little too large for my feet.

'Gloves?'

They were long and white, very fine, but too large also.

'Han's an' fit like a doll,' said Mrs McRibbie, sniffing.

'Like a lady,' I said, surprising myself, speaking with a defiance I was far from feeling.

'Just so, my dear,' said Mrs Gordon. 'And you look like one, except for that distressing shaven head. The silk shawl, Mrs McRibbie. Yes. So . . . And so . . .'

Her hands pushed my head this way and that, with a sort of efficient brutality. (You do not treat gently with spades, or any other unimportant tools.) She wrapped the shawl tight round my head, and gathered it at the nape of my neck, as though it hid a normal amount of female hair.

'Now you can look at yourself, Catriona.'

Suddenly to hear my name was, I think, the greatest shock of all.

Mrs McRibbie opened the cupboard door. Inside it was a full-length looking-glass. I saw myself. Not Jaikie Bogle, but Catriona. A

slender young lady, in blue that matched her eyes. Colour high—
cheeks pink with rage and alarm. Beautiful, people had often said. Innocent, to all seeming.

It was utterly impossible to believe that this elegant, feminine
reflection facing me had been, a bare three-quarters of an hour before,
a grubby little stable-boy, eating porridge among grooms with a tin
spoon.

So we all stood for a moment, I looking in blank disbelief at myself:
the two women looking critically at me.

'An' this is the yin,' said Mrs McRibbie again, 's'al bring puir master
Lancelot his ane.'

'I believe she will,' said Mariota Gordon. 'God send she will.'

I was in the power of two women, neither young. Yet I was as helpless as I had ever been.

The dizzying shock I had had—the bewilderment of finding myself a
girl again—made me unable to guess what was coming to me, what
sort of tool was to be, what sort of work I was to be pressed into.

This was foolish of me, as they had all but told me right out how I
was to be used.

Even if I had seen the next hour as clear as I could see my own foot,
there was nothing I could have done. The spade cannot run away
from the gardener who grips it—and who has an army of gardeners
behind him, to catch the spade if it should learn the trick of running.

More things were pulled out of Mrs McRibbie's cupboard. A voluminous cloak, with a hood like a monk's: and a black lace veil, such as
a pious widow wears at her man's burial. The veil was thrown over
my head, so that I could scarcely see, and the cloak thrown about me,
so that I could scarcely move.

I tried to see myself once again in the full-length glass: but all I
could see was a sort of conical shrouded figure, like a dreadful Inquis-
itor in the illustrated stories of my childhood.

There was no comfort in remembering childhood stories, at that moment.

I glanced at the two women, the terrible women—the one whom I
had never seen before, the other I had thought my kindest benefactor.
More than ever I saw the look of gleeful, almost fearful excitement,
and I thought again of something I had never seen, the face of a gambler on the point of making a last and desperate throw, and certain—
almost certain—of winning.

Mrs Gordon unlocked the door. They took me out of the room.

They kept me between them, all along the back passages to the side door where I had entered. Cloaks and bonnets hung from pegs inside the door. Mrs Gordon wrapped herself up, while Mrs McRibbie held my arm; then Mrs McRibbie wrapped herself up, while Mrs Gordon held my arm. Each had a grip like a man's. We went out of the house, myself between them. I felt like a very small thief, between two very large Constables of Police.

Outside the door was the brougham, with the two sturdy fat ponies harnessed to it. The curtains were drawn over the windows.

I had cleaned the harness, the previous evening, when the brougham was ordered.

By the horses' heads stood Willie the undercoachman. He looked without curiosity at the group which approached the carriage—two familiar ladies, and some small unknown mourning female between them. On the box-seat, ready with his whip, sat Mr Gordon.

A footman I did not know helped Mrs Gordon into the closed carriage, then me, then Mrs McRibbie. I was placed beside Mrs McRibbie. Mrs Gordon sat opposite. When the door was closed on us, it was dark inside the carriage, because of the curtains over the windows.

I was still bemused. I was still angry.

I heard someone climb up onto the box beside Mr Gordon. I heard the swish of the whip, and Mr Gordon's voice telling Willie to let go of the horses. I heard the crunch of gravel under the wheels. We were moving.

I felt that we were going gently downhill. That meant, down the drive to the lochside road. It seemed to me that we turned away from the town, and went along the loch in the other direction. I could see nothing through the curtained windows. I did not know how far we went, or how long we sat jolting on the leather cushions. I felt that we turned off the macadamised road onto a rougher track. The brougham bounced uncomfortably, though Mr Gordon went very slow. Mrs McRibbie, pressed against me, felt like a great man-of-war, like the side of a mountain.

There was no conversation at all, all the way, until Mrs Gordon suddenly said, 'It's a good many years since you were Master Lancelot's nurse, Mrs McRibbie.'

'Ay, mem, ye tuk him awa' tae schule lang syne. But I'll no' forget he's my bairn.'

Mrs Gordon nodded.

I understood that Lancelot Gordon—the bookworm I had still never set eyes on—was the apple of Mrs McRibbie's eye, as well as of his mother's. She would do anything for him, as Mrs Gordon would. She would commit any atrocity. What atrocity were they committing?

We climbed, then descended. The track grew very bumpy. I could not guess where we were. I could hear only the rattle of the horses' feet, the rumble of the wheels, the squeaking of the springs, the thudding of my own heart.

Mrs Gordon's eyes were bright, and her mouth was a little open. She looked like a gambler about to make his last throw, like a bride on her way to the church, like a child being led towards the Christmas tree.

We stopped. I heard the boots of the two on the box, as they scrambled down. The door was thrown open. Mr Gordon held it. Mrs Gordon got down first, ignoring the arm her husband offered.

'Catriona,' she said sharply.

I jumped, at hearing my name. I climbed awkwardly to the ground, hampered by my voluminous cloak. Mrs McRibbie descended, like a gradual avalanche, with Mr Gordon's help. I found myself again between the two women.

We were on the lochside. It was a place I knew, called Barrachrail, where there had once been a farm. I thought it was Ardno ground. The land sloped up from the lochside, dry grass, rocks, then a great sea of empty heather. I heard the chatter of grouse, and saw a small pack, far away, swinging very fast and low to the ground, high up the hillside.

Beside us were the low grey ruins of the farmhouse and steading of Barrachrail. I wondered, numbly, if it was a place the tinkers ever used.

Before us was the loch, steely under a quiet grey sky, for the day was overcast and windless.

The far bank was only a hundred yards away: for this was the point at which Loch Grannom, shaped like an hourglass, narrowed to its central waist. Barrachrail stood on a sort of point; a much sharper and longer point jutted from the far side. There was no road on the far side, no dwelling, no tree, nothing. I could see a few specks of white on the bare ground—sheep: and then the big hills rising behind.

To cross the loch at this point would be the work of a few minutes for a man in a boat, or for a strong swimmer. To go round by land, either way, would be thirty-five miles or more.

At the water's edge, pulled a little out onto a black, gravelly strand, was a boat—an ordinary small rowing-boat, painted dark green, dirty. There were oars in the rowlocks, and a coil of rope in the bows. Beside the boat stood a big man in bonnet and breeches and sea-boots. I had never seen him before. I had never seen before the man who stood at the horses' heads.

There was no other boat at Barrachrail. There was no boat on the far bank.

The boatman looked at me curiously. I thought he tried to penetrate my veil.

Mr Gordon's face showed all the excitement, the expectancy, of his wife's. He was even less able to conceal his feelings, far less strict at controlling himself. He twitched with tension; his hands shook as mine had done, undressing and dressing in the housekeeper's room.

In a hoarse, high, unfamiliar voice, Mr Gordon called to the boatman, 'Good man, John. I'm glad to see you.'

The boatman touched his bonnet. He said nothing. He was still staring at me.

And I was wondering what in God's name we were at, here with carriage and boat and housekeeper at this beautiful desolate place, and myself dressed up as Lady Catriona—as Lady Carnmore . . .

Some waterfowl floated motionless far out in the loch. A hawk wheeled. There was a great silence.

Mr Gordon pulled out his watch from his waistcoat pocket, then nodded to his wife, as though too tense to speak.

Between them, she and Mrs McRibbie took me to the water's edge, to the boat. Brusquely, Mrs Gordon pulled the cloak from about me, and pulled the veil from my face. I stood on the shingle in the blue silk dress, with the silk shawl over my head.

At a nod from Mrs Gordon, the boatman picked me up with both hands to my waist, and lifted me into the boat. He was enormously strong. He was gentler than Mrs Gordon. I found myself sitting on the small wooden seat in the stern of the boat. It was damp. There was no cushion. Nothing could have been less important. There was a little splash of water in the bottom of the boat, and a tin baler: nothing else.

The boatman pushed the bows of the boat clear of the shingle, and once it was afloat climbed aboard. The boat rocked violently for a moment. He picked up the oars, spun the boat round, and began rowing towards the far bank, at the water's narrowest point.

I looked over my shoulder, at the place we had left. None of them had moved. They stood like statues, like herons, at the edge of the water.

We were going to the far bank, to a very empty and deserted place. Why? The boatman and I alone. Why?

'Please tell me what is happening!' I cried suddenly. 'Where are we going? Where are you taking me?'

The boatman put down his oars for a moment. He pulled a sort of face, then touched his ears and his mouth, and shook his head, and shrugged.

He was a deaf-mute.

Or, if not, he was pretending to be, in order not to answer my questions.

When we were half way across, the boatman stopped rowing. He took off his bonnet, and waved it to the shore we had left. I looked back. Mr Gordon was waving his own hat. It was a signal. The boatman was acknowledging it. The signal had ordered him to stop. He back-watered with his oars, so that the boat stopped drifting forward; it floated motionless in the middle of the narrows, fifty yards from either bank.

Once again I was bottomlessly puzzled. To sit in a little boat, in a smart blue silk dress, in the middle of a loch. . .

The idea jumped into my head that I was to be drowned—knocked on the head and dropped into the water. But I could think of no reason why the Gordons should want me dead. Or why, even if they did, they should dress me up as a lady before killing me.

I served some purpose of theirs, sitting in the stern of the boat, dressed in silk, getting rather cold. I was still their tool. I was still tight in their grip.

But was I? Was I? One of the things I could do very well was to swim. I was sure the boatman could not. I had never heard of a Highlander who could. He could row faster than I could swim, but I could dive like a duck, and swim deep under the water, so that he would not know which way I went. I was sure I could do this. In a silk dress? I would get out of the silk dress somehow, once I was in the water. I would swim to the shore, the far shore, landing far from the boatman, where he would not expect, landing as far out of reach of the Gordons as though I were back in France. . .

As this wild hope formed itself in my head, it died. For along the lochside, coming towards the point, came five horsemen at a canter. They approached rapidly. They could not fail to see the boat, sticking up like a pimple on the steely grey face of the loch. They could not fail to see the bright pale blue of my dress.

They were a hundred and fifty yards away—a hundred—and I recognised the leading rider. I would have known that graceful seat among millions. He was a beautiful horseman. It was Carnmore. It was my husband.

The strange letter was explained, and Carnmore's strange expression when he read it. He was promised a sight of his wife, if he came to the lochside at this hour.

Ice seemed to embrace all parts of me. I felt like a fish on an ice-block, alive, helpless, unable to move, at the mercy of anyone. I felt deathly cold.

I supposed that, now Carnmore was come, the boatman would row on. He would deliver me to Carnmore.

I was not so very far from jumping into the water, not to swim but to sink to eternal safety from Carnmore.

The boatman picked up his oars. I felt that my heart had stopped beating. He did not row towards the far bank, but turned the boat so that it was sideways on to the bank—so that the newcomers could see clearly who was in the boat.

The five horsemen, in a close group, cantered to the very tip of the point, to the edge of the water. They reined in their horses. Carnmore jumped off, graceful as a cat. I heard voices over the smooth water, but not what was said. Another man dismounted, and Carnmore gave him his reins. He stood and stared at the boat—at me. I saw the white wedge of his face, between hat-brim and collar. I could not see his expression, at fifty yards' distance. I could imagine it.

Carnmore turned, and took something from his saddle. Something long and slender, with a metallic glint. I thought for a second that it was a gun. It seemed in his hands to grow longer, to telescope outwards.

That was what it was—a telescope, a deer-stalker's spyglass.

He raised it. It disappeared, to my vision, because it pointed directly at me. I might have dived into the bottom of the boat, to hide my face from him. I did not think to do so. I was incapable of movement, caught still in the ice-block of despair. I sat like a stone, staring back at him over fifty yards of water.

At last Carnmore lowered the spyglass. He took something else from his saddle-bag. It was a white cloth, perhaps a towel, a yard square. He took it by two corners, and waved it.

I thought he was waving to me. A flag of truce? Of surrender?

The obvious truth came to me. I looked back at the Gordons. With a similar white flag Mr Gordon was signalling back.

Two white flags. Truce. Peace between Carnmore and Inverdoran, between the Gordons of Carnmore and the parvenu Carnmore. Two flags of truce waved over me.

I was once again ready—almost ready—to spring over the side of the boat and go down, down into the deep cold waters of the loch.

The boatman showed no sign of picking up his oars, of taking me to my husband.

Carnmore took the reins of his horse, and mounted. After one long backward look, he led his men away, briskly, at a canter, so that they became smaller and smaller.

The boatman picked up his oars at last, and rowed back towards the Gordons.

My brain, numbed with the ice packed round it, struggled to find a reason for this extraordinary performance.

And found it. It was supremely obvious. It would have been obvious to anybody else, the moment the women began speaking in the house-keeper's room.

The Gordons had shown Carnmore that they held me. They had allowed him to inspect me, minutely, through a spyglass, so that there should be no mistake. But he could not recover me there and then, for they held me in baulk in the middle of the loch. Seeing me, knowing me, he had waved the white flag. Truce, peace, surrender. He would do something, give them something they had demanded. When he had done so, he could have me. He had agreed to these terms. That was his white flag. He could have me. That was Gordon's white flag.

The Gordons were selling me to Carnmore, in return for their estate.

10

The bows of the boat crunched onto the black shingle. The boatman jumped into a few inches of water. He pulled the boat a yard further onto the land. He lifted me ashore, setting me on my feet on the strand.

I tried to hide my trembling. I tried to stand stiff and straight. I wanted to show no weakness to these treacherous Gordons.

The Gordons themselves had a look of jubilation, of triumph. Well they might. They had won. The most jubilant face of all was Mrs McRibbie's.

My cloak and veil lay in a heap on a tussock of grass by the shingle. I picked up the cloak and wrapped it about me, for I was cold. No one offered to help me. For the moment I was unimportant.

Mrs McRibbie picked up the veil. She shot me a look of anger, amidst her jubilation, that I had left her this horrid task.

'I wonder why Carnmore came with such a squadron?' said Mr Gordon, his voice still hoarse and high with his excitement.

'In case he saw his way clear to kidnap. Which would have been legal.'

'Ha! Yes. Legal, to be sure . . . It is a good thing there were no boats on the other bank.'

'There were,' said Mrs Gordon. 'Two. I had them moved yesterday evening.'

'Ah! Haha! Two! You had them moved! Excellent, indeed!'

'There is a boat at Arichamish. Calum McKechnie takes fishermen out.'

'But that is only three miles away! Carnmore will take the boat, and row across—'

'And find no horses.'

'Aha! Yes! True, my love, true!'

'He must come the long way round by road.'

'Yes indeed! The long way round, to be sure! Either way, it makes no odds which! There is plenty of time, then.'

'There is time enough. We must not dawdle.'

'No! No! On no account. And you think he is sure to come with a Warrant of Search, with a lawyer and a party of the County Police?'

'I imagine he will. Would you not, if you thought your bride was being illegally concealed by a neighbour?'

'I would,' said Mr Gordon nervously. 'I would, indeed, my love! Yes, to be sure, he is certain to take that action—'

'And all will be well.'

Carnmore would come to Inverdoran, armed with documents and lawyers and officers, demanding the surrender of his wife. What then? I should see Mrs Gordon, general in this war, had her strategy ready.

By this time I had been convoyed back, between Mrs Gordon and Mrs McRibbie, to the door of the brougham. We all re-embarked. The curtains were still drawn over the windows. We started.

On the way to the loch, the women had been silent. On the way back, there was a torrent of conversation. Before the throw of the dice, there had been tight-lipped tenseness. Now that the throw had won, there was an almost drunken loosening of tongues. There was no aspect of the Carnmore castle and estate that they did not discuss. The evicted tenants were all to be reinstated. The children and grand-children of each were known to Mrs Gordon, every one. A certain farm was to have a new roof. Master Lancelot should have his own study in the castle, which would one day be his business-room, when he managed the estate. Mrs Gordon had its furniture and decoration planned in detail. Mrs McRibbie was to have a cottage, when she re-tired, very near to the castle so that she should see Master Lancelot as often as she would . . .

'We shall have the Gordon tartan on all the floors again,' said Mrs Gordon almost dreamily, 'instead of whatever dreadful carpets the im-posters may have laid.'

And so it went on. I was ignored. The spade was put aside in a corner, until it was needed again.

Back I was brought to the housekeeper's room. Back I was changed into Jaikie Bogle.

'Now please fetch that chit of Miss Elspeth's,' said Mrs Gordon, unlocking the door.

Mrs McRibbie nodded, and swept out.

Mrs Gordon had no more to say to me, now that we were alone to-gether, than when we were three. God knew I had nothing to say to her. She clasped and unclasped her fingers, and knocked her clenched fists together. There were still battles to be fought. The general was still on edge.

Back came Mrs McRibbie with a maidservant whose face I knew—Ina, the pretty fair girl who looked after Elspeth, the one Angus liked. The one who was, from a little distance, not so very unlike myself.

'Into those clothes, girl,' said Mrs Gordon, as soon as the door was locked.

The blue silk dress, and all the rest, lay over the backs of chairs. The dress was a little dirty, from the boat. The white shoes were dirty, and the gloves.

Ina looked perplexed and bashful. She stared, saucer-eyed, at Mrs Gordon, at Mrs McRibbie, and at me. Of course she thought I was a boy.

Mrs Gordon laughed suddenly, the same thought striking her.

'Turn your back like a gentleman, Jaikie,' she said to me. 'If I catch you trying to peep, Angus shall whip you better than he did last time.'

I turned to face the wall. There were rustlings and whispers and sharp commands behind me. In a few minutes I was suffered to turn round again.

Ina wore the silk dress, the grubby white shoes, the gloves. The dress fitted her better than it had fitted me. Of course, it had been made for her. The shoes and gloves had been chosen for her.

So dressed, she looked very much more like me.

Mrs Gordon took up a kind of pencil—something like a child's crayon. She commanded Ina to sit down, and to hold perfectly still. She cupped Ina's chin in her hand, and tilted her head backwards. Ina looked terrified, as though she thought she was to have a tooth drawn. With the pencil, Mrs Gordon drew a dark spot—a mole—beside Ina's eye. It was my mole—Mamma's mole—the patch of a beauty of Queen Anne's day.

Ina squeaked when she saw herself in the tall glass, though she was too overawed to say anything.

I thought she could not imagine what I was doing in the room. I thought she had no idea what game she was playing a part in.

'Why hae ye waitit sae lang, mem, tae offer this ploy?' said Mrs McRibbie suddenly.

'We wanted to give the gentleman time to brood,' said Mrs Gordon. 'Plenty of time to brood.'

'Och—tae gi' the puddin' a guid boilin'.'

'More than three months' boiling, Mrs McRibbie. I thought that about right. It ought to be ready to boil over.'

I thought she was right. Carnmore would be ready to explode, having known all those three months that I was alive and in the neighbourhood: obliged, all those three months, to save his face by pretending I was ill in my bed.

And when he did get me back, and I had cost him his castle . . .

Two keepers were sent for, who had been waiting by a sidedoor for this summons. They were to take me at once to the middle of the pheasant-preserves, and keep me there quiet until they were sent for. They protested at disturbing the pheasants, but Mrs Gordon said the coverts were not to be shot for another fortnight, and they were to do as they were bid.

She explained that a dreadful man who claimed to be my father was coming with a lawyer to claim me. But he was a liar, and wanted me only as a slave, to carry his coals and his water-buckets. Mrs Gordon was all concern for the poor waif Jaikie Bogle, confirming their opinion of their mistress. They said not a sleuth-hound would find me, the way they'd hide me.

'How shall we find you, then, when the danger is past?' she said, smiling.

They said they would be by the clearing where the hand-reared pheasants had been fed. The place was alive with snares, for foxes and pole-cats and marten-cats. A whole pack of sleuth-hounds, they said, would not get near me.

I knew the kinds of snares some of the gamekeepers set, to protect their precious poults. Some went by other names; and some had been unlawful for years.

'Don't let the boy run away,' said Mrs Gordon. 'He may try.'

'He'll no' ren, Mem,' they assured her.

'Go now,' said Mrs Gordon. 'Take a piece from the kitchen, for you may be there a long time.'

So they took me to the kitchen, and collected hunks of bread and cheese, and wheedled a stone crock of the home-brew from the stillroom. The telegraph system of the servants had been functioning again, and speculation flew about the kitchen like chaff. Strange ploys were afoot. Armies were arriving. Lord Carnmore was concerned.

'He's your sire, laddie?' said one of the keepers, laughing.

I gave a sort of sick laugh, the best I could manage, at the droll idea that Carnmore could be interested in me.

It was a twenty-minute walk to the preserves, through the policies behind the house, and across a strip of bleak park, and over a few wheat and barley fields, stubble now and waiting for the plough. The preserves were recent planting, not beautiful, a tangle of small trees only useful for harbouring game-birds.

'Gae canny,' the men said to me. 'Pu' yer fit whaur we du.'

I knew then that there were illegal gin-traps in the undergrowth. I went very canny, and put my feet exactly in the prints of the leader. At the same time, I tried to mark the path we took. If a chance came to run, I wanted a safe road to run along.

And so we came to a big clearing, where sheaves of wheat had been spread like fans and tied to stakes, to give food and shelter for the young birds. There were birds everywhere, full-grown pheasants and young ones, cocks and hens, tame as the fowls by a steading, strutting forward to the keepers in the hope of handfuls of corn. Most would be dead by Christmas, shot by Mr Gordon's friends: and another population would be bred the following spring.

I envied those doomed pheasants.

We made ourselves comfortable at the edge of the clearing. I could not run away. The keepers were alert, young, active men, absolutely loyal to the Gordons. I could not have run two yards. When they caught me, they would probably tie me up, to prevent my being troublesome again. They would have been sorry to do so, because they were nice men, but duty was duty.

They did not understand why I could not eat bread and cheese.

The house was a mile away or thereabouts, somewhat downhill, and approached by road from the other side. There were two hundred yards of thick wood and undergrowth between the clearing and the open fields. We would hear nothing of the arrival of a regiment of cavalry. I thought Carnmore might bring a regiment of cavalry, to get his wife and keep his castle.

It was very peaceful. The trees were full of long-tailed titmice, bustling along in flocks on mysterious journeys and peeping to each other. The undergrowth was spangled with blackberries, green and red and a few ripe. The sky was still steely-grey but the air was not cold. The keepers smoked their pipes, sitting relaxed each side of me. They were delighted to spend a working day doing such duty.

I had been in despair many times since Midsummer Evening. But this was rock bottom.

The keepers asked me about the brutal false-father Mrs Gordon had invented for them. My brain was not working sufficiently well to invent answers. They must have thought I was feeble-minded. That day, I think I was.

So we stayed, until late in the afternoon.

Then there was a noise of someone pushing through the undergrowth, and a voice called, 'Hamish! Mungo!'

'Hauld still, mon,' shouted Hamish.

He jumped to his feet, and went to guide the newcomers safely to the clearing.

I glanced at the other man, Mungo. Having only one guard doubled my chances of escape. He knew it as well as I. He stood up also, and stood over me. If I had been a greyhound, he could have grabbed me even as I started moving.

Not one man but two followed Hamish into the clearing. One I knew to be a gardener, a middle-aged psalm-singer called McQhae. The other was Angus, the disgraced groom.

'We're tae tak' the laddie tae the hoose in suxty mennit,' said McQhae. 'Tha's fowrty mennit frae the noo.'

He pulled a watch the size of a potato out of his pocket, and looked at it owlishly. He nodded, and pushed it back. We were to set off in twenty minutes, then. For twenty minutes we should stay in the clearing.

All was clear. Obviously all was clear. Carnmore had come and gone, or perhaps not come. I had at least another night at Inverdoran —perhaps several days and nights—before the exchange was made as the Gordons had planned it. I might find chances of escape. At least it was reprieve. I sighed deeply. Suddenly I did want bread and cheese. I was passionately hungry. This, no doubt, was the effect of the sudden passing of danger, lifting of terror. Relaxing, I was ravenous. But the keepers had long ago eaten every bit of their piece, and given the crumbs to the pheasants.

Angus sat down heavily. He looked at me in a way I did not like. There was nothing he could do to me, with the three others by, however bitter his resentment.

'Yon Carnmore steppit intil the hoose wi' the laird,' said McQhae, 'drawin' up a paper. 'Tis tae be writ, wutnessit, seegnit an' sealit an' a' the nicht. We haird the clash, oot ahint the hoose. Verra quair ploys, sirs, verra quair ploys.'

My head swam for a moment. I had to close my eyes, and grip hard at my knees with both hands: or I might have swooned at these casual words.

My hope of reprieve had lasted for ten seconds.

I heard the voices of the others as though from a great distance. I did not know what they were saying. I did not know if I could walk with the others back to the house. But I did not want to show such abject weakness, even to myself. I struggled up through the blankets of nightmare that pressed down on me, and tried to concentrate on what McQhae was saying. God knew, I wanted to know what was happening.

Carnmore, it seemed, had come long before he was expected. He had a lawyer and three policemen in a carriage, and himself and three men on horseback. He must have ridden like the wind, and put the fear of God into Lochgrannomhead, to have done so much so quickly. He had thought to catch the Gordons napping. A man would have to get up very early, to catch Mrs Gordon napping.

Carnmore announced, in the hearing of half the household, that he had reason to believe that his wife was concealed at Inverdoran. To keep a wife from her husband, even by her misguided wish, was against the law of the realm and of God, as all men knew. Therefore he had come with a warrant to search Inverdoran.

Mr Gordon was greatly astonished. He said they had heard that Lady Carnmore was ill, and confined to her bed. That was the clash among the neighbours. They much regretted her ladyship's indisposition, and prayed for her speedy recovery.

Carnmore said that her ladyship had been removed to the Perth Infirmary, ten days earlier, to be under the eye of a particular and celebrated physician. He had not been to see her for three days, owing to pressure of business on his estate. He had received news, the day before, that she had disappeared from the Infirmary, two days previously, going with an unknown lady and gentleman, apparently willingly. The Gordons knew, he said, why he supposed she was biding at Inverdoran.

The lawyer warned the Gordons about the gravity of the offence of which Lord Carnmore was accusing them.

Mr Gordon refused to allow the lawyer, the police, or Carnmore's men to search any part of his house or buildings. It was an imposition he said, an insult, an invasion of his rights. They should accept his word that Lady Carnmore was not there.

The lawyer produced the warrant, and read it out. It empowered them to search where they listed, and required the laird to permit the search.

Carnmore gave to the lawyer and to the police an exact description of Lady Carnmore. When last seen, he said, earlier in the same day, she had been wearing a pale blue gown.

Mr Gordon seemed much enraged by the search, but he could not legally do anything to prevent it.

After three-quarters of an hour of search, a policeman set up a great shout. He had found a young lady in a hayloft, evidently hiding. The young lady exactly matched Lord Carnmore's description of her ladyship, as to clothes and colouring and the rest, and even as to a mole by her left eye.

Carnmore was joyful, until the young lady was brought to him.

His mistake was forgivable. He might easily have mistaken the young woman for his wife. The maidservant Ina did, it seemed, much resemble Lady Carnmore, even to the mole by her eye. At a distance, anybody would mistake them.

The lawyer and the police were sympathetic to Carnmore in his disappointment, after his hopes had been raised so high. They were very apologetic to Mr Gordon, and also to Ina.

Mr Gordon was gracious to the lawyer and the police. They were not to be blamed for the misinformation on which they had acted. They were doing their duty as it had seemed to them.

It was explained that Ina had been hiding in the hayloft from Mrs McRibbie, to whom she had been impertinent. Mrs McRibbie forgave her. Ina did not herself speak, owing to fright and bashfulness. It was Mrs Gordon who gave the explanation.

Ina's fine gown was a gift from her lady, Miss Elspeth, who was generous, like all the laird's family.

The lawyer and the police were anxious to be away home to Lochgrannomhead, where their dinners would be waiting for them. They could do no more good at Inverdoran. They left in the carriage.

Lord Carnmore was very angry, but he kept his anger under control. (McQhae thought he would not do so, and was disappointed that he did.) He said loudly, in front of all the household, that he had seen what he had seen.

Mr Gordon said that Lord Carnmore knew best, as to that. And, that being so, the contract could be drawn up on the terms already agreed.

Lord Carnmore fought a great battle inside himself (so McQhae put it) and at last agreed to the contract. He said he would go inside with Mr Gordon, and together they would draw up a contract. But if Mr Gordon's terms were to be met, Carnmore's terms must be met also.

Mr Gordon said Lord Carnmore need not sign the contract until he had what he sought under his hand. After he had signed, he could take what he sought away with him. Mr Gordon would lend him a carriage and horses, if he had need of them.

Then Mrs Gordon called to two men who were by. She told them to go to the pheasant preserves, to the clearing where the young birds were fed, and call out for Hamish and Mungo. In one hour—no less—they were to bring the lad Jaikie Bogle to the house.

'Carnmore is yer sire,' said Hamish to me, wonderingly. For he still believed the story Mrs Gordon had invented for him.

'Havers,' said McQhae. 'Carnmore's ower young tae be the sire o' siccan muckle lad.'

They did not understand about Ina, or the lawyer, or any part of it. They did not understand why Jaikie Bogle was to be taken to the house.

I had thought to have a night, or days and nights, before I was surrendered to Carnmore. I had twenty minutes—the time it took to walk from the clearing to the house.

Then I was under Carnmore's hand, according to the contract.

'Ye'll no' be needin' fower tae tak' yin wee laddie intil the hoose,' said Mungo.

Angus readily agreed, too readily. I did not like his ready agreement. The keepers went away together, to their crofts or to some evening task.

'I'll no' need twa,' said Angus to McQhae. 'Off wi' ye, auld mon.'

McQhae objected. He had been ordered, by the mistress, to help bring me to the house. Angus clenched a fist, and shook it under McQhae's nose. He swore at McQhae. He was twenty years younger than the gardener, two inches taller, much more solid and heavy. McQhae was frightened. He thought Angus would hit him and beat him, if he did not go away. I thought so too. He went away, picking his way carefully through the undergrowth to the edge of the wood.

'I waitit lang for this mennit,' said Angus softly. 'I waur stoppit frae whuppin' ye yinst. I'll no' be stoppit this tide.'

From inside his jacket he drew the long plaited thong of a hunting-whip. His face was calm, thoughtful. Of course he blamed me for his disgrace. He was standing over me, as I crouched on the ground. I could not run.

I would not cry out. I would not give him that satisfaction.

He raised the whip-thong, and brought it down with all his strength on my hip. I felt the violent flare of the pain. I did cry out. I could not help it. I did not think I could bear any more strokes like that, without fainting.

He raised the whip. He took a step back, to give himself more room, to hit harder and hurt me more. He stepped back into the edge of a mound of ivy which grew round the base of a hazel-clump.

There was a heavy metallic clang. Angus screamed and fell backwards. He dropped the whip. He screamed again, a thin terrible noise like that of a hare that has been shot but not killed.

He had trodden into the jaws of a gin-trap. It had sprung shut, the steel teeth clamped to his ankle. It was meant for a fox, perhaps for a poacher.

He was screaming continuously. Blood was gushing from his leg over the ground and over the metal of the trap. It was terrible to hear a man making that thin girlish noise of agony and terror.

I should have tried to help him. A good person would have done so, because he was in frightful pain and needed help. I should have found a branch, and tried to lever the jaws of the trap apart against the spring. I did not help him. I did not think to. The keepers had hurried away minutes before. They must be far out of earshot of Angus's screams. McQhae might hear. I could not bring myself to care.

I went away through the preserve, not towards the house, nor by the road the keepers had taken, but in a third direction. I went very carefully, prodding before me with a stick pulled from a hazel. Angus's was not the only gin-trap in the wood. Behind me as I went were the terrible screams of the man with the steel teeth biting into his leg.

I prodded at a drift of brambles with my hazel-stick. There was a gigantic metallic clang. The gin-trap almost bounced off the ground with the power of its spring. I gave a scream almost as loud as Angus's. For a sick moment I had a vision of those cruel jaws on my leg.

I thought Carnmore would have been pleased to have me brought to him with a gin-trap on my leg.

I could not free my stick from the trap, so tight were the jaws clamped together. I found another. I was desperate to hurry. McQhae was not far off. He must hear the screams, and run back to Angus. Mrs Gordon would send other servants for me, if I were not brought when she expected. I was desperate to hurry, but I dared not. My knees shook at the thought of the gin-trap. Angus's screams behind me seemed as loud as ever.

The preserve was far larger than I had supposed: or perhaps I took the wrong direction, that gave me the furthest to go. I was in a fever to get on and out, but I dared not put a foot to the ground until I had proved the ground safe.

Picking my way through that wood was the most nerve-racking experience of my life. A voice inside my head was screaming run—run—and take the chance of the traps. I fought down my passionate desire to run, and prodded before me with the stick.

I thought I heard another voice—perhaps more than one—joining Angus's screams. He might be able to tell them which way I went, if they could stop him screaming. Still I could not hurry. With immense self-control I prodded, and advanced one stride, and prodded again, and advanced one stride: and at last I came to a screen of fir-trees, and pushed through a hedge into a field of turnips.

I thought I must get away far and fast, for they would bring out dogs. They would take the dogs all round the outside of the preserve, and find the line of my scent. They would follow me on horseback, hunting me. Every soul on the Inverdoran estate would be hunting me, because of the bargain made with Carnmore.

I must go away far and fast, to England, France, anywhere. I must give up all idea of staying within reach of my parents. That was an appalling decision, but the choice had been taken from me. I must see them once more, to say goodbye, and then go to a distant place.

I must go to Lochgrannomhead, ahead of horses and hounds . . . How? I must have a horse myself. There were ponies out in the pastures near the stables, though the better horses were in. I must manage without saddle or bridle.

The hunt would be up. Every minute that went by increased my danger. I stopped in the middle of the turnip field, and stood listening intently for shouting or the barking of dogs. I could hear only the distant crying of birds.

Salvation lay now in speed. Making a wide circuit round park and policies, I ran, and ran, using what cover there was. My legs began to feel like wet putty, my heart jolted, my lungs seemed like to burst out of my ribs. I was streaming with sweat, which stung my eyes and glued my clothes to my body. I could think only of catching a pony, and riding far and fast away from Inverdoran.

Far behind me I heard the barking of dogs. There were no hounds at Inverdoran, but they had pointers and setters and retrievers and terriers, all with excellent noses. Pouring with sweat as I was, I was leaving a line of scent that even a greyhound could have followed. It was a race now.

Labouring, tottering, almost done, I came up through the fields towards the paddocks. I could see the stable-block, and beyond it the house. It was still broad daylight, although the sky was darkening. I dropped to all fours, and crawled as fast as I could up the side of a field newly ploughed. It was more exhausting than running. Earth stuck to my sweating hands and to my face. I could hear the dogs. The sight of the big house beyond the stables filled me with dread. No doubt Carnmore was still there. I seemed to feel a malevolent beam of black light shining at me from the windows. Again I was torn between the screaming need to hurry and the need to go careful. I must not be seen, not now, near escape but near the house too . . .

I came to the railed fence of the first of the half-dozen paddocks. It was empty, and so was the next. There were three ponies in the third paddock, rough little shooting-ponies, placid creatures, seldom urged out of a walk. A setting-dog would run six times as fast. There were two more ponies in the next small paddock, which was bordered by the back of the stable buildings. There were windows in the upstairs floor of the stables, where the grooms and coachmen lived. The nearest paddock, every inch of it, was commanded by a dozen windows.

I thought I could use one of the shaggy little shooting-ponies as a stalking-horse, to get me unseen to the next paddock. There I could catch a better pony for my escape. I crawled to where the nearest pony stood, sleepily grazing in the thin autumn grass. He looked at me without interest. Bending low, I seized a handful of his boot-brush mane, and tried to persuade him towards the far rail of the paddock. He did not want to go. I thought nothing would budge him. I heard the dogs, still far away but not as far as before. The evening was very still. I thought I heard shouts also. Would somebody guess I was making for the ponies? Would somebody be posted in the upstairs windows of the stables? Had I crawled into a trap?

I might be caught if I went on. I would certainly be caught if I stayed.

I gave the sleepy pony a sharp slap on the rump with my free hand. I was terrified of making such a noise. Reluctantly, sluggishly, he began to move. I half pushed him the whole length of the paddock, bent double behind him. Of course my legs could be seen, below the chest of the pony. I thought a watcher might not notice that a pony had grown two extra legs.

Of the two ponies in the next paddock, one was visibly lame. It had been pulling a small cart with loads of firewood, and had somehow bruised a pastern. I might have to take it, if I could not get to the other, but I hoped not.

Sweat still stung my eyes, and made my hands slippery. I had not properly got my breath back, and my heart was still thudding painfully. My hip was sore where Angus had hit me with the whip.

The second pony in the top paddock was a good one, part Connemara, dun, a young animal of thirteen hands, only half-broken, strong and active. He wore a leather head-collar so that he could be caught more easily. It was not as good as a bridle, but I thought it would be better than nothing. The pony was grazing right up against the wall of the stables. I thought this strange, until I saw that he was rubbing his dock against the wall, as ponies sometimes do. He would be by far the best pony for me to take—the only one I could really hope to get away on—but he was directly under the windows. I thought that perhaps he was so close under the windows that he could not easily be seen, unless a watcher opened a window and leaned out. All the windows were closed. I think few of them were ever opened. I had to get close up under the stable wall, and then catch the dun pony.

I used the lame pony as another stalking-horse, to hide me. He was willing to be pushed along, although he limped as he went. I felt hideously exposed to all those windows, even though I was hiding as well as I could behind my second stalking-horse. I was thankful that there was no bright evening sun, to shine on the bright yellow of my hair. There was not much else to be thankful for.

Every second as I sidled nearer and nearer to the stable, I expected to hear a shout or a whistle from the windows, or from the paddocks behind me. I would rather have gone in any direction, than moved steadily towards the stable windows; but that was where the pony I needed was.

I got to the wall. I flattened myself against it. There had been no shout or whistle. I was still very frightened.

Because I was holding one pony, the other was easy to catch. I pulled the leather belt from the loops in my breeches, and pushed it through the head-collar, to make a kind of rein. I did not think my breeches would fall down.

The paddock had two gates. One led into the next paddock, and so to the rest. That took me back in the wrong direction, towards dogs and pursuers. And paddock led into paddock, and there was no way out. The furthest empty paddock had a gate into a field, but it was always padlocked. The other gate from the top paddock was at the corner of the stable-block. The gate itself was hung from the masonry of the stable. A flagged path ran from the gate, along the front of the stables, to the main stable arch. The pony's shoes would rattle like gunfire on the flagstones. I should have to cross the broad open archway, showing myself to anybody in the stable-yard. Quite likely the pony would try to bolt into the stable-yard, where he knew there was food and company.

I had to jump out of the paddock.

Well, I did so. I scrambled onto the pony's back, feeling most odd, as I had never ridden astride before (riding had not been any part of my life as a stable-lad). The moment had come—I had to risk showing myself. I kicked the pony towards the fence. He refused, swerving so that I had to grab hold of the mane to stay on. He refused a dozen times. Twice he swerved so violently that, riding bareback, I fell off. But I did not let go of my belt. Still there was no shout or whistle. It was getting darker by the minute. At least we made little sound on the grass of the paddock.

I heard the dogs nearer.

At last the pony jumped not over the rails but through them. There was a great splintering crash. Pony and I fell together. I was winded and dizzy, and lay helpless for a moment, but by a providential instinct still held the strip of leather which attached the pony to me. I scrambled on his back again, and we set off.

I could not believe that we would not be seen. I kicked the pony into a canter, and clung desperately to his mane as we bucketed down through the park towards the loch.

All along the lochside road, the park was bordered by a high stone wall. There were doors in it—all kept locked—but only one gate. There were two ugly little lodges there; it was the bottom of the driveway. It was certain that the gateway would be watched, and certain that the gate itself would be closed.

I reached the wall, six or so hundred yards away from the lodges, among small trees. My pony had done almost all for me that he could. I hoped he had not damaged his knees, in breaking the fence. I was well away from the house now, and out of anybody's sight; and I had left no line of my own scent for the dogs. I persuaded the pony close up against the wall, and managed to kneel on its back. Scrabbling at the rough stone of the wall, my fingertips felt the top. I took hold of it just as the pony moved away. I heaved myself up onto the coping of the wall. I called softly down to the pony, 'Thank you. I hope your knees are not hurt. Thank you.'

I looked carefully up and down the road. It seemed certain that the Gordons would have sent watchers there. I saw no one. I heard nothing.

Someone would notice the broken rail of the paddock. If they did not, my pony would go back to the stable. Someone would guess that I had taken the pony. But I did not think they would know which way I had gone. I thought it was already too dark for the print of the pony's feet to be visible.

I dropped onto the grassy verge of the road. It was a longer drop than I expected, and jarred every bone in my body. I picked myself up, and began to walk along the verge towards Lochgrannomhead. I went carefully, watching and listening, prepared at any moment to dive into the ditch.

More and more weary, I plodded on. I thought that if I once stopped, I would fall asleep; and if I slept, I would not wake until noon; and I would wake to find a dozen Inverdoran servants sitting about me in a ring—or a dozen Carnmore servants.

I plodded on, and came to Myrtle Lodge at I knew not what hour. The dreadful little house was dark and silent. Of course it was—my parents went early to bed. Mamma was not well, and Papa exhausted himself with his inventions. I did not think I should try to rouse them. A sudden awakening, a shock in the middle of the night, would be very bad for Mamma. Besides, I would have to bang at the knocker, and shout, and call a great deal of unwelcome attention to myself.

I tried to get into the house stealthily. But, though all the windows rattled and none properly fitted, they were bolted. There was no trap-door into a coal cellar at Myrtle Lodge. I could have broken a window, but I might be heard—caught—hauled before the Sheriff Court . . .

I decided I must wait until the household was stirring in the morning. I could lie hidden in the overgrown jungle of the garden. The navvies in their barrack would wake me early, or the horses in the livery stable on the other side. There was no fear of sleeping until noon in this noisy place.

I crawled into a thicket which should have been a rose-bed, and knew no more until I heard loud singing in an Irish voice, and the neigh of a horse asking to be fed, and felt the morning sun on my eyelids.

It was a long moment before I could think where I was, so deeply had I been asleep.

I peered through brambles at my parents' home. It looked worse than it had in midsummer—more decrepit, more gimcrack. Paint was peeling from the woodwork, and an upstairs window was broken.

Even Papa, I thought, used to have broken windows mended . . .

There was no smoke in the chimney. There was no sound, or sign of any movement.

I crept round to the back of the house, and peeped in through the kitchen window. The kitchen was dark and empty. The table was bare and the range cold. Cobwebs clung to the inside of the window.

I peeped in through other windows, keeping myself hidden from the road. There were dust-sheets over the furniture in the parlour.

The house was empty. My parents had gone away.

11

I crawled back into the thicket where I had slept, to ponder this new problem.

The thought suddenly came to me that Mamma had died. I choked to think she had died without me, without knowing where or how I was. I was full of misery.

Then I remembered the clash of the coachmen and grooms at Inverdoran, and their love of gossip about the great. The death of a Countess, whose name they all knew, would have been discussed a thousand times.

Especially as they so greatly disapproved of the Countess's greedy daughter.

Mamma could not be dead. She might be ill, gravely ill. Would Dr McPhee have put her into a hospital? Surely he would have found women to tend her in her own bed. There would be no difficulty about the fee. Her devoted son-in-law would surely concern himself with that.

Devoted son-in-law. Obviously that was where they had gone. Carnmore had given them refuge in his castle . . .

No. If he expected me back, he would not have them by when I returned. He would keep from them, of all people in the world, the truth about his ways as a husband.

Despair filled me. I could not, dared not, linger in Lochgrannomhead, or anywhere near. I must run a long way away. Yet, once I went, I could never come back. I was still Carnmore's property. He had bought me, and he owned me, and he always would. I could never come back. I could never see my parents again. I had to see them before I went. This was an absolute necessity. As far as I could, I must reassure them about myself. I must ask their blessing and forgiveness. I must kiss them, each, a last time, and then go away for ever.

It was appallingly final—to go away for ever.

I could write, perhaps. They would show Carnmore my letters. Perhaps he would be able to trace them to their source. He would come to Timbuctoo for me—and devise punishments for the trouble I had given him.

To go away for ever—that was right, that was imperative. But to take leave of my parents first—that was just as imperative. I could *not* go until I had seen them.

Someone must know where they had gone.

I considered going to Dr McPhee. But what would he think, what would he do, if Jaikie Bogle came to his door asking what had become of the Earl and Countess of Larrig? I thought he would be very unlikely to tell me anything, and very likely to call a Constable. And if I declared myself to him, threw myself on his mercy, invoked his discretion? The risk was too great. As a professional man, widely known and respected, he more than ordinary people must rigidly conform to the law. What he believed of Carnmore, what he believed of me, was nothing to the point.

Mr Craigie, the Procurator Fiscal, I believed to be a kind man, in spite of his hoodie-crow appearance and his cawing voice. *His* kindness was nothing to the point. If he believed me to be Jaikie Bogle, he must send me back to Inverdoran. If he knew me to be Lady Carnmore, he must send me back to my husband. That Carnmore broke contracts with his tenants did not disqualify him from owning me. Our marriage was a contract I was breaking. So any lawyer must see it.

If there was no help from respectable people, prominent people in the town, then I must look lower down.

I crept from my refuge, and went covertly to the barrack of the navvies, which almost shadowed the Myrtle Lodge garden. They had been friendly to me once. Three hulking men in rough clothes were cooking a mess in a black iron pot over an open fire, on the open ground by the barrack. The smell might have made me hungry—I had not eaten for a day and a night—but I could not think of food without a heaving stomach.

I greeted the navvies with cautious respect. One of them made to cuff me. One offered me food. One swore and spat. Of course I was dirty and unkempt. I supposed I looked what I was—a runaway stable-lad.

'The auld folks,' I said, 'wha bided in yon hoose—'

'Awa',' said one of them shortly.

'Ay, an' yon's an ill ploy, ye ken. The auld mon promissit's a siller shullin', when I ren tae bear a paircel frae the shop.'

'Ye no' had the shullin', laddie?'

'No' a sicht o' ma shullin'! It's no' richt!'

The navvies believed me. They shook their heads. Life as they knew it was full of such betrayals. They sat me down, and gave me a mug of what they called tea, and gravely discussed my shilling.

Most girls of my age would have had hysterics, to hear the language they used.

They did not know where the old people had gone. They were not sure when they had gone—a week or two since, maybe a month. They had seldom seen the gentleman, never the lady, even when they were there. The navvies wanted to help me, but they could not. I was so moved by their goodwill, that I almost wept.

Worry and fright kept me near enough to tears. I did not want to weep. They would think I was crying over a lost shilling.

I did not want to weep, but into my head, for no reason that I knew, came the thought of Sir Richard Grant. My back tingled at the memory of his arms holding me, and my cheek tingled at the memory of his face pressed to mine. And I did weep.

And those rough workmen swore, and looked disgusted, and gave me pennies from their pockets—nine copper pence, to make up for the shilling I said I had been cheated of. I said I would not take their pennies, but with frightful and furious oaths they said that I would.

It came to me that the only people who had ever given me money were Sir Richard Grant and these three sullen navvies.

I wiped my eyes on my sleeve, and tried to face the future more sensibly.

I decided to ask about my parents at the livery-stable. It was possible they had rented a carriage to remove themselves, or that someone had rented one for them. I stood up by the navvies' fire—and then saw the man watching me from the roadway.

A square, clean-shaven jaw, a thin mouth. It was Kenzie. Murdo's man.

I sat down again immediately. I was safe in the company of the navvies—not for ever, for they must go back to their work on the new road, but for a time.

How in God's name had Kenzie followed me to Myrtle Lodge? He could not, for first I was on horseback, and then prowling through the dark. But he was a servant of the Inverdoran estate. He must have heard the clash about my escape. He must have guessed that I would come to Lochgrannomhead.

He must have guessed so: but he could have searched the town for a week, with all the rest of the clan, and not thought to keep watch on Myrtle Lodge.

He must have known, then—Murdo must have known—that Jaikie Bogle would make for Myrtle Lodge. In God's name, how? There was no connection on earth between the Inverdoran stable-lad, and the raw gimcrack villa on the edge of the town . . . But there was. Benjie had taken my message. It must be from Benjie that the tinkers knew. They had recaptured him, or he had rejoined them. Poor Benjie. I wondered what they had done to him, to make him betray me.

I told the navvies that I would ask after the old people in the livery-stable; and they nodded, approving.

'I'm scairt tae gae speirin' o' yon grumes, tae ma lane,' I said anxiously. 'They'll mebbe whup 's, an' no' tell wha' they ken.'

So it came about that those navvies came with me to the livery-stable. It was partly kindness. It was partly curiosity, I think. It was partly indignation that I had been cheated of a shilling. It may even have been the hope of some kind of battle with the grooms.

Kenzie watched me along the road to the stables. I wondered how far away Murdo was.

As we turned in through the gate of the livery-stable, a gig came round the corner of the road from the middle of the town. I knew the gig, for I had often washed its wheels. I knew the cob which pulled it, for I had picked out his feet and combed his mane. I knew the two men in the gig, for one was Willie the Inverdoran under-coachman, and one was Andrew the old groom.

They did not see me, a shrimp in the midst of the three big navvies. Willie stopped the gig outside Myrtle Lodge. Andrew scrambled down, and walked towards the door of the house.

Why had they not come sooner? I supposed the Gordons had not known, exactly, where my parents had been living—might have preferred not to know, to be comfortably oblivious of old friends in new distress. But they could find out, very easily, from doctor or lawyer or tradesmen. They had found out. It was providential that they had had to find out, that the servants had not come sooner. The navvies would have been obliged to surrender me to them.

They were watching the house, and the road on each side of the house. I was safe in the livery-stable, but they would see me the moment I left. So would Kenzie. I wondered if Willie and Andrew would recognise Kenzie, who had worked in the Ardno quarry. I could not see that it helped or hindered me, if they all took tea together.

Carnmore too knew where my parents had lived. Would he not also expect me to come to find them? Why had he no watcher here? The probable answer came to me—Carnmore would think I would know my parents had left Myrtle Lodge. He would think I would know where they had gone. He did not know the sequestered life I had been leading for three months. He would be watching the place where my parents were. Of course he knew where they were. He had probably taken them there. He would be watching there, not here, night and day, sure that sooner or later I would go there. That made the present less perilous than it might have been, but the future more perilous.

The grooms in the livery-stable were alarmed and annoyed at the sudden invasion of the navvies. They looked askance at me, too.

They did not know where the Larrigs had gone. They had been gone for three weeks. A carriage had come for them, in the middle of the morning, three weeks before. The grooms had not paid any attention to the carriage or the coachman or the removal. Simply, two people had got into a closed carriage, and gone away. They might have gone a short distance or a long one—to Perth or Edinburgh or London, or to the other side of Lochgrannomhead. The grooms had not noticed how much luggage had gone with the people in the carriage. They had not noticed if the lady had been ill or well.

The navvies shrugged to each other and to me. The old man had got clear away, without paying his debt to me. That was the way of the world. That was the way poor men were treated.

They must go down to the new Crianlarich road, they said, to break the stones for their bread. They expected me to leave the livery-stable with them. But I picked at some tattered and stitched old harness that hung from a peg in the shed, as though I had a professional interest in it. They shrugged again, and strode away, having served me with more kindness than I had met in most of my life.

There was a good deal of bustle in the stalls and sheds of the livery-stable, as two or three rented carriages were to be sent out, and horses at livery to be taken round to their owners. By keeping out of the way, and keeping in corners, and keeping quiet, I was able to disappear in the midst of the bustle. I had no plan. I had to go into the town to ask about my parents. I did not know where to go. I could not leave the stable without being seen by Kenzie and the Inverdoran men.

I tried to think sensibly, which was the last thing I felt capable of doing. What tradesman would know where Mamma and Papa had gone? One with whom they continued to deal? Were they buying food, or clothes, or coals? It seemed desperately unlikely. What else did they ever buy? Only things Papa needed for his inventions.

It had been chemistry. It was still chemistry when I was married on Midsummer Day. Bottles and jars of heaven knew what were carried to Myrtle Lodge from the Pharmacist, from Mr Thomas Haddow, who looked like a bull and was dissolved into pity by my crocodile tears. His shop was in a little street which led off the Marketplace, an alley called Milkchurn Row. Of course, in three months, Papa might have had a dozen new enthusiasms. He might have been buying not chemicals but steel springs, or wheels, or gunpowder, or darning needles . . .

Thinking like this made me feel the familiar mixture of pity, amusement, exasperation, and love. He *might* still nurture his passion for chemistry. It seemed an extraordinarily good idea to go to Haddow's shop. It seemed impossible for me to get there unseen.

A very battered and tattered country brougham was being manhandled round by three of the men. Harness and horse were called for. The carriage was to go to the Manse, to pick up the Free Kirk Minister, and take him to some village for a marriage or funeral or baptism. A driving-groom was to take him. The driving-groom had a black coat too large for him and a black hat too small for him.

Even as they were hauling the brougham out of the shed into the yard, I was able to open the door and crawl in. I failed to shut the door. It swung wide open. I burrowed into the floor of the carriage, my face full of dust, my arms hiding my head. A man swore, and banged shut the open door. They said they would tie up the catch with a piece of string, and the Minister must use the other door.

So I was carried safe past Kenzie, and Willie, and Andrew, and all the way to the Manse on the other side of the town.

The driving-groom walked the horse every yard of the way. Perhaps he was in no hurry; perhaps the horse could go no faster. I could have jumped out at any moment without any chance of hurting myself: but not without being seen. I peeped out of the window, to look for a chance, but always there were people by, and I would have been gripped for certain. I did something else that was needful, as we went: I spat on the cuff of my shirt, and rubbed my face with it. It was not a treatment a lady's-maid would have recommended for the complexion, but I thought it would lift most of the mud.

Once at the Manse, I was not so lucky getting out as I had been getting in: or I was not so clever. They saw me, and set up a shout. The Minister was not like to run after me, nor the driving-groom: but there was a tall lad in an apron who gave chase. He would have caught me, too, but the Minister called him back in a voice like a bull's.

I went to Milkchurn Row, going very warily. As far as I could, I kept amongst people, indifferent strangers hurrying about their business. I thought I would not be noticed in a press of people. I thought that, as a stable-lad—even a grubby one—I would not be recognised as the tinker-boy who had set the market in a turmoil. And that had happened three months earlier.

At the door of Haddow's shop, I stopped and looked round carefully. There were a dozen people in Milkchurn Row. Most were women. There must have been faces I had seen before, but I knew none of them. I slipped into the shop. The bell jangled over my head as though to call the Procurator Fiscal.

Thomas Haddow looked at me with such gloomy suspicion that, for a moment, I thought he had recognised me. Perhaps he was bothered by a likeness, that he could not put a finger on. Perhaps gloomy suspicion was his usual mien to strangers. His dealings with Papa had been enough to make a man both gloomy and suspicious for life.

I said I was a groom at Inverdoran. (News of Jaikie Bogle's escape would hardly yet have reached Milkchurn Row, and probably never would.) I said my mistress had a message to be delivered to the Countess of Larrig. But the address we had been given, to take the message to, was an empty house. In the livery-stable next door, they had suggested Mr Haddow, because they thought he did much business with Lord Larrig.

'He'll mebby ken, they says, whaur the leddy hae gangit.'

'Ye cam' on yer lane frae Inverdoran wi' the message?' asked Haddow, frowning.

'Na! I cam' wi' Wullie in the wagonit, for Robert Cochrane's no' braw the day.'

'Wha' ails Robert Cochrane?'

'He tuk a wee fa' frae the pole o' the phaeton. He tuk a muckle gesh tae his laig. Mrs Gordon, the mustress, hae pu' a gran' bandidge ower the gesh, ye ken, an' gi'd Robert Cochrane a dram.'

This was satisfactory. My credentials were established. Of course Thomas Haddow knew the names of the Inverdoran coachman and undercoachman, from the number of times they had come to fetch medicines or soap or scent. In a week or a day, or an hour, Thomas Haddow would know that my story was nonsense. He might know I was the runaway. It would not matter. I would not see him again.

Mr Haddow said he knew where Lord Larrig was, because he sent out parcels of chemicals for his lordship's experiments. Lord Carnmore was paying for the chemicals, or Lord Larrig would not have had them. But it was not to Carnmore that the chemicals were sent. It was Strathlarrig.

I goggled at him. It was the last answer on earth I had expected.

'His ane cassel,' said Thomas Haddow, with a sort of glum pride. 'Sir Richard Grant bides there the noo. I doot her leddyship's there, forby.'

I left the shop as carefully as I had entered it. I had an ugly shock. Kenzie was in Milkchurn Row. He had his back towards me; he was inspecting the window of a grog-shop. I recognised the shorn back of his head, and I glimpsed the reflection of his face in the grog-shop window.

My heart was jolting. Kenzie had guessed I had smuggled myself out of the livery-stable in the carriage. He had had no difficulty following it, so slowly as it went. But would he leave the stable unwatched? How if I had not gone out in the carriage? Of course, he had not been alone. He had been joined by one or more of Murdo's other tinkers.

I ran away from Haddow's door. Just before I turned into the Marketplace, I stopped and looked back. Kenzie was still staring, rapt, into the window of the grog-shop. I buried myself in the crowd in the Marketplace. I decided to hide in the town until dark, and then go to Strathlarrig. I dared not cross the country by daylight.

I had nine copper pennies, and now I wanted food. But I dared not buy baps or oatcakes in the market. It was one thing to scuttle through the place, keeping my face turned away from folk; it would have been quite another to march to a stall and make a purchase.

I found the overgrown garden of an empty house. It was as bad as the garden of Myrtle Lodge: or as good. The garden was a comfortable hiding-place until, at noon, it began to rain.

As I crouched, sodden, I realised that Willie and Andrew would know within a minute that Myrtle Lodge was empty. They would realise quite as quickly as I. They would report so, to Mr or Mrs Gordon. One or other of those had almost certainly come to the town, to lead the search for me. The Gordons would ask where the Larrigs had gone. They would adopt my own first idea, probably, and ask Dr McPhee.

Strathlarrig would be watched by their people, and by Carnmore's people. In the dark, and on my own home ground, I was not much worried at the thought of getting past them all. The dirty weather would help me, as it had more than once before.

I began to be sure that I should get to my parents.

I had time, between noon and night, to be amazed that they should be at Strathlarrig. They could not have ended Sir Richard's tenancy. They could not have afforded to. They must be there as his guests. So he was playing the host, to the house's owner? With new furniture everywhere, and new everything? Probably he was not there, and had simply lent them the castle. However it might be, it all seemed strange and uncomfortable, a most awkward arrangement.

To be sure, Papa would not mind, if he could get on with his inventions; and Mamma would not mind, if she saw Papa happily busy.

It was a weary way to Strathlarrig on foot. My clothes were heavy with the rain, and my boots squelched.

I came down out of the hills to my father's castle. I came not from the back, which would have meant a prodigious circuit, for which I did not have the strength: nor from the front, coming up the Larrig River from its mouth at Inverlarrig on the lochside, because that way would be the most easily watched: but from the side, the east. From that direction the castle would have showed me, by daylight, two great towers with a steep-pitched slate roof between them.

I had hurried. Now I went slow. I stared at my home through the darkness and teeming rain. There were a few lights in the great windows of the lower floors, glowing dim behind curtains. There were lights high in the east wing, between the towers.

My nursery, as a child. The little suite of rooms far away from any others, which I shared with my dear Miss MacRae and a nursery maid, chosen for us so that we would neither disturb the rest of the household, nor be disturbed by it. Who could possibly be using those rooms now? I crouched in the sodden heather, feeling cold rain-drops dribbling down the small of my back, and down the valley between my breasts: and my mind lurched back to my golden childhood in those sunny rooms, behind those windows which glowed at me across the valley, welcoming, beckoning . . .

My parents were there. Of course they were. It would have been their own choice, that they should be off by themselves, so that Mamma would not be fatigued by company, and Papa could get on undisturbed with his scientific work. I reasoned so: but it was not reason that made me certain that behind those high bright windows my beloved silly parents were waiting. I simply knew they were there. And that was good, because, once I was in the castle, I knew a dozen secret ways of getting up to those rooms. I had needed them often as a child.

I felt a great wave of love and tenderness for the two behind the windows. I sent it across the teeming darkness, a message, saying that I was near, that I was full of happiness at the thought of seeing them. I jumped up from the tussock of heather where I crouched, and hurried forward, downhill, thinking of nothing except my coming reunion with Mamma and Papa.

Joy made me careless. I fell. I was tripped. It was a cord. It was a kind of snare. Hands gripped me. I struggled, and cried out. But I was on the ground, on bare rock running with water, held, pinned on my back by invisible hands. A shape loomed above me, black against the black sky. I smelled a reek of whisky and decay and carrion. In the sewers of a city I would have known that foul smell for the reek of Murdo's breath. I heard a chink of steel. I could not see the knife. I remembered the knife.

Well, my problems were solved. I need no longer hide from Carnmore, or the Gordons, or the police, or the tinkers, or anyone. I should be spared a weary journey to a place of hiding, and a miserable life of fear and furtiveness. My running and struggles were over. But it was such a pity that I should not say goodbye to my parents.

The rain filled my face; and the reek of Murdo's breath filled my nostrils.

Kenzie had seen me in Milkchurn Row. He had followed me into Haddow's shop, and found out what I found out. After that, they did not need to follow me, but only to wait for me.

There was a shout, and an answering shout. The glare of lanterns blossomed in the darkness, their beams prying through the teeming rain. Murdo's face above me was suddenly bathed in light. Light flared on his knife-blade. I heard the thumps and crashes of fighting men, oaths, a tinkle of glass as a lantern was smashed, a scream, the clash of steel on steel, the crack of a pistol, the big thud of a shotgun so near that it almost stunned me.

Murdo's face disappeared. He seemed to have been knocked away from me. The impact of the shot had pushed him. I was free. The beam of a lantern found me. I wriggled away from it, and jumped up, and ran off into the heather.

'The laddie—whaur's yon laddie?' shouted a voice. It was not the voice of a tinker.

Carnmore's men had saved me, or Inverdoran men.

More lanterns dotted the hillside. Armies were out. I crawled down a sheep-track that I knew of old. Prayers of thanks for my deliverance sang through my head. God had stretched out his hand to save me, so that I could see my parents and comfort them, this one last time. I went very careful now, so as not to waste His intervention. Having been rescued from Murdo's hand, it would be folly to fall into other hands. I went with extreme, with exaggerated care. It was well I did. There were men everywhere, and I heard dogs.

Going like a slow-worm, I came through the gardens to the very walls of the castle. Going like a spider, I crept round to the terrace and to the wall which extended the terrace, and so to the trap-door into the coal-cellar.

I could not budge the trap-door. I heaved at it, incredulous. It did not move. They had discovered it, after the burglary and the murder. They had nailed or bolted it.

The rain was harder and colder.

I knelt shivering by the useless trap-door. If I waited until dawn I should be seen, by Carnmore or Inverdoran or Strathlarrig servants. Before dawn, I must be in the castle and out of it again. By daylight I must be far away.

I began to continue making a circuit of the castle. With so much commotion, I thought, there must be men going in and out. There must be—might be—an open door somewhere.

There was. It was the little door by the kitchens, through which Benjie and I had let in Murdo and his men. It stood wide, in spite of the cold rain. A lamp glowed in the stone-flagged passage inside.

I crept to the open door, and peeped in. I heard a woman's voice, some way away, quacking like a duck.

I slipped in. The squelch of my boots seemed to make a deafening noise. I dripped on the flagstones as I went.

It took me some time to get safely to the east wing and to the top floor of the wing. And at last I knocked on the door of the old nursery.

Papa's voice said, 'Who is that? I am not to be disturbed. I am extremely busy.'

I burst into tears. I could not speak. The door was not locked. I opened it, and went in.

Papa was bent over the table where, long before, Miss MacRae and I had eaten our dinner. The table was the same. Everything in the room was the same. It was the day-nursery, where I had sat to my lessons and played with my toys. It was full of warm light, from lamps and a five-branched candlestick. A small fire flickered from the grate, behind the wire nursery fire-guard of my childhood.

Papa was wearing a flannel dressing-robe and a small velvet smoking cap. On the table were all manner of glass bowls and beakers and jars, some joined together with pipes, one on a little brass tripod over a wick flaming in a saucer of oil. Steam rose from that jar, with a penetrating smell.

Papa looked up as I came in. He was cross at being disturbed. He blinked at me across the room, short-sightedly.

'Papa,' I mumbled, through my sobs.

Papa's face then was the most wonderful thing I had ever seen. He seemed only slowly, slowly, to take in who I was. As he took it in, his face was transformed, slowly, slowly, until it shone with joy. I saw that his hands were trembling, and that there were tears on his cheeks, as well as mine.

He opened his arms, and I flew into them.

'Cat, Kitten, Pussy, darling child,' he murmured into my hair.

As we embraced, laughing and crying, we knocked over the beaker which was heating on the flame. There was a crash, and an acrid smell, and a hiss as the liquid put out the flame. I exclaimed in dismay, but Papa scarcely noticed the accident. He was stroking my head, and touching my face with his fingertips, and the tears of thankfulness were pouring down his dear cheeks.

'Where have you been, little Kitten?' he was able to ask me at last.

'I will tell you everything,' I said shakily. 'But first I must see Mamma.'

'She has been ill. She has been very weak. I have been most gravely worried. That is why we are here.'

'But—'

'Dr McPhee said that we were not to stay at Myrtle Lodge. He said there was damp, you know, which was bad for your Mamma. I daresay there may have been a patch or two of damp. It was arranged that Sir Richard Grant would take us in. I daresay Dr McPhee suggested it. It was somewhat impertinent of Grant, in a sense, to offer to accommodate us in our own house. But I felt obliged to come here, for your Mamma's sake.'

'And to my nursery—'

'Grant seemed unwilling that we should be in the—the midst of his friends and guests. We consented to occupy these rooms.'

'Can I see Mamma?'

'Now at once? No no, little Cat, your Mamma is asleep. She must not be disturbed. You shall see her in the morning.'

'Now at once, Papa. Is she in my bedroom?'

'Kitten, you are *not* to disturb your Mamma, who has suffered enough on your account—'

But before he could stop me, I had crossed the room, and opened the door into what had been my bedroom.

They had put in a new bed, of full size, in place of my child's bed. There were wraps, and gowns, and slippers, and so forth, and things of Mamma's on a dressing-table; but otherwise the room was just the same. There was a nightlight on the bedside table, where I had always had one when I was ill. (In truth I was never ill, but sometimes Miss MacRae thought I was, and sometimes I pretended I was.)

Mamma was asleep. I paused in the doorway, uncertain. Papa was bleating behind me. I did not want to wake Mamma; but I could not linger until morning. I walked forward, quietly, and looked down at her. Her face was calm in sleep. It was unlined. I thought it looked younger than my face. I leaned over her. The rain lashed at the window; a little flame whistled from the burning coals in the grate. There was no other sound. Examined closely, Mamma's face had something haggard about it. There was grief, in the set of her beautiful mouth.

She moaned softly in her sleep, and moved her head. Her eyes opened. She woke, and saw me. There was no delay in her recognition, or in her joy. She stretched up her arms towards me, and I fell on my knees at her bedside, and buried my face in her shoulder, and our happy tears mingled.

'Wicked, thoughtless Puss,' said Mamma at last. 'Why have you cut off your hair? Why are you dressed in those clothes? How wet you are! you must change at once . . . Alexander will be so thankful.'

'Who?' I asked stupidly, dazed with happiness.

'Sandy. Carnmore. Your husband, dearest. He will forgive you. I know he will. He promised us he would forgive you, if only he could get you back. How could you treat him so shamefully, precious child, when he has been so kind to us, so thoughtful? He has been moving heaven and earth—he has become quite drawn and grim with worrying about you.'

'Mamma, I cannot—'

'It is the most extraordinarily lucky chance, is not it,' said Mamma happily from her pillows, 'that he should be here tonight?'

'*What?*'

'I thought you would be amazed!'

'I see the hand of Providence,' said Papa from the door.

'He came to call on us today,' said Mamma, 'as he often does. So kind he is! So thoughtful! And then, when the weather became so dreadful, we persuaded Sir Richard to ask Alexander to stay the night, instead of riding all the way back to Carnmore, and ruining his health . . .'

'Don't tell him I'm here!' I cried. 'Papa, I beg you—'

'But I have told him, Kitten. Of course I have told him. A moment ago, when you came in here to see your Mamma, I rang for a footman, and sent him with a message. What joy, Kitten! Your old parents, and your devoted husband too, to greet and to forgive the wicked little prodigal!'

I jumped to my feet. My mind was racing. Of course, it was no accident that Carnmore was here, when he clearly expected me to come here. He persuaded Papa and Mamma to persuade Sir Richard, but made them think it was their own idea. Sir Richard could not refuse to entertain him, with his parents-in-law in the castle . . .

I could get out of the nursery. I must get out, at once. Once out, I could hide somewhere in the attics or cellars. And slip away under cover of darkness. At once. There was not a second to be lost.

I dropped to my knees, to give Mamma the last kiss I should ever give her. And, as I did so, I heard the voice in the door:

'Catriona.'

I was too slow. He was too quick.

I looked up. He stood in the open doorway, Papa behind him. He was silhouetted against the brighter light in the next room. I could not clearly see his face, but only the smooth butter-coloured hair that framed it. His voice when he spoke my name was gentle. To Mamma it must have sounded loving.

He stretched out his arms towards me. I found that I was cowering away from him, as though trying to burrow for safety into Mamma's bed. I was sure the face I turned to him showed the horror and terror I felt.

'You are dressed as a boy,' Carnmore went on, with a smile in his voice. 'Of course, it was so you started this adventure, wasn't it? In my suit, with my watch and my money in the pockets. What became of the watch? It was my father's, you know. I value it highly, for reasons of filial piety . . . Last time I saw you, you wore a blue dress, not suitable for boating, I think. That Gordon woman is a devil, is not she? Driven by an obsession. Well, I can understand that. I have been driven by my own obsession, my darling Cat, my little wife. As I think you know, I would have sacrificed anything. Any bricks, mortar, people . . . I cannot explain why. We are not responsible for our demons. But now that I have found you again, precious little Cat, I shall never, never let you go.'

'Quite right, my dear fellow,' said Papa behind him.

'My naughty Pussy will not run away again, Alexander,' said Mamma comfortably from her pillows.

Mamma raised her right hand, and very gently patted my head with it, as she had so often done when I knelt beside her sofa when I was a young child. With her left hand Mamma took my hand, which lay on the covers of her bed. She gripped my fingers. I was startled by the strength of her grip. It was as though she were holding me, to stop me running away again from my husband.

So we all remained for a moment. My wet clothes clung to me like seaweed. The unmoving flame of the night-light, within its jar, cast a gentle golden glow over Mamma's face, and, I suppose, my face. I could not see the smile on Carnmore's face, but I knew it was there.

I felt incapable of moving. A sort of paralysis invaded all my limbs. I thought Carnmore would have to carry me away. I thought he would not mind doing that.

He would be angry that I had lost his father's watch. It would be one other thing to anger him.

'We shall go away at once, tomorrow, dear little wife,' said Carnmore softly. 'The arrangements have been made for a long time, because I knew you would come back to me. We shall go to a very quiet and remote place. No one will see us or hear us or bother us. I am looking forward to that so very much. I have dreamed of nothing else, for three months. We can pick up where we left off, just where we left off. You remember, little Kitten, where we left off? We shall start afresh, from that point.'

'You see, Pussy?' said Mamma happily. 'Your husband loves you and forgives you. You are a luckier Pussy than you deserve.'

Where we left off. The branding-iron. I did not know if I could stand that pain. I would smell the roasting of my own flesh. His desire would be aroused by my agony, and he would take me. He would tear into my flesh with his flesh, because I was sobbing with pain. That would be worse than the branding-iron.

Suddenly I stood up. I did not decide to do so, but found that I had done so. Standing, I brushed away Mama's hand from my head, and pulled my fingers from her clasp.

The room had only one door. Carnmore blocked it. There was a window—my bedroom window when I was small. One night, when I was small—the night of the orphaned owlets in their nest in the hole in the chimney . . .

I went to the window, and drew back one half of the heavy curtain. Mamma exclaimed from her pillows.

'A foul night,' said Carnmore, still with a smile in his voice.

The sky outside the window was black as ink. I could not see the ground. Rain thrashed against the glass, like handfuls of gravel thrown by a giant in a temper.

The window was a long way from the ground. The ground below the window was paved with flagstones. There would be puddles of rainwater on the flagstones. Somehow it seemed more shocking to fall a hundred feet onto wet flagstones than onto dry ones.

I had gone out of that window as a child, and climbed to the roof. I was braver then. I could not do it now. I could imagine too vividly the fall through a hundred feet, and the smack onto wet flagstones. Not even the thought of the branding-iron could get me out into the teeming darkness, a hundred feet above the puddled stones. My knees shook at the thought, and fear of the great height tingled the soles of my feet.

I would have expected to become braver, as I grew up. I was disgusted to find that I had become a coward.

'Close the curtain, Catriona,' said Carnmore.

His voice was still soft, but there was in it a small clear note of authority. Well, he had absolute authority over me. He was my owner, body and soul. He had told me so, and it was true. The law of the realm said so, the words of the Sacrament of our marriage said so.

I glanced over my shoulder towards him, from the black and rain-drenched window. He took one step towards me, holding out his arms.

That one step, those outstretched arms, gave me the courage I lacked. I threw open the window. Mamma cried out. The flame of the night-light danced in its jar. The fire glowed brighter in the draught. Cold rain gusted into the quiet little room. In a moment I was out of the window, and clinging to the down-pipe which ran beside it.

Rain and wind battered my senses. The elements tried to prise me from the drain-pipe. The metal of the pipe was cold and wet to my hands. I climbed a few feet upwards, easily, driven by the threat of Carnmore. I scarce knew what I was doing, or where I was going, except that I was getting away from Carnmore. I would sooner have gone down the pipe than up. Carnmore would have seen me going down. He would have been waiting for me at the bottom.

I heard him shout, below me. I supposed he was leaning out of the window. I did not look down. I dared not. The yawning blackness below would have made my head swim.

I clung to the drain-pipe with my hands and with my knees. I could grip well with my knees, because of my stable-lad's breeches. At least I was dressed for climbing.

I went on up the pipe, and heaved myself over the crenellated pediment into the broad leaded gutter behind it. I crouched in the gutter, sheltered a little from the battering of wind and rain. On the inward side, I felt the smooth wet slates of the roof, steeply pitched, a slippery cliff to the ridge which I had once bestridden triumphantly, dreaming of riding a racehorse at the Perth Hunt Meeting.

I did not think Carnmore would follow me up the drain-pipe. For the time, I was safe from him and from everybody.

Safe? Was I safe? How long was I safe? I could not go down, except into his arms. If I returned again by the drain-pipe, there he would be in the window. I could cross acres of roof—slate and stone and leading —and come to any of a dozen skylights, which served various of the attics. They would be bolted, against wind and rain. No matter—I could break the glass with my boot. I could drop down into an attic. Into his arms? Perhaps not. He would not know about the skylights, where they were or even that they existed, a stranger in a strange castle.

Of course he would know about them. Beside him in my nursery stood the owner of the castle, who knew it better than I did. Who was deluded by Carnmore, bewitched by him, bought by him.

All the same, there were many skylights, dotted haphazard amongst the acres of roof. My ploy was simply to go through a skylight where Carnmore was not. He could not watch them all, even if he were told of them all. The noise of the breaking glass might be drowned, perhaps, by the crash of the rain on the roof. The attics were very extensive, and mostly deserted.

He would summon the household. There would be servants and lanterns everywhere, a pair of arms below every skylight. Would he do that? Declare to Sir Richard Grant and to the world that Lady Carnmore was so desperate to escape from her husband, that she crawled on a roof in a rainstorm?

I lay in the gutter, shivering, soaked to the skin, very cold, utterly undecided about what to do. I could not stay where I was for ever, hungry and exhausted and exposed. I could not go back the way I had come. Could I go on? I shuddered at the thought of the steep invisible wall of slates, running with rainwater, which towered beside me.

From the ridge at the top of the roof, the slates sloped down on the inside at the same awesome angle. Below was the east courtyard. It was raised above ground level, but there was still an eighty-foot drop from the roof to the paving-stones. There was no pediment there—no battlements, over an inner courtyard, but simply a narrow gutter. My stomach fluttered at the thought of sliding down that side, with nothing at the edge of the roof but a flimsy gutter.

I was not sure that I could climb the wet roof to the ridge. I was not sure that I dared gain the ridge, to be plucked off it by the wind, and thrown down the inner slope. But I could *not* stay where I was. I could not wait until daylight for my climb: I should be visible on the roof from thirty square miles of hill.

I began to feel the cold and wet creeping and seeping into my bones. I knew my fingers would soon be numb, if I did not move. I should not be able to grip with them. Any climb would be suicidal.

The rain battered into my eyes and ears, driving my senses out of my head. I forced myself to think. I must make for a skylight. The journey to it was hair-raising, but, if it was to be done, it must be done at once. How could I help myself to climb? Well, I could take off my jacket and boots. I had gripped the drain-pipe with my knees, but for the smooth roof I would need the grip of my toes. And my jacket, stiff and sodden, seriously hampered my movements.

I struggled out of my boots and my worsted stockings. I found to my alarm that my chilled fingers were already beginning to grow numb. My feet were no colder bare than shod, because they had been so wet. I thought my back would be no colder without my jacket, but I was wrong. Though sodden with the rain, it had been protection against the icy fingers of the wind. My flannel shirt was no such protection. It was soaking within seconds. I felt that it was glued wetly to my back and shoulders and breasts.

I started up the slope of the roof. Rainwater ran down the slates in a continuous stream, as though the whole roof was the bed of a shallow river. I tried to stick myself to the slates, like a court-plaster on a broken pate, keeping flat to the roof, touching it and holding it with as much of myself as possible; I was even, I swear, holding onto the slates with the skin of my cheek and chin.

I crawled upwards an inch at a time. With every upward inch, I felt in instant danger of slipping down a foot or a yard, or all the way to the gutter. The wind tugged at me, this way and that, as it eddied about the roof. My face was every moment full of rainwater, from the sky above and from the slates below.

It came to me that I had not, after all, kissed Mamma goodbye, because Carnmore came to the door just as I was going to do so.

Once, twice, thrice I slipped backwards, losing inches which I had struggled so hard to gain, my heart jumping into my throat as I thought I should slide clear to the bottom of the roof. I scraped my face as I slid, and hurt my fingers and toes and breasts.

I gained the ridge, and pulled myself up onto it. I could grip with my knees, as though I were riding, but I was far more exposed to the wind. I could see down into the courtyard to my right, because there were lights in windows. They seemed a terribly long way down. I tore my eyes away from them, before I began to get vertigo. I knew I must not look down again.

The climb up the roof to the ridge, and the crawl along the ridge to the chimney, were the worst parts of my journey. Then I got into a valley between roofs, where I was sheltered and perfectly safe; I crossed some flat leading, and then a roof with stones instead of slates, which gave a much better grip.

I felt that my fingers and toes were bleeding. I thought my face and breasts were too, from sliding down the slates when I slipped.

I crossed over the roof of the chapel, which was not difficult. Then there was an uncomfortable stretch of bare ridge, very exposed, which was the peak of the roof of the antechapel. I went along it in a sitting position, crouched against the wind, as I did on the other ridge. There was not far to fall on my left side, where the roof sloped to a high safe pediment, the top of the outer wall of the antechapel. But there was a longer slope on the other side, which ended in no pediment but only a gutter. Below was the main courtyard of the castle, paved with great slabs of granite.

What was bad about that ridge was that it was so exposed, and so wet, and so slippery. What was good about it was that it was much shorter than the other—no more than five yards. And what was even better, supremely good, was that in the roof into which it ran, and with which it formed a right-angle, was let the first of the skylights. Because of the pitch of the roof, this skylight was almost vertical. It was easily reached from the ridge of either roof. I knew it well. I had climbed out of it as a child. It could be opened, with hinges and bolts like a window; as far as I was concerned, it could be broken with a chip of stone from the roof. The skylight gave to an attic where, according to tradition, a madwoman had been kept. She was said to haunt the place, so it was never used. I could not see the skylight, from five yards away in the darkness. There was no light in the attic, then. I greeted the invisible skylight as an old friend, a friend in my very great need.

Rain and wind battered at me with a greater force than ever, as I crawled along that ridge. I supposed the wind was forced into a narrow space by the towers over the gatehouse and the chapel, and that I was in the midst of that narrow space. My flannel shirt, saturated, clung to my skin, and the wind lanced through it.

I was half way along the ridge, and my confidence was climbing like a sky-rocket.

And then a light blazed behind the glass, and the glass was swung open on its hinges, and a lantern was thrust out, and its beam shone on my face.

'There you are, little one,' said Carnmore. 'Do come in out of the rain.'

There was another light behind him and below him in the attic. By its light, I could see that he was kneeling on the sill of the skylight, half out onto the roof, his hand on my ridge. He was no more than eight feet away from me. He was shining the beam of his lantern full in my face.

I began to go backwards along the ridge. It was as easy as going forwards. I could go faster. I went faster. I went too fast. I could not see where I was going. I came, before I expected it, to an irregular bump in the ridge, a kind of patch that had covered a hole. Going forwards, it had not made me any problem. Going backwards, and not expecting it, it was a trap. And I was very frightened that Carnmore was so close to me, and I was distressed by the light glaring in my face. I nudged into the hump, and teetered, off balance. I grabbed at the point of the roof in front of me, suddenly filled with panic. My fingers were sore and cold and numb and wet. The smooth stone was wet. I missed my grip. The effort to grab had thrown me further off balance. I would not have been so incautious but for the terror of Carnmore so near me. I heard a scream. It was my scream. I slid helplessly from the ridge of the roof. Providentially, I slid to my left. Half sliding, half rolling, unable to save myself, I went fast down the slope of the roof, and crashed into the gutter and into the pediment. I heard a crack, and felt a shocking pain in my left leg, which had struck the pediment at an awkward angle. I tried to move, to crawl along the gutter away from Carnmore. I could not move that leg. It hurt very badly.

I had broken the leg. Carnmore was in the skylight. I saw the beam of his lantern poke up over the ridge. He was on the ridge, not sitting as I had been, but crouched on his hands and knees. He shone the beam down at me. I lay in an awkward heap in the gutter. My left leg was in an odd, unnatural position.

'Poor little Kitten,' called Carnmore over the noise of wind and rain. 'You've hurt yourself. How silly of you—that's my job. But I'll come and comfort you. At least, I'll come and look at you.'

He seemed to clip the lantern to his belt; then he began to crawl along the ridge. I saw that he was going to the end of the ridge, to the roof of the chapel, whence he could easily climb down into the gutter.

In no time he was two thirds of the way along the ridge, and beyond the place where I had slipped. He stopped, and unhooked the lantern from his belt. Holding onto the ridge with his other hand, he shone the lantern down at me. I could not see his face, because it was behind the lantern: but once again I knew there was a smile on it.

There was another glare from just the other side of the ridge. Out of my direct line of sight, there was another lantern in the skylight.

'Carnmore!' shouted a voice. 'What in God's name—'

Carnmore jumped, as anybody jumps at something utterly unexpected. I did not see what happened, because it was all behind the glare of his lantern. It seemed that, startled, he lost his balance. Because he did not want to drop his lantern, he was holding with only one hand. It was not enough. He slid off the ridge, exactly as I had done. But he slid off the other side. He slid down the long slope, at the bottom of which there was no pediment. As he slid, he gave a cry which was not a scream but a kind of high drone, like no sound I had ever heard before, like no sound I hope ever to hear again.

The noise of his landing on the granite was like that of an open-handed slap across a face. I think the wind dropped for a moment, at that moment, as though God were making sure that I heard.

'Carnmore,' said the voice from the ridge again, in a tone of shock and misery. It was Sir Richard Grant's voice. To someone behind he called, 'He was doing what? Chasing a boy? Was he demented? There are no boys on my roof . . . At least, I know of no boys on my roof–'

His lantern came up over the ridge. It played along the ridge, and down the inside roof, and down the outside roof, and explored the gutter. Once again I was impaled on the beam of a lantern.

'There is a boy,' said Sir Richard's astonished voice. He added, 'My God!'

I supposed he had recognised me. I was right.

'Bogle,' he said, in a stifled tone. 'So you have reverted to burglary. Is there no end to the mischief you make? You are responsible for the death of my guest–'

'Nonsense,' I called out, as firmly as I could for the pain of my leg. 'You were responsible for Carnmore's death, Sir Richard.' I added, although it was a dreadful thing to say, 'Thank you very much.'

'What in heaven's name has come to your speech?' said Sir Richard. 'Have you turned into a gentleman?'

I burst out laughing. It was not what I expected to do. It was not what a widow of one minute should have done. Perhaps it was strong hysteria. For a moment it seemed exquisitely funny that Sir Richard thought I was a gentleman.

'Come up out of there, Bogle,' called Sir Richard in a very fierce voice.

'There is nothing I would prefer,' I said, 'but I have broken my leg.'

There was shouting and commotion behind him, and in a minute a ladder poked over the ridge, and slid down the slope of the roof until its foot rested against the pediment. Sir Richard came over the ridge and down the ladder. Someone I could not see perched on the ridge with a lantern to light his way. He was in evening dress. I thought he would need new evening dress, after this evening.

'You miserable urchin,' said Sir Richard, sounding seriously angry. 'I suppose thieving is in your blood. You won't go to the Gordons this time, my lad. You'll go to the Sheriff Court, and get the whipping you need.'

He picked me up. He was very strong. I cried out at the pain in my leg. For the second time I felt his arms about me—one arm under my back, one under my knees. I put one arm round his neck, so that I could take some of my own weight. He took a better grip with the arm that was under my back, before he started the business of going up the ladder. His arm went right round me, so that his hand was on my breast. The sodden flannel of my shirt clung to my breast like a second skin. It was there that his hand rested.

I had never before felt a man's hand on my breast. His was the only hand in the world I wanted to feel there. My reaction to the startling fact was not modest. Without thought, I tightened my arm round his neck.

'Dear God,' he said, so astonished that I think he nearly dropped me. 'Bogle . . . You're no more a boy than . . . When you fell down off the hayrack, and I caught you, I thought . . . I was disgusted and appalled at myself, and all along . . .'

'Well, now you know that it's not unnatural to embrace me,' I said, 'I wish you would please do it. Just to take my mind off my broken leg, you know.'

'Catriona. Cat.'

'Well, yes.'

He held me very tight. He held my cheek to his.

'All along, I knew there was something familiar in your face,' he mumbled into my wet hair. 'All along, I was fascinated by you, and drawn to you, and I thought . . . I cannot understand how it is that I didn't recognise you.'

'My own Papa didn't recognise me.'

'He loves you, no doubt. But he's not in love with you.'

'Are you?'

'I . . . Cat, I cannot declare myself to—to a lady just this moment widowed!'

'Oh yes,' I said, 'you can.'

I could not see his face. But I felt his lips on mine. I drowned in the joy of that kiss. I forgot the pain of my broken leg, and all discomfort and wet, and cold; I forgot all modesty.

And all the time, his hand was still on my breast. He was immodest too. I was so glad.

There was a bellow of astonished outrage, from the ridge of the roof. Whoever it was, was so startled that he dropped the lantern. It crashed on the roof, and tinkled all the way down into the gutter.

Of course, not many castle servants see their laird passionately kissing a stable-lad.

'A lad called Benjie,' said Richard. 'He managed to slip those brutes who owned him, and came here to warn us.'

'God be blessed and thanked,' I said, 'for a friend like Benjie.'

'A most improbable angel, to look at and listen to. But we'll turn him into the good man I believe he can be.'

'We? Where is he? What will become of him?'

'Yes, we. He's here. He's to be a stable-lad.'

'Another of those,' I said.

Richard laughed, and kissed me. He had overcome his scruples about making love to a woman so recently widowed.

'When I fell in love with you,' I said at last, freeing myself, with some reluctance, 'I was a boy. It was so awkward.'

'When I fell in love with you, you were a boy,' he said. 'It was more than awkward. That is why I offered for poor Elspeth.'

'Oh. Elspeth. What about Elspeth?'

'I am very sorry for Elspeth,' he said, 'but I am not going to ally myself to a family who behave as they behaved.'

'She is obsessed,' I explained. 'Carnmore was, too.'

'As a matter of fact, I am too,' said Richard.

'As a matter of fact, I am too,' I said.

I was so glad to see Dr McPhee again. My leg had a clean break, and he said it would mend quickly.

Mamma and Papa were greatly shocked. They grieved deeply and sincerely for Carnmore. I had told Richard everything, but we told them nothing. There was no purpose in it, and probably they would not have believed me.

Papa continued a little to resent Richard. This made me angry, but Richard laughed away my anger.

Papa abandoned chemistry—suddenly, one morning in December—and embarked on the invention of a steam-pump which would supply cities with water. Richard was permitted to invest in the Larrig Steam Aquaportation Company; he provided a workshop and tools, and listened gravely by the hour to Papa's explanations of mechanics.

We were married on Midsummer Day, my nineteenth birthday: quietly, in the chapel at Strathlarrig, because I was a widow. A few old friends were there. Mamma was distressed that the Gordons of Inverdoran were not present.

'I *will* try not to be wild and spoiled and wilful,' I said to Richard. 'I *will* try to change, truly I will.'

'I shall be seriously angry if you change in any way,' said Richard, with the savage frown he had worn when I first met him.

Benjie still calls me Jaikiebogle. In other ways—some other ways—he has become a model. But having learned a name for me, he will not unlearn it. He has grown, and put on weight, and looks his proper age, and has become rather a dandy in his dress: but his carroty thatch resists any brush and comb, and his grin whenever he sees me is as broad as the Larrig River.

God be blessed and thanked for a friend like Benjie.

The **Jewish** Mama's Kitchen

Special thanks

I would like to dedicate this book to my mum and dad, who have
always been there for me and to whom I owe so much.

An Hachette UK Company

First published in Great Britain in 2009 by
Spruce, a division of Octopus Publishing Group Ltd
2–4 Heron Quays, London E14 4JP.
www.octopusbooks.co.uk
www.octopusbooksusa.com

Distributed in the U.S. and Canada for Octopus Books USA
c/- Hachette Book Group USA
237 Park Avenue
New York NY 10017.

ISBN 11: 978-1-84601-341-6
ISBN 10: 1-84601-341-0

A CIP catalogue record of this book is available from the British Library.

Printed and bound in China

10 9 8 7 6 5 4 3 2 1

The Food and Drug Administration advises that eggs should not be consumed raw. This book
contains some dishes made with raw eggs. It is prudent for more vulnerable people, such as pregnant
or nursing mothers, invalids, the elderly, babies, and young children to avoid uncooked or lightly
cooked dishes made with eggs.

The Jewish
Mama's Kitchen

Denise Phillips

spruce

Acknowledgments

Being called a Jewish mama is a privilege that not all Jewish women are entitled to. But my mother more than deserves it. She sparked my initial interest in cooking as a child, and she has continued to be so supportive right up to this day. I speak to her at least once a day, and over the past few months I have spent many hours discussing and revising many of her recipes for this book. It certainly provided my mother a welcome distraction from worrying about my father, who had been ill, but who has now, thankfully, recovered. I would also like to acknowledge the contribution of two other mamas of my mother's generation—Freda Skovron and Yehudhit Solomans—who provided plenty of ideas for recipes based on their own childhood experiences. In addition, Sharon Feldman-Vazan helped to balance the content of this book by inspiring me to add a number of interesting Sephardi recipes.

The creation of this book occurred at a very busy time in my life and was made possible only by the support of some key people. I would like to thank my friend Marsha Schultz for her time and effort in editing my efforts, and Masa Segota, my au pair, for all her help with food preparation and cleaning up that enabled me to get on with the next recipe. My close friend Lynne Misner was there to help me bounce around ideas and to confirm my train of thought.

Finally, I would like to thank my new husband, Jeremy, for his help in reading through the recipes and providing his input as a complete cooking novice.

And of course, thanks to my children, Abbie, Samantha, and Nick, for getting on and dealing with their homework while I was busy chopping onions and frying fish!

Contents

Introduction

As one of four daughters whose mother and grandmother (as well as a large group of aunts) all loved to cook and entertain, perhaps it was inevitable that I would develop a passion for cooking when I was very young. I was hooked by the way the women all worked together in the kitchen—gossiping, singing, laughing, and crying (from the onions!) as they peeled and chopped, sifted and sorted, melted and measured (not very accurately—they worked by instinct), and stuffed and grated.

The women would plan their meals and shop together, then create their own individual masterpieces. They would drink numerous cups of tea "to keep them going," and they always burned their mouths tasting soups and stews that bubbled enticingly on the hot stove. The kitchen was always steamy, and it smelled divine—the aromas of baking bread, roasting chicken, and simmering cholent and goulash were always wafting through the air. Everyone talked about how the food should be prepared—and they often argued over whose recipe was the best. The most frequent argument was over whether or not to add sugar to a dish. Those of Polish origin (the Polacks) said no, but those with Lithuanian roots (the Litvaks) put a pinch of sugar in everything—"to bring out the flavor"!

The atmosphere was so focused on the delivery of the Friday night or festival meal that I never considered whether my female role models had lovely clothes, painted nails, or styled hair. These women from Poland, Russia, and Holland, with their grubby aprons (called *pinnies*), fingers stained red from peeling beets, and onion-tired eyes were my mentors. They are my heritage and the real source of my inspiration. They were true Yiddisher mamas, and I am proud to carry on their tradition with this book. I hope that it will provide you, the reader, an insight into the fascinating link between food and the celebration of Judaism.

Cooking and good food have been central to Jews since the time of the Bible. In fact, the Jewish religion places the kitchen as the center of Jewish life as much as it does the synagogue because of its role in promoting family values. The Jewish calendar is studded with a glorious variety of festivals and holidays. Some of them are serious occasions; others are more fun. But they all have one thing in common: a celebratory shared meal, with a signature dish chosen for its religious connection to the holiday.

But good food is not restricted to festivals. Every Friday night we welcome the arrival of the Sabbath, when families come together and celebrate the joy of life by eating the best food that they can afford.

There is no single Jewish cooking style. The Jewish culinary tradition encompasses a wide variety of cultures and cuisines. In order to gain insight into a Jewish mama's world, it's helpful to understand some of the history and traditions of her people.

Judaism is not only one of the oldest religions in the world, but it is also one of the most geographically widespread. Over the last 5,000 years, Jews have traveled to every corner of the globe—sometimes out of choice, other times under pressure or hardship. Wherever they have settled, Jews have incorporated many of the local dishes into their own culinary lives, adapting them to suit Jewish dietary laws. These laws, which are called kashruth, dictate the kinds of meat, poultry, and fish that may be eaten and the way in which fish and animals must be killed and prepared. Great care is taken to ensure that processed foods do not contain any forbidden products (such as shellfish and pork), and dishes are not allowed to contain both milk and meat. Jews who observe the kashruth have separate utensils, crockery, and cutlery that they use in the preparation of meat and in the preparation of recipes that include milk.

Most Jews living in Western Europe originated from Poland, Russia, and the Baltic. These so-called Ashkenazi Jews brought with them a culinary heritage of traditional foods such as soups, stews, stuffed vegetables, and hearty, starchy, sugary, comfort foods that served them well during the long, cold winter months of Eastern Europe.

The other main grouping of Jews are called Sephardi Jews. They originated from Spain and North Africa, and they settled around the Mediterranean and the Middle East. Their food traditions reflect the lighter, spicier foods, such as kebabs, rice, and salads, that are eaten in warmer climates.

When the State of Israel was founded as the Jewish homeland in 1948, both Ashkenazi and Sephardi Jews rapidly settled the area. As a result, a new Israeli Jewish cuisine developed. This cuisine featured the best of both "original worlds." Its tasty, satisfying dishes have been heavily influenced by scores of other cultures, but they feature the finest fresh local produce, and they are made following the ancient dietary laws. From falafel and hummus to goulash with savory rice, Israeli Jewish cooking is a fantastic "melting pot" of cuisines.

Because "traditional Jewish cooking" means different things to Ashkenazi, Sephardi, and Israeli Jews, the challenge in writing a book that deals with traditional Jewish recipes is to decide which "tradition" to follow, or to strike a balance among the three cuisines. In this book I have attempted to capture the geographic and ethnic cultures that have strongly influenced the many different varieties of Jewish cooking.

Welcome to my kitchen—come inside, and let's cook!

Chapter one
APPETIZERS

Eggplant Dip

This is a tasty, versatile Sephardi dip that is usually served with a selection of crudités, sliced pita, or matzah crackers. It has a wonderful texture and flavor, and even those who aren't usually fond of eggplant often find this absolutely delicious. You can make this dish either on a gas stove, outdoor grill, or broiler.

PAREVE: contains no meat or dairy products / Passover-friendly / can be made in advance
PREPARATION TIME: 10 minutes / **COOKING TIME:** 15 minutes / **SERVES:** 6

2 regular eggplants (about 2 pounds total) ◆ **2 large garlic cloves, peeled and sliced thinly**
1 tablespoon mayonnaise ◆ **2 teaspoons fresh lemon juice** ◆ **Salt**
◆ **Freshly ground black pepper** ◆ **¼ cup pine nuts, for garnish** ◆ **2 tablespoons coarsely chopped Italian parsley, for garnish**

◆

1 Cut several 2-inch-long, 1-inch-deep slits in each eggplant. Push the garlic slices into the slits.

2 If using a gas burner, place the eggplant directly on the burner over a medium-high gas flame and roast, turning occasionally until soft (about 15 minutes). If using an outdoor grill, place the eggplant on the hot grill and roast, turning occasionally until soft (about 10 minutes). Remove from the heat and set aside to cool.

3 Remove and discard the skin from the eggplant. Place the eggplant in a large bowl and mash with a fork. Mix in the mayonnaise and lemon juice. Add salt and pepper to taste. Refrigerate covered until chilled.

4 Just before serving, place the pine nuts in a small, dry saucepan over medium-low heat. Toast, stirring frequently until golden brown (3 to 4 minutes). Sprinkle the pine nuts and parsley on the dip and serve.

Chopped Herring

Chopped herring is a much-loved, traditional appetizer in American Jewish households. It is most commonly eaten on slices of Challah (see pages 41 to 42) to break the fast at the end of Yom Kippur. This recipe is my mother's. Even with food processors and the kitchen accessories readily available today, my mother believes that the proper way to make this dish is to chop it by hand, using a large chopping cleaver.

PAREVE: contains no meat or dairy products / can be made in advance
PREPARATION TIME: 15 minutes / **COOKING TIME:** 0 minutes / **SERVES:** 4 to 6

One 24-ounce jar pickled herring, drained
2 tablespoons chopped onion from herring marinade
1 medium green or red apple, peeled, cored, and grated
2 slices challah or white bread ◆ 2 large eggs, hard-boiled and peeled

◆

1 Remove and discard the skins of the herring. Place the herring, onion, and apple on a chopping board and put aside.

2 Briefly dip the bread in warm water. Squeeze dry and place on the chopping board. Chop together with the herring, onion, and apple.

3 Remove and set aside the yolk of one egg. Add the egg white and remaining whole egg to the mixture and chop together to produce a pâté. Transfer the mixture to a serving dish.

4 Grate the reserved egg yolk. Sprinkle on top of the chopped herring and serve.

Falafel

Although the number of ingredients in this recipe may seem daunting, it's quite easy to make these deep-fried chickpea balls, and the taste of homemade falafel is simply without peer. This is the most popular street snack in Israel, and it's sold, wrapped in a pita, in kiosks, markets, and traditional restaurants. Israelis take their falafel very seriously—every year there are competitions to find the champion falafel maker, and there is fierce rivalry between street vendors and chefs. When it comes to falafel, fresh is definitely best; have your guests ready and waiting as the fritters come straight out of the fryer and onto their plates.

PAREVE: contains no meat or dairy products / can be made in advance / can be frozen up to 1 month
PREPARATION TIME: 30 minutes (plus at least 6 hours to allow chickpeas to soak)
COOKING TIME: 55 minutes / MAKES: about 40 fritters

1½ cups dried chickpeas ♦ 3 to 4 tablespoons bulgur ♦ 5 large garlic cloves, peeled
1 large yellow onion, peeled and chopped coarsely ♦ 5 tablespoons fresh Italian parsley
5 tablespoons fresh cilantro leaves ♦ 3 tablespoons ground cumin ♦ 1 teaspoon curry powder
1 tablespoon ground dried coriander ♦ 1 teaspoon baking powder
1 teaspoon cayenne pepper ♦ 1 teaspoon salt ♦ Freshly ground black pepper ♦ 1 large egg,
lightly beaten ½ cup water ♦ 3 to 4 tablespoons graham flour ♦ About 6 cups vegetable oil

♦

1 Place the chickpeas in a medium saucepan and cover with water. Let soak at least 6 hours or overnight.

2 Drain and rinse the chickpeas. Rinse the pan. Return the chickpeas to the pan, cover with water, and bring to a boil over medium-high heat. Reduce the heat to medium-low and simmer 45 minutes or until tender (add more water during cooking, if necessary). Drain.

3 Transfer the chickpeas to a food processor and pulse to a paste. Then empty into a large bowl. Stir in the bulgur and set aside.

4 Place the garlic, onion, parsley, cilantro, cumin, curry powder, coriander, baking powder, cayenne pepper, and salt in a food processor. Add pepper to taste. Process to a paste. Add to the chickpeas.

5 Add the egg and water to the chickpeas. Stir in the flour. If necessary, stir in a bit more water to prevent the mixture from being too dry or too thick. The consistency should be smooth and not too sticky.

6 Using wet hands, shape the mixture into small balls ready for frying.

7 Pour oil in a large, deep skillet to form a 2½-inch-deep layer of oil (or use a deep-fat fryer). Heat the oil over medium-high heat.

8 When the oil is very hot, place several balls into the oil (do not overcrowd the skillet) and cook until golden brown (3 to 4 minutes).

9 Using a slotted spoon, transfer the cooked balls to paper towels to blot any excess oil. Repeat until all balls have been fried. Serve immediately.

Knishes

These stuffed pastries are an American Jewish snack, but they are now also becoming popular with non-Jews from all ethnic groups. The knishes that are sold by street vendors in New York City and other large cities are often quite good—but homemade knishes are, of course, even better.

PAREVE: contains no meat or dairy products / can be made in advance / can be frozen up to 1 month
PREPARATION TIME: 40 minutes (plus 1 hour to allow dough to rest) / **COOKING TIME:** 45 minutes
MAKES: about 45 slices

DOUGH
1 cup all-purpose flour ◆ 1 teaspoon baking powder ◆ 2 large eggs ◆ 2 teaspoons kosher salt
3 tablespoons vegetable oil, divided ◆ 2 to 3 tablespoons cold water

FILLING
3 tablespoons vegetable oil ◆ 2 yellow onions, peeled and chopped finely
2 cups mashed potatoes ◆ Salt ◆ Freshly ground black pepper

GLAZE
Yolks of 2 large eggs, lightly beaten

◆

Mama says...
Be sure to very generously salt and pepper the potato filling to ensure a tasty knish.

1 Make the dough. Place the flour, baking powder, eggs, salt, 2 tablespoons oil, and 2 tablespoons water in a food processor that has been fitted with a dough blade and process until a smooth dough is formed. (If necessary, add 1 additional tablespoon water.)

2 Using the remaining tablespoon of oil, grease a large bowl. Place the dough in the bowl and let stand for 1 hour, covered.

3 Meanwhile, make the filling. Heat the oil in a medium saucepan over medium-low heat. Add the onions and sauté until golden brown (about 15 minutes).

4 Transfer the onions to a food processor that has been fitted with a metal blade. Pulse briefly to finely chop the onions.

5 Place the onions and potatoes in a medium bowl. Salt and pepper to taste, and mix well. Set aside until the dough has rested 1 hour.

6 Assemble the pastries. First, preheat the oven to 400°F.

7 Divide the dough into thirds.

8 Lightly dust a work surface with flour. Place 1 portion of dough on the work surface. Using a hand roller, roll the dough into a 20-inch by 8-inch strip.

9 Place one-third of the potato filling along the length of the strip—over the entire width. Starting at one end of the strip, roll up the strip to form a shape that resembles a jelly roll.

10 Repeat steps 8 and 9 with the remaining two portions of dough.

11 Place the pastries on a baking tray and glaze with egg yolk. Bake 30 minutes.

12 Cut into 1-inch-thick slices and serve immediately.

Hummus

This creamy chickpea purée is a specialty of Middle Eastern Jews, but it has become popular among non-Jews all over the world as well. Although is can be added to sandwiches, it is usually eaten with a hot pita as an appetizer. Traditionally, hummus is made with dried chickpeas, but canned chickpeas work nicely, too—and they make for a much faster preparation time. Tahini, a thick sesame seed paste, can be found in the ethnic section of most supermarkets. Be sure to thoroughly stir the tahini, which will have separated in its can or jar, before using.

PAREVE: contains no meat or dairy products / can be made in advance
PREPARATION TIME: 10 minutes / **COOKING TIME:** 0 minutes / **MAKES:** about 4 cups

**Two 14-ounce cans chickpeas, drained and rinsed ◆ Juice of 1 lemon
3 tablespoons tahini paste ◆ ¼ cup, plus 2 tablespoons extra-virgin olive oil
3 garlic cloves, peeled and crushed ◆ Salt ◆ Cayenne pepper**

◆

1 Place the chickpeas and lemon juice in a blender and purée. Add the tahini, olive oil, and garlic. Salt and pepper to taste. Blend until smooth.

2 Adjust the seasonings, if desired. Spoon into a serving dish and serve.

Mama says...
sprinkle with chopped parsley and olives, drizzle with extra-virgin olive oil, and serve with a hot pita.

Egg and Onion

*This is a simple, traditional dish that is often served alongside chopped liver
(see opposite) on Friday nights. It can be made with raw or cooked onion, and it is
delicious on rye bread, Challah (see pages 41 to 42), or matzah crackers.
For a mild onion taste, use cooked white onions. For a stronger onion flavor,
use raw or cooked yellow onions.*

FLEISHIK: contains no meat *or* **MILCHIK**: contains dairy products *or*
PAREVE: contains no meat or dairy products / Passover-friendly / can be made in advance
PREPARATION TIME: 10 minutes / **COOKING TIME**: 20 minutes / **SERVES**: 6

1 tablespoon chicken fat, margarine (nondairy for a meat meal), or vegetable oil
1 large yellow or white onion, peeled and chopped coarsely
8 large eggs, hard-boiled, peeled, and chopped finely
Salt ◆ Spanish paprika for garnish (if desired)

◆

1 Heat the chicken fat, margarine, or
vegetable oil in a medium frying pan over
medium-low heat.

2 If a light onion flavor is desired, place onion
in the pan and sauté until soft and slightly
browned. Remove from the heat and set aside.

(If a stronger onion flavor is desired, do not
cook the onion.)

3 Finely chop or grate the eggs. Mix with
the onions and salt to taste. Transfer to a
serving bowl and sprinkle with paprika.
Serve at room temperature.

Grandma's Chopped Liver

My mother and grandmother have always made their own chopped liver for the family to enjoy on Friday nights. In fact, Friday nights wouldn't be the same without this delicacy, which is served with large, soft slices of challah (see pages 41 to 42) or matzah crackers. Although many people purchase chopped liver at their local deli, you can control the ingredients, freshness, and flavor, and serve a treat that any deli would be proud to sell by making your own (which is really easy to do).

FLEISHIK: contains meat / Passover-friendly / can be made in advance / can be frozen up to 2 weeks
PREPARATION TIME: 15 minutes / **COOKING TIME:** 10 minutes / **SERVES:** 4 to 6

**2 to 3 tablespoons sunflower oil ◆ 2 large yellow onions, peeled and sliced thinly
9 ounces koshered chicken livers ◆ 3 large eggs, hard-boiled and peeled
Salt ◆ Freshly ground black pepper**

◆

1 Heat the sunflower oil in a frying pan over medium-low heat. Add the onions and sauté until slightly browned (about 10 minutes). Add the chicken livers. Stirring occasionally, fry 5 minutes. Transfer the chicken livers and onions to paper towels to blot any excess oil.

2 Remove the egg yolk from one egg and set aside, then coarsely chop the egg white and remaining two eggs.

3 Place the chicken livers and onions on the work surface with the chopped eggs. Mince together. Transfer the mixture to a medium-sized bowl and mix well. Salt and pepper to taste. Refrigerate covered until ready to serve.

4 Just before serving, spread the mixture over crackers or place in a serving bowl. Grate or mince the remaining egg yolk. Sprinkle the egg yolk over the chopped liver and serve.

Tabbouleh

This satisfying tabbouleh is traditionally served with a selection of other salads and dips as part of an appetizer table, or as a side dish with meat or chicken. The members of my synagogue in North London have regular Friday night meals together where tabbouleh is often served with teriyaki salmon and fish balls. Serve this at room temperature to bring out the full flavor of the onions and tomatoes.

PAREVE: contains no meat or dairy products / can be made in advance
PREPARATION TIME: 15 minutes / **COOKING TIME:** 15 minutes / **SERVES:** 6

**2 cups bulgur ◆ 1 cup boiling water ◆ 10 plum tomatoes
5 scallions, chopped coarsely ◆ 6 tablespoons coarsely chopped fresh mint
3 tablespoons coarsely chopped Italian parsley
3 tablespoons extra-virgin olive oil ◆ Juice of 1 lemon
Salt ◆ Freshly ground black pepper**

◆

1 Place the bulgur and water in a medium saucepan. Bring to a boil over medium-high heat. Reduce the heat to low and simmer uncovered until the bulgur is tender (about 15 minutes). Transfer to a colander and drain off any remaining water. Set aside.

2 Fill a large saucepan with water and bring to a boil over high heat. Place the tomatoes in water and cook 2 to 3 minutes. Remove the tomatoes from the water. Peel off and discard the skins. Remove and discard the seeds. Coarsely chop the tomato flesh.

3 Transfer the bulgur to a serving bowl. Add the tomatoes, scallions, mint, parsley, olive oil, and lemon juice. Generously salt and pepper. Toss to mix.

Mama says...
Scoop individual portions into small Bibb lettuce leaves. Top with chopped, pitted black olives and serve.

Fried Eggplant Salad

I love to serve this salad as a first course for our Friday night meal when it's too hot for chicken soup. This is one of several Sephardi recipes given to me by a friend, who received the recipes from her Tunisian mother-in-law. It's a simple dish that uses few ingredients—but, as is the case with many recipes that have been handed down from generation to generation—the exact measurements of ingredients were never written down. This is the way I like to prepare it, but feel free to experiment with different measurements of your own, to suit your personal taste.

PAREVE: contains no meat or dairy products / Passover-friendly / can be made in advance
PREPARATION TIME: 10 minutes / **COOKING TIME:** 15 minutes / **SERVES:** 8

3 tablespoons olive oil
2 large eggplants, cut into bite-sized cubes (leave the skin on)
About 1 cup salty Israeli pickled cucumbers, chopped coarsely
1 bunch (about 1 ounce) Italian parsley, chopped coarsely ◆ Salt
Freshly ground black pepper

◆

1 Heat the olive oil in a large frying pan over medium heat. Add 1 layer of eggplant. Sauté until golden brown (about 5 minutes). Transfer to paper towels. Repeat until all the eggplant is fried.

2 Place the eggplant, cucumber, and parsley in a large bowl. Add salt and pepper to taste. Toss to mix. Transfer to a serving bowl or to individual salad plates.

Mama says...
Serve this tempting salad in a glass dish, garnished with thin slices of lemon.

Herring Salad

In the old days, herring made a regular appearance at Ashkenazi Eastern European dinner tables, as they were economical and tasty, and they kept forever when soaked in brine. Today a wide variety of prepared herring can be found in delis and supermarkets. The fish is always the same—the variety is in the marinade, which may be sweet, salty, spicy, garlicky, peppery, or lemony. Herring is not a personal favorite of mine, but I've found it to be surprisingly good when combined with beets, as in this salad. This recipe is quick and easy—and, because it requires no cooking, it's a pleasure to make during hot summer months.

MILCHIK: contains dairy products
PREPARATION TIME: 5 minutes plus 15 minutes to refrigerate / **COOKING TIME:** 0 minutes
SERVES: 6 to 8

2 medium golden delicious apples, cored, peeled, and chopped coarsely
20 ounces schmaltz herring, chopped coarsely
2 tablespoons pickled Israeli cucumbers, chopped coarsely
1 tablespoon sugar ◆ 2 teaspoons cider vinegar ◆ 1¼ cups sour cream
1 cup cooked beets, peeled and chopped coarsely

◆

1 In a large bowl, combine the apples, herring, cucumbers, sugar, and cider vinegar. Add the sour cream and mix well. Stir in the beets. Refrigerate until chilled (about 15 minutes) and serve.

*Mama says...
serve this colorful salad in a glass bowl, and garnish it with fresh chives.*

chapter two

SOUPS, DUMPLINGS & BREAD

Borscht

The popularity of borscht throughout the centuries is no doubt related to the availability and cost of its main ingredient—the gloriously purple beet. In the twenty-first century, however, many enjoy it for another reason as well—it is low in fat and high in nutrients. My recipe is based on my great-aunt's. My great-uncle was from Russia, and he and my great-aunt made this every Passover. It was not an easy dish to make back then, as cooked beets were not available in stores during those days. Fortunately, they are available to us today. Borscht may be served hot or cold, chunky or smooth. Traditionally, it's served cold during the summer, with a dollop of sour cream, and hot in the winter, with a garnish of sliced boiled potato. Either way, its vibrant color and flavor will be sure to please. Beware of serving it at a table dressed in a white tablecloth, however!

PAREVE: contains no meat or dairy products *or* **MILCHIK:** contains dairy products
or **FLEISHIK:** contains meat / Passover-friendly / can be made in advance
PREPARATION TIME: 15 minutes / **COOKING TIME:** 40 minutes / **SERVES:** 4

**4 cups water ◆ 1 teaspoon kosher salt ◆ 2 large eggs ◆ Juice of 1 lemon
One 2-pound cooked beet (about a 3-inch diameter), peeled and chopped coarsely
3 tablespoons light brown sugar to taste**

◆

1 Place the water in a large saucepan. Stir in the salt. Add the chopped beet.

2 Bring to a boil over medium-high heat. Reduce the heat to medium-low and simmer for 30 minutes.

3 In a small bowl, whisk together the eggs, lemon juice, and sugar. Add to the soup. Cook, stirring constantly, for 3 minutes.

4 Transfer half of the soup to a food processor. Process until the mixture is smooth. Return the mixture to the saucepan. Serve warm or chilled.

Thick Cabbage and Bean Soup

The original cabbage soup that was made in Eastern Europe was probably created as a way to use up overripe vegetables. Today, many Jewish mamas add cannellini beans for extra nutrition. Hearty and flavorful, with a delightful combination of colors, textures, and tastes, this is the perfect soup to serve on cold winter days.

PAREVE: contains no meat or dairy products / can be made in advance / can be frozen up to 2 weeks
PREPARATION TIME: 25 minutes / **COOKING TIME:** 40 minutes / **SERVES:** 6

2 tablespoons olive oil ◆ 1 medium yellow onion, peeled and chopped finely
3 medium carrots, peeled and chopped coarsely ◆ 2 medium potatoes,
peeled and chopped coarsely ◆ 2 medium zucchini, trimmed and chopped coarsely
3 large garlic cloves, peeled and chopped finely ◆ 4 cups vegetable stock
4 cups coarsely chopped green cabbage ◆ 2 cups drained canned cannellini beans
Salt ◆ Freshly ground black pepper

◆

1 Heat the olive oil in a large saucepan over medium-low heat. Add the onion, carrots, potatoes, zucchini, and garlic. Sauté 10 minutes.

2 Add the vegetable stock, cabbage, and cannellini beans. Generously salt and pepper.

3 Increase the heat to medium-high and bring to a boil. Reduce the heat to low and simmer 40 minutes or until all the vegetables are soft. Adjust the seasonings, if necessary.

4 Serve immediately.

Mama says...
Ladle the soup into deep bowls. Drizzle with swirls of extra-virgin olive oil and serve.

Golden Vegetable Soup

A familiar dish from the shtetls of Eastern Europe, this soup is packed with the goodness of winter root vegetables. I remember my mother serving this to me when I was little. Today, my children enjoy it. The garnish of toasted cashews is a modern touch that enhances both its flavor and appearance. To hide the ingredients from children who refuse to eat vegetables, I make a "no bits" version, which is blended into a completely smooth soup.

PAREVE: contains no meat or dairy products / Passover-friendly
can be made in advance / can be frozen up to 1 month
PREPARATION TIME: 20 minutes / **COOKING TIME:** 30 minutes / **SERVES:** 6

**1 cup coarsely chopped cashews, crushed ◆ 2 tablespoons olive oil
2 onions, peeled and sliced ◆ 1 medium rutabaga, peeled and chopped coarsely
2 medium potatoes, peeled and chopped coarsely
8 medium carrots, peeled and sliced into rounds ◆ 5 cups vegetable stock
Fine sea salt ◆ Freshly ground black pepper**

◆

1 Preheat the oven to 400°F.

2 Place the crushed cashews on a baking tray and toast in the oven 8 to 10 minutes. Remove from the oven and put to one side to garnish the soup later.

3 Heat the olive oil in a large, deep saucepan over medium-low heat. Add the onions and sauté 2 minutes.

4 Add the rutabaga, potatoes, carrots, and vegetable stock and bring to a boil. Simmer until the vegetables are soft (about 20 minutes).

5 Transfer 4 ladles of vegetables and broth to a blender and blend until smooth. Return to the saucepan, stir to mix, and salt and pepper to taste.

6 Pour the soup into individual bowls. Garnish with toasted cashews and serve immediately.

Split Pea Soup

A large number of recipes were invented during World War II, when Eastern European Jews sought to maintain their health and put meals on the table in spite of the lack of fresh food available. These recipes often incorporate dried foods of some sort. This is one such recipe—it features nutritious legumes.

FLEISHIK: contains meat / can be made in advance / can be frozen up to 1 month
PREPARATION TIME: 15 minutes (plus 12 or more hours to allow legumes to soak)
COOKING TIME: 70 minutes / **SERVES:** 6

1 cup dried yellow split peas, rinsed ◆ 2 medium celery stalks with leaves
2 tablespoons vegetable oil ◆ 2 medium yellow onions, peeled and chopped coarsely
1 medium carrot, peeled and chopped coarsely ◆ 6¼ cups beef stock
Salt ◆ Freshly ground black pepper

◆

1 Place the peas in a large saucepan. Cover with cold water and let sit a minimum of 12 hours.

2 Drain and rinse the peas. Rinse the saucepan. Return the peas to the saucepan, cover with cold water, and bring to a boil over medium-high heat. Reduce the heat to low and simmer 40 minutes. Drain and rinse the peas, and set aside.

3 Trim the celery. Coarsely chop the leaves and set aside. Coarsely chop the celery stalks.

4 Heat the vegetable oil in a large saucepan over medium-low heat. Add the onions, chopped celery stalks, and carrot, and sauté until soft (about 5 minutes).

5 Add the beef stock and peas to the vegetables. Increase the heat to medium-high and bring to a boil. Reduce heat to low and simmer 25 minutes.

6 Transfer the mixture to a food processor or a blender (in batches, if necessary). Blend until the mixture is smooth. Salt and pepper to taste.

7 Pour the soup into individual serving bowls. Garnish with the chopped celery leaves and serve immediately.

Hearty Lentil Soup

*This rustic winter soup was a real favorite of my mother's when she was a little girl.
I'm not sure that she was aware that lentils are naturally low in fat, high in fiber,
and rich in protein—she just loved the taste! I like to make this with red lentils, as
they give the soup a wonderful color, but green lentils can be used instead, if desired.*

PAREVE: contains no meat or dairy products / can be made in advance / can be frozen up to 1 month
PREPARATION TIME: 15 minutes / **COOKING TIME:** 45 minutes / **SERVES:** 6 to 8

2 tablespoons vegetable oil ◆ 2 medium yellow onions, peeled and chopped coarsely
2 medium carrots, peeled and chopped coarsely ◆ 2 celery stalks, chopped finely
1 medium potato, peeled and chopped coarsely ◆ 7 cups hot vegetable stock
1½ cups dried red lentils, rinsed ◆ Two 14-ounce cans tomatoes chopped with juice ◆ Salt
Freshly ground black pepper ◆ 6 to 8 sprigs fresh Italian parsley, for garnish

◆

1 Heat the vegetable oil in a large saucepan over medium-low heat. Add the onions, carrots, celery, and potato, and sauté 5 minutes, stirring occasionally.

2 Add the vegetable stock, lentils, and tomatoes. Salt and pepper to taste.

3 Increase the heat to medium-high and bring to a boil. Reduce the heat to low and simmer 40 minutes. Adjust seasonings, if necessary.

4 Transfer to large, individual soup bowls. Garnish the bowls with parsley sprigs and serve hot.

Barley Soup

This is a hearty soup that hails from the farming communities of Poland and the Baltic states. My grandmother loved to make this as an alternative to chicken soup. She considered it "the next best thing to 'Jewish penicillin'," as it contains a nourishing combination of ingredients.

FLEISHIK: contains meat *or* **PAREVE:** contains no meat or dairy products
can be made in advance / can be frozen up to 1 month
PREPARATION TIME: 15 minutes / **COOKING TIME:** 1 hour / **SERVES:** 6 to 8

2 tablespoons nondairy margarine or vegetable oil (for a pareve dish)
2 medium yellow onions, peeled and chopped coarsely
3 medium turnips, peeled and chopped coarsely ◆ 1 leek, trimmed and chopped coarsely
1 cup sliced cremini mushrooms ◆ 7 cups vegetable stock
1 cup pearl barley ◆ ½ cup dry red wine (if desired) ◆ Salt
Freshly ground black pepper ◆ 6 to 8 sprigs fresh Italian parsley, for garnish

◆

1 Heat nondairy margarine or vegetable oil in a large, deep saucepan over medium-low heat. Add the onions, turnips, leek, and mushrooms and sauté 5 minutes.

2 Add the vegetable stock, barley, and, if desired, wine. Generously salt and pepper. Bring to a boil and reduce to simmer 45 minutes.

3 Transfer 4 large ladles of the vegetables, barley, and broth to a food processor or a blender. Blend until smooth. Return to the saucepan and stir to mix.

4 Adjust the seasonings, if necessary. Pour into individual soup bowls, garnish with parsley sprigs, and serve hot.

Knaidlach or Matzah Balls

Although these soft Jewish dumplings add texture and flavor to any soup, they may be most "at home" in Chicken Soup (see next page). Knaidlach are light, fluffy dumplings made from fine-ground matzah meal. Matzah balls are somewhat heavier, and they are made from medium-ground matzah meal. A scarcity of either type of dumpling can cause family disputes, so always ensure that each person is served an equal number of these favorites, and have extras on hand for seconds. Serve these in soup, along with a bit of Challah (see pages 41 to 42), as a first course, or as a light lunch.

FLEISHIK: contains meat / Passover-friendly / can be made in advance
can be frozen, uncooked, up to 1 month
PREPARATION TIME: 25 minutes / **COOKING TIME:** 15 minutes / **MAKES:** about 30 small dumplings

1 cup matzah meal (medium-ground for matzah balls; fine-ground for knaidlach)
2 tablespoons ground almonds ◆ 2 tablespoons chicken fat or vegetable oil ◆ 1 large egg
Kosher salt ◆ Freshly ground black pepper ◆ 2 cups simmering soup

◆

1 In a medium bowl, mix together all the ingredients. Refrigerate 30 minutes.

2 With wet hands, shape the mixture into small balls. Refrigerate covered, or use immediately.

3 Gently drop the dumplings into simmering soup and cook uncovered for 15 minutes. If they have been frozen first, allow them to thaw for 15 minutes before using.

Mama says...
Make the soup for these dumplings a day ahead of time and refrigerate it overnight. Its flavor will be even better, and you can use the schmaltz (fat) that rises to the top of the soup to make your knaidlach or matzah balls the next day.

Ultimate Chicken Soup

Chicken soup is an essential part of the traditional Friday night family meal in most Ashkenazi homes. We welcome in the Sabbath with a meal fit for royalty, and this soup's broth more than meets that standard. Jewish chicken soup is also known as "kosher penicillin," and any Jewish mama will attest to its magical healing properties. Perhaps it's the nutrients in the soup, or perhaps it's the soothing effect of breathing in its tantalizing steam. One thing is for certain, however: no other medicine tastes as good! Every Jewish mama has her own recipe for chicken soup, and every Jewish mama believes that hers is the best. I like to leave the skin on the onions to give extra color and flavor (they're strained out before the soup is served), and I cut the carrots into decorative shapes to encourage the children to eat their vegetables. The secret of any good soup is in its stock, so make sure to use the best that you can. The longer the soup cooks, the more flavorsome it will be.

FLEISHIK: contains meat / Passover-friendly
must be made at least 1 day in advance / can be frozen up to 1 month
PREPARATION TIME: 20 minutes (plus at least 12 hours, to refrigerate)
COOKING TIME: 3 hours / **SERVES:** 12 to 14

½ boiling fowl ♦ 1 pound raw chicken necks and backs
1 package (about 8 ounces) chicken giblets
2 turkey necks (about 8 ounces total), cut into small pieces ♦ 28½ cups water
4 medium carrots, peeled and sliced thinly ♦ 5 celery stalks, sliced thinly
2 parsnips, peeled and cut into large slices
2 turnips, peeled and sliced thinly ♦ 1 rutabaga, peeled and sliced thinly
2 yellow onions, unpeeled, halved ♦ 2 small tomatoes, halved
4 tablespoons powdered chicken bouillon or 3 chicken bouillon cubes
2 tablespoons kosher salt ♦ 3 fresh or dried bay leaves ♦ 3 black whole peppercorns

♦

1 Divide the fowl into large pieces.

2 Place all the ingredients in a large stockpot. Bring to a boil over medium-high heat. Reduce the heat to low and simmer 3 hours, occasionally skimming off the fat from the surface of the mixture (the fat may be refrigerated up to 3 days for another recipe).

3 Remove from the heat and let cool to warm. Place a large strainer over a large saucepan.

Strain the soup mixture. Gently remove the vegetables that are still intact from the strainer and place in the broth. Remove the chicken meat and set aside for another meal. Discard all other ingredients in the strainer.

4 Refrigerate the soup uncovered for at least 12 hours.

5 When ready to serve, reheat the soup over medium heat. Serve piping hot.

Kreplach

*Kreplach are the Jewish equivalent of Italian ravioli or Chinese wontons.
These small, stuffed pasta packages are served in hot chicken soup, and they're
particularly popular during Rosh Hashanah and other festivals. Although they take
a little time to make, they are delicious. Once you've mastered the art of preparing
kreplach, I am sure that you will be making them regularly. If you have a pasta
machine gathering dust, now is the time to use it, as you will be able to make really
thin dough. (You can, of course, roll the dough out by hand, if you prefer.) Be careful
not to overfill the kreplach, and make sure they are well sealed before cooking.*

FLEISHIK: contains meat / can be made in advance
can be refrigerated (prior to boiling) up to 1 week or frozen (prior to boiling) up to 1 month
PREPARATION TIME: 45 minutes (plus 90 minutes to allow dough to rest)
COOKING TIME: 10 minutes / SERVES: 10 to 12 (MAKES: about 80 dumplings)

2 cups all-purpose flour ◆ 2 large eggs ◆ 1 to 2 tablespoons kosher salt, divided
1 or more tablespoons cold water ◆ 1 tablespoon chicken fat or vegetable oil
1 small yellow onion, peeled and chopped very finely
½ cup ground cooked beef, chicken, or turkey ◆ Freshly ground black pepper
1 teaspoon finely chopped fresh flat-leaf parsley
Hot chicken soup (see pages 36 to 37; 1 cup per serving)

◆

1 Make the pasta. Place the flour, eggs,
1 teaspoon kosher salt, and 1 tablespoon water
in a food processor fitted with a dough blade.
Mix, adding a bit more water if necessary, until
a smooth dough is formed (about 2 minutes).
Remove from the bowl and cover with plastic
wrap. Let sit 1 hour.

2 Meanwhile, make the filling. Melt the chicken
fat or vegetable oil in a medium saucepan over
medium-low heat. Add the onion and sauté until
soft (about 5 minutes). Add the beef, chicken, or
turkey and stir to mix.

3 Transfer the mixture to a food processor. Add the pepper, parsley, and 1 teaspoon salt and pulse to combine. Refrigerate until ready to use.

4 Divide the dough into six equal-sized portions. Using a pasta machine, roll one portion through the machine at each of its settings, until the dough has been rolled at the machine's thinnest setting. (If desired, the dough may be rolled out with a hand roller. Roll until the dough is paper thin.)

5 Using a 2-inch round cutter, cut out circles of the dough. Place ½ teaspoon of the meat filling in the center of each circle. Dampen the edges of each circle and fold over to make triangles. Dust some flour to prevent sticking. Repeat with the remaining portions of dough. Set aside 30 minutes before cooking.

6 Fill a large saucepan with water, then add 1 tablespoon salt and bring to a simmer over medium heat. Gently place the kreplach in simmering water and cook until the dumplings rise to the surface of the water and are just tender (about 5 minutes).

7 To serve, place the kreplach in individual bowls of hot chicken soup (6 to 8 kreplach per serving).

◆

Challah

Challah is Jewish bread—it has been in our culture as long as there have been Jews. Details of its preparation are found in ancient religious texts and prayers, and its heritage goes back further than the time of the Great Temple in Jerusalem, where challah was given to the priests as an offering. Although today it is readily available in delis and most supermarkets, nothing beats the smell, taste, and satisfaction of homemade challah. I like to make mine with honey instead of sugar. The wonderful aroma that wafts from the oven indicates when the bread is done. Traditionally, challah is plaited (braided), and it's made of three, four, or six strands. At festival times (especially during Rosh Hashanah), however, challah is baked in round loaves. During the time from Rosh Hashanah to Simchat Torah, I add apples and raisins to the bread, as a symbol of the "sweet and fruitful" new year that we hope is to come. During Purim I glaze the bread with honey and sprinkle decorative cake sprinkles, and on Shavuot I form the dough into the shape of the Ten Commandments. This recipe calls for the challah to be made in three-strand plaits.

PAREVE: contains no meat or dairy products / can be made in advance / can be stored at room temperature up to 2 days, in the refrigerator up to 4 days, or in the freezer up to 2 weeks

PREPARATION TIME: 15 minutes (plus 2½ hours to allow dough to rise)

COOKING TIME: 35 minutes / **MAKES:** 2 large loaves

1 cup warm water, divided ◆ 1 tablespoon active dry yeast ◆ 1 teaspoon kosher salt
4¼ cups bread flour ◆ 1 tablespoon honey ◆ 2 large eggs
¼ cup, plus 1 tablespoon vegetable oil, divided
1 medium green or red apple, peeled, cored, and grated (if desired)
3 tablespoons dark raisins (if desired) ◆ 2 teaspoons cinnamon (if desired)
Yolks of 2 large eggs, lightly beaten ◆ 2 tablespoons poppy seeds

◆

1 Place ½ cup warm water in a large bowl. Stir in the yeast and salt. Set aside until the mixture is foamy (about 10 minutes).

2 Place the flour, honey, 2 large eggs, and ¼ cup vegetable oil into a food processor. Process until the ingredients are well mixed. Add the yeast mixture. If desired, add the apple, raisins, and cinnamon.

3 While processing, gradually add the remaining water to form a smooth, springy dough that comes away from the sides of the bowl.

4 Using the remaining 1 tablespoon vegetable oil, grease a large bowl. Transfer the dough to the bowl and cover with plastic wrap. Set aside in a warm spot for 2 hours or until the dough has doubled in size.

5 Knock back the dough and divide in half. Divide each half into thirds. Roll each piece into a sausage shape.

6 Braid together 3 strands. Set aside. Repeat with the remaining 3 strands.

7 Cover the loaves with plastic wrap and set aside 30 minutes to allow the bread to rise again (this is called "proving").

8 Preheat the oven to 400°F.

9 Brush the egg yolks over the loaves. Sprinkle the loaves with poppy seeds. Place the loaves on a baking tray lined with nonstick baking paper. Bake 35 minutes or until golden brown. Bread should sound hollow when tapped on the bottom.

Soup Croutons

Mandlen are bite-sized soup croutons that are exceptionally quick and simple to make and they are a great family favorite when served with tomato soup or Ultimate Chicken Soup (see pages 36 to 37). I was taught this particular recipe by my great-grandmother, who was brought up in Poland. It calls for the croutons to be deep-fried, but they can be baked instead, if preferred (see "Mama says"). For a modern twist, I sometimes add 1 teaspoon fresh, finely chopped basil or dried herbes de Provence to the mandlen dough.

PAREVE: contains no meat or dairy products / can be made in advance
can be stored in an airtight container up to 1 week
PREPARATION TIME: 10 minutes (plus 30 minutes to allow croutons to dry)
COOKING TIME: 10 minutes / **MAKES:** about 60 croutons

**1 tablespoon, plus about 3 cups vegetable oil, divided ◆ 1 large egg
1 teaspoon kosher salt ◆ ½ cup all-purpose flour**

◆

1 Mix together 1 tablespoon vegetable oil, egg, and salt. Add the flour bit by bit, mixing until a dough is formed (some flour may not be used). Knead 10 minutes.

2 Lightly dust a work surface with flour. Using a hand roller, roll out the dough into a ¼-inch-thick sheet. Using a sharp knife, cut the pastry into ½-inch-wide diagonal strips. Reverse the direction and cut the pastry into ½-inch-wide diagonal strips to produce diamond-shaped croutons. Set aside for 30 minutes to dry.

3 Heat the oil in a deep-fat fryer.

4 Place the croutons in hot oil (in batches) and deep-fry until golden. Transfer to paper towels to remove any excess oil and let cool.

Mama says...
To bake croutons, preheat the oven to 400°F. Line a baking tray with parchment paper. Place the croutons on the tray and bake 10 minutes.

Homemade Bagels

There are as many stories about the origins and significance of bagels as there are different flavors of these breads themselves. The bagel—traditionally made as a humble, plain circle of bread—has now been adopted by America and most of the Western world as an incredibly popular snack food. Despite their almost universal acceptance today, bagels still have a significant role in Jewish life. They are traditionally eaten with hard-boiled eggs by mourners after a funeral, and they are also served to guests at circumcision ceremonies. The bagel's shape is said to symbolize the eternal cycle of life—hence its place at these occasions. Having no beginning or end, the bagel (the German word for "ring" or "bracelet") was long thought to protect from invasion by evil spirits, including the dreaded eyin hora (evil eye). This food of good fortune can, therefore, bring luck, blessings, and prosperity—as well as ward off demons! Unlike most breads, bagels must be boiled before they are baked. This gives them their unique chewy and crispy texture and great fresh taste. Bagels go stale quickly, so if you have extras, cut them into thin slices and toast them for a great snack to enjoy at any time (except during Passover!).

PAREVE: contains no meat or dairy products / can be made in advance / can be frozen up to 1 month

PREPARATION TIME: 10 minutes (plus 2 to 2½ hours to allow dough to rise)

COOKING TIME: 30 minutes / **MAKES:** 12 bagels

1 cup warm water ◆ 1 tablespoon active dry yeast ◆ 1 tablespoon kosher salt
3 teaspoons sugar, divided ◆ 4½ cups strong flour ◆ 1 large egg, lightly beaten
3 tablespoons vegetable oil, divided ◆ White of 1 large egg
1 tablespoon cool or lukewarm water
2 to 3 tablespoons poppy seeds or sesame seeds (if desired)

◆

1 Place warm water in a medium bowl. Stir in the yeast, salt, and 1 teaspoon sugar. Set aside 10 minutes or until mixture is frothy.

2 In a food processor, mix together the flour, beaten egg, 2 tablespoons vegetable oil, remaining sugar, and yeast mixture. Process until the mixture forms a smooth, spongy dough.

3 Grease a large bowl with the remaining vegetable oil. Place the dough in the bowl and cover with plastic wrap. Let sit 60 to 90 minutes or until the dough has doubled in size.

4 Knock back the dough to its original size and knead until all the air is pressed out and the dough is smooth.

5 Dust a work surface with flour. Divide the dough into 12 pieces and roll each piece into 7-inch-long, ½-inch-thick "sausages." Shape each "sausage" into a circle and carefully press the ends together to seal.

6 Line a baking tray with parchment paper. Place the bagels on a tray, cover with a damp towel, and let sit 1 hour to prove (rise again).

7 Preheat the oven to 425°F.

8 Fill a deep saucepan with water, then bring to a boil over high heat. Reduce the heat to medium and place 4 bagels in the pan. Cook for 2 to 3 minutes, until the bagels rise to the surface of the water. Remove the bagels from the water and place on a baking tray. Repeat until all the bagels have been boiled.

9 In a small bowl, mix together the egg white and 1 tablespoon water. Brush each bagel with egg-white wash. If desired, sprinkle the bagels with poppy seeds or sesame seeds.

10 Bake for 20 minutes or until golden brown. Remove from oven and let cool to warm before slicing and serving.

Mama says...
Serve bagels with cream cheese, snipped chives, lox or smoked salmon, and a dusting of black pepper.

chapter three
MAIN COURSES

Smoked Trout Salad

Jewish people have a great affinity for smoked fish of all kinds, and trout is no exception. Whether served as a pâté, as part of a sandwich, or as a main course with potatoes and vegetables, smoked trout is extremely versatile. Because it's now available already smoked, it's also become a quick and easy ingredient for preparing wonderful meals.

PAREVE: contains no meat or dairy products / can be made in advance
PREPARATION TIME: 15 minutes / **COOKING TIME:** 10 minutes / **SERVES:** 4

SALAD
2 cups fresh or frozen peas
2 cups (about 8 ounces) fresh asparagus tips, sliced in halves
2 tablespoons olive oil ◆ **2 zucchini, trimmed and sliced into thin circles**
3 cups (about 8 ounces) mixed salad leaves ◆ **1 cup fresh blueberries or raspberries, rinsed**
4 large fillets (about 2 pounds smoked trout), skinned and flaked

DRESSING
2 tablespoons mayonnaise ◆ **2 tablespoons extra-virgin olive oil**
1 tablespoon sesame seed oil ◆ **Salt** ◆ **Freshly ground black pepper**

◆

1 Make the salad. Place the peas and asparagus tips in a medium saucepan and cover with water, then bring to a boil over medium-high heat. Boil 4 to 5 minutes. Drain. Rinse with cold water (to prevent further cooking and to retain the color of the vegetables).

2 Meanwhile, heat the olive oil in a frying pan over medium heat. Add the zucchini and sauté, turning occasionally, until just tender (about 2 minutes). Set aside 10 minutes to cool.

3 Place the peas, asparagus, zucchini, salad leaves, and blueberries or raspberries in a large salad bowl. Add the trout and gently mix to combine.

4 Make the dressing. In a small bowl, whisk together the mayonnaise, olive oil, and sesame seed oil. Salt and pepper to taste.

5 Place the salad on individual serving plates. Whisk the dressing and drizzle over the salads. Serve immediately.

Halibut with Egg-Lemon Sauce

This is a prime example of a fish dish that tastes better cold or at room temperature than it does warm. It's an ideal Passover supper dish that does not include nuts or matzah meal and is popular with the older generation because of its ease on the digestive system. My mother sometimes makes this recipe using mackerel instead of halibut. It provides a nice change of flavor, and mackerel is less expensive.

PAREVE: contains no meat or dairy products / Passover-friendly / can be made in advance
PREPARATION TIME: 20 minutes / **COOKING TIME:** 25 minutes / **SERVES:** 4

Four 6-ounce halibut steaks, boned ◆ **1 large yellow onion, peeled and sliced thinly**
1 bay leaf ◆ **Salt** ◆ **Freshly ground black pepper** ◆ **Juice of 2 lemons**
2 large eggs, lightly beaten ◆ **1 tablespoon (or more, to taste) sugar**
1 teaspoon cornstarch or (for Passover) potato flour ◆ **Slices of lemon, for garnish**
Sprigs of Italian parsley, for garnish

◆

1 Place the fish in a saucepan that is large enough for all the fillets to lie flat. Cover with water. Add the onion and bay leaf. Salt and pepper to taste.

2 Bring to a boil over medium-high heat. Reduce the heat to low and simmer until the fish is white and firm to the touch (about 15 minutes).

3 Gently transfer the fish to a serving plate. Transfer 1 cup liquid from the pan to a medium saucepan on low heat. Add the lemon juice, eggs, and sugar to liquid. Salt and pepper to taste.

4 Transfer 1 tablespoon liquid to a small bowl or glass. Discard the remaining liquid.

5 Place the cornstarch or potato flour in a bowl or glass with liquid and whisk to blend. Pour into the lemon-juice sauce, whisking constantly.

6 Still over low heat, cook, stirring constantly, until the sauce coats the back of a spoon (about 3 minutes). Do not allow the sauce to come to a boil. Adjust the seasonings, if desired, and remove from the heat.

7 Pour the sauce over the fish. Chill or set aside until the dish has reached room temperature (about 30 minutes).

8 Serve with lemon slices and parsley sprigs.

Mother-in-Law's Boiled Gefilte Fish

My mother-in-law passed this popular recipe down to me. In the tradition of Jewish cuisine, cooks simply added a little of this and a bit of that until the right combination was achieved. My late husband encouraged me to undergo "fish ball training" with his mother as part of our engagement! The fish balls can be cooked in a deep-fat fryer or boiled in fish stock, which is the lighter of the two versions.

PAREVE: contains no meat or dairy products / Passover-friendly
can be made in advance / can be frozen up to 2 weeks
PREPARATION TIME: 20 minutes / **COOKING TIME:** 1 hour / **SERVES:** 10 to 12 (**MAKES:** 40 small balls)

FISH STOCK

4 cups water ◆ 4 yellow onions, peeled and sliced thinly
½ pound bones and skin of fish (any type) ◆ 2 celery stalks
2 medium carrots, peeled and sliced thinly ◆ 2 tablespoons parsley
2 teaspoons kosher salt ◆ 2 black whole peppercorns ◆ 2 bay leaves ◆ 1 to 2 tablespoons sugar

FISH BALL MIXTURE

1 pound boneless, skinless haddock ◆ 1 pound boneless, skinless cod ◆ 1 pound boneless, skinless hake ◆ 1 large yellow onion, peeled and chopped finely ◆ 2 large eggs
2 to 3 tablespoons medium-ground matzah meal ◆ 1 tablespoon vegetable oil ◆ 2 teaspoons kosher salt ◆ 1 teaspoon white pepper ◆ 2 teaspoons sugar ◆ 1 drop almond extract

◆

1 Make the fish stock. Place all the ingredients in a large saucepan. Bring to a boil over medium-high heat. Reduce heat and simmer 15 minutes.

2 Make the fish ball mixture. Mince the fish in a food processor. Add the remaining ingredients. Pulse until light and sticky. Season if necessary.

3 Make the fish balls. Using wet hands, roll fish mixture into egg-sized balls. Using the palm of your hand, flatten the balls slightly. Place balls in fish stock and cook over medium heat 45 minutes.

4 Using a slotted spoon, transfer the fish balls to a serving platter.

Fish Pie

Jewish people love fish. Even the Talmud discusses mystical values surrounding the tradition of eating fish on the Sabbath. This savory pie, made with flaked cooked fish and topped with mashed potatoes, is a delicious, warming dish to serve on cold winter evenings. I like to use a mixture of fresh and smoked haddock, but fresh and smoked cod or trout work just as well. To save time, ask your fish merchant to "pin bone" the fillets for you. Otherwise, use tweezers to remove the bones yourself.

MILCHIK: contains dairy products / can be made in advance / can be frozen up to 1 month
PREPARATION TIME: 40 minutes / **COOKING TIME:** 75 minutes / **SERVES:** 6

PIE FILLING
24 ounces fresh haddock fillets, skinned ◆ 24 ounces smoked haddock fillets, skinned
About 3 cups milk ◆ 1 tablespoon olive oil ◆ 1 yellow onion, peeled and chopped coarsely
◆ 1 tablespoon ground dried coriander ◆ 1 tablespoon butter
1 tablespoon all-purpose flour ◆ 1 teaspoon dry mustard (any variety) ◆ Salt
Freshly ground black pepper ◆ 3 large eggs, hard-boiled, peeled, and chopped coarsely
10 scallions (about 4 ounces total), chopped coarsely
2 to 3 tablespoons Italian parsley, chopped coarsely
(reserve 3 to 5 sprigs for garnish)

POTATO TOPPING
4 boiling potatoes, peeled and chopped coarsely ◆ 3 tablespoons milk
½ cup unsalted butter ◆ Salt ◆ Freshly ground black pepper

◆

1 Make the pie filling. Cut the fish into small bite-sized pieces. Place in a medium-sized saucepan. Cover with 2½ cups milk.

2 Bring to a boil over medium-high heat. Reduce the heat to medium-low and simmer 10 minutes.

3 Place a colander over a large bowl. Drain the fish and set aside. Transfer the liquid to a heatproof 2-cup measuring glass. Set aside.

4 Heat the olive oil in a frying pan over medium-low heat. Add the yellow onion and coriander. Sauté 2 minutes. Set aside.

5 Add enough remaining milk to the liquid in a measuring glass to make 2 cups total liquid. Set aside.

6 Melt the butter in a medium-sized saucepan over medium-low heat. Stir in the flour. Cook 1 minute, stirring constantly. Still stirring, slowly add the milk liquid. Cook, and keep stirring, until the sauce has thickened and coats the back of a spoon (about 5 minutes). Stir in the mustard. Generously salt and pepper to taste.

7 Preheat the oven to 400°F.

8 Flake the fish. Place in a large bowl. Add the egg, sautéed onion, scallions, parsley, and sauce. Gently stir to mix. Transfer to an ovenware dish, approximately 12 inches by 6 inches, and set aside.

9 Make the potato topping. Place the potatoes in a large saucepan. Cover with water and bring to a boil. Cook until very soft (about 15 minutes). Drain. Transfer to a large bowl and, using a potato ricer or a fork, mash. Add the milk and butter. Salt and pepper to taste. Stir to mix.

10 Spread the mashed potatoes over the fish mixture. Bake 1 hour, until the potatoes are crispy and golden brown.

11 Garnish with parsley sprigs and serve.

Mediterranean Salmon

This is a very popular recipe at the cooking classes I teach, and it has become something of a "signature dish" for me. In fact, it has almost reached iconic status at my dinner parties! The wonderful combination of salmon—the most popular fish in Jewish cuisine—red bell peppers, rosemary, and other ingredients provides all the flavors of the Mediterranean on one plate. I like to serve this with shredded green cabbage and mashed potatoes, rice, or crusty bread to soak up the delicious juices. This dish works well with cubed lamb instead of salmon, as well.

PAREVE: contains no meat or dairy products / Passover-friendly / can be made in advance
PREPARATION TIME: 10 minutes / **COOKING TIME:** 15 minutes / **SERVES:** 6

2 tablespoons olive oil ♦ 4 large red onions, peeled and chopped coarsely
3 large garlic cloves, peeled and chopped coarsely
2 red bell peppers, cored, and chopped coarsely
2 tablespoons all-purpose flour or (for Passover) potato flour ♦ 1 cup vegetable stock
1 cup dry red wine ♦ 2 tablespoons fresh rosemary, stemmed
(reserve 3 to 5 sprigs for garnish) ♦ 1 cup pitted black olives
Six 5-ounce salmon fillets, skinned and cubed ♦ Salt ♦ Freshly ground black pepper

♦

1 Heat the olive oil in a large frying pan over medium-low heat. Add the onions, garlic, and bell peppers. Sauté 3 minutes, stirring occasionally.

2 Stir in the flour. Cook 2 minutes, stirring frequently. Stir in the vegetable stock, wine, rosemary, and olives. Increase the heat to medium-high and bring to a boil. Add the salmon. Add salt and pepper to taste. Reduce the heat to medium and cook covered until the salmon is completely cooked (5 minutes).

3 Transfer to a serving platter. Garnish with rosemary sprigs and serve.

Fried Fish

Introduced by Sephardi Jews in the 1600s, fried fish is probably one of the most well-known Jewish dishes, and it is still popular. As it tastes better cold, it is frequently fried in the day on Friday, refrigerated overnight, and served as a main course during Shabbat. Steaks of cod, halibut, and haddock, or fillets of flounder and sole are perfect for frying. I like to lightly salt the fish and let it sit for 30 minutes before frying it. This eliminates excess water and keeps the coating crispy.

PAREVE: contains no meat or dairy products / Passover-friendly
can be made in advance / can be frozen up to 1 month
PREPARATION TIME: 15 minutes (plus 30 minutes to allow salt to draw out excess water)
COOKING TIME: 5 to 8 minutes / **SERVES:** 6

**3 pounds cut white-flesh fish fillets or steaks ◆ 2 teaspoons salt
½ cup fine-ground matzah meal ◆ ½ cup medium-ground matzah meal ◆ Freshly ground pepper
3 tablespoons all-purpose flour ◆ 2 large eggs, lightly beaten ◆ About 5 to 6 cups vegetable oil**

1 Rinse the fish in cold water and sprinkle lightly with salt. Place in a colander and let sit to drain 30 minutes. Using paper towels, pat the fish dry.

2 Combine the matzah meals, salt, and pepper. Place the flour, eggs, and seasoned matzah meal in 3 dishes (one ingredient per dish). Lightly dredge the fish in flour. Shake off the excess flour. Dip the fish in egg, evenly coating it. Dip the fish in matzah meal.

3 Preheat the oven to 350°F. Place the vegetable oil in a deep-fat fryer or a large frying pan to make a 1-inch layer of oil.

4 Heat over medium heat until the vegetable oil is hot (or until a small piece of bread dropped into the oil fries to a crisp within 30 seconds).

5 Place several pieces of fish in the oil. Fry the fillets for 3 to 4 minutes and the steaks for 5 to 6 minutes, then gently turn the fish. Fry until golden brown on the bottom side (about 3 to 5 minutes). Transfer to a baking dish and place in the oven to keep warm while the remaining fish is frying. Repeat until all the fish is fried, adding and heating more oil if necessary.

Friday Night Roast Chicken

My children look forward to this when they come in from school on Friday evenings. Many Jewish people cherish the quality time of Friday nights spent with extended family. My mother cooks her roast chicken plain, with some onion beneath the chicken and a bit of salt and pepper on top, and she keeps the roasting bird covered under aluminum foil until the last 15 minutes of its cooking time. The foil is then removed, which allows the skin to become crispy. To make gravy, she simply adds a little chicken stock and some boiling water to the pan juices. This recipe is a variation of my mother's, and it has evolved partly because I have a healthy spread of fresh rosemary in my garden throughout the year. Adding red wine and water to the roasting pan keeps the chicken succulent and prevents the flesh from drying out. I frequently serve this with Mushroom Rice (see page 73), Roast Potatoes (see page 79), and a selection of seasonal vegetables.

FLEISHIK: contains meat / Passover-friendly
PREPARATION TIME: 15 minutes / **COOKING TIME:** 80 to 85 minutes / **SERVES:** 6

4- to 5-pound roasting chicken (giblets removed)
2 tablespoons fresh rosemary ◆ **1 lemon, sliced into thin wedges**
3 large garlic cloves, peeled ◆ **2 yellow onions, peeled and chopped coarsely**
1 cup dry red wine ◆ **Salt** ◆ **Freshly ground black pepper**

◆

1 Preheat oven to 400°F. Pull the skin from the breast of the chicken and slip some rosemary, lemon wedges, and garlic cloves under it. Place the rest of these ingredients in the chicken cavity.

2 Arrange the onion in a roasting pan. Pour the wine over the onions. Add enough water so the pan is three-quarters full.

3 Place the chicken breast-side down in the pan. Salt and pepper to taste. Cover the pan with aluminum foil.

4 Bake for 80 to 85 minutes. Remove from the oven and leave to rest for 10 to 15 minutes. Carve into portions, and transfer to a serving platter.

Pot Roast

My aunt in New York makes pot roast every Friday night, in a special pot kept just for this purpose. This dish is as important to her family as roast chicken is to mine. I like to serve this with Roast Potatoes (see page 79). The red wine adds a wonderful flavor to the dish and helps to tenderize the meat.

FLEISHIK: contains meat / Passover-friendly / can be made in advance
PREPARATION TIME: 15 minutes / **COOKING TIME:** 2½ to 3 hours / **SERVES:** 6 to 8

1 cup dry red wine ◆ 1 cup beef stock ◆ One 3- to 4-pound beef brisket
2 large yellow onions, peeled and sliced thinly ◆ 2 medium carrots, peeled and sliced thinly
4 celery stalks with leaves, cut in half ◆ 2 tablespoons fresh parsley
4 large garlic cloves, peeled and chopped finely ◆ 2 bay leaves ◆ 2 tablespoons cornstarch

◆

1 Place the wine and beef stock in a large saucepan or roasting pan. Add water until the pan is half full. Bring to a boil over medium-high heat.

2 Add the beef, onions, carrots, celery, parsley, garlic, and bay leaves. Bring back to a boil. Reduce the heat to low, cover, and simmer until the beef is cooked through and tender (2½ to 3 hours). Transfer the meat to a plate and set aside.

3 Place a colander over a bowl. Discard any excess fat from the surface of the pan juices, then pour the juices into a colander. Discard the bay leaves. Set aside the vegetables to serve with the beef (or discard them).

4 Place 2 tablespoons of the juices in a small heatproof glass. Add the cornstarch and blend to make a paste. Return the remaining juices to the pan and heat over medium heat, stirring occasionally, until the sauce thickens (about 3 minutes). Over medium heat, gradually add this to the stock, stirring from time to time until it thickens.

5 Slice the beef. Gently place it in the sauce and warm gently.

6 Transfer the beef to a serving platter. Top with the sauce and serve immediately.

Chicken or Turkey Schnitzel

I don't do everything my mother does—but one thing we do share is this recipe, and we both make it every week! My daughter makes it as well (she adds powdered chicken stock to the matzah meal to enhance the flavor of the dish). I think it is one of those very special dishes that everyone likes. Just cut up the schnitzel for the children and tell them it's nuggets! If you have any leftovers, try slicing them thinly and serving them with a salad for lunch the next day.

FLEISHIK: contains meat / Passover-friendly / can be made in advance / can be frozen up to 2 weeks
PREPARATION TIME: 15 minutes / **COOKING TIME:** 15 minutes / **SERVES:** 6

6 chicken breasts or 6 thick slices of turkey breast ◆ 4 tablespoons flour
Salt ◆ Freshly ground black pepper ◆ 2 large eggs, lightly beaten
1 cup medium-ground matzah meal or bread crumbs
4 to 6 tablespoons vegetable oil

◆

1 Place each piece of meat between two pieces of plastic wrap or parchment paper. Using a kitchen mallet or a rolling pin, pound the meat until thin and flat. (Be careful not to tear the meat.)

2 Place the flour in a shallow bowl. Season with salt and pepper. Place the eggs in a separate shallow bowl. Place the matzah meal or bread crumbs in a separate shallow bowl.

3 Lightly dredge each schnitzel in the flour, then dip in the egg, then dip in the matzah meal or bread crumbs, coating the schnitzel evenly.

4 Heat the vegetable oil in a large frying pan over medium heat. Add the schnitzels in one layer (they may be cooked in batches). Sauté until cooked through and golden brown (about 5 minutes). Turn them once during cooking.

Sweet and Sour Meatballs

One of my earliest memories of my grandmother's kitchen is of standing on a stool and helping her roll meatballs for dinner. We sang together and I told her all my secrets. My own busy daughters still find the time to help me roll meatballs—one of the few food preparations that must be performed in the original way.

FLEISHIK: contains meat / Passover-friendly / can be made in advance / can be frozen up to 1 month
PREPARATION TIME: 25 minutes / **COOKING TIME:** 1 hour / **SERVES:** 6

MEATBALLS

2 pounds ground beef ◆ 1 medium yellow onion, peeled and grated ◆ 1 large egg
2 tablespoons tomato purée ◆ 2 tablespoons medium-ground matzah meal ◆ ½ teaspoon salt
Freshly ground black pepper ◆ 2 tablespoons coarsely chopped fresh parsley

SAUCE

Two 14-ounce cans of diced tomatoes with juice ◆ Juice of 1 medium lemon
¼ cup packed light brown sugar ◆ 1 bay leaf ◆ 1 to 2 tablespoons white or red wine vinegar
2 cups beef stock ◆ 1 tablespoon potato flour ◆ 2 tablespoons cold water ◆ Salt
Freshly ground black pepper ◆ Sprigs of basil, for garnish

◆

1 Make the meatballs. By hand or in a food processor, thoroughly combine all the ingredients. Shape the mixture into 2-inch balls.

2 Make the sauce. Place all the ingredients except the potato flour and water in a large saucepan. Bring to a boil over medium-high heat. Reduce the heat to medium-low and simmer 10 minutes.

3 Gently place the meatballs in sauce. Reduce the heat to low, cover the pan, and simmer 40 minutes.

4 In a small glass, mix potato flour and water to a paste. Stir into sauce. Increase heat to medium and cook until sauce is thick, stirring constantly.

5 Transfer meatballs to a deep serving dish. Top with sauce and garnish with basil. Serve with rice.

Beef Strudel

Meat loaves and strudels (meat loaves with pastry) have always been part of the Jewish mama's culinary repertoire, probably because they are economical and tasty, and because they can be made in different shapes and quantities. Best of all, perhaps—children will eat them! Although I call for beef here, strudels can be made with chicken, turkey, or lamb, as well. For a Passover-friendly dish, omit the pastry and simply serve this as a meat loaf.

FLEISHIK: contains meat / can be made in advance / can be frozen, uncooked, up to 2 weeks
PREPARATION TIME: 40 minutes / **COOKING TIME:** 1 hour / **SERVES:** 8

STRUDEL

2 tablespoons olive oil ◆ 1 medium yellow onion, peeled and chopped finely
3 large garlic cloves, peeled and chopped finely ◆ 1 tablespoon ground cumin
2 pounds beef, ground ◆ 2 tablespoons ketchup or tomato purée
2 tablespoons medium-ground matzah meal ◆ 1 large egg, lightly beaten
2 tablespoons fresh oregano, chopped coarsely ◆ 2 teaspoons salt
1 teaspoon freshly ground black pepper ◆ One 15- by 10-inch sheet (about 12½ ounces)
of thawed frozen puff pastry

GLAZE AND TOPPING

Yolk of 1 large egg ◆ 2 tablespoons raw sesame seeds

SAUCE

2 tablespoons olive oil ◆ 1 medium yellow onion, peeled and chopped finely
4 large garlic cloves, peeled and chopped finely ◆ 1 carrot, peeled and chopped finely
Two 14-ounce cans diced tomatoes with juice ◆ 1 tablespoon tomato purée
½ cup dry red wine ◆ 2 to 3 tablespoons fresh basil, chopped coarsely
(reserve 8 whole small basil leaves for garnish) ◆ 1 teaspoon sugar
Salt ◆ Freshly ground black pepper

1 Preheat the oven to 400°F.

2 Line a baking tray with baking parchment paper. Set aside.

3 Make the strudel. Heat the olive oil in a medium frying pan over medium-low heat. Add the onion, garlic, and cumin and sauté until the onion is soft (about 5 minutes).

4 Place the onion mixture, beef, ketchup, matzah meal, egg, oregano, salt, and pepper in a food processor. Process until well blended. (Or, place the ingredients in a large bowl and mix by hand until well blended.)

5 Lightly flour a work surface. Place the pastry on the work surface and roll out until the sheet is about 15 inches by 10 inches (the pastry should be quite thin). Place the meat lengthwise along the center of the pastry, leaving a 1-inch border on all sides. Brush the edges of the pastry with a bit of water. Fold in the side edges and roll up. The pastry should resemble a jelly roll.

6 Place the pastry on the baking tray. Brush with the egg yolk and sprinkle with sesame seeds. Bake for 40 minutes or until the pastry is golden and crispy.

7 Meanwhile, make the sauce. Heat the olive oil in a medium saucepan over medium heat. Add the onion, garlic, and carrot and sauté 3 minutes. Add the tomatoes, tomato purée, wine, basil, and sugar. Salt and pepper to taste. Increase the heat to medium-high and bring to a boil.

8 Reduce the heat to low and simmer covered 40 minutes.

9 Transfer the sauce to a food processor and pulse briefly to make a smoother sauce. Return the sauce to the pan. Adjust seasonings, if necessary.

10 To serve, cut the strudel into thick slices and place on a serving platter or on individual serving plates. Top with the sauce, and garnish with the reserved basil leaves.

Mama says...
A good meat strudel is highly seasoned. Overdo it a bit with the seasonings, as the spices need to permeate through the pastry layer into the meat.

Goulash

This Hungarian meat stew was a great favorite of my family's when I was a child, and my mother used to prepare it whenever my grandmother came to visit. I have fond memories of my sisters and me—who were always starving after a long morning spent at Cheder (the Jewish equivalent of Sunday school)—running up the drive and being greeted with the wonderful aroma of this dish.

FLEISHIK: contains meat / can be made in advance / can be frozen up to 2 weeks
PREPARATION TIME: 30 minutes / **COOKING TIME:** 2 hours, 20 minutes / **SERVES:** 6 to 8

3 tablespoons vegetable oil ◆ 6 medium yellow onions, peeled and sliced thinly
2 medium red bell peppers, cored, seeds removed, and chopped coarsely
4 garlic cloves, peeled and chopped finely ◆ 1 to 2 tablespoons hot Hungarian paprika
4 pounds good-quality chuck steak, trimmed and cubed ◆ 2 tablespoons flour
2 cups dry red wine ◆ 2 cups beef stock ◆ Two 14-ounce cans diced tomatoes with juice
1 teaspoon sugar ◆ 1 tablespoon caraway seeds ◆ Salt
Freshly ground black pepper ◆ Sprigs parsley, for garnish

◆

1 Heat the vegetable oil in a deep, wide saucepan over medium heat. Add the onions, bell peppers, garlic, and paprika. Sauté 5 minutes. Transfer to a plate and set aside.

2 Using the same saucepan, sauté the meat until it has become brown on all sides (about 5 minutes). Return the onion mixture to the saucepan. Add the flour. Heat, stirring constantly, for 1 minute.

3 Stir in the wine, beef stock, tomatoes, sugar, and caraway seeds. Salt and pepper to taste. Then increase the heat to medium-high and bring to a boil. Reduce the heat to low and simmer covered, stirring occasionally, until the meat is cooked through and tender (about 2 hours). Adjust the seasonings, if desired.

4 Transfer the goulash to a serving platter. Garnish with parsley sprigs and serve.

Cholent

Cholent is one of the most familiar of all Jewish traditional dishes. It is a one-pot meal that features meat, grains, and vegetables, all cooked together for a very long time in very low heat and topped with delicious potato dumplings. In Jewish households, the cooking process starts on Friday, and the dish is normally served for lunch after the synagogue service on Shabbat. As it is prohibited to actually cook on Shabbat, this is the perfect way of providing a ready-to-eat hot meal. In the shtetls of Eastern Europe during the late nineteenth century, pots of cholent were cooked in communal bakers' ovens, which were large enough to generate and retain an incredible amount of heat. The families would go after synagogue to collect their pots of Cholent and partake of their Sabbath meal. One of the best things about Cholent is the incredible aroma it creates as it cooks.

FLEISHIK: contains meat / must be made 1 day in advance
PREPARATION TIME: 40 minutes (plus 6 hours to allow beans to soak)
COOKING TIME: 18 to 20 hours / **SERVES:** 8

STEW

1⅓ cups navy or butter beans ◆ ¼ cup, plus 2 tablespoons olive oil ◆ 2 medium yellow onions, peeled and chopped coarsely ◆ 6 large garlic cloves, peeled and chopped coarsely
28 ounces beef brisket, cut into chunks ◆ ½ cup pearl barley
3 carrots, peeled and thinly sliced ◆ 3 baking potatoes, peeled and cut into large chunks
1 small turnip, peeled and chopped coarsely ◆ 1 celery stalk, chopped coarsely
One 14-ounce can chopped tomatoes with juice
4 cups beef stock ◆ 1 cup dry red wine ◆ 3 tablespoons corn syrup ◆ 8 large eggs
1½ tablespoons Hungarian paprika ◆ Salt ◆ Freshly ground black pepper

DUMPLINGS

2 boiling potatoes, peeled ◆ 1 medium yellow onion, peeled
2 tablespoons fine-ground matzah meal (or more, if necessary) ◆ Salt
Freshly ground black pepper

◆

Mama says...
The secret ingredient of my recipe for Cholent is the corn syrup, which softens and sweetens the other ingredients in a very subtle, unassuming way.

1 Place the beans in a medium saucepan. Cover with water. Let soak at least 6 hours.

2 Make the stew. Heat the olive oil in a large, deep, heavy-bottomed casserole over medium heat. Add the onions and garlic. Sauté 5 minutes.

3 Meanwhile, drain and rinse the beans.

4 Add the beef, beans, barley, carrots, potatoes, turnips, celery, tomatoes, beef stock, wine, corn syrup, eggs (in their shells), and paprika. Salt and pepper to taste. Add enough water so that all ingredients are covered with liquid.

5 Preheat the oven to 225°F.

6 Make the dumplings. Finely grate the potatoes and the onion. Place the potatoes and onions

between paper towels and squeeze to remove excess water.

7 Place the potatoes and onions in a large bowl. Add the remaining ingredients and mix well.

8 The mixture should be very firm; add more matzah meal, if necessary, to achieve this.

9 Shape the mixture into 2-inch balls and place on top of the stew mixture.

10 Bring the mixture to a boil over medium-high heat. Reduce the heat to very low.

11 Using aluminum foil, tightly cover the casserole. Place a casserole lid over the foil.

12 Bake 18 to 20 hours or overnight.

Mama says...
This stew may be cooked in a slow cooker, if you have one that's large enough. Use the lowest heat setting available.

Pickled Tongue or Salt Beef

Life for most people is so much easier today than it used to be in Eastern Europe. Nowadays, most kosher butchers sell prepared pickled ox tongue and brisket (or salt beef)—which is fortunate, because saltpeter, which is used in the pickling process, is no longer available to the public. To get the real "deli" pickled tongue or salt beef experience, just follow this recipe. Cook the meat slowly for a long period of time in order to get the most tender result possible. Use the meat as a filling for a chunky sandwich made with rye bread or pumpernickel, Coleslaw (see pages 82 to 83), and mustard, served on a platter with crispy french fries or Latkes (see page 131) and an assortment of pickles.

FLEISHIK: contains meat / Passover-friendly / must be made in advance / can be frozen up to 1 month
PREPARATION TIME: 10 minutes / **COOKING TIME:** 2½ to 3 hours / **SERVES:** 8 to 10

**6 pounds pickled salt beef, pickled ox tongue, or brisket
2 medium red onions, peeled and halved ◆ 2 medium carrots, peeled and halved
2 bay leaves ◆ 1 tablespoon white wine vinegar ◆ 8 whole black peppercorns**

◆

1 Wash the meat thoroughly under cold running water. Put in a large saucepan and cover with cold water. Add the onions, carrots, bay leaves, white wine vinegar, and peppercorns.

2 Bring to a boil over medium-high heat. Reduce the heat to medium-low and simmer until tender (2½ to 3 hours), occasionally skimming the scum off the surface of the water. (Add more boiling water if necessary during cooking.)

3 Drain. Pour cold water over meat. Remove the skin and any gristle or excess fat from the tongue.

4 Wrap in aluminum foil and weigh down with a plate in the refrigerator. Slice the meat as desired.

Liver with Onions

This is a very tasty meal. I have to be in the right mood for it—liver does have its own flavor—but when I am, this is fantastic. The best side dish for this is mashed potatoes—flavor them with a spoonful of mustard and use them to soak up all those sweet onions. Delicious!

FLEISHIK: contains meat / Passover-friendly
PREPARATION TIME: 15 minutes / **COOKING TIME:** 20 minutes / **SERVES:** 6

**2 tablespoons olive oil ◆ 6 medium yellow onions, peeled and sliced thinly
1 tablespoon light brown sugar ◆ 2 tablespoons medium-ground matzah meal
Salt ◆ Freshly ground black pepper ◆ 2 tablespoons vegetable oil
3 pounds koshered chicken livers or 6 slices (about 3 pounds total) koshered ox liver
½ cup dry red wine**

◆

1 Heat the olive oil in a large frying pan over low heat. Add the onions and brown sugar. Cook 20 minutes, stirring occasionally, until the onions are golden brown and caramelized.

2 Place the matzah meal in a shallow dish. Add salt and pepper. Dust the liver with matzah meal.

3 In a separate frying pan, heat the vegetable oil over medium-low heat. Add the liver. Cook 3 to 4 minutes on each side. Pour the wine over the liver. Cook 2 minutes.

4 Arrange the onions on a serving platter. Top with the liver and serve immediately.

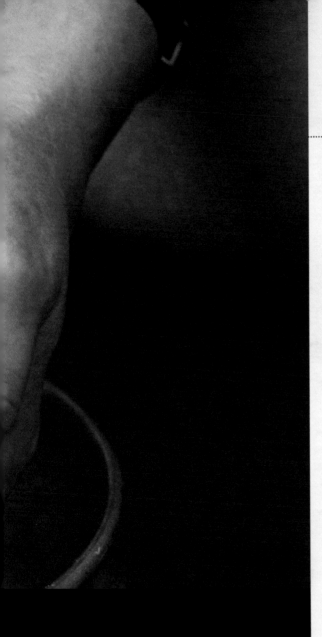

chapter four

SIDE DISHES

Chrain

Traditionally, horseradish is served on the seder plate at Passover to represent the bitterness of the Israelites when they were slaves in Egypt. Seder is the account of the exodus of Egypt led by Moses. It takes the form of a service at the dinner table and the seder plate includes symbolic foods to retell the story. Chrain is used throughout the year as a condiment—it livens up Gefilte Fish (see page 50), cold meats, and chicken. Be careful when grating horseradish, as the vapors it exudes are very powerful and can make you sneeze, cough, or cry (and that's before you've eaten it!). To temper the effect of this powerful ingredient, Jewish cooks mix it with beets, sugar, and vinegar to produce a wonderful relish called chrain. As Passover approaches, it is usually easy to find whole horseradish roots in supermarkets and Jewish delis. At other times of year, they are often only available at specialty food stores. Horseradish is quite easy to grow, however. My brother-in-law has a thriving crop in his backyard that it is always ready to pick just before Passover, when it is most needed.

PAREVE: contains no meat or dairy products / Passover-friendly / can be made in advance
PREPARATION TIME: 10 minutes / **COOKING TIME:** 0 minutes / **MAKES:** 2 cups

1 medium whole horseradish root (about 8 ounces)
3 medium beets (about 12 ounces total), boiled and peeled ♦ ⅔ cup white or cider vinegar
3 tablespoons light brown sugar or honey ♦ Freshly ground black pepper

♦

1 Open the kitchen window to help circulate air. Wearing rubber gloves, peel the horseradish.

2 Using a food processor or a hand grater, finely grate the horseradish. Place in a large bowl.

3 Finely grate the beets. Add to the horseradish. Add the vinegar and brown sugar or honey. Pepper to taste, and stir to mix.

4 Using boiling water, sterilize a 2-cup jar and its lid. Place the horseradish-beet mixture in the jar. Tightly seal. Refrigerate at least 2 hours before serving. Relish may be stored in the refrigerator up to 2 months. The pungency of horseradish varies considerably, so be sure to taste the relish and, if necessary, add a bit more brown sugar (or honey) or vinegar before placing it in the jar.

Mushroom Rice

This is one of my family's favorite dishes. I love to serve this with Roast Chicken on Friday nights (see page 57). I cook the rice in chicken stock to intensify the flavor. For a pareve dish, use vegetable stock instead.

FLEISHIK: contains meat *or* **PAREVE:** contains no meat or dairy products / can be made in advance
PREPARATION TIME: 10 minutes / **COOKING TIME:** 20 minutes / **SERVES:** 8 to 10

2 tablespoons extra-virgin olive oil ◆ 1 medium yellow onion, peeled and chopped coarsely
4 large garlic cloves, peeled and chopped finely
2 cups mixed fresh mushrooms, such as white, porcini, and wild mushrooms
5 cups chicken stock (fleishik), vegetable stock (pareve), or pareve chicken stock
2 cups long-grain white rice ◆ 1 tablespoon dried mushrooms
1 cup cooked, coarsely chopped asparagus (if desired) ◆ Salt
Freshly ground black pepper ◆ 2 tablespoons coarsely chopped fresh parsley

◆

1 Heat the olive oil in a large, deep-frying pan or saucepan over medium-low heat. Add the onions and garlic and sauté 3 minutes.

2 Add fresh mushrooms. Cook 5 minutes. (The mushrooms will release some juices; cook until the juices have been completely reabsorbed.) Set aside 2 tablespoons mushroom-onion mixture.

3 Add the chicken or vegetable stock, rice, and dried mushrooms to the pan. Increase the heat to medium-high and bring to a boil. Reduce the heat to medium-low and simmer 10 minutes. Add the asparagus, if desired.

4 Turn off the heat, cover the pan, and let sit for 10 minutes.

5 Using a fork, fluff the rice. Salt and pepper to taste. Transfer to a serving bowl. Sprinkle with parsley and the reserved mushroom mixture. Serve immediately.

Potato Kugel

Kugels (savory casseroles) are a major feature of Ashkenazi cuisine, especially on Shabbat and during Yom Tov, when there are often extra guests to feed. Kugels freeze and reheat well, and they require little attention while cooking. Here I've taken my mother's recipe, made it healthier (by omitting egg yolks and calling for less oil), and added a stylish twist by making it in individual ramekins. If you prefer not to prepare individual servings, simply place the entire mixture in a shallow baking dish and bake for 45 minutes.

PAREVE: contains no meat or dairy products / Passover-friendly
can be made in advance / can be frozen up to 1 month
PREPARATION TIME: 20 minutes / **COOKING TIME:** 25 minutes / **SERVES:** 10

About 3 tablespoons olive oil ◆ 6 boiling potatoes, peeled
2 medium yellow onions, peeled and grated ◆ 4 tablespoons medium-ground matzah meal
1 tablespoon potato flour ◆ 1 teaspoon baking powder
Whites of 6 large eggs, lightly beaten ◆ 3 tablespoons extra-virgin olive oil
2 tablespoons fresh basil or parsley, chopped coarsely
1 teaspoon sugar ◆ Salt ◆ Freshly ground black pepper

◆

1 Preheat the oven to 400°F.

2 Line the base of 10 individual ramekins with nonstick baking paper. Lightly grease the sides of the ramekins with olive oil.

3 Using a food processor or a hand grater, grate the potatoes. Place the grated potatoes between paper towels and squeeze to remove any excess water.

4 Place the potatoes in a large bowl. Add the onions, matzah meal, potato flour, baking powder, sugar, egg whites, extra-virgin olive oil, and basil or parsley. Generously salt and pepper and mix well.

5 Spoon the mixture into the ramekins. Place in the oven and bake 25 minutes or until the tops are golden brown. Serve hot or chilled.

Pickled Vegetables

My friend Sharon, who is a Sephardi Jew, gave me this recipe, another favorite of mine. Pickled vegetables are generally served as a side dish to couscous in her community, but they are also delicious as part of an appetizer spread, as an edible served with cocktails, or simply as a snack. The process of pickling was created as a way to preserve vegetables, allowing them to be eaten out of season. The need to preserve vegetables in this way is no longer pressing, but pickling still lends enormous flavor and bite to most vegetables, and makes them a tasty addition to most meals. All kinds of vegetables—from turnips and beets to cauliflower and zucchini—may be pickled, and usually an assortment of such vegetables are served together. This recipe calls for one of my favorite combinations.

PAREVE: contains no meat or dairy products / Passover-friendly
must be made at least 1 day in advance / **PREPARATION TIME:** 10 minutes (plus at least 12 hours to allow vegetables to pickle) / **COOKING TIME:** 0 minutes / **SERVES:** 6

1 to 2 medium carrots, peeled and cut into short, fat sticks
1 orange bell pepper, cored and cut into short sticks
1 green bell pepper, cored and cut into short sticks ◆ 2 teaspoons salt ◆ 1 cup water
1 cup white wine vinegar (use kosher for Passover)

1 Using boiling water, sterilize a clean 2-cup jar and its lid.

2 Sprinkle the vegetables with salt and place in the jar. Add water and vinegar. Tightly seal the

jar with the lid and refrigerate at least 12 hours before serving. Use as desired.

3 Leave overnight in the refrigerator and use as desired.

Mama says...
These pickled vegetables may be stored in the refrigerator up to 2 weeks.

Ratatouille

This colorful combination of mixed vegetables is great with most main courses, and it can be served hot, warm, or cold. Even after refrigerating and reheating, this dish tastes fine and presents well.

PAREVE: contains no meat or dairy products / Passover-friendly / can be made in advance
PREPARATION TIME: 15 minutes / **COOKING TIME:** 15 minutes / **SERVES:** 6

3 tablespoons extra-virgin olive oil ♦ 2 medium red onions, peeled and chopped coarsely
1 large or 2 small eggplants (about 1½ pounds total), cut into bite-sized cubes (skin on)
2 medium zucchini, chopped coarsely
1 medium red bell pepper, cored and chopped coarsely
1 medium yellow bell pepper, cored and chopped coarsely
3 large garlic cloves, peeled and chopped finely
One 14-ounce can diced tomatoes with herbs
6 cherry or other small salad tomatoes, halved ♦ Salt
Freshly ground black pepper ♦ 4 tablespoons chopped fresh basil, divided

♦

1 Heat the olive oil in a large saucepan over medium heat. Add the onions and sauté 3 minutes.

2 Add the eggplant, zucchini, bell peppers, and garlic. Sauté 3 minutes.

3 Stir in the canned and fresh tomatoes. Salt and pepper to taste. Cook uncovered 10 minutes.

4 Stir in 2 tablespoons basil. Transfer the mixture to a serving platter and garnish with the remaining basil.

Potato Salad with Lemon Mayonnaise

This salad is also a regular at Shabbat lunches and, being pareve, it's served at Passover meals as well. It is healthy, economical, versatile, and delicious.

PAREVE: contains no meat or dairy products / Passover-friendly / can be made in advance
PREPARATION TIME: 10 minutes / **COOKING TIME:** 20 minutes / **SERVES:** 8

**2 teaspoons sea salt ◆ About 20 baby new potatoes, cleaned and halved
Yolks of 2 large eggs ◆ Juice and zest of ½ medium organic lemon
1 teaspoon dry mustard (any variety) ◆ 1 tablespoon superfine sugar
Freshly ground black pepper ◆ 2 cups vegetable oil ◆ Snipped chives, for garnish**

◆

1 Fill a large saucepan with water and add 1 teaspoon salt. Bring to a boil over medium-high heat. Add the potatoes and cook until tender (about 20 minutes). Drain and set aside to cool.

2 Place the egg yolks, lemon juice and zest, mustard, and sugar in a blender or food processor. Salt and pepper to taste. Blend or process until the mixture is smooth.

3 With the blender running, slowly add the vegetable oil. Blend or process until the oil is thoroughly blended into the mixture. Adjust the seasonings, if desired.

4 Mix together the mayonnaise and cooled potatoes. Transfer to a serving bowl, garnish with chives, and serve.

Mama says...
To save curdled mayonnaise, gradually? add one egg yolk while whisking the mayonnaise constantly.

Red Cabbage with Wine

This is delicious hot or cold, and makes a great side dish to almost any main course.

PAREVE: Passover-friendly / can be made in advance
PREPARATION TIME: 15 minutes / **COOKING TIME:** 30 minutes / **SERVES:** 6 to 8

2 tablespoons extra-virgin olive oil ◆ 2 medium red onions, peeled and sliced thinly
8 cups red cabbage, shredded fine ◆ 1 cup kiddush or sweet red wine
1 cup white raisins ◆ 2 cups chicken stock (fleishik) or vegetable stock (pareve) ◆ Salt
Freshly ground black pepper ◆ 4 tablespoons nondairy margarine

◆

1 Heat olive oil in a large saucepan over medium-low heat. Add the onions and sauté 5 minutes. Add the cabbage, wine, raisins, and chicken or vegetable stock. Salt and pepper to taste.

2 Increase the heat to medium-high and bring to a boil. Reduce heat to medium-low. Stir in the margarine. Simmer 30 minutes, stirring occasionally.

Crispy, Sliced Roast Potatoes

This is a very simple side dish that is delicious served with hearty main courses.

PAREVE: contains no meat or dairy products / Passover-friendly
PREPARATION TIME: 5 minutes / **COOKING TIME:** 30 minutes / **SERVES:** 6 to 8

8 large potatoes ◆ 2 tablespoons extra-virgin olive oil ◆ Salt

◆

1 Preheat the oven to 350°F. Cut the potatoes into 1-inch-thick slices. Rinse in cold water to remove excess starch. Blot dry with paper towels.

2 Place the potatoes on a baking tray. Drizzle with olive oil. Salt to taste. Bake 30 minutes, until golden brown and crispy.

Croquette Potatoes

These are mashed potato parcels shaped into barrels and coated with egg white and matzah meal or bread crumbs. They are a great favorite in my house, and—like latkes—they always disappear quickly. These are usually served as a side dish to fish or chicken. These can be made in advance and refrigerated until ready to use. Just pop them into the oven at 350°–400°F for 10 minutes to reheat them.

PAREVE: contains no meat or dairy products / Passover-friendly / can be made in advance
PREPARATION TIME: 20 minutes / **COOKING TIME:** 15 minutes / **MAKES:** about 20 croquettes

8 boiling potatoes, boiled and peeled ◆ 2 large eggs, separated
3 tablespoons melted margarine ◆ 1 teaspoon freshly grated nutmeg
3 tablespoons finely snipped chives ◆ Salt
Freshly ground black pepper ◆ 1 cup medium-ground matzah meal or bread crumbs
About 4 to 6 cups vegetable oil ◆ Fresh chive blades, for garnish

◆

1 Place the potatoes in a large bowl or pot. Using a potato ricer, mash the potatoes until very smooth.

2 Add the egg yolks, margarine, nutmeg, and snipped chives. Salt and pepper to taste. Stir to mix.

3 Using a fork, lightly whisk the egg whites. Place in a small shallow dish.

4 Place the matzah meal or bread crumbs in a shallow dish.

5 Using wet hands, take 2 tablespoons mashed potato and mold into barrel shapes. Roll in the egg white, then in matzah meal or bread crumbs.

6 Heat the vegetable oil in a deep-fat fryer or a large, deep skillet over medium heat until the oil is 350°F (or until a small piece of bread dropped into the oil fries to a crisp in 30 seconds).

7 Place the croquettes (in batches, if necessary) in the fryer and cook 5 to 7 minutes, until golden brown and crispy. Blot with paper towels. Serve garnished with chives.

Kasha with Mushrooms

Kasha, also known as buckwheat groats, was a popular dish with the poorer Jews in Russia in the early nineteenth century. It is nutritious, high in fiber, and low in fat. I like to serve it with tongue, braised brisket, Pot Roast (see page 58), and Roast Chicken (see page 57). Kasha can be purchased in fine, medium, or coarse grain. If you're looking for a traditional dish, coarse grain is the one to use. The secret to creating a wonderful kasha dish is to toast the grains before they are baked. Toasted kasha is available at some supermarkets—it provides a shortcut to creating this dish, but you can easily toast kasha yourself.

FLEISHIK: contains meat *or* **PAREVE:** contains no meat or dairy products
PREPARATION TIME: 20 minutes / **COOKING TIME:** 1 hour / **SERVES:** 8

2¼ cups coarse-grain kasha (buckwheat groats) ◆ 1 large egg, lightly beaten
4½ cups chicken stock (fleishik) or vegetable stock (pareve) ◆ ¼ cup vegetable oil
2 large yellow onions, peeled and chopped finely
2 cups white mushrooms, cleaned and chopped coarsely ◆ 4 tablespoons fresh parsley, chopped coarsely (reserve 3 to 4 sprigs for garnish)
1 teaspoon fine sea salt ◆ Freshly ground black pepper ◆ 2 tablespoons extra-virgin olive oil

◆

1 Preheat the oven to 350°F.

2 Place the kasha in a large frying pan over medium heat. Toast, stirring constantly, until the kasha gives off an aroma (about 5 minutes). Immediately add the egg and stir vigorously into the kasha. Add the chicken or vegetable stock. Stir to mix.

3 Transfer the mixture to a baking dish and bake covered 45 minutes.

4 Meanwhile, heat the vegetable oil in a medium frying pan over medium heat. Add the onions and mushrooms. Sauté until the onions are soft and the mushroom liquid has been reabsorbed (about 10 minutes). Stir in the chopped parsley and cook 1 minute. Generously salt and pepper. Set aside.

5 Remove kasha from the oven. Stir in the onion-mushroom mixture. Transfer to a serving bowl. Drizzle with olive oil and garnish with parsley.

Homemade Coleslaw

A simcha (party) just isn't a simcha without coleslaw. This versatile, tasty dish is often served on Shabbat, as well as during Passover.

PAREV: contains no meat or dairy products / Passover-friendly / can be made in advance
PREPARATION TIME: 5 minutes / **COOKING TIME:** 0 minutes / **SERVES:** 8 people

4 cups coarsely shredded white cabbage leaves
4 cups coarsely shredded red cabbage leaves
3 medium carrots, peeled and grated coarse
⅓ cup chopped walnuts (if desired)
2 cups mayonnaise
Juice of ½ medium lemon
1 tablespoon honey
1 teaspoon prepared whole-grain or Dijon mustard ◆ Salt
Freshly ground black pepper
12 endive leaves or 6 radicchio leaves
6 green savoy cabbage leaves

◆

Mama says...
As a variation on this classic coleslaw,
try adding 1/3 cup white raisins to the
coleslaw for extra sweetness.

1 In a large bowl, toss together cabbage, carrots, and (if desired) walnuts. Set aside.

2 Place mayonnaise, lemon juice, honey, and mustard in a medium bowl. Salt and pepper to taste. Mix thoroughly.

3 Add the fresh dressing to the cabbage mixture and stir thoroughly to mix.

4 Transfer to a serving dish, garnish with endive or radicchio and savoy cabbage leaves, and serve.

Vegetable Couscous

My friend Sharon gave me this Sephardi recipe. This dish hails from Tunisia, where Sharon's mother-in-law lived until persecution led them to flee to Tiberias in Northern Israel. Times were tough—they lived in a wooden hut, and meat was scarce. Fortunately, vegetables were plentiful, and the family enjoyed them in this dish frequently. Years later—in another country and another culture—we still enjoy its delightful colors, textures, and flavors. The traditional way to eat this is to drain off most of the couscous "soup," garnish it with a few chickpeas, and have it as a first course. The vegetables are placed on top of the couscous, and this is eaten as the main course, accompanied by pickled vegetables. Today, we like to serve this as a colorful side dish to roast meats and fish. This dish calls for a very deep pan, as it requires a lot of liquid to produce both the side dish and the "soup" that can be used as a first course. If you prefer to omit the "soup" part, reduce the amount of vegetable stock used to cook the vegetables to 6 cups (so that 8½ total cups of vegetable stock are required for the recipe), and drain off and discard the liquid from the cooked vegetables.

PAREVE: contains no meat or dairy products / can be made in advance
PREPARATION TIME: 30 minutes / **COOKING TIME:** 25 minutes / **SERVES:** 10 to 12

¼ cup, plus 3 tablespoons olive oil, divided
3 large carrots, peeled and cut into thin sticks, 2½ inches long
2 celery stalks, cut into 3-inch-long sticks ◆ 1 medium zucchini, cut into 1-inch-thick circles
1 medium yellow onion, peeled and cut into 2-inch-thick wedges
1 medium white cabbage (about 8 ounces), cored and cut into 2-inch-thick wedges
1 medium potato, peeled and chopped coarsely ◆ 1 small butternut squash (about
1 pound), peeled and cut into 2-inch-thick wedges
½ teaspoon turmeric ◆ 11½ cups vegetable stock, divided ◆ Juice of 1 lemon
1 cinnamon stick ◆ Salt ◆ Freshly ground black pepper ◆ One 14-ounce can chickpeas, drained
2½ cups couscous ◆ 4 tablespoons parsley, for garnish

1 Heat ¼ cup olive oil in a large, deep saucepan (4-quart or larger) over medium heat. Add the carrots, celery, zucchini, onion, cabbage, potato, and squash. Sauté 10 minutes, stirring frequently.

2 Stir in turmeric. Add 9 cups vegetable stock, lemon juice, and cinnamon stick. Generously salt and pepper to taste.

3 Increase the heat to medium-high and bring to a boil. Reduce the heat to medium-low and simmer until all the vegetables are soft (about 20 minutes).

4 Bring to a boil and simmer for 20 minutes or until the vegetables are quite soft. Remove from the heat.

5 Set aside 2 tablespoons chickpeas. Add the remaining chickpeas to the vegetables. Stir and set aside.

6 Place the couscous in a deep, heat-resistant dish. In a small saucepan, bring the remaining 2½ cups of vegetable stock to a boil over medium-high heat. Pour the stock over the couscous. Immediately seal the dish with plastic wrap. Let sit for 5 minutes.

7 Using a fork, fluff the couscous. Stir in the remaining 3 tablespoons of olive oil. Salt and pepper to taste.

8 Place a large colander over a large saucepan or pot. Drain the vegetables. Remove and discard the cinnamon stick.

9 Transfer the "soup" to individual bowls, garnish with the reserved chickpeas, and serve (or refrigerate the "soup" up to 2 days for later use).

10 Transfer the couscous to a large serving platter. Top with the vegetable-chickpea mixture. Garnish with parsley sprigs and serve hot.

chapter five

FRIDAY NIGHT
DESSERTS

Lemon Meringue Pie

This is a satisfying, sweet, light finish to any Friday night dinner. Although it can be made using cookies as its base, I prefer a real, old-fashioned pie crust.

PAREVE: contains no meat or dairy products / can be made in advance
PREPARATION TIME: 25 minutes (plus 30 minutes to chill) / **COOKING TIME:** 1 hour
SERVES: 6

PIE CRUST DOUGH
2¼ cups all-purpose flour ◆ 1 cup nondairy margarine ◆ 1 large egg
Zest of 1 medium organic lemon, grated finely ◆ 2 tablespoons confectioners' sugar

FILLING
½ cup cornstarch ◆ 4 cups cold soy milk
Yolks of 5 large eggs (whites reserved for meringue)
2 to 3 tablespoons superfine sugar, to taste
Juice and grated zest of 2 medium organic lemons

MERINGUE
Whites of 5 large eggs ◆ 1¼ cups superfine sugar

◆

1 Make the pie crust dough. Place all the ingredients in a food processor that is fitted with a dough blade. Process until the dough forms a ball. Transfer the dough to a work surface, wrap in plastic wrap, and flatten so it is 1-inch thick. Refrigerate 30 minutes.

2 Preheat the oven to 400°F.

3 Lightly flour a work surface. Remove the dough from the plastic wrap and roll out to fit a 2-inch-deep, 10-inch-round springform pie plate. Gently ease the dough into the pie plate.

4 Cover the pie crust dough with aluminum foil. Place some baking beans on the foil, then bake blind 30 minutes.

5 Make the filling. In a medium bowl, mix together the cornstarch and 2 tablespoons soy milk. Heat the remaining soy milk in a medium-sized saucepan over medium heat. Pour the hot milk into the cornstarch mixture and stir well.

Return the mixture to the saucepan and, stirring constantly, bring to a boil over medium heat. Boil 3 to 4 minutes, stirring constantly.

6 In a small bowl, whisk together the egg yolks and sugar until thick and creamy. Add the milk mixture and stir to blend. Stir in the lemon juice and zest. Immediately pour into the cooked pie crust. Set aside to cool.

7 Reduce the oven temperature to 325°F.

8 Make the meringue. Place the egg whites in a clean, medium-sized bowl. Whisk until stiff, but not dry. Whisking constantly, add the sugar 1 tablespoon at a time, until all the sugar has been incorporated into the meringue.

9 Spoon or pipe the meringue high onto the pie filling, completely covering the pie filling.

10 Bake 20 minutes or until the meringue is pale and lightly browned.

Mama says...
To create a perfect meringue, be sure to add the sugar to the egg whites very gradually, whisking constantly.

Apple-Plum Crumble

This is a great fall dessert, when apples and plums are plentiful. I love to serve this with hot Nondairy Custard (see page 93).

PAREVE: contains no meat or dairy products / can be made in advance
PREPARATION TIME: 30 minutes / **COOKING TIME:** 30 minutes / **SERVES:** 8 to 10

FRUIT MIXTURE

2 medium red or green sweet apples, peeled, cored, and sliced thinly
About 15 plums, pitted and sliced thin
1 tablespoon cinnamon ◆ 2 tablespoons raw sugar or dark brown sugar
2 tablespoons all-purpose flour

CRUMBLE

2 cups all-purpose flour ◆ 1 packed cup light brown sugar ◆ ¾ cup margarine
1 cup oats ◆ 1 tablespoon cinnamon ◆ 2 teaspoons baking powder
2 tablespoons shredded dried coconut

◆

1 Preheat the oven to 400°F.

2 Make the fruit mixture. Place the apples and plums in a large bowl. Add the cinnamon, sugar, and flour. Gently mix. Transfer the mixture to a large baking dish.

3 Make the crumble. Place all the ingredients in a food processor. Process until the mixture forms crumbs. Sprinkle the crumbs evenly over the fruit mixture.

4 Bake uncovered for 30 minutes.

Mama says...
For an even better-tasting, crunchier crumble, cook the crumble in advance, then reheat it when you are ready to prepare the dessert.

Chocolate Roulade

This is an easy-to-make sponge cake that is filled with cream cheese and grated chocolate, then rolled. For a delicious pareve dessert, use nondairy cream cheese.

MILCHIK: contains dairy products *or* PAREVE: contains no meat or dairy products
can be made in advance / Passover-friendly
PREPARATION TIME: 25 minutes (plus about 30 minutes to cool)
COOKING TIME: 15 minutes / SERVES: 6 to 8

¼ cup good-quality bittersweet chocolate ◆ 6 large eggs, separated
½ cup superfine sugar ◆ 2 tablespoons cocoa ◆ 2 teaspoons vanilla extract
2 cups cream cheese (milchik), heavy cream—whipped for Passover, or nondairy
cream cheese substitute (pareve) ◆ ¼ cup, plus 2 tablespoons grated bittersweet chocolate
1 cup raspberries (if desired) ◆ ¼ cup confectioners' sugar

◆

1 Preheat the oven to 350°F. Line a 9-inch by 13-inch jelly-roll pan with parchment paper.

2 Melt the chocolate in a double boiler.

3 In a large bowl, whisk together the egg yolks and superfine sugar until thick and creamy. Stir in the cocoa and melted chocolate.

4 In a medium bowl, whisk the egg whites until very stiff. Stir in the vanilla extract. Gently fold into the chocolate mixture. Pour into the pan and spread evenly to the edges of the pan.

5 Bake 15 minutes or until the mixture has risen and is firm to touch.

6 Invert onto a clean piece of parchment paper. Peel off the parchment-paper lining. Set aside until cool (about 30 minutes).

7 In a medium bowl, mix together the cream cheese or nondairy cream cheese substitute and the grated chocolate. Add the raspberries, if desired. Stir in the confectioners' sugar last.

8 Carefully spread the chocolate mixture over the cooled cake. Starting at one of the wider ends, carefully roll up the cake—use the parchment paper to help guide the cake. Using a spatula or a cake slicer, carefully transfer to a serving platter.

Mama's Best-Ever Apple Pie

Apple pie is a common, beloved dessert on Friday evenings. The cinnamon permeates the apple, giving the pie a wonderful flavor. This particular recipe creates an old-fashioned, double-crusted treat. I love to serve it with hot Nondairy Custard.

PAREVE: contains no meat or dairy products / can be made in advance / can be frozen up to 2 weeks
PREPARATION TIME: 40 minutes (plus 30 minutes to allow pastry to rest) / **COOKING TIME:** 40 minutes
MAKES: One 9-inch pie

PIE CRUST DOUGH
2½ cups all-purpose flour ◆ ½ cup margarine ◆ 1 teaspoon salt ◆ 2 teaspoons cinnamon
2 tablespoons superfine sugar ◆ 1 large egg ◆ 3 tablespoons cold water

GLAZE
Yolks of 1 to 2 large eggs, lightly beaten

FILLING
6 medium Granny Smith apples, peeled, cored, and sliced thinly ◆ 1 tablespoon cinnamon
2 tablespoons all-purpose flour ◆ 2 tablespoons dark brown sugar
Juice of ½ medium lemon ◆ 1 tablespoon margarine, cut into small pieces

◆

1 Make the pie crust dough. Place all the ingredients in a food processor that is fitted with a dough blade. Process to form a dough.

2 Remove the dough, wrap in plastic wrap, and flatten to 1-inch thick. Refrigerate for 30 minutes.

3 Preheat the oven to 400°F. Lightly flour a work surface. Remove the dough from the refrigerator and unwrap. Transfer two-thirds of

the dough to the work surface. Rewrap the remaining dough and set aside.

4 Roll out the pastry to fit a 9-inch by 1-inch-deep, round pie plate (allow for a bit of overlap).

5 Gently place the dough over the pie plate and ease into the plate. Brush the edges of the dough with the egg yolk glaze just before the top dough is put on the pie.

6 Make the filling. Place all the ingredients in a large bowl and gently mix. Place the filling in the pie. Set aside.

7 Make the pie dough top. Lightly flour the work surface. Transfer the remaining dough to the work surface and roll it out to fit the pie plate (allow for a bit of overlap). Gently place on top of the pie filling. Squeeze together the dough edges to seal. Glaze the dough with the remaining egg yolk.

8 Using a sharp knife, cut three curved slits in the top layer of the dough (to allow steam to escape).

9 Bake for 40 minutes or until the pie crust is golden brown.

Nondairy Custard

PAREVE: contains no meat or dairy products / **PREPARATION TIME:** 10 minutes
COOKING TIME: 15 minutes / **SERVES:** 10 (makes about 2½ cups)

Yolks of 6 large eggs ◆ ½ cup superfine sugar ◆ 2½ cups soy milk
2 tablespoons custard powder (available at specialty food stores and at some grocery stores)
2 teaspoons vanilla extract

1 Place the egg yolks and sugar in a medium-sized bowl. Beat until pale and thick.

2 Place the soy milk in a medium-sized saucepan. Bring to a boil over medium heat. Remove from the heat.

3 In a small bowl or glass, mix together the custard powder, vanilla extract, and 2 tablespoons hot soy milk.

4 Whisking constantly, pour the mixture into the soy milk. Pour the soy milk mixture into the egg mixture. Stir to mix.

5 Return the mixture to the saucepan and heat over low heat, stirring constantly, until the mixture thickens and coats the back of a spoon (about 10 minutes).

Berry-Peach Salad

There is always a place for fruit at the Jewish table. Use the ripest berries you can find for the best flavor.

PAREVE: contains no meat or dairy products / Passover-friendly / can be made in advance
PREPARATION TIME: 15 minutes (plus 2 hours to chill) / **COOKING TIME:** 0 minutes
SERVES: 6 to 8

3 medium, very ripe peaches ◆ 2 cups fresh blueberries, rinsed
1 cup fresh blackberries, rinsed ◆ 2 cups fresh raspberries, rinsed ◆ ½ cup sugar
1 teaspoon cinnamon ◆ 2 tablespoons Kiddush wine or kir
Fresh mint leaves, for decoration

◆

1 Remove and discard the pits from the peaches. Cut the peaches into small segments. Place in a large bowl. Add the blueberries, blackberries, and 1 cup raspberries and gently toss to mix. Set aside.

2 Pulse the sugar and remaining raspberries in a food processor or a blender until puréed. Pour the mixture through a very fine strainer into a bowl.

3 Add the cinnamon and wine or kir to the freshly puréed berries, then stir to mix. Pour over the fruit mixture and gently toss to mix. Chill in the refrigerator for 2 hours.

4 Spoon the mixture into individual glass dishes or Champagne glasses. Decorate with mint leaves and serve with Mandelbrot (see page 113).

Chocolate Pavlova with Raspberries

This recipe has been in my family for years, but it has been adapted over time to take advantage of modern cooking techniques and availability of key ingredients. Strawberries, blueberries, peaches, or nectarines can be combined with the whipping cream, but my favorite remains fresh raspberries. Frozen or canned raspberries may be used as well, provided they are thawed, if frozen, and well drained.

PAREVE: contains no meat or dairy products / must be made 1 to 2 days in advance
PREPARATION TIME: 25 minutes / **COOKING TIME:** 2 hours / **SERVES:** 8 to 10

Whites of 6 large eggs ◆ 1 cup superfine sugar, divided
2 tablespoons cornstarch or potato flour ◆ 1 teaspoon vanilla extract
2 teaspoons white wine vinegar ◆ 1 cup coarsely grated bittersweet chocolate
1 cup nondairy whipped topping ◆ 1 cup raspberries

◆

1 Preheat the oven to 225°F. Line a large baking tray with parchment paper. Set aside.

2 In a large bowl, whisk the egg whites until stiff. Whisking constantly, gradually add ⅔ cup sugar, 1 tablespoon at a time.

3 Sift in the cornstarch or potato flour and the remaining sugar. Continue to whisk the egg whites. Stir in the vanilla extract and vinegar. Whisk again. Fold in the chocolate.

4 Spoon or pipe the mixture into a 9-inch circle on the lined baking tray.

5 Bake 2 hours. Turn off the oven and let sit in the oven until completely cooled (about 40 minutes).

6 Transfer cooled meringue to a serving platter.

7 Place whipped topping in a medium bowl. Fold in the raspberries. Spoon onto meringue and serve.

Hot Chocolate Soufflé Pudding

Everyone loves chocolate soufflé pudding, and this recipe is perfect for family Friday nights. Coated with a trufflelike chocolate sauce, this cocoa-based pudding will satisfy any chocoholic. Quick and easy to make, it can also be made in advance and reheated.

PAREVE: contains no meat or dairy products / can be made in advance
PREPARATION TIME: 25 minutes / **COOKING TIME:** 35 minutes / **SERVES:** 6

SOUFFLÉ PUDDING

1 tablespoon margarine ◆ 3 tablespoons hot water ◆ ⅓ cup bittersweet chocolate
1½ cups self-rising flour ◆ 1 teaspoon baking powder ◆ ½ teaspoon baking soda
3 tablespoons cocoa ◆ ½ cup sugar ◆ 4 large eggs ◆ 1 cup soy milk
2 tablespoons corn syrup ◆ 1 cup sunflower oil

SAUCE

⅓ cup margarine ◆ ¾ cup plain bittersweet chocolate ◆ ¾ cup soy cream
1¼ cups confectioners' sugar

◆

1 Preheat the oven to 350°F. Grease with the margarine and line a 7½-inch by 3-inch-deep, round cake pan. Set aside.

2 Melt the chocolate for the soufflé pudding. Place in a food processor with 3 tablespoons hot water and whip together.

3 Make the pudding. Sift together the flour, baking powder, baking soda, cocoa, and sugar into a large bowl. Add the melted chocolate, eggs, soy milk, corn syrup, and sunflower oil. Beat until smooth. Pour into the cake pan.

4 Bake 25 minutes or until the pudding has risen and is springy to touch.

5 Make the sauce. Place the margarine, chocolate, and soy cream in a medium-sized saucepan and melt over low heat. Whisk until smooth. Remove from the heat.

6 Sift a third of the confectioners' sugar into the mixture and whisk until smooth. Repeat until the sauce is glossy.

7 Invert the pudding onto a warm serving plate. Cut thick slices and pour the sauce over.

Lokshen Kugel

Lokshen kugel, or noodle pudding, is an unusual and exclusively Jewish way of eating pasta as a dessert! It may sound strange, but my children are addicted to it, and the sweet ingredients make for a very filling and satisfying dessert. Although Lokshen kugel can easily be reheated, or even served cold, we find that it rarely lasts beyond Friday night. This particular recipe is really quick and easy, and it's extremely delicious. I like to use flat egg noodles that are at least ½-inch wide.

PAREVE: contains no meat or dairy products / can be made in advance
PREPARATION TIME: 20 minutes / **COOKING TIME:** 40 minutes / **SERVES:** 8

¾ cup margarine ◆ 1 tablespoon salt ◆ 3 cups egg noodles ◆ ½ teaspoon baking soda
4 red or green sweet apples, peeled, cored, and grated coarsely ◆ 1½ cups superfine sugar
2 teaspoons cinnamon ◆ 4 large eggs, lightly beaten ◆ 1 teaspoon vanilla extract
3 tablespoons dark raisins ◆ 3 tablespoons apricot jam ◆ 1 tablespoon water

◆

1 Preheat the oven to 350°F.

2 Using 1 tablespoon margarine, grease a 2-inch-deep, 9-inch by 14-inch baking dish. Set aside.

3 Fill a large saucepan with water. Add the salt. Bring to a boil. Add the noodles and cook until al dente (about 5 minutes). Drain and place in a large bowl.

4 Melt the remaining margarine in a small saucepan over low heat. Toss into the noodles. Add the apples, sugar, cinnamon, baking soda, eggs, vanilla extract, and raisins. Place the mixture in a baking dish.

5 Bake 35 to 40 minutes or until golden brown.

6 Place the jam and water in a small saucepan and melt over low heat. Stir to mix. Drizzle the mixture onto the kugel.

Mama says...
Dust individual serving plates with cinnamon. Spoon a generous helping of kugel onto plates and serve.

Baklava

*This is a traditional Middle Eastern dessert that features layers of phyllo filled with
chopped nuts and honey syrup. Despite being rather sweet, it is quite irresistible.
I serve it with pareve vanilla "ice cream" or with coffee or lemon tea on Friday
evenings. For a true Sephardi dessert, serve this with Turkish coffee or mint tea.
Baklava is expensive to buy, and you may think that it's difficult to make at home.
However, I promise that my recipe is not challenging, that it is economical, and that
it serves a large number of guests.*

MILCHIK: contains dairy products / can be made in advance / can be frozen up to 1 month
PREPARATION TIME: 30 minutes (plus 30 minutes to chill) / **COOKING TIME:** 30 minutes
SERVES: 10 to 12

1 tablespoon unsalted butter, for greasing, plus 2 cups, melted
¾ cup blanched almonds ◆ ¾ cup raw pistachios
1 cup sugar, divided ◆ 12 sheets (about 16 ounces) phyllo, thawed if frozen
¾ cup honey ◆ 1 cup water
¼ cup rosewater ◆ 2 tablespoons lemon juice

◆

Mama says...
Decorate baklava with coarsely chopped pistachio
nuts. Serve with yogurt.

1 Grease with butter and line a 12-inch by 8-inch jelly-roll pan. Set aside.

2 Place the almonds, pistachios, and ½ cup sugar in a food processor. Pulse to chop rough.

3 Cut the phyllo to fit the baking pan. Place one layer phyllo on the bottom of the pan. Brush with melted butter. Repeat twice. Sprinkle 3 tablespoons of the nut mixture evenly over the third layer of the phyllo.

4 Repeat until all the phyllo sheets are used, finishing with three layers of phyllo on the top. Refrigerate 30 minutes.

5 Preheat the oven to 350°F.

6 Using a sharp knife, cut the chilled baklava in diagonal strips. Cut across the strips to form diamond shapes.

7 Bake 25 to 30 minutes or until golden brown.

8 Meanwhile, place the honey, water, rosewater, and lemon juice in a medium saucepan. Heat on low 10 minutes. Remove from the heat and cool.

9 Using a sharp knife, cut the baklava pieces again. Pour the syrup over the baklava. Serve hot, warm, or chilled.

chapter six
TEA AT BOOBA'S

Booba's Dried Fruit Strudel

This is one of my mother's recipes and she received it from her mother. It's easy, and it makes a little piece of dough and some dried fruit go a long way.

MILCHIK: contains dairy products *or* **PAREVE:** contains no meat or dairy products
can be made in advance / can be frozen up to 1 month
PREPARATION TIME: 25 minutes (plus 30 minutes to chill)
COOKING TIME: 20 minutes (plus 10 minutes to cool before serving) / **MAKES:** 35 pieces

3½ cups self-rising flour ◆ 1 cup unsalted butter (milchik) or margarine ◆ 2 large eggs
1 to 2 tablespoons cold water ◆ 4 to 6 tablespoons raspberry or black currant jam
2 cups mixed dried fruit, such as raisins, currants, and dried cranberries
½ cup candied cherries, halved (available at specialty food stores and at some grocery stores)
½ cup chopped walnuts ◆ 2 teaspoons cinnamon

◆

1 Place the self-rising flour, butter, eggs, and 1 to 2 tablespoons water in a food processor that is fitted with a dough blade. Process, adding the remaining water, a bit at a time, if necessary, until the dough is soft and smooth. Remove the dough from the food processor, wrap in plastic wrap, and flatten to 1-inch thick. Refrigerate 30 minutes.

2 Preheat the oven to 350°F. Line a baking tray with parchment paper. Set aside.

3 Lightly flour a work surface. Cut the dough into four equal-sized portions. Place one portion on the work surface. Using a hand roller, roll out the dough into a 13½-inch by 6-inch rectangle. Cover the remaining dough with plastic wrap.

4 Spread a thin layer of jam over the entire surface of the dough. Sprinkle ¼ dried fruit, cherries, and walnuts evenly over the dough, then repeat with the remaining portions of dough.

5 Fold each of the dough's long sides 1 inch. Starting at one short side, roll up the dough, so that it resembles a jelly roll.

6 Place the dough on the baking tray. Cut small slits in 1-inch intervals in the dough to allow steam to escape. Sprinkle cinnamon onto dough.

7 Bake 20 minutes or until golden brown and firm to touch. Let cool to room temperature, about 10 minutes.

Ultimate Apple Cake

Certain recipes become family heirlooms that are treasured by generations. This is definitely one of those. All of my sisters have this recipe. Although we have tried out many variations, using plums, apricots, and pears, the cake just seems perfect with apples. It is suitable for serving at tea and as a hot or cold after-meal dessert.

PAREVE: contains no meat or dairy products / can be made in advance / can be frozen up to 2 weeks
PREPARATION TIME: 20 minutes / **COOKING TIME:** 70 minutes / **SERVES:** 8

1 tablespoon vegetable oil ◆ 2 large eggs ◆ 1 cup superfine sugar ◆ ½ cup margarine
1½ teaspoons baking powder ◆ 1 teaspoon almond extract ◆ 1 cup self-rising flour
4 to 5 sweet, green, medium apples, peeled, cored, and sliced very thinly
1 tablespoon vanilla sugar ◆ 1 tablespoon light brown sugar, for decoration (if desired)

◆

1 Preheat the oven to 350°F.

2 Grease with vegetable oil and line an 8½-inch round springform cake pan. Set aside.

3 Place the eggs and superfine sugar in the bowl of an electric mixer. Mix until blended.

4 Melt the margarine in a small saucepan over low heat. Add the melted margarine, baking powder, and almond extract to egg-sugar mixture.

5 While mixing, slowly add the flour. Mix until well blended (mixture should be very thick).

6 Put two-thirds batter in the cake pan. Top with the apples, completely covering the batter. Top the apples with the remaining batter (the batter will not completely cover the apples).

7 Sprinkle the vanilla sugar over the top of the batter.

8 Bake until the cake is golden brown and a toothpick inserted into the center of the cake comes out clean (50 to 60 minutes). Remove from the oven and let cool to warm.

9 If desired, sprinkle with brown sugar just before serving.

Booba's Kiddush Kichels

These simple little cookies bring back memories of fun visits to my grandparents' house for Shabbat tea. They are quick to make, and they keep well in an airtight container for 4 to 5 days. In this recipe, I call for vanilla and almond extracts to flavor the cookies, but a pinch of dried ginger, allspice, or cinnamon would make a pleasant alternative.

MILCHIK: contains dairy products / can be made in advance / can be frozen up to 2 months
PREPARATION TIME: 15 minutes / **COOKING TIME:** 20 minutes / **MAKES:** about 55 cookies

1 cup unsalted butter ◆ Yolk of 1 large egg ◆ ¾ cup confectioners' sugar
2 cups all-purpose flour ◆ About ¾ cup ground almonds ◆ ½ teaspoon salt
1 teaspoon vanilla extract ◆ 1 teaspoon almond extract

◆

1 Preheat the oven to 350°F. Line a baking tray with parchment paper. Set aside.

2 In a medium bowl, cream the butter. Beating constantly, gradually add all the remaining ingredients.

3 Shape the dough into small balls (each about the size of a teaspoon). Place carefully on the baking tray.

4 Bake 15 to 20 minutes or until firm to touch. Do not allow to brown.

Mama says...
For added visual excitement, create these in different shapes—cut circles in half to make crescents, or lightly roll out the dough and use cookie cutters to make any shapes you desire. These may also be decorated with candied cherries or nuts.

Oatmeal Cookies

This is an old recipe that I inherited from my grandmother's sister. These cookies are extremely delicious. Fortunately, the ingredients are relatively healthy.

MILCHIK: contains dairy products *or* **PAREVE:** contains no meat or dairy products
can be made in advance / can be frozen up to 1 month
PREPARATION TIME: 15 minutes (plus 30 minutes to chill) / **COOKING TIME:** 15 to 20 minutes
MAKES: about 55 cookies

1 cup honey
9 tablespoons unsalted butter (milchik) or margarine ◆ 6¼ cups rolled oats
1 cup whole-wheat flour ◆ 1 teaspoon baking soda ◆ 2 teaspoons cinnamon

1 Preheat the oven to 350°F. Line 2 baking trays with parchment paper. Set aside.

2 In a large bowl, cream together the honey and butter or margarine. Stir in the oats, flour, baking soda, and cinnamon.

3 Wrap the dough in plastic wrap and refrigerate for 30 minutes.

4 Roll 1 tablespoon of the mixture into a ball. Gently flatten and place on a baking tray. Repeat, leaving 1 inch of space between the cookies on the baking trays.

5 Bake for 15 to 20 minutes, until golden and set.

Mama says...
Just before serving, dust cookies
with confectioners' sugar.

Chocolate Marble Cake

This is a very traditional Jewish cake. Although it is quite plain, it is addictive. My family calls this the "cut and come again" cake, because everybody always goes back for seconds! It is also good for small children, as it contains no nuts or strong flavors. Try it warm from the oven—the cake melts in your mouth.

MILCHIK: contains dairy products *or* **PAREVE:** contains no meat or dairy products
can be made in advance / can be frozen up to 1 month
PREPARATION TIME: 15 minutes / **COOKING TIME:** 45 to 50 minutes / **SERVES:** 8

1 tablespoon vegetable oil ◆ 4 ounces bittersweet chocolate
2 tablespoons milk (milchik) or soy milk (pareve) ◆ ¾ cup self-rising flour
1 teaspoon baking powder ◆ ¾ cup superfine sugar ◆ 3 large eggs
¾ cup margarine, softened ◆ 1 teaspoon vanilla extract

1 Preheat the oven to 325°F. Grease with vegetable oil and line an 8-inch-round springform cake pan.

2 Melt the chocolate in a double boiler over medium heat. Add the milk or soy milk and mix well. Remove from the heat and let cool to room temperature.

3 In a large bowl, mix together the flour, baking powder, and sugar. Add the eggs, margarine, and vanilla extract. Mix well.

4 Place the batter in the pan. Drop spoonfuls of chocolate batter on top. Using a wooden skewer or a spoon, swirl the chocolate into the cake batter to give it a marbled effect.

5 Bake 45 to 50 minutes or until a wooden toothpick inserted into the cake comes out clean.

Carrot Cake

Healthy eating is not normally high on the agenda during tea at Grandma's, but this yummy carrot cake manages to combine the best of both worlds—great taste and nutritious ingredients (and no butter or cream)! I love the combination of crushed pineapple, carrots, and walnuts—not only does it make this cake taste delicious, but it also creates a wonderfully moist texture. This is an ideal treat to pack in lunch boxes and picnic baskets.

PAREVE: contains no meat or dairy products / can be made in advance / can be frozen up to 1 month
PREPARATION TIME: 15 minutes / **COOKING TIME:** 1 hour / **SERVES:** 8

1 tablespoon vegetable oil ◆ 1 cup all-purpose flour ◆ ¾ cup superfine sugar
1 teaspoon baking soda ◆ 1 teaspoon baking powder ◆ 1 teaspoon cinnamon
2 large eggs ◆ 1 cup vegetable oil ◆ 1 cup grated carrots
1 cup crushed pineapple with juice ◆ ⅓ cup walnut pieces

◆

1 Preheat the oven to 350°F. Grease with vegetable oil and line a 9-inch round springform cake pan. Set aside.

2 In a large bowl, mix together the flour, sugar, baking soda, baking powder, and cinnamon.

Add the eggs and vegetable oil. Mix well. Stir in the carrots, pineapple, and walnuts.

3 Bake 1 hour or until golden brown and a toothpick inserted into the center of the cake comes out clean.

Mama says...
Just before serving, dust the cake with a bit of confectioners' sugar.

Lamington Squares

In the 1960s my grandmother went to South Africa to visit relatives. When she came back she brought this recipe with her. Today my mother still makes this for special teas. We all love its combination of ingredients and the contrast of flavors that a plain sponge cake, coated in chocolate and dipped in coconut, offers.

MILCHIK: contains dairy products *or* **PAREVE:** contains no meat or dairy products
can be made in advance / can be frozen up to 1 month
PREPARATION TIME: 20 minutes / **COOKING TIME:** 20 minutes / **MAKES:** 36 squares

1 tablespoon vegetable oil ◆ ¼ cup superfine sugar
½ cup unsalted butter (milchik) or margarine (pareve)
2 large eggs ◆ ½ cup milk (milchik) or soy milk (pareve) ◆ ½ teaspoon baking soda
1 teaspoon cream of tartar ◆ Zest of 1 medium organic lemon ◆ 1½ cups self-rising flour
1 cup water ◆ ¼ cup cocoa ◆ ¼ cup confectioners' sugar
2 teaspoons vanilla extract ◆ ¼ cup, plus 2 tablespoons shredded coconut

◆

1 Preheat the oven to 350°F. Line and grease with vegetable oil a 9½-inch-square baking pan. Set aside.

2 In a large bowl, cream together the superfine sugar and butter or margarine. Beating constantly, add the eggs, one at a time. Still beating, add the milk or soy milk, baking soda, cream of tartar, and lemon zest.

3 Gradually fold the flour into the mixture. Spoon the mixture into the pan and level off.

4 Bake 20 minutes. Remove from the oven and cut into squares. Set aside to cool.

5 Place the water in a small saucepan and bring to a boil over medium-high heat. Reduce the heat to medium low. Stir in the cocoa, confectioners' sugar, and vanilla extract. Simmer 2 minutes. Remove from the heat and let cool to room temperature.

6 Dip each square of cake into the chocolate mixture and roll in coconut.

Stuffed Monkey

When I was asked to write this book, my mother presented me with a little black book that had belonged to a great-great-aunt who had lived to well into her nineties. Inside was a recipe for something called "stuffed monkey." There were no directions; just a list of ingredients. After doing some research and experimenting, I discovered that this is actually a type of sweet pastry sandwich, and I was able to re-create the complete recipe. The dried cranberries are a modern twist, and I think they add just the right finishing touch. Coarsely chopped dried cherries may be substituted for the cranberries, if you wish.

MILCHIK: contains dairy products *or* **PAREVE:** contains no meat or dairy products
PREPARATION TIME: 20 minutes (plus 30 minutes to chill) / **COOKING TIME:** 30 minutes
SERVES: 6

PIE DOUGH
1 tablespoon vegetable oil ◆ 1¼ cups self-rising flour
½ cup unsalted butter (milchik) or margarine
½ cup packed light brown sugar ◆ 1 large egg ◆ 1 teaspoon cinnamon

FILLING
4 tablespoons unsalted butter (milchik) or nondairy margarine (pareve)
¼ cup superfine sugar ◆ Yolks of 2 large eggs (whites reserved for glaze)
¼ cup dried cranberries ◆ ¼ cup white raisins
¼ cup mixed dried, organic citrus peel ◆ About 1½ cups ground almonds

GLAZE
Whites of 2 large eggs

◆

1 Preheat the oven to 375°F. Grease with vegetable oil and line a 9-inch by 1½-inch-deep, square baking pan. Set aside.

2 Make the pie dough. Place all the ingredients in a food processor that is fitted with a dough blade. Process until the dough forms. Remove from the food processor, wrap in plastic wrap, and flatten so that it is about 1-inch thick. Refrigerate 30 minutes.

3 Lightly flour a work surface. Divide the dough into 2 equal portions. Roll out each portion into a square the size of the baking pan (8 inches by 3½ inches). Place one dough square in the bottom of the pan. Set aside the remaining dough square. Cover the remaining dough to prevent it from drying out.

4 Make the filling. Melt the butter in a medium saucepan over medium-low heat. Stir in the sugar, egg yolks, cranberries, raisins, citrus peel, and ground almonds.

5 Spread the filling over the dough square in the cake pan. Top with the remaining dough square. Glaze with egg white.

6 Bake 30 minutes or until golden brown. Let cool before slicing.

Mama says...
Cut into squares and dust with confectioners' sugar.

Mandelbrot

Mandelbrot (Yiddish for "almond bread") are hard almond biscuits that are double baked to create a dry cookie similar to Italian biscotti. In fact, these treats were probably introduced to the Italians by the Spanish Jews. Their unique texture and taste make them perfect for dipping into coffee, tea, punch, wine, and soup. I sometimes like to flavor the mandelbrot with chocolate chips, a variety of different nuts, or dried fruits. This is my favorite version—it's made with chocolate, hazelnuts, and almonds. This recipe makes about 50 cookies—that may seem like a large number, but if your family is like mine, they won't last long!

PAREVE: contains no meat or dairy products / can be made in advance / can be frozen up to 2 months
PREPARATION TIME: 20 minutes (plus 15 minutes to cool) / **COOKING TIME:** 40 minutes
MAKES: about 50 cookies

**4 cups all-purpose flour ◆ 1 cup superfine sugar ◆ 1 teaspoon baking powder
½ teaspoon salt ◆ 3 large eggs ◆ 1 teaspoon almond extract
½ cup chocolate chips or coarsely chopped bittersweet chocolate ◆ About 1 cup skinned
hazelnuts, chopped coarsely ◆ About 1 cup blanched whole almonds, chopped coarsely**

◆

1 Preheat the oven to 350°F. Line a baking tray with parchment paper. Set aside.

2 Place the flour, sugar, baking powder, salt, eggs, chocolate, and almond extract into a food processor that is fitted with a dough blade. Process until a dough is formed. Stir in the hazelnuts and almonds.

3 Lightly flour a work surface and transfer the dough to the work surface. Divide the dough into three equal portions. Roll each piece into 12-inch-long, 2-inch-wide sausage shapes. Place on the lined baking tray.

4 Bake 25 minutes or until just firm. Remove from the oven and set aside 10 minutes to cool. (Do not turn off the oven.)

5 Using a serrated knife, cut the "sausages" into ½-inch-thick diagonal slices. Return to the oven.

6 Bake 15 minutes, until the centers are dry and the cookies are crisp and golden brown.

Old-Fashioned Fruit Cake

*This is a very old recipe that my grandmother passed down to me.
My mother remembers having this delicious cake at her aunt's house during tea
more than 60 years ago. I love the addition of cocoa—the hint of chocolate in this
rich fruit cake is just delicious. This cake may be frosted, decorated with chopped
almonds, or served plain. Rich and dense, it's suitable for serving not only at tea,
but also at weddings, bar mitzvahs, and other formal festive occasions.
The cake does take some time—six weeks—to set up (otherwise, it's too fresh
to slice), but the result is well worth the wait. During the weeks that it's setting,
occasionally drizzle brandy over the cake, allowing the liquor to soak into the
fruit and flavor it over time.*

MILCHIK: contains dairy products *or* **PAREVE:** contains no meat or dairy products
must be made at least 6 weeks in advance
PREPARATION TIME: 25 minutes (plus 6 weeks to set) / **COOKING TIME:** 2 hours, 30 minutes
SERVES: 15

1 tablespoon vegetable oil ◆ 1¼ cups unsalted butter (milchik) or margarine
2½ cups self-rising flour ◆ ½ teaspoon salt ◆ 7 large eggs ◆ 1⅓ cups superfine sugar
About 1¼ cups ground almonds ◆ Zest and juice of 1 medium organic lemon
Zest and juice of 1 medium organic orange ◆ 1 tablespoon cocoa
1 teaspoon ground allspice ◆ 1 teaspoon cinnamon ◆ 5 cups dried currants
5 cups white raisins ◆ 1 cup candied cherries, chopped coarsely
1 cup mixed, dried organic citrus peel
6 tablespoons brandy (or rum, if desired), divided

◆

1 Preheat the oven to 325°F. Grease with vegetable oil and line a 10-inch round cake pan. Set aside.

2 Place the butter, flour, and salt in a food processor and process until well combined. Add the eggs, sugar, almonds, zests and juices of lemon and orange, cocoa, allspice, and cinnamon. Pulse to mix.

3 Transfer the batter to a large bowl. Stir in the currants, raisins, cherries, and citrus peel. Spoon the batter into the cake pan.

4 Bake until the cake is firm to the touch and a wooden skewer inserted into the center of the cake comes out clean (about 2½ hours). Remove from the oven and set aside to cool.

5 Place the cooled cake in an airtight container (or wrap the cake in plastic wrap, then in aluminum foil). Let sit 6 weeks (unrefrigerated), occasionally drizzling 1 tablespoon brandy (or rum) over the cake.

Chapter seven
FESTIVAL COOKING

ROSH HASHANAH
"Head of the Year"

"Leshana tova tikotevu."
"May you be inscribed for a good and sweet year."

This is the familiar greeting exchanged by family and friends as they gather to celebrate Rosh Hashanah, which are the two holy days at the start of the Jewish New Year. It is a time of reflection and contemplation as we repent for the sins of the past year, but it is also a time of joy and hope for the year to come, as we pray that God will forgive us and look after us in the future.

The festival is celebrated not only in the synagogue, but also in the home, where the dinner table is often lavishly laid out with fruits of the new season, such as pomegranates, figs, persimmons, apples, and pears. Bowls of honey symbolize the wish for a sweet year and a special golden, coiled, circular challah bread, a sign of the year's cycle—round, complete, and uninterrupted—is torn into chunks for dipping into the honey. Apples are another popular fruit, as their round shape expresses the time of the season, and its sweetness reflects the hope for a sweet new year. Combining these two symbolic foods, I like to include apple and honey in the making of my challah during the time from Rosh Hashanah to the end of Succot.

Another favorite recipe of mine is chicken tagine, which is made with apples, prunes, and honey, and Tzimmes (see pages 120 to 121), a sweet carrot stew that uses sliced carrots that resemble coins in the hope that we will be blessed with a prosperous New Year. Honey cake, Lekach (see page 122), is another predominant feature at the festival table and every Jewish mama will have her own variation on the recipe.

Honey-Roasted Chicken

Apple and honey represent our wishes for a good, sweet new year. This popular, family-friendly recipe captures both of these ingredients in one dish. The glaze, which is made with apple juice and honey, gives the chicken a beautiful, crispy coating.

FLEISHIK: contains meat / Passover-friendly / can be made in advance
PREPARATION TIME: 15 minutes / **COOKING TIME:** 85 minutes / **SERVES:** 6

½ **cup apple juice** ♦ ½ **cup dry white wine**
¼ **cup, plus 1 tablespoon honey, divided** ♦ **One 5-pound whole chicken**
Salt ♦ **Freshly ground black pepper**
1 medium yellow onion, peeled and chopped coarsely
4 medium red or green apples, peeled, cored, and cut into thick wedges

♦

1 Preheat the oven to 400°F.

2 In a small bowl, whisk together the apple juice, wine, and ¼ cup honey.

3 Place the chicken breast-side down in a large roasting pan. Pour the honey mixture over the chicken. Salt and pepper to taste.

4 Arrange the onions and apples around the chicken. Cover the pan with aluminum foil or use the pan lid.

5 Bake 1 hour.

6 Remove the foil or uncover pan and bake 15 minutes more.

7 Remove the pan from the oven. Transfer the chicken to a carving board. Let sit 5 minutes.

8 Meanwhile, pour the pan juices into a saucepan. Discard the apples and onions. Add the remaining tablespoon honey and heat over medium-low heat. Cook 10 minutes, stirring frequently. Adjust the seasonings, if desired.

9 Cut the chicken into portions and transfer to a serving platter. Serve with fresh green apple wedges and honey sauce.

Tzimmes

*Perhaps it is because sliced carrots symbolize coins that we eat Tzimmes on
Rosh Hashanah, when we are hoping to be blessed with a prosperous new year.
Although it may be served as a main course, most people think of Tzimmes as a side
dish. Although I call for dried apricots, white raisins, or dates, my grandmother's
recipe (on which this is based) offers no such alternatives. She was strictly in favor
of apricots. The honeyed chicken or vegetable stock softens the fruit (whichever type
you choose to use) and gives the dish a delicious flavor.*

FLEISHIK: contains meat / Passover-friendly / can be made in advance / can be frozen up to 2 weeks
PREPARATION TIME: 20 minutes / **COOKING TIME:** 50 minutes / **SERVES:** 6

DUMPLINGS

1 cup all-purpose flour or medium-ground matzah meal
2 tablespoons chicken fat or margarine ◆ 2 teaspoons salt
1 teaspoon freshly ground black pepper
1 large egg, lightly beaten ◆ ½ cup vegetable or chicken stock

STEW

2 tablespoons vegetable oil ◆ 1 medium yellow onion, peeled and chopped coarsely
4 cups thinly sliced carrots ◆ 2½ cups vegetable or chicken stock
2 tablespoons honey ◆ 2 tablespoons lemon juice ◆ 1 teaspoon cinnamon
2 cups dried apricots, white raisins, or dates, or a mixture of these
Salt ◆ Freshly ground black pepper

◆

1 Make the dumplings. In a large bowl, mix together the flour or matzah meal, chicken fat or margarine, and salt and pepper until the mixture resembles fine bread crumbs.

2 Add the egg and 2 cups vegetable or chicken stock and mix together to make a pliable dough. (If necessary, add more stock, a bit at a time.)

3 Roll the dough into walnut-sized balls. Wrap in plastic wrap and refrigerate 15 minutes.

4 Meanwhile, make the stew. Heat vegetable oil in a large saucepan over medium-low heat. Add the onions and sauté 2 minutes. Add the carrots and sauté 5 minutes.

5 Add the chicken or vegetable stock, honey, lemon juice, cinnamon, and dried fruit. Salt and pepper to taste.

6 Gently place the chilled dumplings in the stew. Simmer uncovered over low heat 45 minutes.

Mama says...
Just before serving, dust the stew with a bit of cinnamon.

Lekach

One of the major topics of conversation at Rosh Hashanah is what honey cake recipe to make. Well, this will certainly keep the family happy. It is my favorite classic recipe, and it produces a wonderful cake that is richly spiced with ginger, cinnamon, and other spices. Although it's customary to eat apples and honey during Rosh Hashanah, my family seems driven to eat them together in as many ways as possible. For this reason, my honey cake even features apple juice! Although this cake may be eaten right away, I find that its flavor improves if it's allowed to sit at room temperature at least 3 days before eating. I always make two batches of this recipe—I serve one cake for tea during Rosh Hashanah, and I freeze the other, to be used later for breaking the Yom Kippur fast.

PAREVE: contains no meat or dairy products / must be made 2 weeks in advance
can be frozen up to 1 month
PREPARATION TIME: 25 minutes / **COOKING TIME:** 50 minutes / **SERVES:** 6 to 8

1 tablespoon vegetable oil ◆ 1½ cups all-purpose flour, sifted
3 tablespoons superfine sugar ◆ ½ teaspoon dried ginger ◆ 2 teaspoons cinnamon
1 teaspoon allspice ◆ 1 teaspoon baking soda ◆ ¼ cup vegetable oil ◆ 1 cup honey
Zest of 1 medium organic orange ◆ 3 large eggs, lightly beaten ◆ ¼ cup apple juice

◆

1 Preheat the oven to 350°F. Grease with vegetable oil and line a 9-inch by 5-inch loaf pan. Set aside.

2 In a large bowl, combine the flour, sugar, ginger, cinnamon, allspice, and baking soda.

3 Add the vegetable oil, honey, orange zest, eggs, and apple juice. Beat until smooth, then pour into the pan.

4 Bake 50 minutes or until a toothpick inserted into the center of the cake comes out clean. Remove from the oven and let cool to room temperature in the pan.

5 Tightly wrap the cooled cake in aluminum foil and let sit 2 to 3 days at room temperature, to allow flavors to blend together.

Cinnamon-Apple Strudel

Apple strudel has been a standard Jewish dessert for decades; it's also good for afternoon tea. True Viennese-style apple strudel is made with fresh dough that is rolled out to a paper-thin consistency. It takes considerable skill and time, but we now have access to prepared phyllo, which offers an easy alternative.

MILCHIK: contains dairy products *or* **PAREVE:** contains no meat or dairy products
can be made in advance / can be frozen (before baking) up to 2 weeks
PREPARATION TIME: 25 minutes / **COOKING TIME:** 35 to 40 minutes / **SERVES:** 6

**6 medium Granny Smith apples, peeled, cored, and sliced thinly ◆ 2 tablespoons raisins
2 tablespoons slivered almonds ◆ 2 tablespoons ground almonds ◆ 2 teaspoons lemon juice
2 tablespoons bread crumbs ◆ 3 tablespoons light or dark brown sugar ◆ 1 tablespoon
cinnamon ◆ About 12 sheets phyllo (thawed, if frozen) ◆ 1 cup unsalted butter (milchik) or
margarine, melted ◆ 4 tablespoons slivered almonds, toasted ◆ 1 tablespoon raw sesame seeds**

◆

1 Preheat the oven to 400°F. Line a baking tray with parchment paper. Set aside.

2 In a large bowl, mix together the apples, raisins, slivered and ground almonds, lemon juice, bread crumbs, brown sugar, and cinnamon. Set aside.

3 Place one sheet of phyllo on a work surface. Brush with melted butter or margarine. At each layer, add some toasted almonds. Place another sheet on top and brush with melted butter or margarine, then place one more sheet on top and brush with melted butter or margarine. Repeat three times, so you have four separate three-sheet stacks.

4 Organize the pastry stacks into a large, overlapping rectangle.

5 Place the filling mixture in the center of the pastry. Roll the short sides of pastry inward. Brush the pastry with butter or margarine and roll together like a parcel.

6 Brush with butter or margarine, completely coating the strudel. Sprinkle with sesame seeds. Place the strudel on the baking tray.

7 Bake 35 to 40 minutes or until the strudel is golden brown.

TABERNACLES
Succot

The week-long festival of Succot begins on the fifth day after Yom Kippur (around September/October). The word *Succot* means "booths" and refers to the makeshift huts, or *succahs*, that the Jews called home during their 40 years of wandering in the wilderness following their escape from Egypt. The walls are normally made of wood or canvas and the whole structure is covered by *sekhakh*, a covering that must be made of material that grows in the ground and has been detached from it—usually sticks, bamboo, and branches. The sekhakh should loosely cover the roof so that people inside the succah can see the sky. Today, Jewish families all over the world build succahs in their backyards and children eagerly decorate them with pictures and seasonal fruits and vegetables. Throughout the festival, it is a requirement of Jewish law that all meals be eaten in the succah, unless it rains heavily, in which case the requirement is suspended!

Despite its biblical origins, it is the Jewish Thanksgiving for some because it is also known as the "Festival of the Harvest." It is a time of rejoicing for the goodness and bounty of the earth; therefore, food plays an important role in its celebration. To symbolize the richness of the harvest, stuffed foods of all kinds are served as both savories and sweet dishes. The most popular are Holishkes (stuffed cabbages—see pages 128 to 129) with ground beef, served with a sweet and sour tomato sauce. In Israel, stuffed eggplant or peppers are filled with rice, tomatoes, and herbs. On the sweeter side, recipes like apple strudels and fruit pies with large platters of the new fruits make popular Succot desserts.

Zucchini-Stuffed Tomatoes

When I was little, my family used to go on "Succah crawls," visiting friends and having something to eat in their succahs. Today, my children bring their friends, and this recipe is one of their favorites. When I know that there will be several visitors, I fill smaller tomatoes with the stuffing and serve this as part of a buffet.

MILCHIK: contains dairy products *or* **PAREVE:** contains no meat or dairy products
can be made in advance / **PREPARATION TIME:** 15 minutes / **COOKING TIME:** 15 minutes
SERVES: 4 (as an appetizer) or 2 (as a main course)

2 medium zucchini ◆ 2 tablespoons olive oil
2 cups coarsely chopped cremini or brown cap mushrooms
2 teaspoons fresh, grated, and peeled ginger ◆ 4 large garlic cloves, peeled and crushed
1 cup bread crumbs ◆ ¼ cup ground almonds
1 cup soft goat cheese (milchik) or nondairy cream cheese substitute (pareve)
¼ cup pine nuts ◆ Salt ◆ Freshly ground black pepper ◆ 4 medium beefsteak tomatoes

1 Preheat the oven to 350°F.

2 Grate the zucchini. Place between paper towels and squeeze to remove any excess water.

3 Heat the olive oil in a large saucepan over medium heat. Add the zucchini, mushrooms, ginger, and garlic. Sauté 3 minutes. Drain off any liquid in the pan.

4 Transfer the mixture to a large bowl. Add the bread crumbs, almonds, goat cheese or cream cheese substitute, and pine nuts. Generously salt and pepper to taste.

5 Slice off the tops of the tomatoes. Scoop out and discard the cores and seeds.

6 Gently stuff the tomatoes with the zucchini mixture. Place the tomato "lids" back on top of the tomatoes.

7 Bake 10 to 15 minutes or until the stuffing is golden brown.

Holishkes

*Stuffed cabbage leaves are a traditional dish that is used to celebrate Succot.
My contemporary twist—chopped apricots—provides a nice contrast to the
sweet-and-sour sauce. Serve this as part of a Succot buffet or as a
first course in a Yom Tov meal.*

FLEISHIK: contains meat / can be made in advance
PREPARATION TIME: 35 minutes (plus 30 minutes to chill)
COOKING TIME: 2 hours / **SERVES:** 8 to 10

STUFFED CABBAGE LEAVES

3½ pounds lean ground beef or lamb ◆ ½ cup long-grain white rice
2 medium yellow onions, peeled and chopped finely ◆ ½ cup finely chopped dried apricots
5 large garlic cloves, peeled and chopped finely ◆ 1 teaspoon salt
1 teaspoon freshly ground black pepper ◆ 2 large eggs, lightly beaten ◆ 3 tablespoons water
16 large white or savoy cabbage leaves (select thick leaves in perfect condition)

SWEET-AND-SOUR SAUCE

Two 14-ounce cans diced tomatoes with juice ◆ 2 medium yellow onions, chopped coarsely
1 cup dark raisins (if desired) ◆ 3 tablespoons light brown sugar
2 tablespoons lemon juice ◆ 2 tablespoons ketchup ◆ 1 cup dry red wine ◆ Salt
2 teaspoons cinnamon ◆ Freshly ground black pepper ◆ ½ cup pine nuts, toasted, to garnish

◆

1 In a large bowl, combine the beef or lamb, rice, onions, apricots, garlic, salt, and pepper. (For a smoother mixture, pulse the ingredients in a food processor.) In a small bowl, beat together the eggs and water. Add to the meat mixture and combine. Refrigerate the mixture covered for 30 minutes.

2 Fill a large saucepan with water. Bring to a boil. Plunge the cabbage leaves in the boiling water. Blanch 2 minutes. Transfer the cabbage leaves to a colander and rinse immediately with cold water—this will prevent them from continuing to cook.

Mama says...
This sauce is quite versatile, and it can be used to top many other dishes, such as meatballs or whitefish. Simply cook the sauce ingredients over medium-low heat for 15 minutes, stirring occasionally.

3 Transfer the cabbage leaves to a work surface. Using a sharp knife, carefully remove any hard stalks, while doing minimal damage to the leaves.

4 Preheat the oven to 300°F.

5 Shape the chilled beef mixture into egg-sized ovals. Wrap each oval in one or two cabbage leaves, folding and overlapping the leaves so the mixture is completely enclosed in a tight parcel.

6 Place stuffed cabbage leaves in a baking dish.

7 In a medium bowl, mix together all the sauce ingredients. Pour over the stuffed cabbage leaves.

8 Cover the dish and bake 2 hours.

9 Gently transfer the stuffed cabbage leaves to a serving dish. Spoon the sauce over the stuffed cabbage leaves. Sprinkle with pine nuts and serve.

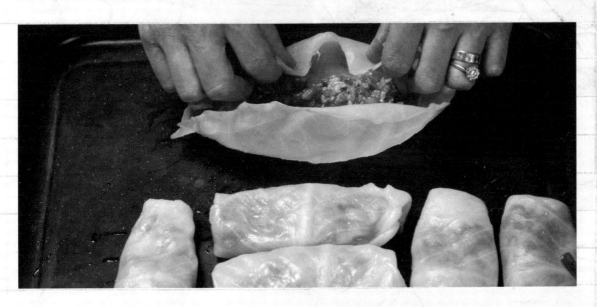

CHANUKAH

Festival of Dedication/Festival of Lights

This winter festival celebrates a great Jewish military victory by the Maccabee army against the Hellenistic occupiers of the land of Israel around 150 B.C. It also celebrates a major miracle: when the Jews recaptured the sacred oil in the temple in Jerusalem, there was only enough holy oil to light the candelabra for one day. Amazingly, however, the candelabra burned for eight days, until new supplies of holy oil were obtained. To commemorate the miracle of the oil, lots of fried foods such as Latkes (see opposite) are eaten at Chanukah. Although it is reported that the Maccabee soldiers ate latkes on the battlefields, they were not the latkes of today, as potatoes were not available until the sixteenth century. They were most likely made from cheese, vegetables, or fruits.

All Jewish homes have a menorah—a nine-stick candelabra. In ancient times, olive oil was used in Chanukah menorahs, but over time, the oil has been replaced by colorful candles, and cards and gifts are exchanged by the family.

Each day of Chanukah is a celebration of the greatness and growth of the miracle. So on the first night, one light is lit and another one on each successive night until the eighth night, when all the lights are lit. Candles are placed in the menorah from right to left, but lit from left to right. The ninth candle is also slightly higher than the others and is known as the Shamash, or servant. It is used to light the other candles.

This festival is a wonderfully joyful occasion for all the family. It tends to fall around Christmastime; as a result, it has become very commercialized.

Latkes

These potato pancakes, called Latkes, are most often enjoyed at Chanukah, when the family gathers together to light the menorah candles, exchange gifts, and play Chanukah games. I like to make "mini" pancakes, which the children love to dip into apple sauce. Latkes are not just for Chanukah, however. They go well with most meals, including roast chicken, cold meats, fried fish, and breakfasts or brunches that include fried eggs. Eat them sweet, sprinkled with superfine sugar and topped with applesauce and sour cream (milchik) or nondairy sour cream substitute (pareve).

PAREVE: contains no meat or dairy products / Passover-friendly
can be made in advance / can be frozen up to 1 month
PREPARATION TIME: 20 minutes / **COOKING TIME:** 15 minutes / **MAKES:** 10 to 12

**5 boiling potatoes, peeled ◆ 1 small yellow onion, peeled ◆ 2 large eggs, lightly beaten
3 tablespoons fine-ground matzah meal (or self-rising flour, during times other than Passover)
Salt ◆ Freshly ground black pepper ◆ About 4 cups vegetable oil**

◆

1 Grate the potatoes and onions. Place between paper towels. Squeeze to remove excess water. Transfer to dry paper towels and squeeze again.

2 Place the potatoes and onions in a large bowl. Stir in the eggs and matzah meal. Generously salt and pepper to taste.

3 Pour enough vegetable oil in a large, shallow frying pan to create a ½-inch-thick layer of oil. Heat over medium heat.

4 Drop spoonfuls of batter into the hot oil. Do not overcrowd the pan—pancakes may be fried in batches, if necessary. Fry until golden brown on the bottoms (about 4 minutes).

5 Turn the pancakes and fry until golden brown on the other sides (about 3 minutes).

6 Transfer the pancakes to paper towels to absorb excess oil. Serve.

PURIM

Festival of Lots

This joyous festival celebrates the overthrowing of a plot by Haman—a wicked advisor to the king of Persia—to kill all the Jews of the land of Persia. The story of Purim is recounted in *The Megillah*, and is known as the story of Esther. Esther was a young Jewish woman who caught the eye of the king and married him and made him very happy. However, her uncle Mordechai overheard Haman plotting to kill all the Jews and destabilize the country. Mordechai reported it to the king and Esther saved her people.

So Purim is a time of feasting and carnival—gifts of food are exchanged, people wear fancy clothes, and everyone has a ball!

Though synagogues are mostly solemn places, the atmosphere changes at this time of year as children dress up as their favorite Purim characters and make huge amounts of noise at every mention of Haman's name in the telling of the story from *The Megillah*.

The focus is on vegetarian food, including nuts, seeds, and legumes, as this was the diet that the Jewish queen Esther ate in the nonkosher palace of the king. It was her way of keeping the laws of kashrut in a non-Jewish world. Bobs (chickpeas) and nahit (black-eyed peas) dusted with paprika, and Hamantachen—the three-pointed biscuits that symbolize Haman's ears (see pages 134–137)—are often served during Purim.

Fritlach

This recipe for Fritlach, fried pastries, comes from my friend Simone's grandmother—another true Jewish mama! Fritlach is the generic Yiddish word for anything fried, and Simone's grandmother used to fry these during Purim. Simone's mother and her sister had Purim parties, and the fritlach were the highlight! Resembling half moons, these fragile golden bubbles are meant to represent Haman's ears (Hamans Ohren).

PAREVE: contains no meat or dairy products / can be made in advance / can be frozen up to 1 month
PREPARATION TIME: 10 minutes (plus 30 minutes to rest) / **COOKING TIME:** 15 minutes
MAKES: about 40 pastries

**2 large eggs ◆ 1¼ cups all-purpose flour ◆ 2 tablespoons, plus 1 cup vegetable oil
2 to 3 tablespoons superfine sugar**

1 In a food processor that is fitted with a dough blade, process the eggs, flour, and 2 tablespoons vegetable oil until combined. Process the mixture to make a soft dough, gradually adding a bit more water if necessary. (The dough should clean the bowl.)

2 Transfer the dough to a work surface and knead until smooth. Wrap the dough in plastic wrap and refrigerate 30 minutes.

3 Lightly flour a work surface. Remove the dough from the plastic wrap and roll out as thin as possible. Using a cutter or a glass, cut the dough into 3¼-inch circles. Cut each circle in half to form half moons.

4 Allow the dough shapes to dry (they should be dry, but not brittle). To speed up the process, either place the shapes near a window on a sunny day or use a hairdryer to dry the shapes.

5 Pour enough vegetable oil in a large, shallow frying pan to create a ½-inch-thick layer of oil. Heat over medium heat.

6 Gently place the dough shapes in hot oil (do not overcrowd the pan; fry the dough in batches). Turning once or twice, fry until very pale golden yellow (about 4 seconds). Transfer the fried dough to paper towels to blot any excess oil. While the pastries are still hot, dust them with sugar.

Hamantachen with Poppy Seeds

These classic triangular Purim delicacies are filled with poppy seeds, prunes, or apricot preserves. The fillings in hamantachen are hidden—this symbolizes the belief that God always has a plan for the Jews, even if they themselves can not always see it clearly. The triangular shape symbolizes Haman's hat, and the size can vary quite considerably, from small, cocktail-sized morsels to large, heavy treats. Hamantachen can be made with either sweet yeast dough or cookie dough. Both varieties are delicious, but most families have a "tradition" of making one or the other. This recipe uses yeast dough; the next calls for shortbread pastry dough.
Try them both and see which you prefer!

MILCHIK: contains dairy products *or* **PAREVE:** contains no meat or dairy products
can be made in advance / **PREPARATION TIME:** 30 minutes (plus 2 hours to allow dough to rise and 10 minutes for mixture to cool) / **COOKING TIME:** 15 minutes / **MAKES:** 40 small pastries

DOUGH
1½ cups warm water, divided ◆ 2 tablespoons active dry yeast
2 teaspoons salt ◆ 8 tablespoons sugar, divided ◆ 2 large eggs
½ cup unsalted butter (milchik) or margarine (pareve)
1 teaspoon vanilla extract ◆ 6 cups bread flour

FILLING
1 cup poppy seeds ◆ ¼ cup water ◆ ½ cup white raisins
1 tablespoon corn syrup ◆ 1 tablespoon superfine sugar

GLAZE
2 tablespoons honey ◆ 2 teaspoons warm water

◆

1 Make the dough. In a medium bowl, mix together ½ cup warm water, the yeast, salt, and 2 tablespoons sugar. Let sit until the mixture becomes foamy (about 10 minutes).

2 Place the eggs, butter or margarine, vanilla extract, and remaining sugar in a food processor fitted with a dough blade. Process to blend. Add the flour and yeast mixture. Process until the mixture is smooth and well combined (about 5 minutes).

3 Transfer the dough to a large bowl, cover with a clean kitchen towel, and let sit about 2 hours, until the dough has doubled in size.

4 Lightly flour a work surface. Transfer the dough to a work surface and roll out to a ¼-inch-thick sheet. Using a cutter or a glass, cut 3-inch circles in the dough.

5 Make the filling. Place all the filling ingredients in a medium saucepan and heat over medium-low heat. Simmer, stirring occasionally, until the liquid has been absorbed and the filling thickens (about 5 minutes).

6 Cool the filling for 10 minutes before using. Place 1 tablespoon filling in the center of each dough circle.

7 Fold the edges of the dough over the filling to form little triangles.

8 Make the glaze. In a small bowl, combine the honey and warm water. Brush the glaze onto all the pastries.

9 Line 2 baking trays with parchment paper. Place the pastries on the trays. Let sit 30 minutes to rise.

10 Preheat the oven to 350°F.

11 Bake the pastries 15 minutes or until golden brown.

Mama says...
Just before serving, dust the pastries with confectioners' sugar.

Hamantachen with Apple

Fans of shortbread will love these delicious treats. The filling combines apples, walnuts, and raisins for a rich, tasty complement to the subtly sweet pastry dough.

MILCHIK: contains dairy products *or* **PAREVE:** contains no meat or dairy products
can be made in advance / can be frozen up to 1 month / **PREPARATION TIME:** 30 minutes
COOKING TIME: 15 to 20 minutes / **MAKES:** about 30 small pastries

DOUGH

2¼ cups all-purpose flour ◆ ½ cup unsalted butter (milchik) or margarine (pareve)
Zest of 1 medium organic lemon ◆ 2 teaspoons lemon juice ◆ 1 large egg
3 tablespoons superfine sugar

FILLING

3 tablespoons white raisins ◆ ¼ cup chopped walnuts
¼ cup unsalted butter (milchik) or margarine (pareve) ◆ ¼ packed cup light brown sugar
1 teaspoon cinnamon ◆ 1 medium red or green sweet apple, peeled

GLAZE AND TOPPING

White of 1 large egg, lightly whisked ◆ 2 tablespoons poppy seeds
2 tablespoons decorative cake sprinkles

◆

1 Make the dough. Place all the ingredients in a food processor that is fitted with a dough blade. Process until a dough is formed.

2 Remove the dough from the processor and wrap in plastic wrap. Flatten the dough to ½-inch thick. Refrigerate for 30 minutes. Clean the processor bowl.

3 Meanwhile, make the filling. Place the raisins, walnuts, butter or margarine, brown sugar, and cinnamon in the food processor. Pulse gently until the ingredients are combined.

4 Grate the apples. Place between paper towels and squeeze any excess water from the apples. Stir the apples into the raisin-nut mixture.

5 Preheat the oven to 400°F.

6 Lightly flour a work surface. Remove the dough from the plastic wrap and roll out to a ¼-inch-thick sheet. Using a 3-inch cutter or a glass, cut circles into the dough.

7 Place about 1 teaspoon of the raisin-nut mixture in the center of each circle.

8 Fold the edges of the dough over the filling to form little triangles.

9 Line two baking trays with parchment paper. Place the pastries on the trays and glaze with the egg white. Sprinkle with poppy seeds and decorative cake sprinkles.

10 Bake 15 to 20 minutes, until golden brown.

PASSOVER
Pesach

Passover is an exciting time of year, especially for children, and it includes many time-honored rituals. A thorough "spring cleaning" of the house helps to symbolize (and achieve) an atmosphere of freshness and renewal. This is the oldest Jewish festival, and it marks the flight of the Israelites from slavery in Egypt into freedom. They left in such a hurry that their bread did not have time to rise. Thus, for eight days a year, Jews eat only unleavened foods.

During the first two nights of Passover, in a service performed at home called Seder, Jews retell the story of the exodus. This is followed by a meal full of symbolic foods. The Seder plate contains foods with special meaning: Charoset (a mixture of chopped walnuts, wine, cinnamon, and apples; see page 141) represents the mortar the Jewish slaves used to assemble the pharaoh's bricks; parsley (symbolizing springtime) is dipped in salt water to remind us of the tears of the Jewish slaves; eggs are a symbol of spring and the cycle of life; shank bones are symbolic of the sacrificial lamb offering; and bitter herbs such as grated horseradish reflect the bitter affliction of slavery.

During the Seder, four glasses of wine are poured to represent the four stages of the exodus: freedom, deliverance, redemption, and release. A fifth cup of wine, the Cup of Elijah, is poured and placed on the Seder table as an offering for the prophet Elijah. The door to the home is opened to invite in the prophet Elijah.

There are many strict rules surrounding Passover: only special Passover foods, utensils, and dishware are allowed and none of them should be used at other times of year. Similarly, when buying in supermarkets, only foods that are specially marked "Kosher for Passover" are permitted, as they have been supervised and kept away from any hint of leavened foods or grain. During Passover, Coconut Pyramids (see page 147), Cinnamon Balls (see page 148), and My Almond Macaroons (see page 145) are all created in accordance with the prohibition against leavened products.

Dried Fruit Compote

The most difficult meal during Passover is breakfast. I think this is because we have become so accustomed to eating bread, toast, cereals, rolls, and other flour-based foods, which are prohibited at this time. Passover cereals are available, but they are not very satisfying. Matzah meal and butter are delicious, but they are not very filling or nutritious. My mother solved the "Passover breakfast" dilemma by serving a large bowl of this delicious compote. Served with ice cream or sponge cake, this also makes a good dessert.

PAREVE: contains no meat or dairy products / Passover-friendly / can be made in advance
PREPARATION TIME: 10 minutes (plus at least 2 hours to chill) / **COOKING TIME:** 0 minutes
SERVES: 4

1⅓ cups raisins and currants ◆ ½ cup dried cherries
½ cup white raisins ◆ 10 dried pitted prunes ◆ 10 dried apricots
About 2 cups hot, freshly brewed fragrant tea (such as Earl Grey or jasmine)
2 tablespoons sugar ◆ 1 medium lemon, sliced

◆

1 Place the dried fruits in a medium bowl and cover with hot tea. Add sugar and lemon slices.

2 Cover the bowl with a plate. Set aside to cool to room temperature.

3 Refrigerate uncovered for at least 2 hours (and preferably overnight).

Mama says...
For a tasty Passover breakfast, serve this with plain yogurt and a bit of honey. For a tasty Passover dessert, stir in about 1/4 cup Passover-friendly liqueur.

Charoset

This fruit and wine pâté is one of the symbolic foods that we have on the Passover Seder table. It represents the mortar with which the Jews were forced to make bricks when they built the cities of Pithom and Ramses for their Egyptian taskmasters. The word "Charoset" means clay in Hebrew. This is a classic Ashkenazi dish that combines apples, walnuts, cinnamon, kiddush wine, and sugar. Charoset is a good example of a dish that varies according to the country in which it's made and the local ingredients that are available. Middle Eastern Jews tend to make Charoset with dates, dried apricots, and raisins. I like to make a large bowl of Charoset, and I hide the leftovers, as I thoroughly enjoy having some of it for breakfast the morning after Seder night. This chunkier version of Charoset includes lemon, which represents the sourness of slavery, and dates, which represent the sweetness of freedom.

PAREVE: contains no meat or dairy products / Passover-friendly / can be made in advance
PREPARATION TIME: 10 minutes / **COOKING TIME**: 10 minutes / **SERVES**: 8 to 10

**1 cup almonds ◆ 6 red or green, sweet apples, peeled, cored, and chopped coarsely
1 cup coarsely chopped pitted dates ◆ 1 teaspoon cinnamon
Zest and juice of 1 medium organic lemon ◆ ⅓ cup kiddush Passover-friendly red wine**

◆

1 Preheat the oven to 400°F. Place the almonds on a baking tray. Bake 10 minutes. Remove from the oven and let cool.

2 In a large bowl, mix together the apples, dates, and almonds.

3 Stir in cinnamon, zest, lemon juice, and wine.

4 Cover the bowl. Refrigerate until chilled.

5 Transfer the chilled mixture to a serving bowl and serve.

Matzah Omelet

This is a very popular Passover breakfast, light lunch, or supper dish among Ashkenazi Jews. My children like these sweet, so I top them with sugar. For a savory omelet, top them with salt instead. Serve these with applesauce and sour cream, and a dusting of cinnamon.

PAREVE: contains no meat or dairy products / Passover-friendly / can be made in advance
PREPARATION TIME: 10 minutes / **COOKING TIME:** 5 minutes / **SERVES:** 2 to 3

**6 large, plain matzah broken into bite-sized pieces ♦ 5 large eggs, lightly beaten
2 teaspoons salt ♦ 3 tablespoons vegetable oil**

1 Place the matzah crackers in a large bowl. Cover with cold water. Let sit 2 to 3 minutes. Drain. Add the eggs and salt to the crackers and mix well.

2 Heat vegetable oil in a medium frying pan over medium heat. Add the matzah mixture and fry until the bottom of the mixture is golden brown (about 2 minutes).

3 Using a spatula, break up the omelet into pieces. Turning frequently, fry until the pieces are crisp and browned on all sides (about 3 minutes). (The pieces will continue to break as they are turned.)

*Mama says...
Sprinkle with salt or sugar and serve immediately with applesauce and sour cream.*

Boobelach

It's tradition to serve boobelach for breakfast or as a snack during Passover, but they may be enjoyed at any time of the year. My mother makes these pancakes for my children every Sunday. Early Sunday mornings I drive to her house, where she is waiting for me with the pancakes all wrapped up in a napkin. My children eat them in the car on their way to Cheder (Sunday school).

MILCHIK: contains dairy products / Passover-friendly
PREPARATION TIME: 10 minutes / **COOKING TIME:** 10 minutes / **MAKES:** 12 pancakes

**3 large eggs ◆ 1 teaspoon salt ◆ 4 tablespoons fine-ground matzah meal
(or cake flour or self-rising flour, during times other than Passover) ◆ ¼ cup milk
About 2 to 3 tablespoons vegetable oil**

◆

1 In a medium bowl, whisk together the eggs and salt until the mixture is light and fluffy. Stir in the matzah meal and milk.

2 Heat the vegetable oil in a large frying pan over medium heat.

3 Drop tablespoons of the mixture in hot oil (do not overcrowd the pan; pancakes may be fried in batches). Turning once, fry until golden brown on both sides (about 2 to 3 minutes per side).

4 Place the pancakes on paper towels, then transfer to a serving plate and serve immediately.

Mama says...
I like my pancakes light and fluffy, so during times other than Passover, I make them with cake flour or self-rising flour. Many, however, prefer the Passover-friendly, heavier matzah meal all year round.

My Almond Macaroons

Passover is not quite Passover unless my family is munching on almond macaroons—the traditional favorite treat of this festival. This recipe uses coarsely chopped almonds as well as ground almonds, and brown sugar instead of white sugar—which makes them a little different than my mother's macaroons. This recipe works well with pecans, too. These may be frozen, or they may be stored in an airtight container at room temperature for up to 5 days.

PAREVE: contains no meat or dairy products / Passover-friendly
can be made in advance / can be frozen up to 1 month
PREPARATION TIME: 10 minutes / COOKING TIME: 20 minutes / MAKES: about 48 macaroons

2 cups ground almonds ◆ ¼ cup whole almonds, chopped coarsely
1 packed cup light brown sugar ◆ 1 teaspoon vanilla extract ◆ Whites of 5 large eggs
½ teaspoon salt ◆ About 48 almond halves (about 2 ounces total)

◆

1 Preheat the oven to 375°F. Line two baking sheets with parchment paper. Set aside.

2 In a large bowl, mix together the ground almonds, chopped almonds, brown sugar, and vanilla extract.

3 Place the egg whites and salt in a medium bowl. Whisk together until the egg whites are stiff, but not dry.

4 Stir the egg whites into the nut mixture, a tablespoon at a time, until the mixture is stiff, but not too wet. (Some egg whites may be left over—discard any that remain.)

5 Gently drop 1 tablespoon of the mixture, spaced about 1 inch apart, onto the baking sheets. Push one almond half onto the top of each macaroon, flattening the macaroons slightly.

6 Bake 20 minutes or until the macaroons are golden brown and just set. (The macaroons will harden as they cool.)

7 Transfer to a cooling rack and let cool.

Matzah Pudding

My family often requests this dessert for our family get-together for Seder. It's delicious and generously sized, and it contains all the flavors of Passover (such as ground almonds, cinnamon, lemon, and apples). It can be eaten hot or cold, and it keeps well, making it an ideal Shabbat dessert as well.

PAREVE: contains no meat or dairy products / Passover-friendly
can be made in advance / can be frozen up to 2 weeks
PREPARATION TIME: 30 minutes / **COOKING TIME:** 50 minutes / **SERVES:** 8 to 10

8 large, plain matzah broken into bite-sized pieces ◆ ½ cup boiling water
3 red or green apples, peeled and grated ◆ ½ cup dark raisins
½ cup coarsely chopped dried apricots
½ cup coarsely chopped walnuts or almonds ◆ 4 tablespoons fine-ground matzah meal
5 tablespoons, plus 1 teaspoon superfine sugar, divided ◆ 2 teaspoons cinnamon
½ teaspoon freshly grated nutmeg ◆ 2 tablespoons honey
Juice and zest of 1 medium organic lemon ◆ 4 large eggs
2 tablespoons margarine, melted ◆ 4 tablespoons apricot jam ◆ 1 tablespoon water

◆

1 Preheat the oven to 325°F. Grease and line a 9-inch square or round baking pan. Set aside.

2 Place the matzah crackers and boiling water in a medium bowl. Let sit 5 minutes. Drain. Place the crackers between paper towels and squeeze out any excess water.

3 Place the soaked crackers in a large bowl. Add the apples, raisins, apricots, walnuts or almonds, matzah meal, 1 tablespoon superfine sugar, cinnamon, nutmeg, honey, zest, and lemon juice.

4 In a separate bowl, whisk together the eggs and remaining superfine sugar until the mixture is light and fluffy. Add to the matzah mixture. Add the margarine. Mix well and pour into the pan.

5 Bake 50 minutes or until a knife inserted in the center of the mixture comes out clean.

6 Place the jam and water in a small saucepan. Cook over low heat 3 minutes, stirring frequently. Brush the jam glaze onto the dessert. Let sit at least 10 minutes before serving.

Coconut Pyramids

These are pyramid-shaped treats that represent the pyramids that the Israelites built for the Egyptians. My mother taught me to get the shape right by using an egg cup, but I have found that molding the treats by hand is quicker and easier. These may be frozen, or they may be stored in an airtight container at room temperature for up to 5 days.

PAREVE: contains no meat or dairy products / Passover-friendly
can be made in advance / can be frozen up to 1 month
PREPARATION TIME: 15 minutes / **COOKING TIME:** 15 minutes / **MAKES:** 24 pyramids

2 large eggs ◆ ¾ cup superfine sugar
Zest and juice of 1 medium organic lemon ◆ 3¾ cups shredded coconut

◆

1 Preheat the oven to 375°F. Line a baking tray with parchment paper.

2 In a large bowl, whisk together the eggs and sugar until the mixture is thick and creamy. Stir in the zest, lemon juice, and coconut. Mix well.

3 Using wet hands, shape about 1 tablespoon mixture into a pyramid. Repeat using all the mixture. Place the pyramids on the tray.

4 Bake 15 to 20 minutes or until the pyramids are lightly browned.

Mama says...
Sprinkle shredded coconut on a serving plate.
Decoratively arrange the pyramids on the plate.

Cinnamon Balls

I seem to spend more time in the kitchen at Passover than at any other time of the year. A good part of this time is spent baking. The cakes and pastries are fantastic, but they're somewhat labor-intensive. That's where the children come in handy! I prepare the mixture and they roll out the dough, so baking is done in next to no time.

PAREVE: contains no meat or dairy products / Passover-friendly
can be made in advance / can be frozen up to 1 month
PREPARATION TIME: 25 minutes / **COOKING TIME:** 15 minutes / **MAKES:** 20 balls

2 cups ground almonds ◆ **1 cup superfine sugar**
1 tablespoon, plus 1 teaspoon cinnamon, divided ◆ **Whites of 2 large eggs**
½ cup confectioners' sugar

◆

1 Preheat the oven to 325°F. Line a baking tray with parchment paper. Set aside.

2 In a medium bowl, combine the almonds, superfine sugar, and 1 tablespoon cinnamon. Set aside.

3 In a small, clean bowl, whisk the egg whites until they form soft peaks.

4 Stir the egg whites, a tablespoon at a time, into the almond-sugar mixture until the mixture is stiff. (Some egg whites may be left over—discard any that remain.)

5 Using wet hands, shape the mixture into small balls. Arrange 1 inch apart on the tray.

6 Bake until golden brown (about 15 minutes).

7 Meanwhile, place the confectioners' sugar and remaining cinnamon in a small bowl. Mix well.

8 Remove the baked pastries from the oven. Roll each ball in the sugar-cinnamon mixture and place on a cooling rack. Let cool.

9 Roll the cooled balls in the sugar-cinnamon mixture again. Serve.

Plava

This light, lemon-flavored sponge cake is traditionally made during Passover, when Jews are not permitted to eat foods made with flour. The most common substitutes used during this time are potato flour, matzah meal, and cake meal. Although this recipe calls for a lemon glaze, the cake may also be served plain or with Dried Fruit Compote (see page 139) or ice cream.

PAREVE: contains no meat or dairy products / Passover-friendly
can be made in advance / can be frozen up to 1 month
PREPARATION TIME: 25 minutes / **COOKING TIME:** 40 minutes / **SERVES:** 6 to 8

CAKE

1 tablespoon vegetable oil ◆ 6 large eggs, divided ◆ 1 cup superfine sugar, divided
¾ cup fine-ground matzah meal ◆ ¼ cup ground almonds
½ teaspoon cinnamon ◆ Grated zest and juice of 1 medium organic lemon
3 tablespoons slivered almonds

GLAZE

¾ cup superfine sugar ◆ ¼ cup water ◆ Grated zest and juice of 1 medium organic lemon

◆

1 Preheat the oven to 350°F. Grease with vegetable oil and line an 8½-inch square springform cake pan. Set aside.

2 Make the cake. Place the egg yolks and sugar in the bowl of an electric mixer. Mix 3 to 5 minutes, until thick and smooth.

3 In a medium bowl, whisk the egg whites until soft peaks form. Gradually add the remaining sugar, beating well after each addition, until the mixture forms stiff peaks. Set aside.

4 In a medium bowl, combine the matzah meal, ground almonds, cinnamon, zest, and lemon juice. Fold into the egg yolk mixture.

5 Using a metal spoon, fold 1 tablespoon egg white mixture into the egg yolk mixture. Gently stir the remaining egg white mixture into the egg yolk mixture.

6 Pour the batter into the pan. Sprinkle with slivered almonds.

7 Bake 40 minutes or until the cake is golden brown and a toothpick inserted into the center of the cake comes out clean.

8 Remove from the oven and let cool in the pan. (The cake may sink a bit.)

9 Make the glaze. Place the sugar and water in a small saucepan. Bring to a boil over medium-high heat. Reduce the heat to medium-low and simmer 4 minutes.

10 Stir in the zest and lemon juice.

11 Drizzle the glaze, 1 tablespoon at a time, over the cooled cake. Take the cake out of the cake pan to serve.

SHAVUOT

Pentecost/Festival of Weeks

Shavuot, the Feast of the Weeks, is the Jewish holiday celebrating the harvest season in Israel. Shavuot, which means "weeks," refers to the timing of the festival that is held exactly seven weeks after Passover. Shavuot also commemorates the anniversary of the giving of the Torah and the Ten Commandments to Moses and the Israelites at Mount Sinai.

It is customary on Shavuot to decorate the home and synagogue with fruits, flowers, and greens, as the first fruits of the new season were harvested around Shavuot in the days of the Temple. In addition, the sages say that although Mount Sinai was situated in a desert, the mountain bloomed and sprouted flowers when the Ten Commandments were given to Moses.

There is also the custom of eating dairy foods on Shavuot. Therefore, recipes like Old-Fashioned Cheesecake (see pages 154 to 155) and Classic Cheese Blintzes (see opposite) are popular. There are a number of reasons for this custom: with the giving of the Torah, the Jews became obligated to observe the laws of Kashruth. As the Torah was given on Shabbat, no cattle could be slaughtered nor could utensils be koshered (in hot water, etc.), so they could only eat dairy products.

Classic Cheese Blintzes

These treats go by many names: the French call them crêpes, the Russians call them blini, and the Jews call them blintzes. They are very thin, crêpe-like pancakes that are filled with cream cheese or cottage cheese and even fruit.

MILCHIK: contains dairy products / can be made in advance / can be frozen up to 1 month
PREPARATION TIME: 20 minutes / **COOKING TIME:** 20 minutes / **MAKES:** 8 blintzes

PANCAKES
1 cup self-rising flour ◆ 1 large egg ◆ 1 cup milk ◆ 1 teaspoon salt
2 to 3 tablespoons sunflower or vegetable oil

FILLING
1 cup cream cheese, softened ◆ 1 large egg ◆ Zest of 1 medium organic lemon
1 tablespoon superfine sugar

◆

1 Lay a large (12 inches by 12 inches) sheet of parchment paper on a work surface. Set aside.

2 Make the batter. In a blender or a large bowl, combine the flour, egg, milk, and salt until smooth.

3 Heat the sunflower oil in an 8-inch skillet over medium heat. Pour 3 tablespoons batter into the hot oil. Tilt the pan so the mixture covers the pan in a thin, even layer. Cook until the batter sets and the pancake edges begin to lift (about 2 minutes).

4 Flip the pancake onto the other side and cook about 10 seconds. Gently transfer the pancake to the parchment paper. Repeat, heating more oil in the pan as needed, until the batter is used. Avoid overlapping the pancakes on the parchment paper; instead, stack them. Reserve the pan for later use.

5 Make the filling. Place all the ingredients in a medium bowl and combine well, then place 1 tablespoon filling in the center of each pancake. Fold 2 opposite sides of the pancake over the filling, then fold the remaining side over those. Roll the pancake to enclose the filling.

6 Pour 1 to 2 tablespoons oil in the pan over medium heat. Fry the blintzes until just golden brown (about 2 minutes). Gently turn the blintzes and cook 1 minute. Serve immediately.

Old-Fashioned Cheesecake

Shavuot is sometimes teasingly referred to as "the cheesecake festival" because of the popularity of this dessert during this festival. Shavuot celebrates the time when God gave the Jews the Ten Commandments and all the laws, including the laws of Lashrus (kosher). Because the Children of Israel were not immediately familiar with all the commandments relating to kashrut, they decided to avoid meat, and they ate only dairy instead. This recipe is both quick and easy to make, and it uses few ingredients.

MILCHIK: contains dairy products / can be made in advance
PREPARATION TIME: 10 minutes (plus about 4 hours to cool) / **COOKING TIME:** 35 minutes
SERVES: 8 to 10

For variety, try making cheesecakes with any of the following:
1 tablespoon lime juice, zest of 2 organic limes, and 2 tablespoons shredded coconut (plus zest of 1 lime and 2 tablespoons shredded coconut for decoration)
1 tablespoon instant coffee
4 tablespoons fresh raspberries (plus raspberries and mint sprigs for decoration)

For this recipe, with chocolate and cinnamon:

CHEESECAKE
1 tablespoon vegetable oil ♦ 3 cups crushed graham crackers
¾ cup unsalted butter or margarine, melted
2 cups cream cheese or large-curd cottage cheese ♦ 2 large eggs
1 cup superfine sugar ♦ ¼ cup finely grated bittersweet chocolate ♦ 2 teaspoons cinnamon

TOPPING
1½ cups sour cream ♦ 2 tablespoons superfine sugar

♦

1 Preheat the oven to 350°F. Grease with vegetable oil and line a 9-inch x 3-inch-deep, round springform cake pan. Set aside.

2 Make the crust. In a medium bowl, mix together the graham cracker crumbs and butter or margarine. Press the mixture in an even layer into the bottom of the pan.

3 In a medium bowl, beat together the cream cheese or cottage cheese, eggs, and sugar. Beat in the chocolate and cinnamon (if making a cheesecake using the other suggested ingredients, beat those in at this time).

4 Pour the mixture over the graham cracker crust in the pan.

5 Bake 30 minutes. Carefully remove from the oven and set aside. Do not turn off the oven.

6 Make the topping. In a small bowl, mix together the sour cream and sugar. Pour over the cake.

7 Return the pan to the oven. Bake 5 minutes.

8 Turn off the oven. Let the cheesecake sit in the oven until it has completely cooled (about 4 hours). Then invert it onto a serving plate.

Glossary

Ashkenazi: Jews originating from Eastern Europe.

Bagel: a doughnut-shaped, yeast-dough, bread roll that is boiled, glazed with egg white, and baked.

Blintz: a thick pancake, Russian in origin and similar to the French crepe, that is stuffed with various fillings and often topped with sour cream.

Booba: a term of endearment for a Jewish grandmother.

Borscht: a Russian-style soup, usually made with beets, that can be served hot or cold, with either sour cream or boiled potatoes.

Cake meal or matzah cake meal: cake meal is very fine matzah meal, perfect for use during Passover when all-purpose flour is prohibited.

Challah: Sabbath bread, traditionally made with egg yeast dough, that is eaten during Sabbaths and festivals.

Chanukah: the festival of lights during which especially foods fried in oil are eaten.

Charoset: A mixture of chopped fruits, nuts, spices, and red wine that is eaten as part of the Passover Seder service.

Cheder: Jewish Sunday school.

Cholent: a traditional meat and vegetable stew that is prepared on the eve of the Shabbat, left to cook slowly overnight, and eaten for lunch on the Sabbath.

Chrain: a sauce made of grated horseradish and beets.

Compote: a mixture of dried fruits that are sweetened and cooked.

Falafel: a deep-fried chickpea ball that is served as an appetizer or is stuffed into a pita bread with salad and tahini or hummus.

Fleishik: Food that contains meat.

Gedempte: Stewed or braised.

Gefilte fish: a mixture of ground fish, matzah meal, ground almonds, and eggs, which is shaped into balls and poached or fried.

Haimisher: Jewish home-style.

Hamantachen: triangular pastries that are usually filled with poppy seeds and jam, prunes, or another similar fruit. These are served during Purim as symbols of the three-cornered hat that Haman used to wear.

Holishkes: cabbage leaves stuffed with meat and rice and baked in a sweet-and-sour sauce.

Hummus: a Middle Eastern dip made from chickpeas and tahini.

Kasha: buckwheat groats, usually served with meat, but also in soups or salads, or as a breakfast cereal.

Kichel: a cookie.

Kiddush: the ritual blessing made over wine at the start of a meal on Sabbaths and festivals to sanctify the day.

Kneidlach: light dumplings made of fine-ground matzah meal and served in chicken soup. (Alternative name for a matzah ball.)

Knish: pastry filled with potatoes, meat, cheese, or rice and baked.

Kosher: "fit to be eaten," according to the laws of the Old Testament.

Kreplach: Pockets of pastalike dough, stuffed with meat or cheese and boiled or fried.

Kugel: a casserole that is usually made with potatoes or noodles, and which may be either sweet or savory.

Latke: a small potato pancake that is traditionally eaten during Chanukah.

Lekach: a dark honey cake that is traditionally served during Rosh Hashanah and after the fast of Yom Kippur.

Lokshen: egg noodles that are usually served in soup or used in kugel.

Mandelbrot: twice-baked almond cookies.

Matzah: unleavened bread, traditionally served during the eight days of Passover.

Menorah: the seven-branched candelabra lit during Chanukah.

Milchik: food that contains dairy products.

Pareve: "neutral" food that contains neither meat nor dairy products and may therefore be eaten with milchik or fleishik foods.

Pareve cream: nondairy cream substitute.

Passover or Pesach: an eight-day festival commemorating the exodus of the Jews from Egypt. Families gather to enjoy lavish meals called Seders.

Pita: a Middle Eastern flat, round bread with a pocket that can be filled with falafel, hummus, tahini, salad, and other ingredients.

Purim: the most festive of the Jewish holidays, with prizes and costumes to celebrate the story of Esther who became the king's wife and foiled a plot to kill all the Jews in the kingdom.

Rosh Hashanah: "the head of the year" when Jews repent their sins and hope for a prosperous new year.

Schmaltz: rendered chicken fat taken from the top of chicken soup.

Seder: a ritual service and meal at the start of Passover, which includes the story of the Jews' exodus from Egypt.

Sephardi: Jews originating from Spain, Morocco, or the Middle East.

Shabbat: the Sabbath (Saturday), the Jewish day of rest. Beginning at sunset, Friday evening, it ends approximately twenty-five hours later.

Shavuot: The Feast of the Weeks occurring seven weeks after the first day of Passover.

Shtetl: a small Jewish settlement in Eastern Europe.

Shtetlach: a small Jewish settlement.

Strudel: a pastry made of very thin sheets of dough, with sweet or savory fillings.

Succot: the jubilant Festival of Tabernacles, which falls five days after Yom Kippur.

Tahini: sesame seed paste that is used as a condiment or as an ingredient in dips.

Tzimmes: carrot stew that is sweetened with honey or sugar.

Varnishkes: bow-shaped noodles that are traditionally served with kasha.

Yom Kippur: the Day of Atonement, the most sacred of Jewish holidays. All work is replaced by prayers and fasting on this day.

Yom Tov: a Jewish festival or High Holy Day.

Index

Passover-friendly index

Use this at-a-glance list to find recipes suitable for Passover.

Picture Credits

Mama says...

Be careful when grating horseradish as the vapors are very powerful and can make you sneeze, cough, or cry (and that's before you've eaten it!)